RICOCHET

RICOCHET

KELLYN CARNI

CamCat
Books

CamCat Publishing, LLC
Fort Collins, Colorado 80524
camcatpublishing.com

Hardcover ISBN 9780744311051
Paperback ISBN 9780744311075
eBook ISBN 9780744311112
Audiobook ISBN 9780744311204

Library of Congress Control Number: 2024935805

Book and cover design by Maryann Appel
Interior artwork by Ba888, Lyubov Ovsyannikova, Strizh

5   3   1   2   4

For my grandmother, Mary Black.

And for anyone who ever wished things had turned out differently.

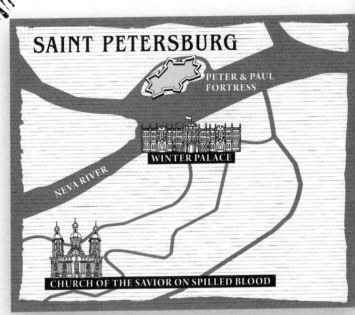

SAINT PETERSBURG

PETER & PAUL
FORTRESS

WINTER PALACE

NEVA RIVER

CHURCH OF THE SAVIOR ON SPILLED BLOOD

TSARSKOYE SELO

ALEXANDER PALACE

1918

THE RUSSIAN EMPIRE

SAINT PETERSBURG

TSARSKOYE SELO

YEKATERINBURG

LUGA

MOSCOW

CHAPTER ONE

"Obviously, at that moment they did not imagine what awaited them ... But the daughters had on bodices almost entirely of diamonds and [other] precious stones. Those were not only places for valuables but protective armor at the same time."

—Yakov Yurovsky's account of the execution of the imperial family

SILENCE FILLED THE CELLAR in the moments before the gunfire.

Sweat beaded on my forehead, my skin prickling with giddy anticipation. We were getting out. Over a year of imprisonment, and we were finally getting out. I suppressed my smile, only because of the worry that creased my father's brow as he paced. He still held his chest high, despite losing his crown, his palace, his freedom—but his unease shadowed the room, hanging heavily in the stale air.

Beside me, my younger brother shifted in his chair as our mother ran her hand absently through his hair like she had when he was little. "Soon, Alexei, my love. We'll be safe soon."

My sisters huddled together against the wall, too nervous to speak. Maria caught my eye, softening her gaze as though to say, "Us, too, Anastasia. She means us, too. We'll all be safe soon."

We would be safe. We would be free. We would be out of the Bolsheviks' captivity, out of this dreadful Ipatiev House, perhaps even out of Russia. Leaving my country, my kingdom, my home—it would have been unthinkable before the rebellion. I yearned to go back to how things were, back when my father still reigned. To go back to our comfortable home in the Alexander Palace, taking springtime rides through the countryside and summer trips to the Crimean shore. Back to freedom. Back to living.

But we'd been ousted from our palace. For a year and a half, we'd been prisoners. We'd been dragged from Tsarskoye Selo to Siberia to Yekaterinburg, and confined within the miserable walls of the Ipatiev House with nothing but each other. Hundreds of years of Romanov tsars, and now here we sat, captives in a musty old cellar. So now, leaving was our only hope.

An hour earlier, guards had burst into the bedroom I shared with my sisters, roused us from our sleep, and ordered us to ready ourselves for an immediate departure. My sisters and I had clambered from our beds in a flurry of excitement and confusion. Had our royal English cousins sent for us at last? Or would we be escaping under cover, taking new identities? Maria was certain it was the former. Even in our haste, she'd combed her golden hair and donned her finest gown, ready to impress the London nobles. But Olga and Tatiana had used those precious minutes to prepare for a life on the run, quickly stuffing their bodices with diamonds and rubies and emeralds.

In my jittery excitement, I'd done neither. I'd scrambled into my usual plain navy dress and left my thick sandy hair unkempt. The only jewel I'd bothered with was my garnet necklace, hidden beneath my collar as always. A palace in England, a hideaway in Poland—it didn't matter. Wherever we went, however we got there, we were getting out.

Catching Maria's eye from across the room once again, I offered what I hoped was a comforting smile. We were finally, *finally*, getting out. The cellar door lurched open and a guard appeared in the doorway. Not one of our usual guards. No, the man in the doorway was unfamiliar, his expression one of cold disdain. A rifle hung at his side, a spiked bayonet capping its end.

My father stopped pacing. My sisters watched eagerly, and my mother brought her hands to her heart in an unspoken prayer. I took Alexei's hand, shifting in front of him instinctively. But the guard looked past my siblings, my mother, and me—addressing my father when he spoke.

"You are to be executed."

Hope froze in my veins.

My father whirled to face him, stunned. "What—"

But the guard raised his rifle without hesitation, without flinching, and the sharp drum of gunshots cut the silence of the cellar. My father staggered. Dropped to his knees. Crumpled to the floor as the guard filled his chest with bullets. I screamed—or was it my sisters? The room filled with shrieking and slamming and bullets, bullets, bullets as more guards stepped through the door, firing their guns.

Alexei's hand tightened in mine and my heart pounded against the coolness of the garnet necklace, concealed under my dress. My forehead burned as the screams dissolved into the ringing in my ears. My vision became a tunnel, blurring away the sight of my mother and sisters collapsing to the floor in a sea of bullets and blood. I only saw the barrel of a gun, pointed straight at my chest, and the guard's finger, pulling the trigger.

The impact bore into my chest with unimaginable force. Then the room faded, and I was floating in a sea of perfect darkness. Sinking in an endless, soundless swamp. Thick nothingness surrounded me, filled me, and swallowed me whole.

CHAPTER TWO

"Life is just one small piece of light between two eternal darknesses."

—*Lolita* by Vladimir Nabokov

N OT DEAD.

No, the wall of darkness before me was just the backs of my eyelids, too heavy to wrench open. Uneven floorboards dug into my spine as cool air nudged me awake. I shivered, and the corner of my mouth twitched upward.

Not dead, because neither Heaven nor Hell ought to be so drafty.

It had been a nightmare, then, surely. The cellar, the bullets, my sisters screaming . . . I was waking up, so it must have been only a terrible dream.

My whole body felt heavy, as though I'd been dragged by a weak magnet through a pit of sand. It wasn't unlike the morning after my fifteenth birthday—the last one before my family was imprisoned—when my sister Maria and I had snuck a bottle of wine for ourselves, drinking the entire thing in our shared bedroom. But there had been no wine, not in that miserable Ipatiev House. So why was I so groggy?

My sternum ached, like I'd been punched in the chest. A bruise was forming there, just behind the garnet necklace hidden beneath my dress.

The thin gold chain was cool against my neck, the gemstone sitting heavily against my chest. The garnet necklace—a secret I'd kept even from Maria.

The floorboards creaked beneath me as I shifted. I peeled my eyes open, and inhaled sharply as my own gray-blue eyes stared back at me. No, not my eyes—

"Alexei, you scared me. You don't just hover over someone as they're waking up, you little creep."

My brother raised his brows as he rose to stand, appraising me with disapproval. "It's about time you woke up. I've been awake for . . ." He fumbled for his heirloom pocket watch out of habit, furrowing his brow as he remembered that the Bolsheviks had taken it, just as they'd taken his kingdom. "I've been awake for a while, anyway. And in case you haven't noticed, we are not in the Ipatiev House."

I glanced around, my eyes widening as I took in the dingy walls and stark furnishings. He was right. This was not the Ipatiev House, the fortified mansion we'd been imprisoned within all those months. Somehow, we'd awoken in a neat but shabby sort of cabin, clearly someone's home. The main room was nearly empty, but for a wooden chair and a crooked table, set with a single plate and a half-burned candlestick.

"Has one of our guards snuck us out, then? Is it . . . is it just us?" I glanced around again, seeing no sign of our parents or sisters, nor the guards. Pulling myself to my feet, I stepped across the small room in just a few strides, peering down the short hallway leading to the bedroom. "Maria? Tatiana? Olga?" Where were they? Where were we? "Mother? Papa?" I looked to Alexei, bewildered, but he only stared at me.

"Ana." His hard tone softened. "Do you . . . do you not remember what happened?"

We'd had a meager dinner, the seven of us, and gone to bed. Then I'd had a horrible nightmare and woke up here. It had been a nightmare, hadn't it? The cellar, the bullets, the screaming . . . the gun pointed right at my chest. My throat tightened. I could still see it all so clearly. As though . . . as though it had been real.

My eyes met Alexei's. Steely blue shields, well-practiced in hiding his emotions. He was only thirteen, but so hardened. Perhaps because he'd confronted his own mortality at such a young age, his hemophilia having pushed him to the brink of death again and again. He would have died years ago, were it not for Rasputin.

My eyes, however, were not shields. Alexei could see my thoughts written clearly on my face. He nodded.

"You do remember."

"No." I shook my head, willing my words to be true. "No, it—" my voice cracked, the words coming out in a broken whisper. "It was a bad dream." But tears welled in my eyes as I relived the nightmare—no, the memory.

The cellar. The guard, addressing my father with his casual announcement.

"You are to be executed."

My father, startled, having no time to respond before the guards fired their guns.

The bullets. Everywhere, bullets and blood.

My sisters, my parents . . . gone.

But Alexei and I, here.

Through tear-filled eyes, I looked again to my brother, his own eyes soft, his hard shell melted by my grief. He held my gaze, his chin quivering just slightly. A moment of understanding passed between us.

It was just us.

I studied Alexei, then. He was no longer my baby brother, to be pampered and doted upon. He was no longer my little playmate, my tenacious partner in crime. He'd grown into a brooding teenager. The months of confinement had brought me closer to my sisters. But Alexei . . . he'd withdrawn. And as we stood there, staring at one another in the wake of our family's massacre, I didn't know what to say.

Alexei looked away first. He swallowed, tightening his jaw as he studied the floor. "I don't know if one of the guards snuck us out. I don't know how we got here. But I think we'd better get out while we can."

With that, Alexei moved toward the door, his limp more pronounced in his exhaustion. Truthfully, he looked quite pathetic. Weakened by the extended bed rests that had become more frequent as he'd gotten older, his arms and legs were too thin. He stood with his weight off his left knee, where it had never truly healed after his hemorrhage at Spala. Since Rasputin's death, since our imprisonment, Alexei had suffered these last few years. He'd become more difficult to protect, more resistant to being coddled, and therefore more prone to injuries that would be but minor bruises for a non-hemophilic boy.

But Alexei stood proudly, still. What he lacked in a tsarevich's appearance, he made up for with his superior attitude. "Well, Anastasia, aren't you coming?"

With a final glance around the stark cabin, I followed him out the door.

The residential streets were empty during the brief dark hours of a July night. We wandered in numb silence, passing more small cabins scattered amongst gardens and pastures and pine trees. The fresh air was foreign to my lungs—too clear, too cool. For a year and a half, we'd been confined within walls, without sunshine, without moonlight, without feeling the crisp coolness of a gentle breeze. But we'd been together. Our whole family. I shivered, wrapping myself with my arms as I walked.

There was no way to know how long we'd been unconscious, but I doubted we'd been taken too far from the Ipatiev House. And while neither of us knew where we were or where we were going, we had to keep moving. One foot in front of the other, creating more space between ourselves and the trauma behind us.

Alexei broke our silence, speaking rather matter-of-factly. "I saw each of them shot. Father. Olga and Maria, standing together. Tatiana and . . ." His voice shook just a bit. "And Mother." My throat tightened as he described the scene I so badly wished to erase from my mind. But Alexei continued.

"And even as I sat there holding your hand, I saw a guard point his gun at you. And he fired." Cocking his head to the side, he eyed me searchingly. "You were *shot,* Ana. But you survived."

I could still see the barrel of that gun, pointed at my chest. The guard's finger, pulling the trigger. I shuddered, my heart quickening. Yes, I was shot. The garnet clanged against the stone-sized bruise on my sternum as we walked, a constant reminder.

Taking a deep breath, I reached beneath the collar of my dress and lifted the garnet by its golden chain. Then I gave the gemstone a little squeeze and opened my palm, exposing the secret I'd carried for nearly two years. Alexei's eyes widened and he opened his mouth to speak, but I beat him to it.

"The guard pointed his rifle right at my chest. The bullet struck here," I pressed my finger to the garnet, "but it ricocheted and that's the last I remember before waking up in that cabin." I raised an eyebrow at Alexei, meeting his incredulous stare with my own. "Why weren't you..." I trailed off, the words sticking in my throat. *Shot. Killed. Executed, like the rest of our family.*

Squaring his shoulders, Alexei held his head high as he eyed the necklace curiously. "Destiny, I suppose."

Despite the weight in my chest, I snorted. "Of course, my tsarevich." Our father's abdication, our imprisonment, our family's execution ... what would it take for Alexei to accept that the throne would never be his? But it wasn't the time to push the issue. I fiddled with the garnet necklace, inwardly debating whether to tell Alexei the rest of the story. Clearing my throat, I decided the information was quite pertinent.

"So, Alexei. About this necklace ..." I paused, unsure how to begin.

"Rasputin gave it to you," Alexei said flatly.

"I—how did you know?"

"Maria told me. She saw him, when he snuck into your shared room. Said she saw him hand you a jewel in the moonlight. Said he whispered something to you and left."

"I—well, yes. Yes, Rasputin did whisper something. But it didn't make any sense." I paused, baffled that Maria had known, that she hadn't said anything—or at least, not to me. Alexei was looking at me expectantly, so I continued. "He said, 'When the time comes, *malenkaya*, you'll escape. Take it, and promise you'll find me.'"

Like a shadow in the night, he'd appeared at my bedside, placing his hand on my shoulder and drawing me into the waking world. It was before my father's abdication. Before those so-called revolutionaries forced us into imprisonment. Back when I was a princess, not a prisoner. I'd had no idea what Rasputin might have meant, when he pressed the garnet necklace into my hand and whispered those words. Though I was startled, there was a soft kindness in the shadowed lines of his face and an air about him that comforted me. I'd drifted back into peaceful sleep, and would have thought it a dream had I not awakened with the garnet still clutched in my palm, like a child with a doll.

Since that night, I'd worn it every day, as one does when a mysterious healer appears in the night to gift one a necklace.

Alexei shrugged. "Well, the first bit was true enough. The time came, and we escaped. But I don't think we'll be finding Rasputin."

I winced. He was right. My mother and father had trusted Rasputin fully—he was, after all, Alexei's savior—but no one else had. I'd heard the whispers, that his powers were unnatural and unholy. Rasputin had been shot down by the Bolsheviks just a month before the self-righteous *svolochy* forced my family into confinement. "*I promise*," I'd whispered back that night. "*I'll find you.*" A promise I would never be able to keep.

We were just rounding a bend along the path as the rising sun burst from the horizon, silhouetting the city before us. The July sunrise was a rare sight, the sun peeking back around the top of the globe at too early an hour for witnesses. I was lost in thought—how could the sunrise be so beautiful in the wake of such tragedy?—when Alexei stopped short.

"This is not Yekaterinburg."

I stopped, too. "What?"

"Look. You can see the Neva River, the canals winding through the city. You can see the Winter Palace, there in the distance." He shook his head in disbelief. "We're in St. Petersburg."

"That's absurd, Alexei . . . How? How could we have traveled across all of Russia in our sleep? It's illogical, it's—"

My declaration of impossibility was cut short, however, by a round of gunshots erupting from an alleyway between storefronts. "Get down," I instructed rather unnecessarily, as I hugged my brother to the ground. I did so gingerly, even in my panic, wrapping him in my arms and landing him on top of myself before rolling him away from the sound of the bullets. A bullet would kill him undoubtedly, but even a tackle to the ground could injure him fatally. He wouldn't stop bleeding, not without Rasputin.

A second round of gunfire answered the first, as black-haired soldiers emerged from the alleyway. One of them yelled something—was it in Japanese?—and the unit sprinted down the street. More bullets, as opposing soldiers shot after them. What the hell were Japanese soldiers doing in St. Petersburg? Had the war progressed so drastically?

"We've got to try to crawl to the buildings, Ana. We need cover, we . . . we must be in the middle of some military operation. *Pizdets*—" Bullets shattered a nearby storefront window in an explosion of broken glass.

Bullets, flying across the street, whizzing over our heads as we sprawled on the ground. Bullets, filling my father's chest as he dropped to his knees. A burning pain scorched through my skull as I shook the image from my mind. Move. I had to move. No way had I survived execution to die in the street.

We crawled on our bellies across the brick-lined road, moving as quickly as we could toward the alcove by the doorway of the nearest shop. More gunfire, but growing distant. We reached the storefront and Alexei scrambled into the little nook by the doorway, audibly exhaling. I clenched my jaw and pressed myself against the brick pillar, shielding my little brother from the street. A moment passed. Quiet. I sighed then, too, and slumped to the ground.

"What *was* that—" I started.

Alexei interrupted me, stammering over his words as he pointed over my head.

"It's a . . . Ana. Look . . . look up."

As I craned my neck to look skyward, my eyes widened at what I saw.

An enormous armored airship hovered above us, its metallic plates glowing orange in the rusted light of the sunrise. The long barrel of a mounted weapon swiveled around, as though seeking its target, and cast a sharp beam of red light directly at my chest. I peered downward, frozen in fear as a red dot of light appeared, bright against my navy dress as it mirrored the garnet beneath.

Perhaps I was going to die in the street, after all.

I squeezed Alexei's hand, found his eyes, and was for once speechless, not knowing how to say good-bye in the seconds preceding our most certain deaths. But there wasn't time anyway, because then—

BANG.

The bullet pounded the garnet into the bruise on my sternum as I screamed, and then everything went dark.

CHAPTER THREE

"The question is, what do we consider supernatural? When, not a living man but a piece of stone attracted a nail to itself, how did the phenomena strike the first observers? As something natural? Or supernatural?"

"Well, of course; but phenomena such as the magnet attracting iron always repeat themselves."

—The Professor and Sahatof, *Fruits of Culture* by Leo Tolstoy

ALEXEI POPPED HIS EYES open, muscles tensed, immediately on alert. But the room was dark and quiet. There were no soldiers, no guns, no armored airship targeting him. There was only the even tide of Anastasia's breathing as she slept, and the soft whine of the wooden floorboards as Alexei scrambled to sit. He hurried to his feet and in his excitement, he forgot himself, moving too quickly. His bad knee buckled, nearly dropping him to the floor, but he didn't stop to scowl. He was elated. It was just as he'd hoped.

Again, the garnet was shot. And again, they awoke on the cabin floor.

They would need a gun, then, he supposed.

His crooked gait evened as he hurried toward the bedroom, his heart pounding wildly. Rasputin had been right. There would be a way. There *had* to be a way. There had to be a world where his blood was not cursed, where his family still reigned, where his crown was not stolen.

Crouching by the bed, he swiped his hand beneath the mattress, fumbling blindly until his fingers brushed the cool metal of a handgun. He'd been around weapons plenty. Learned to shoot, as any tsarevich should. But his hands trembled as he gripped the handle, tracing his quivering finger along the barrel. When had he last held such power in his hands? A lifetime ago, before the Bolsheviks came, he supposed. *Before Father gave up my throne*, Alexei thought bitterly, *throwing away my birthright to appease those self-righteous traitors.* Alexei bristled, remembering how childishly he'd sobbed when his father had told him.

"I've abdicated," he'd said.

Alexei's jaw had dropped. There had been a nasty rebellion—a series of them, he supposed—but he had never expected to hear those words. He'd assumed his father was doing *something* to maintain his authority. He was astonished. Horrified. His father was no longer tsar. Then he'd gasped, his face lighting with realization. *If my father is no longer tsar . . .*

"So I'm . . . I'm tsar? Tsar of all of Russia?" His voice had raised with excitement, already envisioning his coronation.

His father had frowned, pain filling his eyes as he spoke. "For our family's safety, I've abdicated myself, and on your behalf, as well."

"You . . . how . . . how could you?" Alexei had stuttered, the weight of the words crushing his soul. His destiny, shattered. His idol, deposed. Over the months that followed, his disillusionment had festered into resentment. He still hadn't forgiven his father, even as he'd watched him die. And now he didn't know what to feel, as shock and grief and anger and hunger all tangled in his chest.

"Alexei?" Anastasia's voice called from the other room, groggy and confused.

His eyes didn't leave the handgun. "In here, Ana."

So much power, there in his hands. The power to end lives. For a moment, an image of the cellar flashed through his mind. The guns, firing at his father, his mother, his sisters. But he pushed the image away, burying it deep within his gut. He steeled himself, focusing once more on the gun in his hands. The gun and the power it held, not just to end lives.

No, with the garnet, the gun held a power far greater than death.

CHAPTER FOUR

"Two fixed ideas can no more exist together in the moral world than two bodies can occupy one and the same place in the physical world."

—*The Queen of Spades* by Alexander Pushkin

"ALEXEI, BE CAREFUL WITH that thing—we've been here for what, five minutes? And you've found a gun?" I had followed his voice, ambling into the bedroom. My eyelids weighed a ton, my body aching as though I'd slammed through a wall. And my mind was reeling. Somehow, we'd been transported yet again to the shabby little cabin. To the very same square of uneven wooden floor. It had happened again.

He didn't look up, absorbed in his methodical search through the closet. "And ammunition, hopefully." He paused, glancing at me. "Seems we ought to have one, if that's how this works."

My brother could be such a prat. He was clever, and he loved to make a show of just how much cleverer he was than everyone else. I rolled my eyes. "Go on and tell me, then. Tell me what in the world you're talking about."

Taking an exasperated tone, he enlightened me. "Well clearly something magical is happening when Rasputin's necklace is shot. It's happened twice now. So, we need a gun. And ammunition. Aha!" His hand landed on a small metal tin, its contents clinking as he waved it triumphantly.

It was my turn for exasperation. "Magical? Alexei, *that's* your explanation?"

"Twice the gemstone was shot. Twice we've woken up in this place. Magical, you could say. Or metaphysical, maybe."

I rolled my eyes again, opening my mouth to argue, but Alexei continued, twirling the gun in his hands as he paced the room. "Rasputin was tending me once—I was bleeding too much again. And I was . . . sad. I was realizing that I might not live to be tsar, that I might not live long at all." His eyes met mine. "So our old friend was trying to comfort me, I suppose. He told me unfathomable things. About infinite worlds, infinite possibilities. He said that every version of reality we could imagine exists, in side-by-side worlds. So in another reality, or in many, I would live to be tsar."

I understood. The old starets had told me these things, too. But he'd also told me many things that I hadn't believed.

"Think about it," Alexei went on. "From Yekaterinburg to St. Petersburg? Japanese soldiers? An iron-plated battle blimp in the street? And now, we've awakened *here* again. We've traveled to a parallel universe, Ana."

There was such hunger on his face. He wanted so badly for it to be true. For there to be some world in which his own blood didn't betray him. A world in which his kingdom hadn't rejected him. A world in which he would be tsar. I couldn't blame him. What wouldn't I give for a world in which my parents were alive? A world with my sisters. Where I wasn't a prisoner, but a person. A world that still wanted me.

My eyes softened for a moment as I studied Alexei. Shaking my head, I frowned. "If that were possible—which it's not—what then? What would we do?" I was thinking aloud, truly. Alexei couldn't have an answer for such a loaded question. Without our parents, our sisters, our home . . . we were lost. What would we do with ourselves, in an alternate world?

"Well, *I* would find a way to my throne. Just like Rasputin said. Every version of reality we can imagine exists, in side-by-side worlds. So in some world, I can be tsar." He shrugged, feigning nonchalance, but desperate longing haunted his eyes. "I want to find that world."

"I would save them." The words surprised me as they tumbled from my mouth, but I felt their truth. "I mean hypothetically, if anything was possible—I would save our family. I wouldn't let it fall apart. I would do whatever it took, to keep them alive."

Alexei looked down, perhaps a bit ashamed that he hadn't said the same.

I kept talking, as I tend to do, in an attempt to assuage his guilt. "But it doesn't matter anyway. Because we *can't*—" I paused, sniffing the air. "Alexei . . . do you smell smoke?" The smell was quickly overwhelming. Alexei was holding his shirt collar over his nose, while I was reaching for the door to air the place out. Where was it coming from? As my hand wrapped the metal doorknob, I reeled back and shrieked, my hand immediately blistering. I kicked the door hard, it easily fell open, and my jaw dropped at what I saw.

The whole world was on fire. Outside of the cabin, it was a burning wasteland. My eyes darted to take it all in, my mouth hanging open. What buildings remained were toppling, consumed in flames. The streets were mostly empty of people—just blackened corpses. Nearby was a woman's scorched remains, the singed scraps of a brown woolen dress curling into ashes. The cabin we stood within was alone untouched by the raging fire— but the flames were leaping toward us rapidly.

"Anastasia! The garnet! Again!" Alexei grabbed my hand, pulling me toward him as he drew the gun. What did we have to lose? I looped the chain around my free wrist and slammed the garnet on the table. Alexei met my eye, and I nodded.

BANG. For a moment, everything went black, and then . . . I awoke. My body felt heavy. The floor beneath me, creaky. I blinked my eyes open, finding myself on the cabin floor once more.

It worked.

BANG, HEAVY, CREAKY, blink, bang, heavy, creaky, blink—the cycle repeated, each world as wrong as the last. It was always the cabin. Always the gun.

Sometimes it began as the first world had: an empty cabin, seemingly peaceful at first. But then a Bolshevik would arrive home, or a knife-throwing Kazak, or once, a crying baby that Alexei simply didn't want to deal with.

There were other times that we arrived in the midst of some postapocalyptic hellscape, not unlike the raging fire. In one world, exploding boulders were raining from the sky, and I had to laugh at the ridiculousness as I quickly produced the garnet, Alexei pulling the trigger without hesitation. *Bang, heavy, creaky, blink*—and we'd arrived in the middle of a shoot-out within the cabin. The shooters' eyes had widened in disbelief when we'd magically appeared on the cabin floor. Immediately alert, I had clenched my brother's hand and swung the garnet by its chain, intercepting a bullet in the crossfire. *Bang, heavy, creaky, blink*—the next time, the cabin had existed in an otherwise empty void, floating in nothingness.

There were times when I'd marveled at Alexei's marksmanship, each shot finding the garnet with precision. As though drawn to the jewel. As though the garnet wanted the bullet, *wanted* to be used. I'd voiced such to my brother, to which he'd scoffed. "You speak as though the gemstone has sentience. I—*we* are in control, Anastasia. We are. You've just never seen me shoot."

I'd sighed and extended my hand, dangling the jewel by its chain as Alexei pointed the gun, pulling the trigger yet again.

As we bounced through dimensions, my mind went to Lower Dacha—our little palace by the sea. When we weren't at the Alexander Palace, we had bounced from one grand home to another, but my favorites were those on the water. "Find a flat one," Maria had instructed me, as we stood together on the rocky shore. And I had found the flattest stone—it was like a large coin—and I had whipped my wrist to fling it along the water's surface. The rock had skidded along the top of the water for as long as it could, bouncing across the surface until eventually it ran out of momentum and sunk to the bottom of the sea.

Bang, heavy, creaky, blink.

CHAPTER FIVE

"But I think that I have already been moving too long in a sphere which is not my own. Flying fishes can hold out for a time in the air, but soon they must splash back into the water."

—Ivan Turgenev

T HE MONTHS OF IMPRISONMENT leading up to my family's execution had been terribly boring. Entertainment had been scarce, and so we had created our own. Alexei, Maria, Tatiana, even Olga, when I could persuade her, became the cast and crew for my plays. Pushkin, Gogol, Tolstoy—I would direct my siblings through any script I could find in our prison of a mansion's considerable library.

I knew my sisters participated mostly to appease me, and perhaps to ease their own boredom. But not Alexei. He would become consumed in the works—his connection to the outside world, his view into the soul of his kingdom. He would analyze the characters' interests and beliefs to ascertain their political leanings. He would get caught up in the details, unable to find meaning in the larger story.

"*. . . yet this ring came from there.*" Olga inanimately recited her line, the play doing nothing to ease her boredom.

"*From there? What do you mean?! From where?*" Alexei, at least, could act.

"From the other world. Yes."

"That's very interesting—Wait." Alexei broke character, flipping the page of his script. "Wait, that's all they say about that? They mention 'another world' and then go right back to the silly story?"

I had vaguely wondered, then, if Alexei had bought into Rasputin's ramblings, his impossible belief in other worlds. The ramblings that to me had been irrelevant fiction. But to Alexei, this world had forsaken him. His illness, the Bolsheviks, the realities of this world—they had usurped his throne, his identity, his destiny. For Alexei, there *had* to be another world, another chance for him.

These were the thoughts that filled my cloudy mind as I awoke again on the cabin floor, my body feeling the heaviest it'd been. I allowed myself a moment to sit, waiting for the grog to clear. Alexei was already peeking out the window, holding the curtain back with the barrel of the gun. "It seems peaceful," he announced.

"Excellent. Let's try to keep it that way."

Appearing pensive, Alexei turned the gun in his hand, then let his arm drop by his side. "I suppose that would be novel." He glanced around the cabin. "Best get out of here, then, before someone arrives home."

As I peeled myself from the floor, the garnet dropped with a clink as though yanked from my hand. I was muttering profanities and searching the floor when the door cracked open. We froze, looking at one another from opposite ends of the room with wide eyes. The soft click of a readied gun echoed in the silence. Someone was arriving home, indeed. A vigilant someone.

A young soldier appeared in the doorway, and my first impression was that he was quite handsome despite the gun in his hand. The gun . . . My heartbeat quickened, and for a moment I could only see the barrel of the gun.

I gasped, and my vision blurred. Then through the haze, there were the harsh, cold eyes of the Yekaterinburg guard, rifle raised. My feet hadn't left the ground, but it was as though I was once again captive in the tense silence of the cellar, broken by the guard's pronouncement—*"You are to be executed"*—and the bullets, bullets, bullets. I couldn't breathe, couldn't see, couldn't move, could only hear the gunfire, the screaming—

"Can you hear me?" A voice penetrated the cellar walls that had entrapped my mind. I latched frantically to the voice. Followed it. And just as suddenly as I'd left, I found myself in the cabin once again. I blinked. Took a shaky breath. Exhaled. What was *that*?

The soldier stood before me, still holding the gun, but his green eyes were lit with concern. "Can you hear me?" he repeated.

Almost imperceptibly, I nodded.

Across the room, Alexei raised his brows, pointing his own gun at the soldier's back.

"Okay, then. Who are you, and why are you in my house?" The soldier spoke slowly, as though expecting some perfectly reasonable explanation. As I was unable to conjure a more sensible answer to these questions, a version of the truth would have to do.

"Well, our . . . our family . . ." I trailed off, swallowed, and made myself say the words. "Our family has been killed. We've been . . . on the run. And we wound up here, and we just need a place to rest, and—"

"And I'll shoot if you shoot so drop the gun." Alexei's hand was trembling but he spoke with the authority of a tsarevich accustomed to giving orders. "My sister and I will require a loaf of bread, and water . . . and a bar of chocolate—and we'll be on our way."

The soldier's mouth twitched toward a smile—he appeared rather amused, and not so bewildered as I would be had a bossy thirteen-year-old boy with a gun stuck me up for a loaf of bread in *my* living room. "I see . . ." His eyes met mine, his expression transforming to one of genuine sympathy. "I'm sorry for your loss, my lady." Then, smirking rather devilishly, he took the tone of a simpering servant as he responded to Alexei's demands. "And you're right that I've been undeniably inhospitable. While it seems unwise to drop the gun, I'll fetch the bread and water straight away." As he made his way past us into the small kitchen, his hands moved in a flash, pressing Alexei to the wall with his left, while snatching the gun with his right, all before Alexei could say a word. Perhaps disarming a sickly boy was not such a feat, but I was startled by the soldier's agility. Then he gestured toward the dumpy table and chair in the corner. "Have a seat."

Out of other options, and quite honestly refreshed to be told what to do next, I took a seat, moving the garnet along with me beneath my boot.

There was only the one chair, so Alexei stood beside me at the table. "Now what?" he whispered.

"We eat," I whispered back. "And if things get ugly, we run. We find a gun," I bent to the floor, scooping the necklace from beneath my boot, "and go."

STALE BREAD AND plain boiled water had never tasted so good. Alexei and I nearly choked on the dry bread in our haste to fill our stomachs. Looking up from the empty plate, I found the soldier studying us, brow furrowed in scrutiny. Then his eyes widened in recognition. "Unbelievable . . . it's you, isn't it? The tsarevich! The whole imperial army must be searching for you." He was already pulling the windows closed, locking the door. "You'll get me killed, kid. I've got to get you back to the Winter Palace."

Alexei froze, his face a puzzled mix of pride and embarrassment as he stared at a breadcrumb.

The soldier was running his hands through his dark waves, pacing— rather comically flustered. Despite the situation, I bit my lip to hide a smile. Muttering more to himself then to me, the soldier continued, "And you must be the Grand Duchess Maria. Two Romanov kids in my cabin, of all places. Unbelievable."

I balked. "Maria?" I was both flattered and offended, my closest sis- ter being the beauty of the bunch, but still, I did not take kindly to being mistaken for her or anyone but myself. And then I conjured the image of her wide eyes, quietly comforting me from across that horrible cellar. The indignance dropped from my face, my tone softening. "Anastasia, actually. And I'm not a kid." He couldn't be more than a year or two older than me. "I'm seventeen."

He looked at me then. "Anastasia who?"

"Romanov. Obviously."

"Never heard of an Anastasia. You said you were on the run, that your family . . ." He trailed off, looking solemn. "Why've you got the tsarevich with you?" He gestured toward my little brother. "He doesn't look well."

Alexei hadn't moved. He stood with his hands folded, staring impassively at his feet. I saw the wheels turning in his mind. He hadn't decided yet if this recognition was to our benefit or not. What we needed was time to learn about this new world we had arrived in, and time to form a plan. What we did not need was to be carted off to the Winter Palace with neither. But then again, what did we have to lose? The garnet lay hidden beneath my dress.

My mind raced to organize what data I could. "*Never heard of an Anastasia,*" he'd said. And yet he knew of my sister, and he'd recognized my brother on sight. Perhaps there was no Anastasia—not here in this world. I realized then that the soldier was still looking at me expectantly, awaiting my answer. I certainly did not have one. So I tried to deflect.

"Well who are you? How can I entrust a stranger to safely return the tsarevich to the palace? How do I know you aren't—" I paused. A Bolshevik, I'd been about to say. But how could I know if there even were Bolsheviks in this world? "—an enemy?" I finished.

The soldier let out an exasperated sigh that was almost a laugh. "I could ask the same of you! For all I know, *you* work with the rebels. Look, I want no part in whatever is happening here, but as the tsarevich is sitting in my kitchen, it seems to be too late for that." He looked at Alexei. "It'd be my duty to return you to the tsar. To your father." He stopped pacing, and then, as an afterthought, "I'm Lev."

My brother finally looked up. As I was apparently an insignificant nobody in this world, the next move would be up to Alexei.

"To the Winter Palace then. And the bar of chocolate?"

⁓⁓⁓⁓⁓⁓

ATOP AN OLD mare Lev had industriously procured in the hour that had passed, I hugged Alexei's swaddled form to me with one arm, my other hand fidgeting with the garnet as we rode. Was it any good, without a gun? I furrowed my brow, growing anxious as the ease of trans universal travel waned.

Wrapped in a blanket, Alexei didn't need much of a disguise to appear as a sickly child seeking the palace physicians. Lev thought it best that no one recognize the tsarevich as he led our horse through the bustling streets of St. Petersburg. The sun was shining, and shoppers were out in hoards, enjoying the July warmth. They chattered and laughed as they went about their business. Scents of fresh fudge, apple cakes, and vanilla *kartoshka* wafted temptingly from a crowded bakery. It was all offensively normal, given the trauma, the suffering, the *absurdity* of the situation.

With every step, we narrowed the distance between ourselves and our family. Or at least, some otherworldly version of our parents and sisters. But oh, how I ached to see them. Alive. Unhurt. My heart fluttered with eager anticipation, a desperation that had allowed such recklessness to progress this far. Recklessness, or perhaps just plain stupidity. Because inevitably, we would encounter another version of Alexei, too.

As we neared the palace, my heart no longer fluttered, but raced. This was a terrible idea. We needed time to form a plan. Time to learn about this world.

"Alexei," I whispered faintly, but urgently, "demand we stop. Say you need . . . something. Anything. Say you want something sweet. Get Lev to stop somewhere, and we'll steal the horse. We'll ride somewhere we can hide out while we make a plan."

He squeezed my hand in response.

"Stop the horse, soldier." Alexei spoke with authority from beneath his crumpled blanket. "I've had nothing to eat but stale bread. Stop and I'll buy us all some *kartoshka*."

Lev sighed, but did not stop walking. "Your Highness, we're nearly there. When we reach the Winter Palace, you can have all the sweets you desire—"

"But Lev," I interrupted, "I really *must* use the facilities. Can't we stop for just a moment?"

"Sorry, my lady. So do I. But what I need most of all is to unload our precious cargo safely and wash my hands of it."

"Well sorry to burden you, but I won't be able to hold it, and your horse wouldn't like that very much at all."

Alexei elbowed me in the ribs. "Gross, Ana."

Biting my tongue, I raised my palms unapologetically. We were desperate, weren't we?

Looking over his shoulder, Lev raised his eyebrows. "Look, I don't know which is a greater risk to my life: bringing you two to the palace, or doing anything except that. But I'll sleep better having returned the boy to his home. I don't know who *you* are, or how you and the boy came to be in my house, or what else you might be plotting. And I don't want to know. I'm delivering you to the palace. And then I'm going home."

I wasn't without sympathy for his position. We had indeed burdened him, and he had been kind to us. But, our only semblance of a plan—if one could call our hasty whispers just moments before a plan—consisted of avoiding the Winter Palace at all costs and was quite at odds with Lev's mission. He was not interested in my words, so it must be action.

"Just faint," Alexei whispered. "We'll have to stop, then."

Whether by choice or by fate, I resorted to the oldest trick in the book.

I took a breath, and in my mind, I was eight years old, standing upon the ledge of the garden wall, my sisters behind me with their hands interwoven, creating a basket to catch me. *"Just fall,"* Maria had said. *"I promise we'll catch you. That's why they call it a Trust Fall."* That had been all I'd needed. I remembered the feeling—the faith, the certainty. I had closed my eyes, and fallen without fear.

After the day we'd had, this should have been easy. But the prospect of willingly falling off of a horse—falling like a brick, to sell it as a faint—was causing me to sweat. My sisters were not here to catch me. No one was. My heartbeat throbbed in every vein. My skin prickled. *"I've never heard of an Anastasia,"* he'd said. Who was I, if not Princess Anastasia, daughter of Tsar Nicholas II and Tsarina Alexandra? Who was I, without my sisters? Who was I, without my kingdom? My forehead burned and my vision began to blur. I was no one's daughter, I was no one's princess, I was no one. I did not exist.

I-did-not-exist-I-did-not-exist-I-did-not—

I fainted.

THROUGH MY HEAVY lashes, emeralds danced before me, twinkling in the late afternoon sun. Then the image began to clear, and my eyes found Lev's. Kneeling over me, he pressed two fingers to my neck, finding my pulse. "You swooned," he informed me, rather unnecessarily.

A small crowd had formed around us, as my fall from the horse had attracted the attention of the townsfolk on the street—and the attention of several nearby soldiers. Clad in the same silver-buttoned black coats as Lev, the soldiers approached him genially. They were inquiring as to my health, Lev hurriedly attempting to move them along, when a nosy bystander spotted Alexei and cried out, "The tsarevich!"

The friendly concern for my well-being vanished, and the next moments were a whirlwind.

"He's been kidnapped!"

"Kidnapped by a soldier, no less!"

"Traitorous rebels, likely!"

And Alexei—"You're mistaken, I'm not who you think!"—even then, could not bring himself to say the words, "I am not the tsarevich." But it wouldn't have mattered, the crowd was frenzied, the soldiers in action.

"Now let me explain before—" Lev's voice, pragmatic, but raised to be heard over the commotion, was cut short as a soldier tackled him from behind, knocking the reins from his hand and the gun from his side. Silver buttons flashed in a tangle of fists and kicks and grunts, and the crowd was momentarily distracted. Alexei seized this moment to toss off the blanket and slide from the horse, diving for the gun.

"Ana! The garnet! Now!" Alexei's voice trembled as he grasped for the gun stock with his right hand, and reached to me with his left. I snapped out of my daze and sprung toward him, my fist clenching the gemstone. But soldiers were swarming us then, blocking my path to my brother.

"She was with them!"

"Arrest her!"

The soldiers seized me by my middle, nearly knocking the wind from my lungs as they easily pinned my small frame to the ground. I flailed, kicking and cursing as they bound my wrists and ankles with thick rope. My fingernails dug into my palm as I was still clasping the garnet tight in my fist.

"Alexei!" I screamed to be heard over all the commotion. "Alexei, don't let them take you! Alexei, tell them—"

A soldier stuffed a crusty handkerchief in my mouth, and I nearly gagged.

Alexei was handled more gently but was equally incapacitated, restrained by soldiers on both sides. I could only see the back of his head. Would he have fought, if he were able? Would he have resisted restraint, refusing to be separated from his sister? As it were, he stood quietly, allowing the dutiful soldiers to escort him away.

I struggled against my constraints, determined to catch up to my brother. My only family, my only tie to the world I'd known. The little boy I'd spent my life protecting. As he marched on, he stood tall, his shoulders rolled back, assuming his usual air of authority despite his frailty. Turning his head, he looked over his shoulder and his eyes found mine. There was fear in his eyes, but I saw something else there, too. Excitement. Ambition. Then he looked forward and kept moving, onward to the Winter Palace.

As my brother faded into the distance, the soldiers were patting me down less-than-gently as they inspected me for weapons. "What have we, here?" A tall soldier peeled my fingers open, wrenching the garnet from my grasp as I squirmed, jerking the chain off my neck. He held the oversized gemstone up to the light, the prism glimmering in the sunlight, casting planes of red light on the street.

"Kidnapper, traitor, and thief," the soldier proclaimed, pocketing the necklace. I could only glare, seething at the unfairness of it all.

Outnumbered three to one, Lev continued to struggle, but was securely bound. He was still protesting, demanding his explanation be heard as he repeated his true but thin account of what had transpired—"I found these two in my home, I don't know how they got there, I was returning the boy to the palace!"

The soldier cracked the butt of his rifle against Lev's back. "Save your story for the tsar."

CHAPTER SIX

"Better the illusions that exalt us than ten thousand truths."

—Aleksander Pushkin

LEXEI BIT HIS LIP to avoid gawking as his captors ushered him to the throne room. In his own world, the Winter Palace had been reserved for state affairs, a grand castle that gleamed with a magnificence unlike any of the lesser palaces he'd called home. *Could I belong here?* His eyes traced the opulent halls wistfully as he walked, taking in the ornate details of the wall hangings, admiring the grandeur of the golden columns. *The air itself even seems to glisten,* Alexei thought as he stepped through the enormous oak doorway into the throne room. Then his gaze settled on the man on the throne, and his mouth hung open in wonder.

The man was the image of his father, from his kind eyes to that immaculate handlebar mustache. He even kept his sleeves rolled to the elbows, displaying the green dragon tattoo circling his muscled forearm. But there were subtle differences, too.

The tsar's face was less lined than his father's had been. His dark hair less grayed. He sat upon his throne with the easy demeanor of a king who still held his kingdom. Alexei's throat tightened. *A father who hadn't failed.*

For a moment, his anger softened. *Who hadn't been sentenced to die.*

"My son, why have you come home so early, and without your sisters?" Even his voice was the same, the deep tones carrying easily across the room, nearly shattering Alexei's desperate grip on reality.

For a moment, it was as though Anastasia had been right. That it had all been a terrible dream. And he was safe now, with his father, the tsar. He was where he belonged. *No,* he told himself. *No, it was not a dream, you are not safe, and this man on the throne is not your father. Your father lost his throne. Your father is dead.* His lip quivered. A tear welled in his eye, threatening to escape down his cheek, but he blinked it back. Weakness would accomplish nothing. *You don't belong here, but you could. If you can keep your wits about you.*

"Alexei?" The tsar raised his brow, waiting for an answer.

Alexei didn't have a story, didn't know how to lie the right way to support this charade.

Honesty, then.

"I wanted to see you." He forced a tight smile.

"Well," the tsar grinned back, "come, then. Let's have a game of chess and you can tell me about your time with your uncle. I'm curious to hear if you and your sisters had any success in taming his wild notions."

A soldier cleared his throat. "Your Majesty. The young tsarevich was discovered on horseback, wrapped in rags, accompanied by a soldier and a young woman. Kidnapped by the rebels, it would appear."

The tsar looked alarmed, but doubtful. "I see." His thumb and forefinger twirled the long ends of his mustache. "Indeed, the rebels have been gaining courage. Emboldened by my brother's idiocy, unfortunately." He looked to Alexei knowingly, as though the boy ought to understand the reference. "And what do you say to that, Alexei? Were you kidnapped?"

"No, Father." Could it be that easy? Ana and Lev would be released from prison, if there were no charges. He would play chess with the tsar, and tell him about—where had the man said he'd been? His uncle's house. Mikhail, then? He would need to stay sharp if he were to continue this façade.

But the tsar's easy demeanor hardened as he narrowed his eyes, assessing him. "You look pale, and weak. The journey from your uncle's estate is not *so* taxing. There is something you aren't telling me."

The meddlesome soldier piped in again. "Your Majesty, he resisted coming into our custody. He attempted to deny his identity."

Alexei shrunk under the tsar's piercing gaze. What could he possibly say? He couldn't refute it, there were too many witnesses. His mind raced. Why would he have unexpectedly returned home from his uncle's estate, pale and wan? He thought of his Uncle Mikhail, his father's younger brother. He'd never liked Alexei much—Mikhail had been heir to the throne until Alexei was born. But Alexei hadn't liked him so well either—he'd always felt as though Mikhail had been waiting for him to die—hoping for an incurable bleed that even Rasputin couldn't whisper away. From what he could glean, there was some conflict arising between his father and his uncle already, and an idea came to him, then. He didn't care who it might damn.

"I wanted to be discreet, until I could talk to you, Father. But I had to leave the Luzhsky Uyezd. Your brother—he was poisoning me. At first, I thought I had just fallen ill, but it was him. That's why I'm so . . . weak." He winced. His mother had always told him that he was strong despite his illness, that anyone who said otherwise was a traitor and a heretic.

The magnitude of this revelation spurred the palace into action immediately. Believing his son's admission without question, the tsar was livid. He ordered extra guards to the palace entries. He ordered that Alexei be taken to the palace physicians without delay. He looked past Alexei to the soldiers by the door. "Alert my council that we meet at midnight. Alert the first regiment that we ride to the Luzhsky Uyezd at dawn."

In all the madness, no one asked him again about Anastasia or Lev.

EVERYTHING IS JUST *as it ought to be.* Alexei sank deeper beneath the foamy bubbles as he soaked in the warm bath water. The physicians, having been predisposed to believing Alexei's story given his pallid appearance and the court's general distrust of Mikhail Romanov, had validated the lie, while offering a prognosis for full recovery. As he was not in any acute physical distress, the physicians had recommended a warm bath, full belly, and comfortable bed.

Less than twenty-four hours had passed since the execution, but Alexei had felt as though his skin was caked in a lifetime's worth of dirt and dried blood. While he'd kept clean over the last year and a half, the warm bath, bubbling with soap, was a luxury he hadn't experienced since before his family's imprisonment. *This is how the tsarevich should be treated.*

Since his revelation in the throne room, he had been pampered and fussed over, and the palace was abuzz with gossip.

"An attempted poisoning of his own nephew!"

"He's always been after the throne."

"The tsar must retaliate!"

And retaliate, he would. *He's a strong leader in this world,* Alexei thought approvingly.

There was a knock at the door, and a servant entered the bathing chamber, a folded blanket and silken pajamas in hand. A second servant appeared behind the first, with a tray of cheeses and sliced apples. They smiled warmly at Alexei, but he could see their concern for him in their faces.

Alexei rose from the water, bubbles rolling off his pale skin, and the servants' mouths hung agape. The first servant dropped the pajamas, rushing to wrap him in the blanket.

"My precious boy! You're so thin, and these bruises!"

Alexei flinched—he did not welcome pity. "I'm not your precious boy, I'm the tsarevich—you should address me as such." He snatched the blanket and wrapped himself.

The servant stepped back, exchanging a glance with his companion. Alexei wondered if they were used to being so overly familiar with the tsarevich, or if it was just that his feeble form commanded no respect. He had learned to be stern with people, to maintain his dignity.

"Of course, Your Highness." Clearly dismissed, the servants left the pajamas and the tray, scurrying from the room.

As Alexei stepped from the bath, his left knee buckled slightly, but he caught himself. The knee could straighten now, at least, but the events of Spala had left him forever weakened. As soapy bubbles dripped from his bony frame, his mind went back to the impetus of it all. Spala. He had been eight, out for a row on the pond with his father. Such a simple thing—he'd merely slipped in the boat, the oarlock catching his thigh. It had hurt a bit, but it was the months of bleeding inside his leg that had been agonizing. As young as he had been, he remembered how certain he'd been that he was dying. The doctors had thought so, too. And he had looked forward to his death, as the only imaginable end to the pain.

But then, Rasputin intervened. Alexei had been on the brink of death, his mother barely clinging to her senses. She had telegraphed Rasputin, begging for the starets's prayers, and the healer had proclaimed that the little tsarevich would not die. "Don't let those doctors bother him," he'd advised. Rasputin's message was received and it was so. Slowly, Alexei recovered. And Rasputin had sealed his position of influence within the palace.

As he dressed, delighted by the soft silk against his clean skin, Alexei turned his mind to the important matters at hand. He considered the distance to the Luzhsky Uyezd and calculated that he had two days, at best, to enjoy the comforts of the palace before the tsar would discover that his son remained at Mikhail's estate, and it became apparent that Alexei was an imposter. But he wanted more than two days. He needed to concoct a plan that would allow him to replace the Other Alexei, reclaim his kingdom, and live to be tsar. *And free Ana*, he added to his list, having almost forgotten.

Snug beneath the soft blankets in his oversized bed, Alexei crafted plan after plan, but each was problematic. Word of his presence at the palace, and his simultaneous presence at his uncle's estate, would inevitably reach the ears of the tsar. He could not be seen in two places at once. He struggled to stay awake, to think, to form a plan that would work. But his body was so exhausted. *Tomorrow,* he thought, and nestled into the feather pillows.

CHAPTER SEVEN

"Where pleasures, love, and happiness shone brightest, in health's golden glow, now the blood freezes in the veins and sorrow agitates the soul."

—*On the Death of Prince Meshchersky* by Gavrila Derzhavin

"ARE WE GOING TO talk about it, then?" Lev sat with his back to me, staring through the heavy metal bars of our prison cell as I sulked behind him in the corner.

Awaiting our judgment, we'd been locked in the royal dungeon, deep in the basement beneath the Winter Palace. I was imagining my family many meters above my head—perhaps they were having dinner, drinking wine, laughing together . . .

I snapped out of my reverie.

"Talk about what? Your thoughts on our glorious accommodations? Or our upcoming trial with my fa—" I stopped, catching myself. ". . . with the tsar?"

Lev's shoulders tightened. "How did you know where it was?"

I studied the back of his head, as though perhaps one of his dark curls might enlighten me as to what in the world he was talking about.

"What in the world are you talking about?" I inquired, his curls having forfeited no information.

An exasperated sigh. "The necklace, Anastasia, what else? It looks as though we've answered the question of why you were in my house. But how did you find it?"

"Find it? I didn't find it. It was given to me. It's mine!"

"Mm." He shook his head in disbelief. "You're clearly deranged. Gallivanting around St. Petersburg with the tsarevich, breaking into other's homes. You expect me to believe you when you say you aren't a thief?"

He wasn't wrong—he had no reason to trust me. But what could I tell him, besides the truth? I bristled at the unfairness of it all. On top of everything I'd endured in the last day, now I was locked in a prison cell, defending my morality to a grumpy stranger. Huffing indignantly, I crossed my arms over my chest. "As I said. It was given to me. It's mine."

Lev spoke slowly, his voice accusatory, as he looked at me over his shoulder. "Then whoever gave it to you, stole it from me. From my house. I inherited it. It's mine."

I blinked. Behind his gruff tone, there was earnestness on his face. As though he truly believed the garnet belonged to him. It was impossible, though. Rasputin had given it to me nearly two years ago, before my family had been confined to house arrest. And he had been with our family for years before that as my father's advisor, my mother's magician, my brother's healer. He surely hadn't been ricocheting between worlds. Biting my lip, I tried to make sense of his words. Could it be possible that he was telling the truth? He certainly seemed to think he was. But it just didn't make any sense. Unless . . .

"Maybe there are two."

Turning his back to me once more, Lev returned to staring through the cell bars.

"There can't be two."

<hr />

AT LEAST AN hour had passed in complete silence, and I'd never in my life gone so long without speaking. I sat studying Lev's back: lean but strong, his spine curved slightly to the left. His shoulders were slumped in exhaustion, his elbows propped on his knees, holding his head in his hands. I twirled a sweaty blonde lock around my finger, my dirty hair holding the curl. Aside from the noise of a few repairmen moving in and out of the dark basement, the dungeon was dismally empty.

"So we'll just sit here silently, then? Can't you tell me a story? How about your favorite vacation?"

Silence. Then, "I've never had a vacation."

"Never? Well, your favorite place, then, surely you've been outside of St. Petersburg."

Silence.

"Okay, something else then. When's your birthday?"

He sighed. "November."

I supposed a one-word response was better than none. "Ah, mine's June—"

"Look," he cut me off, his voice sharp. "I don't want to make small talk with you. You've lied, you've stolen from me, you've landed me in prison. So yes, let's just sit here silently. Please."

I flinched. That wasn't fair. I had withheld the truth, but I hadn't lied. And I certainly hadn't stolen his garnet. As for landing him in prison, that was really due to Alexei more so than me. No one seemed to care about me in this world, anyway. No one cared where I went or what I did. I blinked, unsure what to make of that realization. It was a freedom I'd never known and wasn't sure I wanted. Not for what it'd cost. I blinked again slowly, not allowing myself to cry. Not now. No, now I needed to think. This lonesome world was where I would be staying, at least until I found my necklace. Where would I even begin? Would the soldier keep it? Or would he deliver it to the tsar?

Even if I could recover the garnet, what would I do with it? Did I really mean to keep traveling from one world to the next, floating through the universe, anchorless? What sort of world would I even be looking for? My family existed here in this world—they were so close, separated from me only by the stone ceiling above. If I could just catch a glimpse of my mother, or share one laugh with my sisters . . . My head began to ache. They wouldn't know me. What was the point?

Regardless, I needed to get out of this prison. And that would be easier with an ally. I looked to Lev. "Listen, I'm sorry. There are . . . things I can't tell you. I mean, I could, but you wouldn't believe me anyway. But I haven't lied to you about anything. Really. I'm not very good at lying, to be honest. And I promise I didn't steal your necklace. A sort of magician gave it to me, a long time ago."

He inclined his head, turning his body to face me. "Magicians haven't existed for nearly nineteen years."

"Well. This one did, and he gave me the garnet. I didn't steal it."

"You're telling me the gemstone is a *kolodets*."

"A what?" The words were out before I could stop myself.

But Lev mistook my ignorance for disbelief, raising his palms defensively. "I'm not saying I believe in them, either, but you said a *magician* gave you a *gemstone* . . ." He flicked his hands meaningfully, as though the implication was obvious.

A *kolodets*—a well. I had no idea what to make of that, and so I remained silent. For a long moment, we both sat quietly, lost in our own thoughts.

When Lev spoke again, his voice was kinder. Less grumpy. "Tell me about this magician."

Lifting my head, I met Lev's eye. "He was like family." I smiled, despite myself. "Like a strange uncle, you could say. My parents often sought his advice. My brother was sick, and he was the only one who could heal him. He loved my sisters and me. But . . ." My smile faltered. "He's dead now."

"And your family . . . you said they were killed."

"My parents and my sisters, yes."

"I'm sorry."

"Me too. It was horrific." And then the words spilled from my mouth. It was cathartic, to remember it, to release it. It hadn't been a dream. Neither was I dreaming now. This was real. And I began to feel it. "My family had developed many enemies over the years. People who didn't like the way we lived. They forced us out of our home, and for over a year we were imprisoned. In different places, different houses—even in Siberia for a while. I thought that we would just go on like that, our enemies moving us from one place to another. We were captives, but we were together. It could have been worse." I took a breath and closed my eyes. Here it was. My voice cracked as I continued. "Then one night—last night—we thought we were being moved again. We were told to get dressed, and we were escorted to the basement. We were excited—we thought . . . we thought that we would be going somewhere better. That we would be free. But a guard told us then—well, told my father—that we would be executed. And before my father could even respond, they shot him. They started shooting at all of us and . . . I saw them all killed. My father. My mother. My sisters. I saw a guard point his gun at me, and I saw him pull the trigger. I clung to my brother's hand . . . we were going to die. But the bullet—it ricocheted. It hit my necklace. And somehow, we . . . escaped. "

It was as though a violent river of grief had been dammed up, held back as I kept moving forward from one fiasco to the next. But now, when I stopped speaking, my skull swelled with the silence, and the dam was going to break. I didn't fight it—I let the tears pool in my eyes and leak down my cheeks. Lev watched me, his face softening, his eyes full of deep sadness. Like maybe he too knew loss.

He shifted, as though to come to me, but then stayed put. He furrowed his brow. "These enemies, are they after you now?"

"No," my voice caught in my throat. I shook my head and met his eye. "No, they are very far away."

Holding my gaze, Lev nodded. "Good."

NIGHTFALL CAME, OUR prison cell becoming a black abyss. The air was stale. No breeze permeated the thick stone walls of the dungeon.

Sleep was impossible, my mind cycling through sinister images on a loop. I imagined my father—or rather, the tsar of this world—realizing Alexei's deception. Sentencing us to the Peter and Paul Fortress. Condemning us to death. Or worse, separating me from my brother forever. And then images of the night before flooded my consciousness, the silent tension of the cellar erupting with gunfire, the darkness painted red with blood. I thrashed and sobbed and groaned in frustration. I was exhausted, but consumed by dread for the future and memories of the horrific past.

Hours passed in fitful agony, but at some point during the night, I scooted myself just close enough to Lev to hear the rhythmic evenness of his inhales and exhales. And slowly, I matched his breath with my own. His presence was comforting. Calming. The chaotic images in my mind became a soft blur, and I slipped into a deep, dreamless sleep.

CHAPTER EIGHT

"For darkness restores what light cannot repair."

—Joseph Brodsky

"**M**Y SON, HOW I'VE missed you!" The tsarina stood up from the table, setting down her quill and pushing her half-written letter aside. She was beautiful, her red-gold hair shining in the soft morning light, her gray eyes looking lovingly upon her son. Alexei stared, awestruck. Between his fruitless scheming and his total exhaustion the night before, he hadn't prepared himself for the impact of seeing the tsarina's face—his mother's face. Perfect. Unmarred.

"And I've missed you, Mother." Grinning despite himself, he allowed himself just a moment of softness, just a moment to be a little boy, sinking into his mother's comfortable embrace. He breathed in deeply, closing his eyes. She even smelled the same—of sweet white rose and just a hint of smoked tobacco. Familiar, and yet somehow . . . different.

She patted his back, one, two, three times and then kissed the top of his head, just as his own mother had done. Then she pulled away—carelessly, almost—and Alexei snapped his eyes open. *That's the difference.* It'd been a simple hug between a mother and her son, without the desperate urgency that haunted his own mother. She had never pulled away first. She'd clung to him as though he might bleed away to nothing, should she ever let him go.

But this woman was unburdened. Happy. More present. *She has no reason to be melancholy,* Alexei realized. *No reason to place her faith in a mystic like Rasputin.* He frowned, fixing his eyes upon the marble floor. *She's not in constant fear of her son's imminent death. I haven't broken her, here in this world.*

She took his hand, humming softly as she led him to sit with her at the drawing table. "Alexei, my sweet child, I'm so sorry. We never should have sent you to Mikhail's. We thought that being with you—his darling nephew and nieces—would bring him to his senses. We just never imagined . . . but don't fret. Your father and his soldiers left for the Luzhsky Uyezd an hour ago. Your sisters will be safe. This rebellion will be halted. Your uncle Mikhail will be brought to justice."

Alexei pushed away the thoughts of his mother and his own role in her depression, and swallowed the guilt that arose with the tsarina's words. *Mikhail must deserve it,* he told himself. *If he's so untrustworthy, it's surely his own fault.*

Now was not the time for pity, for himself nor anyone else. Shaking his head, Alexei turned his mind to the bigger issue. How could he sustain this deception?

Even with their numbers, the tsar's regiment would arrive at Mikhail's estate by the next day's noon. The tsar would find his true son there, and Alexei would be recognized as a pretender. He would be banished from the palace. He would be imprisoned, or worse.

Alexei's head pounded, his palms clammy. There had to be a way.

He could leave now, hide, give himself some time. But still, his father would arrive at his uncle's estate and discover that he had been duped. That an imposter existed. He would still lose his chance.

The easiest way out would be to use the garnet and start over in another world. He could sneak to the dungeon, free his sister, and teleport. His mind flashed through the numerous worlds they had traveled through the previous morning. How many more gunshots to the garnet would it take to find another world as perfect as this one? No, he was finally where he belonged and he did not wish to leave. His mother, his father, his sisters— they were *here*. He could be with them, he could be the tsarevich, he could live his life as he was meant to. He could do this. But he could only take his rightful place as tsarevich if the Other Alexei ceased to exist in this world.

This one obstacle was an iron wall, separating him from his destiny. But as a dozen impossible schemes churned in his mind, he began to see the smallest crack in that wall—a thin crack—but perhaps it was possible . . .

His only hope was Anastasia. Yes . . . the path became clear in his mind. Would she do this evil thing, for him? Would she, *could* she, ride fast enough to the Luzhsky Uyezd? If she could get there in time, could she dispatch the Other Alexei, so that he was the Only Alexei?

He thought that she probably could. But he did not think she would. *Unless* . . .

"*I would save them,*" she'd said. "*I would save our family.*"

Well, here is your chance, big sister. I'm the only family you've got. In his desperation, he concocted a plan. It would be dependent on his sister's capability. Her love for her brother. And her misplaced trust in him.

"Mother, the prisoners. The two that were arrested when I was brought in. I know what it looked like to our men, but the lady and the soldier were only helping me—escorting me home. The poison had made me so weak, I needed assistance. They should be freed."

"Of course, my son. I'd nearly forgotten. If you say they helped you, all charges shall be dropped. I'll send a guard now."

This was it. He swallowed. "But wait—I must send a note—to thank them."

She smiled. "You've a big heart, Alexei." She slid her quill and a piece of parchment across the table.

There was no time to contemplate the consequences. He hastily scrawled his note as she called for a guard.

Ana—If you're reading this, I've been taken by the rebels. I believe they are taking me to Mikhail's near Luga. He is an enemy. Save me. Then use the garnet. There is no time to waste.
Alexei

Alexei read over his words. *If she succeeds, I'll never see her again.* But a tsarevich had to make sacrifices. He imagined her anger, when she realized that he had deceived her. Would it be in this world, or the next? Would she know immediately? *Of course she will. The Other Alexei won't know her, and Anastasia will see that the note is a lie.*

For a moment, Alexei paused, dropping the pen. His fingers clenched the edges of the parchment, ready to crumple the useless note and discard it. *This plan won't work. Not unless . . . she somehow expects me to be different. She must expect my mind to be addled.* His eyes widened as an idea occurred to him, and he snatched the pen, scribbling a postscript.

P.S. They have a magician. He may wipe my memory.

He folded the parchment, sealed it. His heart was racing. If he paused even for a moment, he might not go through with it. He thrusted the note toward the tsarina.

"All done, dear?" The tsarina didn't seem to notice Alexei's hand quivering as she took the sealed parchment and handed it to the guard. "For our prisoners. Convey our regret for their hardships, and release them at once."

CHAPTER NINE

"Humor is an affirmation of dignity, a declaration of man's superiority to all that befalls him."

—Romain Gary

MORNING HAD COME, THOUGH the sun remained hidden behind the thick walls of the dark dungeon. Despite the hard stone I lay upon, I awoke with that distinct sort of comfort one feels when awakening from a satisfactory sleep. And then, that comfort was darkened by the gloom that sets in during those first moments of wakefulness, when one remembers the terrible realities of the waking world. Despite the awfulness of it all, I nearly choked on my own tongue as a snort of laughter intercepted my yawn—what was Lev *doing*?

Standing on his hands, his feet pressing into the stone ceiling, Lev was performing some absurd type of push-up and grunting rather unabashedly.

"I thought perhaps you'd gone into hibernation." His voice strained under the effort as he straightened his arms. "You missed breakfast," he added, bending his elbows and flicking his head toward the corner of the cell.

More stale bread sat upon a rusted metal platter. What I wouldn't give for a boiled egg, cold sturgeon, an apple. But I was famished, so I dragged myself to my feet and shuffled over to the unappetizing platter. I looked to

Lev. "You know, I didn't peg you for a show-off. A do-gooder, maybe, but I'm quite surprised to see you working so hard to impress me."

Snapping his feet to the floor, he was standing upright in an instant. "Nonsense. It's my daily routine, whether at home, on the road, or imprisoned. You should move your body, Anastasia. A thief must stay fit."

Brushing aside the accusation, I tied my skirts into a knot between my knees. "Do you make a habit of being imprisoned, then?" Placing my hands on the floor, I kicked my feet over my head, landing them against the wall.

"I would prefer to be at home, or on the road, but here we are." Lev shrugged, and raised a brow at me. "Show-off."

The sound of approaching footsteps and a jangling of keys prompted me to return my feet to the ground. My heart fluttered with nervous anticipation. No matter the results of the trial, I was eager for the waiting to come to an end. I was anxious to see my brother. To look upon my father's face.

The guard nonchalantly sorted through the keys on his ring, and finding the right one, slid it into the lock. The cell door fell open.

"You're free to go."

My brows shot upward, my mouth hanging open as I stared in disbelief. Just like that?

"The tsarina apologizes for the inconvenience, Private." He addressed Lev—I was but a nameless girl, after all. "This is for you." He handed Lev a sealed note and turned to walk away. "Better get a move on, the palace is raising defenses. This place will be a fortress by noon."

I TRIED TO remember the last time I had ridden a horse. Really ridden a horse—my time atop the old mare on our way to the palace didn't count. How long had it been since I'd surrendered so completely to the power of such an animal, trusting that the magnificent creature would deliver me whole as we bolted across a field? We'd left the old mare cobbled in the care of the tsar's stablemen and opted for an upgrade. No one seemed to notice. The soldiers, the servants, the court—everyone was quite preoccupied, the castle buzzing with anticipation and preparation for whatever was at hand. Lev had chosen a strong stallion, who had remained nearly alone in the stables. He was young and perhaps lacked the caliber of training that the imperial army required.

But he was fast. And that was what mattered. My brother was out there, somewhere. Kidnapped, he'd written. The note was bewildering, the circumstances implausible. But Alexei was all I had left, and he needed my help. I had to find him.

As the palace grounds passed by us in a gale, I couldn't help but admire the lush green gardens dotted with bright July blooms and the golden summer sunrays glinting off the rippling surface of the Neva River. It was surprising, in a way, to see that such simple beauty still existed, despite the urgency of my quest. Despite the pain and horror that haunted my mind.

I swallowed, steeling myself, and allowed the steady rise and fall of Lev's chest against my back to calm my frayed nerves. His thighs framed mine, holding me in my place atop our steed. A hint of guilt clouded my conscience. But Lev's continued involvement in this mess was his own choice, wasn't it? He had read the note and was compelled to rescue his tsarevich. Other than telling him the truth, how could I convince him that the Alexei who wrote this note was not the Alexei he served? The less considerate side of me was glad to have him along for this adventure. I knew the way to my uncle's Luzhsky Uyezd estate, in the wooded lands near Luga. But I didn't know this world. I didn't know what this rebellion was. A difficult mission lay before me, full of unknowns, but with Lev here, I could succeed. I would succeed. I had to.

We rode hard until the sun began to set, the sky aglow and the air around us hued pink. Lev dismounted agilely. I could hardly move my legs. "Let's be quick about it, then, Anastasia. There's a small offshoot of the Oka just down this bank. We can bring water up for ourselves and for Molniya."

"Molniya?" Lightning. "Because he's fast, I suppose? Not the most creative, Lev."

"I'm open to suggestions." He tied Molniya to a low branch, and began lowering himself down the steep bank toward the stream. "And anytime that you'd like to enlighten me as to why the tsarevich has pinned his hope for rescue on *you*, I'm all ears."

He wasn't wrong. I was small, unskilled, and rather average when it came to scheming. Nothing qualified me to rescue the tsarevich—nothing but my dedication to protecting my little brother. But Lev couldn't know that Alexei was my brother. Wouldn't believe that I was a Grand Duchess, truly. No, I would remain anonymous in this world. I was no one.

I bit my lip, refocusing on my balance as I followed Lev down the ridge. "Mm-hmm. As I said. There are things I cannot tell you. But I will do my best not to lie to you."

"Well that instills the utmost confidence, Anastasia. As long as you're trying your best not to lie. It must take significant effort."

It was indeed a ridiculous promise, and it did not foster the trust one might hope to have in one's designated rescue-the-tsarevich-from-rebels partner. But what else could I say? The truth was out of the question. He'd think me insane.

Then again, he did claim to have a garnet of his own, enough like mine that he couldn't let go of his notion that I'd stolen it. If he *did* have one like mine, did he know what it could do? It was hard to conceive that he did. He was so logical, so down-to-earth, and he'd been so adamant that magicians didn't exist—not anymore, anyway. Had magicians flourished, nineteen years ago? And what else had he said? *"You're telling me the gemstone is a kolodets."* As though I should know what that meant.

Clinging to a root, I stretched my leg downward, landing my foot on a ledge created by Lev's boot in his competent scramble down the slope. "What takes significant effort is climbing—*Ach!*" The root sprung free from the ground, and I slipped down, landing in an undignified pile at the bottom of the bank. My tailbone was likely bruised, but not so bruised as my ego. I considered myself a competent woman. I would have scaled the bank just fine, had I not spent the last eight hours on a sprinting horse.

Lev was there in an instant, extending his hand to help me up as he fought laughter. "All right, my lady?" He grinned, and I glowered, red-faced.

Ignoring his outstretched arm, I pushed myself to my feet. "Fine. I'm fine. Just give me the bucket." I snatched the pail from his hand, inwardly grateful that he had thought to grab it from the stables. Filling the bucket, then filling my mouth with cold stream water, I began to regain my poise.

I could do this. I would do this. I had to.

I filled the bucket again, squaring my shoulders as I walked it to Lev. "Here, drink. But *you're* carrying it up."

BY THE TIME we stopped again, my eyes were well adjusted to the darkness, and my legs felt like they could fall off my trunk and I wouldn't notice. Having next to nothing with us, we made camp quickly. We didn't need a fire—it was a warm July night, and we had nothing to cook. Aside from some berries I'd spotted by the river earlier, our stomachs were empty, but we were exhausted enough that the prospect of preparing a meal was uninviting anyway. We'd settled in a small clearing in a grove of pines, not too far off the road. Molniya was so tired that he'd flopped down on his side, and Lev lay propped up against the giant horse's back as though he were a piece of furniture. Our grumpy pillow swatted his tail and let out a low bray as I positioned myself beside Lev.

"Well, my favorite vacation was with my family, to Livadiya in the Crimea. It was beautiful there, and peaceful. The air smelled of lilac blooms, wild violet, and sea salt. My sisters and I—we slept beneath the stars, like this. The sound of the sea lulled us to sleep."

"You must miss them terribly."

I blinked. It was too much. That world felt very far away. My family, my life, my identity. How could I continue to exist without them? And now, to be separated from Alexei, too . . . I turned my head toward Lev, his company my reminder that I did continue to exist.

"What about your family?"

Lev was silent for a moment, then, "Hmm. There's not a lot to tell. Not now. I had a brother, a twin brother. Luka. But he's gone now." He sighed. "As for my parents, I never knew my father. He disappeared the day after we were born. And my mother . . . she's gone now, too."

His words landed heavily on my heart. He was an orphan. The word tumbled about uncomfortably in my mind. Orphans were to be pitied, aided, looked upon with sad eyes and then passed by. The awkward blankets I'd knitted as a child—they'd been for the orphans, my instructor had said. *How kind*, I'd thought. But now I was parentless, too. I imagined Lev and I, wrapped beneath one of those poorly knitted atrocities as we lay against the horse.

Turning my head, I looked at him. The whites of his eyes caught the moonlight as he watched me, solemnly. My hand lifted involuntarily, moving to take his. But I caught myself and brought it back, brushing my tangled hair from my face. "I'm sorry, Lev."

Even in the dark, I sensed him shrug. "Such is life," he said gruffly. "I'm doing all right on my own."

"So, isn't there something you should be doing, besides trailing along on my quest?" I hoped he'd appreciate my attempt to lighten the mood.

"Well, I suppose I'd be put to use squelching this rebellion, or at least, guarding some less-important castle wall. But as I was imprisoned while those orders went out, I suppose I'm free to trail along with you." His voice lowered as he peered sidelong at me. "I hope my presence isn't terribly burdensome."

I took a deep breath, the smells of horse and pine and Lev filling my senses. "Not terribly burdensome." I closed my eyes, drifting into sleep.

IT WAS STILL dark when Lev shook me awake. "Anastasia. We must be going. A storm is coming, but I think we can outride it if we leave now." My head clunked to the ground as Molniya arose. Taking Lev's offered hand, I allowed him to pull me to my feet, as much as my sore thighs protested. As if on cue, lightning flashed in the distance, a low roll of thunder following. Molniya showed no great affection for his namesake, whinnying dubiously.

We rode hard, leaving the ominous sky in our wake. We didn't stop again until we reached the Luzhsky villa grounds.

CHAPTER TEN

"Moral maxims are surprisingly useful on occasions when we can invent little else to justify our actions."

—*Tales of Belkin* by Alexander Pushkin

THE HOUR WAS LATE, an unlikely time for a knock at the door.

"Come in." Mikhail closed his book of accounts and looked up from his desk, first annoyed at the interruption, then pleased when he saw his wife at the door. "Ah, my love. Come sit. Have a chocolate, aren't you craving one?"

Dina's skirts swished the floor as she swept into the room, closing the door behind her.

"Mikhail, my sweet. The people want action. You've talked, you've presented yourself as a man of the people. My people. But you sit behind your desk, with your books and your chocolates."

He smiled. For once, he was a step ahead of her.

"The time has come. I've gathered the girls in the basement. We'll be sending them to Ivan's in Luga, as it would seem that I will be needing witnesses. You see, I've received word that my brother and his forces are drawing near. Absurdly claiming that I've made an attempt to poison the tsarevich."

Dina nodded slowly, taking in the startling information. "An idiot. But the little Duchesses will tell the truth. And the boy?"

Scratching his chin, Mikhail regretted that his nephew had made a habit of these nightly hunts. The stubborn child was adamant that he should take down a moose single-handedly before leaving the Luzhsky Uyezd. As it was, he'd returned with naught but a raccoon and some grouses.

"Out. But my men are about in the woods and will bring him to join his sisters before sunrise."

Dina leaned across the maple desk, gazing over Mikhail's shoulder to the fireplace, alight with dancing flames despite the July heat. Then she brought her lips to his ear and whispered, "Be sure they do." And she stood, flashing a smile over her shoulder as she whirled from the room.

Mikhail admired his wife as she made her exit, then relaxed back in his chair, kicking his feet onto his desk. He just couldn't understand his brother's stupidity. Nicholas would be caught in this obvious lie, and the people would only resent him more. They would call for the very reform that Mikhail had been promoting for years—since the boy had been born. He had no need to poison the child—the *people* would rise up against the tsar and his heir. Nicholas had become desperate, and it would ruin him. Mikhail popped a chocolate into his mouth, savoring the sweetness. The throne would be his.

CHAPTER ELEVEN

"As the future ripens in the past, so the past rots in the future—a terrible festival of dead leaves."

—Anna Akhmatova

DAWN WAS BREAKING, THE stars fading as the black sky dissolved to a purple-gray above the trees. My aching legs were relieved just slightly when Lev slowed Molniya to a walk. The muscles of his chest tensed against my back as he leaned his chin to my ear and whispered, "Listen."

I listened. The forest was quiet, as the nocturnal creatures had returned home to rest, and the daytime animals had not yet stirred. But when I really listened, I heard it, too. Distant, to be sure, but there were riders in the woods. Would it be the rebels? At this hour, who else?

For what must have been the thousandth time as we rode, I turned my mind to my brother. I desperately wanted to know what had transpired during his time at the castle. How had he been kidnapped, within hours of returning to the castle after an *alleged kidnapping*? Were these Romanovs so careless? I thought of my mother, how she had cherished her son. For his whole childhood, Alexei had been sheltered, coddled, his fragile life protected above all else. If my brother had been returned home by soldiers, while his suspected kidnappers sat in the dungeon below, my mother would have stormed to the basement and executed them herself. Not here, it seemed. Such carelessness. I tried to wrap my mind around it.

Then I had another thought. Would the royal family even realize that my brother had been taken? Likely not. Because he was an extra. Wouldn't his alter ego be safely within the walls of the Winter Palace, with his parents and sisters? But if they didn't think that the tsarevich had been kidnapped by rebels, why was the palace raising defenses?

I had so many questions. How had Alexei freed us? How had he known where the rebels would be taking him? And how had he sent us the note? It didn't make any sense. The worst part was that these questions would likely go unanswered. It seemed quite the long shot that I—or that we, Lev and I—could rescue Alexei from these rebels. Even if we could, what of this magician? If Alexei's memory were wiped, would he even know who we are, who *he* is? My head ached.

And then there was the garnet. "*Save me. Then use the garnet,*" he'd written. "*There is no time to waste.*" I wouldn't know where to begin looking for the necklace—and some help he would be, if he were without his memory. And even if I found the garnet, did he really think our best chance was to skip another stone along the surface of the universe, dipping into world after world, until finally we landed in one in which we could live peacefully?

He didn't care about living peacefully, though, did he? He wanted his crown, his throne, his destiny. And if he wanted to leave this world, that meant he didn't see a path here. He would keep searching for the rest of our lives. I frowned. The idea of leaving this world . . . it didn't feel quite right. This Russia seemed to be on the brink of its own revolution—was this version of my family doomed to the same fate as my own? Could I . . . could I stop it? I wouldn't know where to start. My mind reeled, becoming quickly overwhelmed. Taking a deep breath, I refocused on the task at hand. We were going to free my brother from his captors. We just had to find him.

I turned to look at Lev over my shoulder and spoke quietly. "What do you know of these rebels?"

Again, his muscles tensed and then he exhaled, his breath a soft breeze to the back of my neck. I flushed. Had I ever sat so close to anyone outside of my family? Lev hesitated, then whispered, "More than I should."

I sat up a little straighter in the saddle. "Are you involved with them?"

"No," Lev answered quickly. "No. It's just, my brother, Luka . . ." He trailed off, then started again. "The rebel group is the Narodnaya Volya. Have you heard of them?"

Indeed, I had. In my own world, they had been an anti-tsarist terrorist group many years ago. In fact, they'd assassinated my great-grandfather, ending his reign. They'd bombed the Winter Palace, sneaking dynamite into the basement. And they'd eventually evolved into the Bolsheviks, the very men who had murdered my entire family.

Yet, who were they, in this world?

I looked over my shoulder. "Remind me?"

Lev cleared his throat. "Well. They're most notorious for killing the last two tsars. They were gaining quite a bit of power, until Tsar Nicholas came along and eradicated magic, exiling all the magic-wielders. After that, the Narodnaya Volya disappeared for a while." He paused. I remained silent as I absorbed his words.

"But they're back," he continued. "For the last few years, they've been reorganizing. The war in Europe hasn't helped matters. When His Majesty began sending our resources to England and France, people started getting angry. People don't understand the necessity of international relations— they just think the tsar is wasting money and—" He stopped, as though realizing he was diverging on a tangent.

"Anyway, the rebels started gaining momentum. They found an unlikely ally in Mikhail Romanov, who was not subtle in his criticisms of the policy. He didn't think it was enough that the tsar kept Russia out of Europe's war. He thought that our country should isolate itself completely, forgoing our commitment to support our allies.

"Then when he married his sister's handmaiden, the rebels began to see him as an icon for the common people, despite his ties to the royal family.

But this was all happening quite subversively. The majority of the country doesn't know that the Narodnaya Volya have reorganized, and they certainly don't know that Mikhail has any connection to them. That Mikhail still lives is testament that the tsar has no idea how deeply involved his brother has become. Well, perhaps until now."

I nodded, taking it all in. On the surface, this world seemed much like my own. But here, we hadn't joined the war. My uncle was a traitor. And . . . magic. Lev spoke about it so casually, as though it was widely accepted—or had been.

Before the tsar exiled the magic-wielders.

"These magic-wielders . . . They were working with the Narodnaya Volya?" Unable to contain my curiosity, I hoped my ignorance wasn't too conspicuous.

"Some. Not all." Lev seemed to accept that my level of general knowledge was rather low—a fact I resented, despite its convenience.

"And they all were exiled?"

"I thought so. You seem to suggest otherwise." His tone grew accusatory again, and I knew he still didn't believe me about the garnet. Or the *kolodets,* or whatever it was.

He sighed then, his voice resigned. "And that note seems to suggest otherwise, too. So who knows."

"What if it's true, about the magician? What if they've truly erased my brother's memory? What do we do then?"

Lev raised his brows. "Your brother?"

Oops. "The tsarevich, I meant to say, I was just—"

Lev grabbed me, then, wrapping his muscled arms around my torso. "Get down!" He pulled me from the horse, pinning me to the ground beneath him, as Molniya reared and bolted. There was the sound of a gunshot, and the tree behind us erupted in an explosion of bark and leaves.

Then, a voice I knew echoed from the ridge above. "Oy! Who's there? Travelers shouldn't be about at this hour, my uncle says. I nearly shot you! Thought your horse was a moose."

Kellyn Carni

FOR ALL HIS ferocity, Molniya was turning out to be quite a coward. He couldn't have strayed far, but the gunshot had startled him sufficiently, and he had dashed.

The three of us were trekking along a narrow deer trail, dimly lit ahead of the sunrise. Lev was tracking the runaway horse, studying the ground and surrounding shrubs and branches for signs of movement. Alexei chattered incessantly, offering unhelpful advice based on his experiences hunting moose in these woods.

It had been quite immediately apparent that Alexei's memory had been modified—but beyond that, it was as though my shrewd brother had been replaced with a bumbling half-wit. Introductions had been made—and he clearly had no recollection of me or Lev. Yet he still joined our search without hesitation. He was entirely too trusting, as though he had never been wronged.

". . . and they say that moose are best hunted in the autumn but I say that the beasts must be about, and my father says I'm quite a good shot. I'm sure I'll take one down one of these nights."

"Hmm. Certainly," Lev replied offhandedly, as he stooped low to the ground. The deer trail split, and he determined that we should continue to the left. Then he shushed my brother and paused, listening. "Ah." He clicked his tongue. "Molniya, my boy. Found some grasses, have you." And around the bend, the great coward stood, munching fescue in a small clearing.

"Oy! A majestic beast! The exact image of my own horse—in training still, but will be fine for riding in a few months." Alexei approached the horse confidently.

Trailing behind the boys, I was quite lost in thought. I wasn't sure what to say to my brother. While I needed to explain to him all that he had forgotten, many of those details could not be spoken in front of Lev. As it was, I had hardly gotten a word in amid his long-winded accounts of his moose-hunting efforts. I could only guess how Alexei had come to be

56

out hunting alone on the grounds of our uncle Mikhail's estate. It would seem that the rebels were covering their tracks. I assumed their magician had modified my brother's memory so that he would not remember having been kidnapped and would believe instead that he had been visiting his uncle, enjoying nightly moose-hunts. If that was true, they had been quite thorough.

Alexei had his rifle and a string of what appeared to be pheasants slung over his shoulder. I was a bit startled, as he had never been given much opportunity to hunt in our former life, or to do any sort of dangerous activity that might result in blood.

He had been amenable to aiding us in finding our horse. Or at least, he seemed to think his presence had been of utmost assistance. But how would we convince him to come with us further? And if we could, where would we go? Dutiful to a fault, Lev would want to return him to the palace—again. But Alexei had been right about the kidnapping, Mikhail's estate, and his memory. Hadn't his next instruction been to find the garnet, to use it? What had he known?

Alexei continued prattling on about horses until Lev interrupted him. "Shh—listen." We all stopped moving. Lev looked to me meaningfully. "Riders. The rebels."

It seemed that they had heard us, too—well, heard Alexei anyway—and four horses were approaching us rapidly. My oblivious brother continued talking at full volume—"Uncle Mikhail's men are never out at this hour—"

Lev shushed him again. "Quickly, on the horse." Lev was lifting Alexei, and Alexei was reflexively reaching his foot for the stirrups. "And you, up, hurry now." He was taking me by the hand with a strong grip, then lifting me after my brother.

It was just dawning on me what was happening, as I sat behind Alexei on the horse. Two riders were a tight fit upon Molniya's back. There was no room for a third rider. "But what about you?" I still held Lev's hand tightly. His green eyes met mine, resolute, resigned.

"Get the tsarevich to safety. His letter was written to you. Not me."

Releasing my hand, Lev clapped Molniya's rump and the horse broke into a run. Then he turned to face the approaching rebel riders, arms raised, blocking their path.

And we were gone.

CHAPTER TWELVE

"I did not bow down to you, I bowed down to all the suffering of humanity."

—Raskolnikov, *Crime and Punishment* by Fyodor Dostoyevsky

"SAY THAT AGAIN, I must have misunderstood you." Mikhail stopped pacing, leaned his hands on his desk, and looked pointedly at the young stable hand, who stood wide eyed in the doorway.

"Okay, er, well . . . The tsarevich could not be brought in. He rode away, and . . . he isn't here. Your Grace."

Mikhail raked his fingers through his graying hair. "And how did the boy come to be on a horse?"

"Well, he . . . um, he wasn't alone, Your Grace. There were, er, well, they think they saw two others. They believe one went with him, and the other, the guards have him. But, um, they didn't know what they should do with him."

Bravo, Nicholas. Mikhail balked at his brother's nerve, a quiet rage simmering within him. He continued to pace, muttering to himself. "Nicholas will be pleased. His men have succeeded in removing the boy in stealth. The boy's absence will substantiate his ridiculous lie, no matter what his sisters say."

"Um, Your Grace, sir, the men wanted to know what to, uh, do. With the prisoner."

The prisoner. A man Nicholas trusted fully, then, if he were sent to remove Alexei from the estate and sneak him back to the palace. A man who had been trusted with the truth—that the tsarevich had never left his uncle's estate. That there was no poisoning. That the first regiment rode with their tsar to defend a lie. An important prisoner, then, who would know things.

"They will bring him to me for questioning first. And if he is not forthcoming, Ivan may see fit to draw information from him by other means."

"Yes, Your Grace. I'll deliver the message." The stable hand scurried from the room.

Alone in his study, Mikhail took a deep breath and sighed as he sunk into his heavy wooden chair. Through the window, darkness. But northern nights were brief this time of year and the sun would be rising soon. His brother's regiment would be arriving within the hour.

Mikhail had the Grand Duchesses. He had witnesses. Yet without the boy, he could not easily disprove the tsar's outlandish claim. Would the people believe that he had poisoned his own nephew? *Was it so farfetched?* Shame washed over him. When had his brother become his enemy?

The two brothers had always disagreed on political matters. While Nicholas strived to follow in the footsteps of his father and the generations of tsars before him, Mikhail knew that the tides were changing. The people would not tolerate a system of such absolute power much longer—America and France were evidence enough of that. *The people haven't tolerated it here,* Mikhail thought. *They just haven't reached a true breaking point. Yet.*

Like the frozen Neva in winter, unrest churned tumultuously beneath the empire's unyielding surface. The people's displeasure had surfaced on occasion, the malcontents placated by some small act of rebellion. His father's assassination, even his grandfather's gruesome murder—had changed nothing. If anything, it had delayed reform by temporarily appeasing the revolutionaries. Mikhail had been a young boy when he and his siblings were called to the study to say good-bye to their grandfather as he lay dying. Tsar

Alexander II had once been a formidable presence, but he'd died an oozing pile of inverted flesh, ravaged by Russia's disdain. Even he—Alexander the Liberator, champion of the serfs—hadn't been able to appease the people. Bones had been thrown, so to speak, but the people didn't want concessions. They wanted representation. And so the powerful magic-wielders of the Narodnaya Volya had done their worst, ending Alexander II's reign.

Still, what had it changed? Alexander III had inherited the crown, the title, the absolute power. And he'd ruled more harshly than his father, perhaps in response to the assassination, or perhaps to prevent his own. He'd been unyielding, both as a tsar and as a father. Yet the Narodnaya Volya struck again. They'd acted more discreetly this time, working beneath the veil of magic to slowly drain his life away. Mikhail had been only sixteen when his father died, but he'd been old enough to see that in the grand scheme of things, nothing had changed. Another tsar dead, another tsar took the throne.

After his father's death, Nicholas began his reign with a ruthless vendetta—not against the Narodnaya Volya, but against magic itself. His plan had been thorough, aimed at systematically eradicating magic from the country in every form of its existence. He'd recruited magic-wielders to his cause, promising them they'd be rewarded, or perhaps simply spared from the fate of their cohorts. He'd ordered them to draw the magic from the air, to drain it from the ether, and to obliterate it, removing it from existence.

Then he'd rounded up all the magic-wielders, sparing none. Even those who'd followed his command, who'd aided his cause—even they were shackled and detained. It had been a time of great turmoil, the people living in fear, watching as soldiers raided their homes, searching for magicians. They watched as friends and neighbors were arrested, and those charged with magic-wielding were never seen again. Exiled, supposedly, but Mikhail knew they were more likely executed.

With that, the magic that had always been as natural to Russia as the summer sun or the winter moon was gone. The world had felt rather empty, at first. Then, as with any great change, people became accustomed to it more quickly than one would think. There were those who still hoped that bits of magic had survived—those who searched for *kolodtsy*, studying gemstones and physics and lore. Thus far, there had been no substantial evidence that the mythic magic-vessels had ever existed.

And so Tsar Nicholas had begun his reign. It was ironic, in a way, that a Romanov tsar should extinguish the very force that once flowed freely through his ancestors' veins. He'd eliminated the very force that brought the Romanovs to power centuries before, and he established himself as a tsar of great power, more powerful than magic itself. Many hated him, some revered him as an all-powerful god, and everyone feared him.

The tsardom survived on this fear, and it was not sustainable. Unrest was stirring, and the Narodnaya Volya were active once again. But Mikhail thought that perhaps tsarism and the demands of the rebels were not mutually exclusive. It was a fine line he walked. It would require the tsar to be a man humbler than his brother. A man more intelligent than his nephew.

He rose from his chair. There would be time for contemplation later. Now he must act. First, there was the matter of the prisoner. *Better to deal with that now,* Mikhail thought, *before Nicholas and his regiment arrive.*

THE LUZHSKY HOUSE was comfortable, though not well-suited for conducting trials. The dining room now doubled as the interrogation quarters, Mikhail seated at the head of the table, with Dina to his left. The prisoner sat alone at the opposite end, wrists and ankles bound. The Duchess was the first to speak. Flashing her catlike smile from across the table, Dina addressed the prisoner teasingly.

"Have you a name, soldier?"

The soldier shifted in his seat, as though deciding how truthful he ought to be. "Lev," he answered, and paused. "Lev . . . Lukavich."

This should be easy enough, Mikhail thought smugly. *The boy's honest face can't even hide the smallest of lies.* The three sat silently for a moment,

Mikhail assessing his interviewee. He was not far beyond boyhood, perhaps eighteen. Slim, but strongly built. The young man did not appear nervous, rather, he seemed as though his mind were otherwise occupied.

Mikhail spoke next, seeing no need for further introduction, but rather getting straight to the point. "You were found in the woods, seen aiding the tsarevich in his hasty exit from our estate. Why?"

The young man answered carefully. "The tsarevich requested help. He was kidnapped by a rebel faction. He was brought to you. I came to return him to his home."

Sensing no dishonesty, Mikhail thought that Mr. Lukavich might believe his own words to be true. But why would his story not match his tsar's?

"Kidnapped, you say? Not poisoned?"

"Kidnapped."

"And you were sent here, by my brother, the tsar?"

"No."

Mikhail raised his eyebrows. "Then who sent you?"

"No one. I came of my own volition." Again his words rang true, but Mikhail was sure there was more to tell.

"And your companion? Will he be taking the tsarevich to the palace?"

The soldier paused, thinking. "I hope so."

"Mm." Mikhail looked sidelong at his wife. Her face was thoughtful, but unreadable, and he wondered what she made of their prisoner's vague account of the incident. Though he thought the soldier wasn't lying, he thought he was likely omitting certain truths. But he might be valuable as a witness, come the trial, and it would certainly please Ivan if Mikhail could hand him a soldier who was in on the farce, whose story could expose the tsar for a liar and warmonger.

"Dina, shall we send him to Luga with the girls? Or on to Tsarskoye Selo? Perhaps our friends within the headquarters would like to speak with him. To better understand the tsar's rationale behind this dreadful accusation. To hold him for us, until the trial." As Dina nodded, Mikhail looked back to Lev. "Kidnapping, was it? Poisoning, imprisoning—what a horrid uncle I'm thought to be." They held each other's gaze, and Mikhail whistled sharply, summoning a guard from outside the dining room door. "Arrange a carriage—this soldier must be delivered to the Narodnaya Volya."

———

IT HAD BEEN agreed that the brothers would meet in the garden. As Mikhail descended the pinewood staircase, he cursed himself for ever having mentioned to his nephew the possibility of downing a moose in his forests. If Alexei had not been out hunting, he would be in the basement with his sisters, bound for Ivan's in Luga, and proof to all that Nicholas was either desperate or delusional. Mikhail was quite keen to learn which it was.

What had compelled his brother to orchestrate this hoax? To what degree was Nicholas aware of Mikhail's involvement with the revolutionaries? *More so than I thought,* Mikhail reasoned, *if he's fabricated an excuse to arrest me.*

The prospect of his certain arrest troubled Mikhail, as he had never been one to allow things to happen to him. He preferred to dictate his own circumstances. From his marriage to Dina—she was merely his sister's handmaiden at the time—to his denunciation of absolutism, he had rebuked tradition in favor of following his own intuition. And while his intuition led him to feel quite opposed to imprisonment, he saw no way around it. *All will be revealed in the trial,* he told himself. Dina was, at that moment, preparing the carriage for the witnesses.

The girls. While they knew nothing of the alleged poisoning nor their father's arrival, they did know that their brother was present for dinner, in perfect health, before he left for his nightly hunt. And the prisoner. Though his story had been convoluted, it certainly didn't corroborate the alleged poisoning. Mikhail would be arrested, yes, but then there would be a trial. The girls, the prisoner—they would all be questioned, and his brother's lie would be exposed. Perhaps this arrest was not such a terrible thing. The accusation alone would win him the hearts of the revolutionaries. When it became known that he had been arrested on false accusations, that the tsar had lied to his soldiers, to his people, then he might win the hearts of those still loyal to the tsar. The imperial family would be exiled, and Mikhail would take his place at the head of a new Russian parliament, as Tsar of Russia.

"BROTHER." NICHOLAS STOOD solemnly, his hands clasped behind his back. The sun had just cleared the horizon, the air holding the distinct morning glow unique to that hour. Dina's sunflowers were in bloom, teasingly cheery for the occasion. Several meters back, a guard paced, listening.

"Your Highness." Mikhail bowed formally. Brimming with curiosity, he fought the urge to interrogate his brother. Better to wait, to let the tsar speak first.

Nicholas nodded curtly, and took a deep breath. It clearly hurt him to be here, having this conversation. However, the tsar had never hesitated to do what he thought needed to be done, to the point of ruthlessness at times. Looking to his brother, Nicholas began.

"My son returned home to me last night. Unexpectedly. He has been poisoned, his body weakened, his skin bruised, and he has identified you as the poisoner."

Mikhail raised his eyebrows. "So I've heard."

"Do you deny it?"

Nicholas spoke with utter conviction, his voice bristling with a calm rage. It was odd. Mikhail knew his brother well, but as he reflected, he realized that he did not know whether his brother was a good liar or not, quite simply because he had never known his brother to lie. Perhaps it did not matter to Nicholas the details of the accusation. He could deliver the fictitious details with conviction, because the basest layer of the charges *was* true: Mikhail had betrayed him.

"Of course I deny it, Nicholas, because it is untrue. You know this, and you didn't ride here to question me. You're here to arrest me. Do it, then."

Nicholas sighed heavily. He considered Mikhail's words for a moment, and then he seemed to concede that indeed, there was no purpose in delaying the inevitable. He lifted his hand, and in an instant the guard had drawn his pistol, pointing it at Mikhail's chest. "You stand accused of attempted murder of your nephew, a botched assassination of the heir to the throne. I ask you again. Do you deny it?"

It took great self-discipline for Mikhail to refrain from rolling his eyes. "Yes, Nicky, I deny it. Your man can lower his gun, I will not fight. You will know that I have your daughters in my custody." He intended no threat, though Nicholas could take it that way if he wished.

"I have with me twenty men. My daughters will be extracted from the house with ease."

Oh, how idiotic his brother thought him to be. He trusted that Dina had acted swiftly. "Your daughters will remain in my wife's custody until I stand trial, as they will serve as my witnesses. I'm allowed witnesses, no? They will report that until your men removed Alexei last night, he remained here at my estate. Should they speak truthfully, they will report no signs of poisoning." Mikhail looked at his brother hard, assessing his reaction to the words spoken. Nicholas's face remained stern and skeptical, as though he truly believed Mikhail to be guilty.

Nicholas rubbed his chin, thinking. "You'll have your trial, brother, and your witnesses. But you stand accused of poisoning my son. I will not allow my daughters to remain in your custody."

"I assure you that your daughters will not be harmed," Mikhail spoke slowly. Could he assure such? "However, you will not find them here, nor will you see them before the trial. I cannot have a fair trial, should their recollections be . . . influenced."

When Nicholas opened his mouth to reply, Mikhail cut him off. "I know this is not to your liking, but as your prisoner, I do not particularly care."

At that, the tsar turned on his heel, motioning his guard to bring the prisoner along. Were it not for the gun at Mikhail's back, the brothers could have been walking back to the stables after a picnic in the garden. But they had crossed a line now, from which there was no return. Brothers, yes, but enemies now, each wishing the empire to fit his own mold. *Nicholas's plan for Russia is selfish,* Mikhail told himself. *It's unsustainable, of centuries past. Russia is ready for progress, to drop the notion of tsar as God, to shift power to the proletariat.* Mikhail accepted his current role, brother and prisoner of the tsar, knowing that in a short time, Russia would be forever changed.

CHAPTER THIRTEEN

"People speak sometimes about the 'bestial' cruelty of man, but that is terribly unjust and offensive to beasts, no animal could ever be so cruel as a man, so artfully, so artistically cruel."

—Fyodor Dostoyevsky

T HE CARRIAGE WAS NOW rather crowded.

Lev had been the sole cargo at first, when he was gagged, wrapped in a blanket, and tied down beneath several bundles of hay. He'd heard muffled whispers, followed by the sound of light feet scurrying from the carriage house. The coachman had then thumped the bale of hay atop Lev's bundled form, and whispered, "Stay hidden." An unspoken "or else" seemed to follow, and given his confinement, Lev had determined it was a good moment for compliance.

He had waited there, actually quite comfortable despite his restraints. It was cozy, lying in the hay, and he supposed that after his imprisonment, after the ride from St. Petersburg, it was the closest he'd been to a bed in days.

The last few days had been a whirlwind, since the moment Anastasia and the tsarevich had appeared in his life. Hours had passed since they had parted—would they have made it to the Winter Palace? He hoped that it had gone smoother than their first attempt to return the tsarevich home. Anastasia was small, he thought, but rather capable. Cheeky, yet intelligent.

Would she have landed in the prison beneath the palace again? Or would she be rewarded as a hero, having rescued the tsarevich from his captors?

Anastasia. He had so many questions for her that he hadn't asked. She wouldn't have answered, anyway. Her arrival in his cabin had completely erupted his life, had sparked all of this, hadn't it? Lev closed his eyes. *We were imprisoned together . . . hell, she was cradled against me on that horse for hours. And yet she remains a mystery.*

It was all quite bizarre, and perhaps the bit that stunned him the most was the complete amnesia that Alexei had exhibited when they stumbled upon him in the forest. "*They have a magician,*" the tsarevich had written. How? Had magic somehow survived annihilation all those years ago? Had Luka been right?

It certainly seemed that way.

Lev took a moment to allow that to sink in. He had always appreciated the physical realities of life: the beauty of snowcapped mountains, the rejuvenation of ice-cold water, the vitality of the human body. The metaphysical had been his brother's realm.

"Into the carriage, careful around those hay bales, better you three sit along the benches," it was Dina Romanov's voice, followed by the clunking of boots as several more bodies arrived within the carriage. Then, more loudly, she addressed the coachman, "And we're all aboard, so onward now and with haste."

As the carriage sprung forward, Lev distinguished four separate exclamations of surprise amid the sound of sliding trunks and horse hooves. Dina, and who else? Stowed beneath the hay, Lev listened.

"Well, Auntie, now that we're settled, if you please, what is going on?" A sweet voice, somehow familiar and yet not, seemingly addressed Dina. Two different voices chimed in with sounds of agreement.

Dina's tone was calm, soothing. "My darlings, a conflict has erupted at the estate. I cannot tell you more because that is all I know. I'm terribly sorry this has happened during your holiday with us. I can tell you that we're going now to a safe place in the city."

A safe place, with the Narodnaya Volya? Lev's mind raced. Were they all bound for the same destination? *A safe place . . .* Somehow, he doubted it. If he waited quietly, could he learn where the girls were being taken?

"What of little Alexei? I've not seen our brother since last night's supper. Did he never return from his hunt?" A different speaker, perhaps a bit older than the last.

Lev had gathered that the three passengers were Olga, Tatiana, and Maria Romanov. But what was this about Alexei? How could he have dined with his sisters whilst kidnapped by rebels? Lev considered the timeline he had formed for yesterday's events and supposed it *may* have been possible.

"He is safe. It would seem that your father found it advantageous to remove him from the Luzhsky Uyezd last night." Dina's tone darkened just for a moment. She continued. "Now, I believe it may be important that you remember what you did, who you saw, anything that happened yesterday quite clearly. Maria, can you recall for me your day?"

The gentle voice again. "Well, Auntie, let me think. I awoke rather late in the morning, and had a bit of porridge and fruit. Alexei had slept late too, as he was out hunting again the night before. We had our breakfast together, and then it was a rather unremarkable day, I'm afraid. I did some needlework, read . . ."

While Lev could reorganize his mental timeline to allow Alexei's presence at his uncle's villa for supper, breakfast was quite difficult to figure. The ride from St. Petersburg to Mikhail's estate took nearly a day. *Unless there was a train running to Luga . . . but at that hour? Then a ride from the train station would still take at least three hours. Still possible to make breakfast, if he had been kidnapped during the night.*

"Oh but Auntie, the day before yesterday, what fun we had! We had the most marvelous picnic, Alexei showed us how he learned to build a fire with his Scouts, and we roasted apples . . ." She continued to prattle on delightedly, but Lev had stopped listening. Because whether he traveled by train, horse, or flying dragon, there was no way Alexei could have been picnicking with his sisters at Mikhail's estate while simultaneously standing in Lev's cabin in St. Petersburg, pointing his gun and demanding chocolate. It was physically impossible.

Unless there were two of him.

THE CARRIAGE ROLLED to a halt at long last, and Lev cursed the bumpy roads of the Luzhsky Uyezd. From his hideaway, bundled beneath the hay, he had overheard enough to surmise that Dina and the Grand Duchesses would be moving to some safe house in Luga. While he hadn't been able to put together exactly why they'd needed to leave the estate, he gathered that there had been a conflict of sorts, certainly involving the tsarevich.

Reflecting on his earlier conversation with Mikhail Romanov, Lev supposed that no one seemed to have a clear picture of what had truly happened. Poisoned or kidnapped, at the Winter Palace or the Luzhsky estate—the tsarevich was at the center of all this duplicity. That the heir to the throne had been standing in his living room was only the beginning of what was proving to be quite a mystifying chain of events.

". . . and my hat, just there—thanks, Maria." One of the Grand Duchesses—Tatiana, Lev thought.

"Of course. Let's go then. Now, aren't you coming, Auntie Dina?"

"Go on, my sweets, I'll be right along. I must attend to some cargo. But the Lady of the house is there to greet you."

With no small amount of noise, the girls exited the carriage, leaving only Dina and Lev, bound and gagged beneath the hay bales. Those bales shifted suddenly, allowing the morning sunlight to burst through, absurdly bright after what had felt like hours of darkness. As Lev's eyes adjusted, Dina's face appeared before him. She abruptly removed his gag and held water to his mouth.

"Drink," she instructed coolly. Then she produced a boiled egg, which she shoved into his mouth whole. "Chew. We must keep you well, mustn't we? The Narodnaya Volya will be very interested in your story." He was still quite involved in the chewing when Dina instructed again, "Swallow." Once satisfied that he was unlikely to choke, she crammed the gag back into his mouth. Another shifting of the hay bales. Darkness, again.

He could hear Dina exit the carriage and then command the coachman, "On to the train station, now. Our men will meet you there."

Muffled by the gag, Lev made every effort to shout, to call out, to make his presence known, wishing he had done this when the girls were on board. The train station—they could be sending him anywhere. He thought of Luka and tried to remember all he could about the Narodnaya Volya. Where did they operate? All across Russia, as far as he knew. His muted screams unheard by anyone but perhaps the indifferent coachman, he felt the nearly empty carriage lurch forward once again.

WHILE THE LUGA train station was not particularly busy at this early hour, there were enough people about that Lev considered yelling for help, making a break for it. However, his chances were slim. Ankles and wrists bound, gag in place, and escorted by two monstrous men dressed as imperial soldiers, he certainly appeared as a legitimate prisoner. He didn't see any way around getting on that train, not now.

Not that he hadn't fought. As the carriage had pulled to a stop at the train station, he had wedged his feet under a wooden beam for leverage. Then when the hay bales were removed, he'd hinged from the waist and thrusted himself upward, solidly headbutting his enormous new companion in the chin. He'd reached his tied wrists over the man's head, tightening the rope around his neck. The man's eyes had widened, bulged, he'd been bested—and then there'd been a loud clang, and everything had gone black. When Lev had come to, he'd found himself accompanied by a pair of towering men in soldiers' uniforms, one with a bloodied chin, and the other with an air of satisfaction that seemed to correlate with Lev's splitting headache.

He was shoved along through the station. Passersby glanced at Lev and his formidable escorts with nervous interest, demurely avoiding eye contact with the prisoner or his guards. The ticket collector waved them through and they boarded the train, as their fellow travelers hastily moved on to more favorably inhabited train cars.

Exhausted, sore, likely concussed, Lev stumbled as he tried too long of a step onto the train, caught by the rope at his ankles. The guards hoisted him forward, shoving him into a seat as the engineer announced, "All aboard! Departing now for Tsarskoye Selo."

CHAPTER FOURTEEN

"That aching feeling of loneliness which always overcomes us when someone dear to us surrenders to a daydream in which we have no place."

—*Mary* by Vladimir Nabokov

M Y SORE MUSCLES PROTESTED adamantly, my thighs quite displeased to be charging forth atop our stallion once again. This time, I held the reins, Alexei in front of me, as I drove the horse back the way we'd come. Northward, back toward St. Petersburg.

The first hour of our ride had been spent in impossible deliberation. What were we to do next? Hungry, thirsty, physically and mentally exhausted—my brain had struggled with the dilemma. I'd done it: I'd rescued my brother, and he was safe for now. But unease still churned in my gut, my head still aching with misgivings.

My brother's mind was totally addled. I hadn't expected the magic's effect to be this . . . complete. His head of sandy hair bounced in front of me in rhythm with the horse. My brother was in there, I knew, but his mind was clouded by a thick web of illusions, keeping him from his memories, estranging him from me. He didn't know me, not at all. Would he ever?

And what of Lev? In my mind was the silhouette of his strong frame, standing alone with his arms raised, blocking the path as the horses approached.

He had given himself over to those men—the rebels, or whoever they were—enabling our safe passage to the palace. I'd let Lev sacrifice himself for a lie. My head ached, my stomach knotting with guilt. Where would he be, now?

Anxious and exhausted, we kept riding north, because I didn't know what else to do. I still held Alexei's note in my pocket. My only guidance, my only connection to my brother's brain. I had read the words a dozen times, his tidy scrawl imprinted in my mind. "*Save me. Then use the garnet. There's no time to waste.*" If only he could tell me something about his brief time at the Winter Palace, what he had learned, or how he had been warned what would soon befall him. About his kidnapping, about the rebels, what they had done to his mind, and why. It was so puzzling. Why would they have kidnapped him, only to set him free in the woods, having planted within his scrambled mind this absurd notion of moose hunting? And if the rebels had set him free, why had they approached us in the woods? Or was that . . . someone else? Unable to work it out in my tired head, my thoughts turned back to what I must do next. I had to find the garnet.

We had been riding at a full run for quite some time, the sun now peeking above the thick wall of trees behind us. While moving at such speed did not allow for much conversation, Alexei still managed to protest the arrangement continuously. While he did not seem to mind being whisked away to God-knows-where, he did mind that I drove the horse. He felt strongly that his maleness—or perhaps his status as tsarevich—earned him control of the reins.

That stubbornness, that entitlement—those characteristics were purely Alexei. But something felt off about him, and I couldn't quite place it. Too tired for much thought, I attributed it to the magician. Having one's memory tampered with would certainly alter one's behavior, I could only assume.

By the time the sky had lightened to a glowing pink, it finally felt safe to slow our pace. Alexei and I had quite a lot to talk about, and I wasn't sure where to begin. I supposed he would need to trust me quite a bit, if he were to believe me when I would tell him about his memory, the magician, the kidnapping, the note . . . ah, and the parallel universes, and the garnet, and the execution . . . It was too much. What would he make of what I had to say? Clearing my throat, I thought it best to start simply.

"Alexei." I looked to the sky, begging aid from the cosmos, or from God, or from anyone willing to help me break through to my brother's swirled mind. "Although you don't remember me, we know each other very well, and you need to trust me. It seems that your memory has been altered by a magician, who is working with the rebels. You were kidnapped. You warned me that this might happen—I don't know how you knew. You did, though. You warned me with a note. Because of that note, I am here now. To keep you safe."

Turning as we rode, Alexei met my serious look for a moment, then broke into a laugh. It startled me—it was a laugh I had never heard before. It was not a sarcastic laugh, nor was it at my expense. It was jovial—the sound of a carefree boy who had just heard something hilarious. And it went on and on, until he finally stopped laughing to catch his breath and replied, between chuckles and wheezes, "Ah! You had me for a moment there!" He took a deep breath and continued. "Whew. A magician! That's wild, you delivered it with such conviction. Bravo, lady! Do tell, what is this adventure we've set upon?"

Unamused, I summoned my best impression of Olga, hoping to affect her stern big-sister authority. "Alexei. I'm not fooling around. I'm quite serious."

He shook his head. "Nice try, lady. I've been hunting out in the woods since dusk—hadn't seen another soul until you and your husband showed up. On a horse rather identical to my own young horse, I must say. Two of a kind, truly. A mirror image . . ."

And just like that, he had moved to another subject of greater interest to him. His blasted horse. His words grinded in my mind, bothering me more than they should have. I sighed, unable to contain my frustration. If Alexei couldn't be convinced of the memory-wiping, if he wouldn't believe that he is my brother, that he was kidnapped—then he would never believe me about the parallel universes, or about our lives before. I would have to show him.

The thought of leaving this world—and the people within it—still unsettled me.

But I had to show Alexei the truth. I had to trust that he'd known something when he wrote that note. "*Save me. Use the garnet,*" he'd written. That's what I would have to do.

While I had no idea where to begin in search of my gemstone necklace, I thought I knew where I might find another, and thus we rode for St. Petersburg. Toward the Winter Palace, though that wasn't our destination. I would have to lie, or make some excuse, or hijack the horse—somehow, I had to get us to Lev's cabin. *Sorry Lev,* I silently pleaded. *You were right. I shall become a thief, after all.*

I RECOGNIZED THE small opening in the thick pines from the trail. I'd heard the gentle trickle of the stream, smelled the wetness of the soil, and deduced that we must be nearing the watering hole. Quite pleased with myself, something like pride welled in my chest as I steered Molniya off the path. Perhaps I was more capable than I'd ever had the opportunity to discover as a princess. Here in this world, there was no one to do things for me. It was up to me.

Just me.

Then my smile quickly faded, my momentary pride swallowed by heavy loneliness as the familiar barrage of grief and guilt overtook me once more.

Despite the dark swirl of emotions clouding my mind, the summer sun beamed brightly in the mid-morning sky. It was a warm day, even for July, and my most primary need was water. My already-dirty hair was now wet with sweat and my throat crackled with thirst. As we came upon a small break in the pines lining the road, I welcomed the sight of the steep bank where Lev and I had stopped the day before.

I pulled Molniya to a stop and attempted to swing down from the horse, the soreness of my muscles prohibiting any semblance of grace. While my dismount was more of a rolling crawl, I was grateful to have my feet on the ground again.

Alexei swung down from the horse after me, landing on strong legs as he readjusted his hunting rifle and the string of pheasants he had slung over his shoulder. "I'm rather hungry. Perhaps you can cook us some breakfast." He tossed the string of dead birds to the ground. It wasn't rudeness so much as an innocent expectation, since I supposed he thought me to be some sort of servant. He smiled and sniffed the air, unshouldering his rifle. "Ah, the river runs nearby. I'm going to have a drink of water."

I stared. I hadn't noticed while atop the horse, nor in the darkness of the Luzhsky forest. But Alexei *looked* different. Stronger. Healthier. Happier. The thought gnawed at me; there had to be an explanation. Perhaps the limp had become a learned habit and had disappeared with his memory. Perhaps the fresh air was revitalizing his pallid complexion. That was it, wasn't it?

Limp or not, Alexei couldn't handle a tumble down the ridge, so I retrieved the bucket from Molniya's saddle. "I'll get it." I brushed past him, bound for the river.

"Oy, it looks a bit difficult for a woman. I shall go. You could start preparing the pheasants." He spoke genially, if a bit condescendingly, and reached for the bucket.

My nerves were already frayed and I'd had quite enough. "You'd hurt your fragile self, my precious *tsarevich*."

Yanking the bucket back from his outstretched hand, I hustled to the edge of the bank and began the scramble down. Before, my brother would have been enraged. He was always so defensive and intolerant of pity. Now, he just stood looking rather confused. He shrugged. Did he remember *anything*?

I handled the bank without incident this time, returned to our opening in the woods, water bucket in hand. Alexei was crouched beside the beginnings of a crackling fire, blowing and fanning the small flame, and for a moment, he was the image of our father. I thought of our family picnics, on the beaches of Livadiya.

My father had thought it important that we experience nature, that we knew how to build a fire. My mother had thought it important that we roast potatoes and apples and relax together by the sea as a family. Would Alexei remember these things? Was there anything I could say to break past the barrier in his mind?

"Alexei, do you remember Livadiya?"

He rose from his crouch, looking thoughtful. "Livadiya. Well, I went there with my family when I was very young. But I can't say I remember much about it. Why do you ask?"

As I opened my mouth to answer, he continued talking. "And here, would you pluck the birds? And do you know how to cook them? I'm quite famished, I think I could eat two myself. I could eat an entire goose! Possibly an entire moose!" He chuckled at himself.

It was useless. I pulled a bird from the string and started plucking.

"Me too, Alexei."

We managed to cook an edible meal, and having filled our bellies, Molniya, Alexei, and I snoozed in the late morning sun. I must have fallen asleep immediately, because I awoke hours later with a pheasant bone still clutched in my hand. I had awoken to the sound of Molniya, braying restlessly, wrestling with his cobble. My eyes flew open, and I saw what had the horse dancing nervously. My heart dropped into my stomach. A brown bear was sniffing his way through the woods, approaching our breakfast-turned-slumber party.

"Alexei." I kept my voice as even as I could. The bear did not seem bothered, and I hoped we could keep it that way while quietly making our exit. I tried to remember what I knew about bears and found that it was not much. "Wake up, Alexei." He stirred, opened his eyes, and yawned. He reached his arms overhead, stretching, and the bear turned its head, observing the movement.

"Ah, that was just the ticket—"

"*Shhhh!*"

Alexei followed my gaze over his shoulder and stiffened. He saw the bear, and he saw the bear see him. His eyes shot across our camp, to where he'd carelessly strewn his rifle by the string of uncooked birds. And he slowly lay back down. Keeping his voice low, he spoke seriously. "Anastasia, it's spotted us. You should lie down and try not to move. Even if the bear comes near, try not to move, okay?"

I supposed that sounded familiar. My brother would know, anyway, as he had humored my father with his participation in the Scout Troops despite his inability for outdoorsmanship. Moving slowly, I lowered myself to the ground, wishing it were possible to distance myself from the remains of my breakfast.

Unbothered by Molniya's stomping and braying, the bear sauntered toward us, sniffing, allured by either the scent of roasted pheasant, or that of terrified Romanovs. I closed my eyes, opened them, closed them again. Was it better to see the bear coming? I was sweating profusely, my heart beating rapidly, and I peeked an eye open. It was close enough now to see the gray on its muzzle—an old bear, then. Fully grown.

The bear came upon Alexei first. As the bear pawed at my brother's boot, Alexei remained completely still. I wasn't sure either of us were breathing. As I appreciated Alexei's ability to lie so motionlessly, I was unsure of my capacity to do the same. From my angle, three meters or so from my brother, it was surreal, like watching a film. But then the bear jerked his head upward, as though it had caught a whiff of something intriguing. Roasted pheasant.

Covering the distance in just a few ambling steps, the bear dipped his snout to sniff my hands, still coated in pheasant grease. The nose was wet against my palm. And then my heartbeat began to slow—everything seemed to slow. My mind stopped racing, and it was a moment of clarity. There was nothing I could do in this moment except wait. At the mercy of forces beyond my control, my life would end, or it would continue. And despite the hardships of the last few days, months, years . . . I rather hoped it would continue.

To my immense relief, the bear sniffed again and left me, moving toward the remaining uncooked pheasants on their string. An easy meal. We lay in stillness as the bear had its fill, snacking casually. The bear pawed the last remaining pheasant and then looked to me, his big brown eyes meeting mine for a moment. And the look in the animal's eyes was not malevolent. As though he'd come to some decision, the bear left that last bird uneaten and sauntered onward into the forest. Perhaps there was some goodness in the world, after all. We waited silently for several minutes, still afraid to move, afraid to draw the bear back from wherever it had meandered, until at last it felt safe to sit up.

"Whew." Speaking softly, I looked to Alexei. He too had pushed himself up to a seated position, a strange look on his face. I thought he was perhaps in need of comfort and offered, "You were quite brave."

He blushed, not meeting my eye.

"Not brave. I . . . well, I'm going to need another pair of pants. Before, um, arriving at the palace."

Nearly choking on a laugh, I managed to hold it in, only because he looked like he might die of embarrassment. "Not to worry, Your Highness. We'll be arriving during the night." Ah. Convenient. "If you'd like, we can stop at my cabin along the way, find you some breeches."

Nodding curtly, he stepped behind a spruce tree to shed his soiled bottoms and emerged looking rather ridiculous, with his knobby knees poking out awkwardly between the hem of his shirttails and the top of his socks. Chicken-legged thirteen-year-old that he was, his legs were more muscular than I remembered. To be fair, I couldn't remember the last time I'd seen his bare legs, so I shoved the notion away. But in the back of my brain, an alarm sounded, faint beneath the jumble of thoughts that preoccupied my mind. I shook my head, turning my thoughts to the mission before me, clinging to my brother's words like a beacon in the night. "*Save me. Use the garnet.*"

As I mounted the horse, I mapped the route to Lev's cabin in my head. Alexei scooped up his rifle and the remaining pheasant, then motioned for me to look away, careful not to expose himself as he climbed into Molniya's saddle.

We rode on into St. Petersburg, a nameless girl and a pantless amnesiac, aspiring jewel thieves and travelers of the universe.

THE CABIN WAS just as we had left it, breadcrumbs and empty tin cups atop the dingy table. In the darkness of the late night, I felt my way along the wall to the table and found the candlestick. The single flame illuminated the room, casting shadows at odd angles.

Alexei entered behind me, by now rather unembarrassed by his pantlessness. "Wow." He seemed truly intrigued as he took in the simplicity of the home. "This is . . . this is where you live?" He looked upon me then with a new curiosity and . . . was it concern? I met his eye. Despite my recent practice, I was still quite unskilled at lying, so I simply nodded.

"Feel free to raid the cupboards, if you're hungry. I'll find you some clothes, and . . . I need to look for something."

As Alexei continued to look around in wonder, I began my search. I started with the closet, of course, quickly finding a pair of Lev's pants, and continuing to hunt under each folded garment, of which there were few. No garnet. I searched under the lumpy straw mattress and over the door. Nothing.

There weren't many possible hiding places, and it didn't take long to exhaust my mental list of likely choices. How long could I convince my confounded brother to linger around this cabin before he would demand we continue to the palace?

I stepped back into the main room, the floorboards creaking beneath my boot. That sound of whining wood brought to mind my many arrivals in this cabin. Hadn't it been this very spot, where I'd landed each time, in each world? I looked down to my feet and noticed for the first time a small leather tab, poking up between the floorboards. Kneeling to the floor, I pulled the tab, and the rickety board lifted, revealing a small cubby of belongings. Lev's belongings. My heart panged as I pictured him, arms raised, sacrificing himself as I rode away. Was it just guilt that I felt?

At the top of the cubby sat a small stack of drawings—charcoal on parchment—each signed with a single name: "Polina." Intrigued, I set my candle down and held the pictures to the light, taking a moment to examine each one before moving it to the bottom of the stack. The first depicted the cabin itself. The next, a woman standing tall, cradling an infant in each arm. A sleeping dog. A portrait of two identical young boys, one smiling charmingly, the other quite serious. And then the last picture—I drew a sharp breath. Bearded, but younger than when I knew him. I would recognize those piercing, otherworldly eyes anywhere: Rasputin. How?

A shadow blocked the light, Alexei moving behind me to peer over my shoulder. "Did you draw these? They're quite good."

I set the drawings aside, dumbfounded, and reached absently for the next item in the cubby. "No . . . no I didn't." My hand located a small iron box, heavy for its size, and I gave it a gentle shake. There was something inside. I snapped alert. This had to be it. Using both hands, I struggled to unlatch the tight fastening, and Alexei intervened in an act of condescending chivalry.

"Here, let me—"

"No, hand it back!"

"Just, let me help you—"

And in my effort to maintain my hold of the iron box, I pulled, and Alexei lost his footing, his foot plummeting into the cubby. His bare leg slid against the splintered edge of the flooring, and a jag of wood split the skin of his calf.

"Yach!" He sat heavily on the floor, pulling his leg toward him. A small stream of blood trickled down his leg, and then a thicker drop blotted over the puncture, thickening, stopping.

My eyes shot from his clotting wound to his face—his healthy cheeks, his glowing skin. And it all made sense, the truth hitting me like a hammer to the head.

This boy was not my brother.

CHAPTER FIFTEEN

"To do evil a human being must first of all believe that what he's doing is good."

—Aleksandr Solzhenitsyn

THE WINTER PALACE HAD always intrigued Alexei. Unlike the Alexander Palace and the other smaller palaces he had known, the Winter Palace was truly a grand castle, a fitting home for the imperial family. It was the legacy of the Romanov dynasty, though he couldn't remember ever having been inside. And so he explored the vast corridors, taking in the splendor of the stonework, marveling at the glistening marble staircase as the first rays of the morning sun shone through the ornate windows above.

Despite the early hour, the palace was bristling with nervous energy. Servants bustled about, carpenters came and went, guards stalked the halls—the walls almost seemed to buzz, the air lightly humming. News of the attempted poisoning and the tsar's subsequent crusade to the Luzhsky Uyezd had traveled quickly, and the inhabitants of the palace were outraged on Alexei's behalf, shocked that his uncle could attempt such a thing. It hadn't seemed such a stretch to Alexei. To die by assassination would, after all, be to follow in the footsteps of generations before him. Had the tsars been subject to such a bloody history here in this world? They certainly seemed to enjoy a greater sense of security. That was, he supposed, why the Winter Palace remained their home.

He was unsure of the story—he wished he had paid better attention to his tutors. There was some reason that his family hadn't lived within the castle. *Something to do with a bomb*, he thought. *In the basement?* Whatever had happened, it had been long ago. *Was it during my grandfather's reign? My great-grandfather's?* The story resided somewhere deep within his memory, buried, and it nagged him.

Regardless of the details, he had the strong sense that in his own world, the palace had been deemed not secure, too difficult to guard from attack. And his family had too many enemies.

The imperial family in this world seemed to have its share of enemies too. But this tsar acted swiftly and decisively. He'd rallied his regiment and ridden to the Luzhsky Uyezd without hesitation to defend his son. Would his own father have done the same? Alexei frowned. *Unlikely.*

The image of his father flashed in Alexei's mind. His strong frame, his kind eyes. And in his final moments, his startled expression as he turned to face the guard in that cellar. His knees buckling as he fell helplessly to the ground. Alexei pushed the memories away, burying his conflicting anger and resentment and grief deep inside and turning his thoughts to the dilemma at hand.

Alexei supposed the tsar and his men would have reached Mikhail's estate by now, and Mikhail would stand accused of attempted poisoning. Anastasia would have either failed or succeeded in finding the tsarevich and traveling to another world. And it was all driven by Alexei's lies. Necessary lies. How else could he fulfill his birthright? How else might he become tsar?

A weak voice inside his head begged him to confess. What if he did? Would it bring the tsar home? Would it keep his sister by his side? Would it stop a war?

Maybe.

All he knew for certain was that it would cost him his chance, dooming him to a life of worthlessness. Confessing was not an option.

He silenced that voice and told himself the story again. This world, he told himself, wasn't so unlike his own. Perhaps unrest had been brewing below the surface for a long time, awaiting an impetus.

The whisper of a rebellion had become a shout in mere moments, catalyzed by his lie, not caused by it. *I'm entitled to my destiny,* he told himself. *I'm doing nothing wrong.*

THE DINING TABLE was set only for two, the nervous bustle within the Winter Palace having settled into an anxious quiet. Despite the uneasy mood within the palace, Alexei had settled into tsarevich life quite well. Even the luxuries to which he'd been accustomed prior to his family's imprisonment did not compare to the lavish lifestyle the imperial family enjoyed in this world. Every meal was a feast, every comfort provided for. There were servants to command, countless games, and no one restricting, coddling, or babying Alexei for his condition. Even with the castle on lockdown, he could explore freely and live richly as a tsarevich ought to. It was the life he deserved, the life to which he was entitled.

However, looming over Alexei's content was a deep dread. Dread for that moment when he would know for sure. When too much time had passed, with no Other Alexei, no Anastasia surfacing. When he would know that she had succeeded in finding his double, using the garnet, and traveling to another world.

With no chance of return. It was terrifying, and he had brought it on himself, and he still saw no way around it. Would he be fated to live forever with his secret, and no one to share it with? Or worse—if she did not succeed—would his secret be discovered? Would he be outed as a fraud, sentenced to a life outside the palace walls?

Lost in thought, Alexei slowly pressed his fork into the soft smush of a boiled egg, watching as the white and the yolk crumbled together, oozing between the silver sprigs of metal.

"... and of course, the reparations in the basement must continue, but poor Petrov is now managing both entrances, and it must be quite the ordeal. Won't you assist him, Alexei?"

He was only half listening, lulled by the sweet sounds of his mother's voice, even as she prattled on about mundane palace upkeep. *What had she asked him?*

"Of course, Mother."

As she continued talking, the sound of her melodic voice rambled on like a song, and Alexei sank back into his reverie. His thoughts turned to his former life, his family, his father.

Alexei's father had been a decently competent ruler when left to his own devices. But Alexei had heard the whisperings. His own savior had been his father's downfall. *Rasputin.* His mother's faith in the old starets, his own dependence upon the mysterious healer, his father's trust in the unlikely advisor—these misplaced affections for the magician had allowed him undue influence on the Russian empire. And he had led the tsar astray. Alexei wondered where he would be today, were it not for Rasputin. Would Alexei be in his own world, with his own family, in his own palace? Would his father have kept hold of his rule? Or would Alexei have bled to death, years ago?

"... Alexei?" His mother had asked him something.

"Hmm, yes Mother?"

"You're quite distracted, my son. I only said such. You've endured so much, my sweet boy. But fear not, your uncle will be held accountable. Your father will see to it." She tilted her chin, flashing a conspirative grin. "But we can still have fun, you and I. How about a game of backgammon?"

Alexei nodded, smiling despite himself. "Of course, Mother."

~~~~~~~

IF BACKGAMMON WERE to be the cure for Alexei's restiveness, it would be only after the tsarina had bathed, restyled herself, and taken several social calls. It was late afternoon by the time Alexei was called upon to meet again with his mother in her entertaining chamber.

Comparatively speaking, it was a rather small room, housing several bookshelves, an ornate chest, and a game table set with two chairs and a backgammon board. The tsarina stood behind one of the chairs, facing the door, awaiting her son. She looked beautiful as always, her red-gold curls cascading down her back, her deep-set blue eyes illuminating her face. She stood tall and slender, resting her smooth hand on the table and absently tumbling a die beneath her index finger.

She is rather like a strawberry-haired Anastasia, Alexei thought. *But Anastasia would not wear such an extravagant gown. Nor would she wear such jewelry. Except . . . could it be?* Set against the white silk bodice of the tsarina's elegant gown, the necklace was striking. The thin gold chain sparkled, the oversized red gemstone gleaming in the light. *The garnet.*

Conflicting emotions flooded Alexei all at once, the mix of surprise and relief and dismay astounding him. Surprise, as he had not considered that the jewel might have been stolen, or confiscated, or otherwise removed from his sister's possession. Relief, because if the gemstone was here, then Anastasia remained in this world, another soul that knew his own, his sister. But at the same time, dismay. If Anastasia remained in this world, then so did his doppelgänger. No. *He* was the doppelgänger. This Other Alexei was the true tsarevich here. Yet Alexei had replaced him so seamlessly, hadn't he? Couldn't he, still?

"Roll the dice, Alexei." The tsarina gestured to the board. "Let's see who wins."

CHAPTER SIXTEEN

"One must love life before loving its meaning . . . Yes, and when the love of life disappears, no meaning can console us."

—Fyodor Dostoyevsky

SINCE HIS ARRIVAL THAT morning, Lev had been awed by the luxury of his accommodations. Lounging comfortably across his cot, he slowly gnawed on a roll of bread and glanced around the room. He supposed his chamber to be at least the size of his cabin in St. Petersburg and was but one room in what seemed to be a gargantuan house.

Though he'd been blindfolded for the entirety of his trip from the Tsarskoye Selo train station to his present location, he'd paid attention to the journey. It had been a short carriage ride, and though restrained, he hadn't been buried in hay.

He'd felt the eastern morning sun shining into the carriage, warming the right side of his face. Northeast, then, for most of the journey, before exiting the carriage and turning sharply southwest on foot.

As he'd stepped into the shadow cast by the enormous structure, his mind had registered the west-facing entry. He had noticed the change in the air when he'd stepped inside, felt the solid smoothness of marble beneath his boots. His mind had then rather automatically begun counting paces, scrambling to remain oriented to the space he moved within. If he would be held prisoner, he would know his way to the exit.

Prisoner, again. Anastasia's voice came to mind, teasing him, *"Do you make a habit of being imprisoned, then?"* He hadn't previously. Not until she had shown up in his cabin and uprooted his life.

Not that my life had been all that rooted to begin with, Lev thought as he arose, stuffing the bread roll in his pocket. He found himself pacing as he considered all that had happened in the last few days—in the last few years, truthfully—that had led him here to this lavish prison, a captive of the Narodnaya Volya.

The recent chain of events was straightforward enough, he supposed. He'd found the tsarevich and the mysterious Anastasia in his cabin upon arriving home from patrol, had been mistaken for a kidnapper, arrested, and imprisoned beneath the Winter Palace.

He'd then been released from prison without trial and followed Anastasia on a strange rescue mission instigated by a note from the tsarevich. Found the tsarevich in the Luzhsky forest. And then captured, questioned, hidden in a carriage, dragged on a train, and brought to the Narodnaya Volya's Tsarskoye Selo headquarters.

The details, though . . . they just didn't add up. The garnet, for one. How had Anastasia found it? How had she known it existed? The gemstone had remained hidden beneath the floor for almost nineteen years. And then there was her bold claim that a magician had given her the gem. A magician, as though they weren't extinct like magic itself. That was perhaps the piece that bothered Lev the most, because it too-closely echoed the beliefs of his twin brother.

Luka had always been drawn to the more unusual aspects of reality, and had grown quite obsessed with Russia's history of magic. He'd learned all he could about it—taboo as it was—and had refused to believe it was gone from the world. Like many, he was entranced by the idea of *kolodtsy,* wanting so badly to find the wondrous power of the past preserved. He'd become convinced that the garnet beneath their floorboards was itself a *kolodets.* That their father had been a magic-wielder. That he'd pulled magic from the air and infused the gemstone with some special power.

But that was just it, wasn't it? Luka had clung to the idea that *they* were somehow special. That their father had been something more than their mother's biggest mistake. Luka had wanted so badly for there to be *more.* He'd had quite a few theories on the matter—theories that he'd once shared excitedly with his brother. But how many times had Lev smiled doubtfully, replying, "Sure, Luka," before cracking a joke? Enough that eventually Luka had stopped sharing his ideas. Stopped saying much at all.

After Luka's death and their mother's, Lev had thought about selling the gemstone. A garnet of that size would have fetched a substantial payout—money that Lev could have certainly used. Nevertheless, he couldn't bring himself to part with the gemstone.

It felt like a betrayal to their memories—or at least, that's what he told himself. In truth, every time he'd considered it, every time he'd taken the garnet from its cubby, he felt overwhelmingly drawn to it, as though he and the gemstone were one and the same. He'd begun to understand how Luka had become obsessed, and he might have, too, had he allowed it. Instead, Lev stashed the garnet away again beneath the floor. Hidden, yet comfortably close.

When that soldier yanked the necklace from Anastasia's throat, holding it up for all to see, Lev had been furious at her, and he'd wanted to remain furious. But she was so inconveniently likeable. She didn't *seem* like a thief and a liar. Her voice came to mind once again. *"Maybe there are two."*

Maybe there are two.

The tsarevich—that was the other troubling detail. He'd been there, in Lev's cabin, in St. Petersburg. And yet, to hear the Grand Duchesses talk, he'd been at the Luzhsky estate, picnicking and riding with his sisters. *Maybe there are two.* Twins, like Luka and him? Implausible.

Maybe there are two.

He couldn't quite connect the pieces. *But there was something else, wasn't there?*

There was the note. Strange enough that the tsarevich had known he would be kidnapped and had thought to tell Anastasia. And the post script ... It was bewildering. "*They have a magician. He may wipe my memory.*" How had he known? He had been right, hadn't he?

Lev thought again of the garnet, stowed beneath the floorboards for all those years. What if Luka was right? What if it was indeed a *kolodets*? If the legends were true, then anyone—wielder or not—could release its power. If they knew how, anyway.

Luka had theories on that, too. He'd proposed boiling them, or freezing them, or colliding them with kinetic energy at a high velocity. Lev had once caught Luka singing to the garnet and teased him about it relentlessly. But now ... Lev couldn't see any other explanation. Either the Narodnaya Volya were indeed working with a magician as the note predicted, or they'd sang just the right tune to a memory-wiping *kolodets*, because the tsarevich in the Luzhsky forest clearly did not possess the same mind as the tsarevich who had appeared in Lev's cabin the day before.

He sat again at the edge of the bed, leaning his elbows on his knees and resting his head in his hands. His mind swam with images of the garnet, the tsarevich, Anastasia. Anastasia. She held the answers to his questions, didn't she? Wasn't that why she occupied his thoughts perpetually?

In his mind, he was back in that prison cell, Anastasia before him, her sorrowful eyes glazed with uncried tears. Lev knew what it was to swallow one's grief, to hold it in. Then she had seemed to loosen, to soften just a bit as she had spoken, putting into words the fate of her family—perhaps speaking it for the first time. What had her family done? Who had they been? And who had executed them all—leaving only one survivor? Or was it two? "*My brother,*" she'd said, back in the Luzhsky forest. He had forgotten what Anastasia had been speaking about at the time. But the way she'd reacted when she realized what she'd said—she'd been mortified, stammering as though she'd revealed a dire secret. His mind churned with unanswered questions.

Finding the sudden need to turn off his thoughts and occupy himself otherwise, Lev stood from the bed and began his exercise routine. High step-ups, first. Lev scanned the room for a firm surface of adequate height. The old metal trunk in the closet would do. As he hiked himself up, down, up, down, his mind returned to Luka. He and Luka had come up with the routine as boys, though it had evolved over the years as they'd become stronger, more flexible, and, for Lev anyway, quite bored with the exercises in their basic form. Squats became single leg squats, one leg crossed over the other, a balancing act. More fun.

Luka hadn't been one for fun. The routine for him was an act of self-discipline. Means to an end, a necessary training of the body, preparing himself to meet any physical challenges that might stand between him and his greater goals. His political goals, Lev supposed. He'd become devoted to the Narodnaya Volya, preaching endlessly about inequality and social reform. Even then, his resentment for the tsardom seemed rooted in his obsession with *kolodtsy*, his belief that magic still existed, trapped in the depths of gemstone wells. Luka had grown ever more distant, disconnecting from their mother, but remaining tethered to his brother through that unbreakable connection that only twins share. Luka had nearly disappeared into the shadows, an echo of his former self, by the time the news of his death arrived. On their shared seventeenth birthday, the letter came. The brief message was signed anonymously, but Lev never doubted that it came from the Narodnaya Volya. That his brother had become too reckless, too involved, and gotten himself killed.

As dark as Luka's presence had become, his absence was somehow darker. Lev had felt it before he'd heard it, and he'd known it to be true: Luka was gone.

Lev placed his hands on the floor, kicking his feet to the ceiling. More difficult than regular push-ups. More fun, usually. But in his mind, Lev could see his mother, frozen with shock at the news, not believing it until she'd met Lev's eyes. He'd nodded, answering her silent question, and she'd collapsed to the floor in a puddle of grief, from which she never truly arose. She'd gone through the motions of life for several months after, sure. But she never smiled, hardly spoke, rarely looked at Lev. Smiling, joking, good-natured Lev—he was like her, she had always claimed. And Luka was like their father. That was all she'd ever said about their father. Still, her heart had died with Luka, and that said more than words ever could. Her heart had died and her body had followed, succumbing to the sadness.

And Lev had carried on without them. Just continued to exist, at first, alone, only seventeen, and unsure who he was without his twin, without his mother, without anyone. But in time, he'd learned. A year had passed since then, and he knew now. He was Lev. He would live his life and enjoy it as best he could, because what other option was there?

CHAPTER SEVENTEEN

"Oft have I heard that grief softens the mind, and makes it fearful and degenerate; think therefore on revenge and cease to weep."

—Queen Margaret, *Henry VI* by William Shakespeare

THE IRON BOX SAT unopened in my hands as I knelt by the open cubby, the creaky board set aside, the drawings scattered behind me. With my departure from this world no longer eminent, I felt quite suddenly as an intruder, my exploration of Lev's hideaway a violation of his privacy. I imagined him shrugging, suppressing a grin. He would say something like, "Aren't you going to take it then, thief?" Reacting to the unspoken words, I shoved the box back into the hole in the flooring.

Looking once more to the stranger who stood before me, I couldn't believe I had ever thought this buffoon was my brother. No, my brother was no idiot. He was *too* clever. Clever enough to use my own trusting nature against me, to use Lev's loyalty against him, to find a way to trick me into removing the only obstacle between him and his precious throne. And at the same time . . .

It dawned on me then, the magnitude of Alexei's lie. Had this *other* Alexei not sliced his leg, would I have realized in time that he was not who I thought he was? Would I have opened the box and found a garnet identical to my own? And would I have shot it, used it, and left this world forever with a complete stranger, never to see my brother again? Yes. Yes, I would have. The confusion, the shock, the hurt, they all receded, as a quiet rage boiled within me. My own brother would have cast me to another universe, for his precious crown.

The weight of the revelation sat heavily on my heart, threatening to crush my already-bedraggled spirit. My parents and sisters were gone forever. My brother . . . I knew he was obsessed with becoming tsar. I knew he cared about that more than almost anything. I hadn't thought that he cared about that more than he cared about me. I wanted to scream. To cry. To bury my head in my arms and collapse in a dark room, alone. I loved my brother. But what was he becoming?

As I struggled to hold back tears, the tsarevich extended his hand, offering to assist me to my feet. "Come along, then. Aren't you ready to go on to the palace? I should think my mother and father will have quite a feast for us when we arrive."

Ah. The puzzle before me subdued my rage just a bit, as I needed presence of mind to figure out how to accomplish what needed to be done next. Idiot though he may be, the tsarevich was a sweet kid. He belonged at home in the Winter Palace. My brother, on the other hand, was a selfish, scheming *zasranets*, and he belonged with me, whether he liked it or not. Alexei thought he could just discard his sister, banish the true tsarevich to another world, and waltz to his coronation? We'd see about that. I would switch them back. I would sneak the true tsarevich in and drag my conniving little brother out. I would put an end to Alexei's plot to steal the throne. And if it wouldn't cause a deadly bleed, I would punch him right in the face.

"Anastasia?"

I blinked, taking a deep breath and unclenching my fists. Right. "Yes, of course, Your Highness. I'll ready Molniya, and we'll be off."

Before accepting the tsarevich's outstretched hand, I reordered the drawings into a neat stack, replacing them into the cubby as I had found them. All but one. Even in my anger—my heartbroken disappointment—

still I panged with curiosity, and so I rolled the image of Rasputin into a tight cylinder and tucked it in my pocket. A thief, indeed. Rising to my feet, I turned my mind to the more immediate issue: how would I swap the two Alexeis without alerting the tsarevich of his double? How would I get into the palace so covertly? I supposed I would have to form a plan as we rode.

MY BROTHER MUST have been six or seven—it was before Spala, anyway—when we'd conspired together to free him of his caregiver and go riding. Our parents had thought riding too dangerous for their hemophilic son, and so Alexei had never ridden a horse beyond a walk, and even then, always accompanied.

My sisters and I had been close—inseparable, really, playing together as little girls, knitting and chatting together as young women, knowing each other as only sisters can. Collectively, Olga, Tatiana, Maria, and I had been called OTMA, the acronym of our first names. However, Alexei and I had shared a bond, too. As the youngest two siblings, our connection was strengthened by our mutual tendency for mischief. I cherished my brother, I always had, and had thought it tragically unjust that his illness should rob him of the purest joys in life. I didn't understand then, the reality of the risk a simple injury posed to my brother. Death had been abstract, and my brother had always been resilient in his recoveries. I loved nothing more than an uninhibited ride on a fast horse, and so to me, it was worth the risk. I'd sworn to myself that I wouldn't let him fall.

Alexei had agreed emphatically. "A tsarevich must learn to ride, to lead his troops to battle!" My little brother, even then, was quite singularly focused.

The particulars of our plot were murky in my memory. Still, I remembered that moments after I had posed the idea of shirking the babysitter and heading to the stables, Alexei had formed a plan, and it had worked. We had enjoyed a glorious ride around the fields of Tsarskoye Selo, an hour of freedom, all without incident or injury. And we had almost gotten away with it. Almost. When our parents discovered what we had done, they were furious.

"*It was worth it,*" Alexei had said, peeking in on me as he'd passed my door. His punishment was an early bedtime, no supper. As he was unable to take a belting, I'd taken one for us both. "*It better have been,*" I'd said, lying sore-bottom-up on my bed. We never saw that caregiver again.

I supposed that since that day, Alexei had learned that he could employ his wits to use people, to manipulate his circumstances to his liking. Sometimes he had gotten away with it, and other times he hadn't. This time, he hadn't. I loved my brother, yes, but he was *not* going to get his way. He had to learn that he couldn't just use people. He couldn't just discard me for his blasted throne. He was stuck with me, and I would not let him replace the tsarevich in this world, no matter how much it meant to him.

"My parents will be so thrilled to see me," the tsarevich spoke over his shoulder, ahead of me in the saddle once again. "And you, too! I can just imagine my mother's face when we tell her of the bear!"

His words intrigued me, and I didn't immediately realize why.

"But my sisters, I suppose, remain still at Uncle Mikhail's. I shall miss them."

And then it occurred to me that the simpleminded tsarevich would have answers to questions I hadn't thought to ask. Because if Alexei's note was a lie, then what was the tsarevich doing, alone in the woods of the Luzhsky estate? Was he truly just out moose-hunting? And his sisters . . . were the Romanov siblings simply visiting their uncle?

"Alexei, will you tell me about your sisters?"

"Of course, lady! My sisters are just marvelous, and they love me so much. Olga, Tatiana, Maria, and Alexei—we call ourselves OTMA. We have the most splendid picnics and rides, and . . ." I half-listened as he prattled on, my heart sinking to my boots. This was what the world looked like without me. I didn't exist, and my siblings didn't even know to miss me. OTMA were content in their foursome. In a world in which I had never been born, Alexei was healthy. A bit slow, perhaps, yet healthy.

And here, the imperial family still reigned. Rebellion was brewing, yes, but the tsar retained his crown, and his family was not imprisoned. Conditions were certainly better here. Here, where I had never been born. Was it that fate would only allow my parents four healthy children? And, without Alexei's hemophilia, had my mother remained healthier—physically, mentally? Had Rasputin ever entered the palace? Without Rasputin's council, had my father ruled differently? Would my family, my Russia, my *world* have been better off without me? Was that why it had spit me out, sent me tumbling aimlessly through the endless universe? My forehead burned with the effort of holding back tears, a solid lump forming in my throat as I swallowed my grief. This was no time for self-pity. I was on a mission.

"...and of course, Papa hoped that having us around would raise Uncle Mikhail's spirits, and help him to see that everything is just fine, you know, in our country. But we never really talked about that much, we just had a nice time mostly. Hey, who were those men, do you think, who were riding upon us when your husband sent us off?"

My husband. He meant Lev, obviously, still I blushed, his mistake momentarily distracting me from my anguish as I considered his question. Indeed, who were those men?

"I—" A flash of movement caught my eye, moonlight on steel, as three riders wielding long knives blocked our path. Silhouetted by the white light of the July night sky, the shadow horses stood tall, the riders with their knives creating a fearsome image before us. "I think the more immediate question is, who are *these* men?" I hadn't lowered my voice. Clearly, they heard me.

"We are the Narodnaya Volya. And you are coming with us."

But I'd had quite enough of being arrested, transported, shoved along from one place to the next. I was returning the tsarevich to the palace. I was finding my brother.

"Like hell we are." I pulled Molniya through a tight turn, the horse more than willing to create distance between himself and the three strange horses. The road was long and straight, only two directions one might go.

And so we bolted in the direction from which we'd come, the shadows on the street churning by in a dark whirlwind.

The sound of hooves against the pavement filled the quiet street as the Narodnaya Volya kicked their horses into pursuit. Molniya sensed the chase and increased his speed beyond what I had imagined possible. It was like flying. In front of me, the tsarevich fumbled for his rifle, struggling to hold onto Molniya with his free hand. Did the fool really think so highly of his marksmanship to suppose he could hit a moving target from the back of a sprinting horse?

"No! Leave it! You'll fall—" As the tsarevich twisted, the rifle slid from his shoulder and he succeeded in both dropping the rifle and tumbling gracelessly from Molniya's back. Unbothered, or perhaps even spurred on by the lightened load, Molniya charged forward at an unbelievable pace, leaving the fallen tsarevich behind. "Whooooa, boy! Stop!" Though I jerked the reins, Molniya only ran faster, uninterested in my commands.

In different circumstances, I would have been completely immersed in the high that can only be experienced when riding a fast horse at a full run. As it was, the tsarevich landed on the ground behind me, with enemies quickly advancing upon him. I couldn't let these men take him. The boy was nearly a stranger, but he was innocent. And I needed him, if I were to extract my *zasranets* brother from the Winter Palace. I jerked the reins again, "Molniya! Whooa!" My efforts were futile. I was at the stallion's mercy as he sprinted on. When I looked over my shoulder, the tsarevich and the riders had been encompassed in the darkness as I rode away uselessly tugging at the reins.

A few minutes passed, and Molniya at last began to slow, perhaps sensing that we were no longer being chased. "Whoa, you ill-trained coward. Stop then, won't you?" I jerked the reins again, and this time the stubborn horse responded, tossing his head back and snorting as he stopped abruptly. When I tried to turn him, he would have none of it, wary still of his pursuers.

The street was quiet. The rebels had captured their intended target, then. I slid from the horse, my body aching from the exertion of the last two days. Where would they be taking him? As the road offered only two directions, I supposed I had as good a place as any to start. But even if I could catch up with them—what then?

The moon, nearly full, reflected in a puddle along the street's edge, rippling as a soft breeze unsettled the surface. I absently led Molniya over for a drink, contemplating what I must do next.

My brother—the selfish *zasranets*— would be safe enough for the moment, living in undeserved luxury at the Winter Palace. And if he was facing any hardship, it was his own fault. I loved him, of course. But oh, how I hated him, too. The tsarevich—the well-meaning dimwit—he needed me. I had no choice, truly, except to make some attempt at rescuing him. Where would they take him, this Narodnaya Volya?

Although my knowledge of the Narodnaya Volya was relatively slim, I did remember a few things from my history lessons. They were the reason we'd never lived in the Winter Palace, as it was deemed unsafe after the bomb. The Narodnaya Volya had used carpenters to sneak dynamite into the basement, blowing up the dining room in their first attempt to kill my great-grandfather. And they were the reason we had a duplicate of our imperial train, always running simultaneously to ours when we traveled to Livadiya, because they'd blown up my great-grandfather's train car, too. That hadn't killed him either, though eventually they were successful in his assassination.

I remembered my father's face, when he'd told us the story. He had been only thirteen, he'd said, when he and his siblings were called to his grandfather's study. Tsar Alexander II's mangled body had been brought there, still clinging to life, but doomed to death. He'd been blown to pieces when the Narodnaya Volya had thrown a bomb right beneath his feet. While I'd never known my great-grandfather, everyone said he'd been a generous man. A good tsar. I couldn't understand the hatred, the horrible violence of it—just to prove a point?

I'd witnessed violence even worse, now, and I couldn't understand that, either. "*You are to be executed,*" the guard had announced. An image of my father's kind face flashed in my mind, utterly shocked as he spun to face his executioner. And then . . . I shook my head, refusing to relive the scene once again.

Here in this Russia, it seemed that the Narodnaya Volya were decades behind the organized Bolsheviks of my own world. They'd assassinated the last two tsars, Lev had said. Had they attacked the train? Had they bombed the Winter Palace? Or had they relied on magic for their violence? Perhaps that was it. That would explain why they'd disappeared when Tsar Nicholas rid the country of magic. Regardless, the Narodnaya Volya had returned. And they were a threat to my family once again.

"*I would save our family,*" I'd told Alexei. "*I would do whatever it took, to keep them alive.*" I could see to that here in this world. Not my family, per se, but the Romanovs as they existed in this world. In that moment, I made a silent vow: I would do everything I could to keep my family safe from the Narodnaya Volya. The tsar, the tsarina, and the Grand Duchesses. The tsarevich. My brother. In this world, they could live. In this world, I could save them.

Those men had taken the tsarevich, and it would be up to me to find him.

DETERMINATION FUELED ME as I steered Molniya onward, after the Narodnaya Volya and their hostage. We moved at a walk—as eager as I was to chase down the *svolochy*, I needed stealth, I needed a plan. I racked my brain as we retraced our steps, desperately reaching for any inkling of a clue as to where the terrorists might be taking the tsarevich. It could be anywhere in St. Petersburg. We weren't far from the train station—it could be anywhere in Russia.

A gleam of metal on the street caught my eye, reflecting the bright swirl of night sky illuminated by the peripheral sun, waiting just over the horizon. The tsarevich's rifle. Halting Molniya, I swung down from the horse and knelt to examine the gun. I traced my finger along the dark wooden stock, the shiny metal barrel . . . I supposed I should learn to handle it. Then something else caught my eye, the tight pattern of yellow and black stripes standing out against the road. A pheasant feather.

I led Molniya along for a bit, the muscles of my legs happier to walk than ride. I hadn't taken five steps when I noticed another feather along the road, and then another. Could it be . . . had the tsarevich left me a trail? Was he that clever? I supposed the feathers could have fallen on their own accord. But they seemed to be spaced quite evenly. I smiled to myself, hearing the voice of my old English tutor, "Even a blind squirrel will find a nut, once in a while."

My skin tingled with excitement. *Yes! Lead me to them, tsarevich*! My mind began to spin, figuring what I might do when I reached my destination, how I might rescue the boy when I arrived. It was exhilarating. I was going to find him, free him, and return him to the palace. The Narodnaya Volya couldn't stop me—I would find a way. The rifle, slung over my shoulder, bumped my behind as I walked along, demanding my attention. Would I use it?

As the sky continued to brighten, I supposed I could spot the feathers well enough from horseback, and I mounted Molniya once again. Once I'd ridden nearly one hundred meters without spotting a feather, I redoubled my steps to be sure I hadn't missed some clue marking a turn. But I examined each cross road thoroughly and saw no indication to veer from the long, straight road, so I continued onward.

The sun peeked over the horizon to my left, as the moon sank to my right. The streets were still quite empty, as the sun rose quite a bit earlier than most Russians this time of year. I found that as I rode in solitude along the empty streets, witnessing the spectacular sunrise, the storm of emotions in my mind was settling into a quiet resolve. The anger, the trauma, the hurt, the bewilderment, the fatigue . . . it all began to converge into a stagnant storm cloud within me. A dark, heavy cloud that sat waiting. Alexei had tricked me, used me in the most terrible way. And yet, as I imagined all the awful things I might say to him upon our reunion, I found an odd sense of comfort. Despite how deeply he'd hurt me, I craved the normalcy of yelling at my little brother.

I took a deep breath, watching as the pinks and oranges of the east overtook the indigo of the west. Would the sun be rising on a new day in my own world? Three days, it would have been, since that night in the cellar. I could hardly imagine my Russia continuing to exist without me, without my family. Without a tsar. My head began to ache, and I pushed the thoughts from my mind, reflecting instead upon the last few sunrises.

The previous, I'd been riding from Mikhail's Luzhsky estate with the tsarevich—still thinking him to be my brother. That was before I had learned that to my brother, I was disposable. That I was an instrument to be used, that it didn't matter if I disappeared from Alexei's world, as long as I took with me his double, removing the obstacle that stood between him and his throne. I took another deep breath and turned my eyes to the swirling pastels of the clouds above me.

I'd missed the sunrise before that, I supposed, as I'd slumbered in a prison cell beneath the Winter Palace. With Lev. Who were those men, who had ridden upon him? Since there had been no kidnapping, no rebel plot, no memory mangling magician—who were they? Would they have harmed Lev? Perhaps it had all been a misunderstanding. Perhaps Lev would have taken a train from Luga, and would be safely sleeping in his cabin now. Surely.

I turned my mind back to replaying sunrises. The dawn before that, I'd been walking along the path from the cabin with Alexei. Worlds away. We hadn't even realized yet where we were, or what the garnet was capable of.

The sunrise before that, I had been asleep on my cot, in the sleeping quarters I'd shared with my sisters at the Ipatiev House in Yekaterinburg, our final prison. My mother and father, my sisters, all alive, all sleeping soundly, all unaware that it would be the last rising of the sun they might witness.

Shaking the wistful thoughts from my mind, I rode onward. I spotted another feather, and another, and followed the trail southward as the urbanity of the densely packed St. Petersburg streets faded into the grandeur of Tsarskoye Selo—the Tsar's Village. My home, in another world. My heart fluttered. Would the Alexander Palace look the same, here in this world? As I arrived at the turn toward my childhood home, I peered down that road. Feathers. It wouldn't be far, now.

I couldn't help but gasp when we arrived before the palace. Stopping Molniya in the empty street, I gazed upon my old home. The regal white columns, the welcoming archways—I could even see the window to the room Maria and I had shared. I knew every window, every door, every passage. But it would be different inside, wouldn't it? No tsar lived here, not in this world. Would it be the home of some cousin? Molniya stomped and snapped his tail—flies were bothering him. And as I looked to the dusty street, I saw why the flies had gathered.

A dead bird, plucked featherless, had been cast to the street, marking the end of our path. They were here, then. At the Alexander Palace. A place I knew better than anyone. I smiled and swung down from the horse. As I reached to pat Molniya's nose, he sneezed, blowing thick yellow slime on my outstretched arm, clearly rejecting the affection. "*Bood' zdeorov*, you magnificent brute." I wiped my snot-covered arm on Molniya's black coat. "We'll need to find you a safe place to rest. I have work to do."

CHAPTER EIGHTEEN

"All around me there is treachery, cowardice, and deceit."

—Tsar Nicholas II

THE TSARINA WAS WRONG.

Managing the Winter Palace entrances was not an enthralling and integral task befitting the tsarevich, but was rather a tediously boring waste of Alexei's morning. He'd just begun to slump against the gold embellished walls of the entry hall when a visitor arrived. As the heavy wooden doors swung open, Alexei straightened, forcing a polite smile.

"Excellent to see you, young Highness." The woman, whom Alexei vaguely recognized as a courtier who also existed in his own world, curtsied and stepped through the doorway. Some distant Romanov cousin, perhaps. He narrowed his eyes, unsure how well-acquainted he might be expected to act with this woman.

"Excellent as always, my lady," he spoke gallantly and stepped aside, allowing her entry, as Petrov slowly traced the letters of her name into the log.

Visitors and palace workers alike required identity verification before entry. This task was overseen by a burly but good-natured guard called Petrov who seemed to know every palace worker by name, which greatly

eased the burden of this undertaking. Alexei, who had somehow unknowingly agreed to assist, found the task quite burdensome nonetheless.

The woman lingered, looking at Alexei expectantly. Clueless as to what
she might be expecting, he avoided eye contact, wishing she would move
along. A moment passed in awkward silence.

Petrov looked up from his log. He coughed. "My Lady, a guard will
be right along to accompany you to meet with the tsarina. Unless, perhaps
Master Alexei—?"

Alexei did nothing to hide his annoyance. This minor quest would be
yet another performance without a script as he strove to pass as the Alexei
these people knew. He'd done well enough thus far, he supposed, in his brief
interactions with each arrival at the palace entry. There had been a steady
stream of kitchen workers, servants, and maids that morning, and then the
traffic had dwindled. With the tsar and the Grand Duchesses away, only the
tsarina was receiving visitors.

Looking to the door, and then to the waiting Lady, Alexei considered
the burden each task proposed. He turned to Petrov. "You take the Lady
along. I'll manage the visitor's log."

And so Alexei found himself alone at the main entry to the Winter Palace, having bullied his way into the unwanted responsibility of screening visitors. A formality, Alexei thought, as no one had been turned away thus far.

Petrov's absence passed rather uneventfully, the only arrivals being
three carpenters in well-worn coveralls. Noting the men's appearance, Alexei vaguely remembered the tsarina saying something about repairs in the
basement. Grateful to recall some information that validated his role, Alexei
nodded knowingly at the men and waved them through. "You know your
way to the basement?"

The men nodded.

For good measure, Alexei added, "And how go the repairs?"

The men exchanged a glance, and the oldest of the three replied, "Quite
well, Your Highness. We expect the job to be complete within the week."
They proceeded into the grand hall, moving toward the dungeon stairwell.

"*Workmen,*" Alexei penciled neatly in the log.

His mind then turned to what was perhaps the most pressing matter at hand: recovering the garnet from the tsarina. He found himself pacing before the door as he contemplated how he might steal the necklace without being discovered. It would be tricky—the tsarina was rarely alone, and Alexei found the prospect of sneaking into her dressing chamber to search for the garnet quite intimidating.

While Alexei did not intend to use the garnet—not for himself anyway, he thought, as he imagined his doppelgänger—he did consider it immediately crucial that the mystical gemstone come back into his possession. It was dangerous, wasn't it, for the tsarina to wear such a force around her neck, not knowing the power it held? That was what he told himself, but in truth, he was somewhat bothered by his own mad desire to possess the garnet. Was it greed? Did he simply crave control?

His contemplations were interrupted by Petrov, who hustled to the door rather clumsily. "Alexei, Your Highness, the tsar and his regiment have arrived upon the palace grounds. And with them, your uncle, the prisoner. Your mother wishes for you to join her in the throne room."

Alexei froze, taking a moment to consider what this might mean for him, for his charade. Would he be outed as a liar, an imposter? "*Your uncle, the prisoner,*" Petrov had said. Accused of poisoning the tsarevich? Whatever had taken place at the Luzhsky estate had apparently not shaken the tsar's faith in his son's story, then. As Alexei worked all of this out in his mind, he released a sigh of relief and looked to Petrov.

"Then I shall join her in the throne room."

CHAPTER NINETEEN

"Pain and suffering are always inevitable for a large intelligence and a deep heart. The really great men must, I think, have great sadness on earth."

—*Crime and Punishment* by Fyodor Dostoyevsky

SUNBEAMS POURED THROUGH THE thick glass windows of the throne room, illuminating the dust in the air and striking the gemstone around the tsarina's neck just so, speckling the marble floor with red light. The tsarevich stood beside her. *He does look weak,* Mikhail thought, noting the boy's thin face and pallor.

Not that I'm looking my best, either, Mikhail reasoned. The journey from the Luzhsky Uyezd was decidedly less pleasant as a prisoner on horseback than as a Grand Duke on the imperial train. He supposed it was his rather contradictory statuses as prisoner and Grand Duke, along with the enormity of the charges against him, that had merited such an unusual journey.

Mikhail had hardly spoken with his brother since their meeting in the garden. In fact, he hadn't really spoken to anyone. The tsar's men had guarded him as instructed, but had interacted with him awkwardly, as though unsure whether to treat him as a prince or a traitor. *Unconvinced,* Mikhail smiled to himself. The soldiers, the court, the people—they wouldn't believe the tsar's nonsense. Political differences aside, the people knew Mikhail's character. They would never believe he'd poisoned his own nephew. Surely they wouldn't after the trial, anyway, once they heard the tsar's own daughters discredit his story.

The Grand Duchesses' role in this affair was rather regrettable, in Mikhail's mind. For now, they would be secure at Ivan's, safe under Dina's care. But their future was dim—a shame, as his kind and innocent nieces bore no blame for the sins of their father. Even Nicholas wasn't fully culpable, just resistant to inevitable change. The sun had been setting on the age of kings for quite some time, the Russian tsardom already having survived longer than it should have. What was there to do but exile them? Banishment was surely a better option for Nicholas and his family than whatever else the Narodnaya Volya might suggest.

The Narodnaya Volya. Dina placed her faith in them. Urged him to use them as his forces. Would they prove trustworthy? Mikhail hoped so, because he'd done as Dina wished. He'd placed his own faith in the rebel group—in Ivan.

Ever since Nicholas's eradication of magic, the once-fearsome group had dissolved into a scattered disarray of malcontents. There had been no leader, no ranks, just disordered cells united in their hatred of tsarism, their passion for change. What type of change, precisely, had not been agreed upon, nor had the methods to obtain it. Without magic, their resources were limited.

Then Ivan had emerged. Charismatic and clever, the group had rallied around him, believed in him. Ivan's alliance with Mikhail had illuminated a path forward for the Narodnaya Volya that hadn't existed before. Ivan had brought to them a plan that could work, and in Mikhail, a leader who could merge tsarism and representative government.

Mikhail gazed upon the empty throne before him, the tsarina and the lying little tsarevich beside her. He rubbed at the ropes at his wrists and swallowed, his dry throat groaning around the effort, and he became quite aware of the silence of the room. Then the doors swept open, breaking the silence, and the guards stirred to attention as the tsar burst into the throne room.

Nicholas strode in powerfully, the very air seeming to part before him as his boots echoed across the marble floor He reached the dais and pivoted on his heel, surveying the small crowd of the tsar's advisors, nosy courtiers, and palace staff who had gathered for the address. Without so much as glancing at Mikhail, Nicholas then sat upon his throne, his wife and son at his side.

"Before us stands the accused, my brother Mikhail Alexandrovich Romanov, Grand Duke of Russia. He stands accused of attempted murder upon my son, Alexei Nikolaevich Romanov, Tsarevich of Russia, by use of poison. By the mercy of our Lord, my son recovers and stands with me here today. And by that same mercy, I shall allow my brother Mikhail a fair trial, to be held in two days' time. Until that time, he will reside in the palace dungeon, alone."

Nicholas met his brother's eyes then, anger and compassion dueling on his face, and he spoke directly to Mikhail. "For the next two days, your needs will be provided for. For the next two days, you will remain comfortable. And then you will have your trial."

Mikhail nodded. He couldn't resist. "And then?"

Nicholas's eyes darkened, unamused by his brother's lack of humility. He held Mikhail's gaze for a moment longer. Then his eyes flicked away, beyond his brother.

"Guards."

Mikhail was escorted from the throne room.

As THE GUARDS paraded their prisoner through the palace halls en route to the dungeon stairwell, Mikhail took in the activity of the Winter Palace. *Undeterred,* he thought. But wasn't that just like the rulers, to remain largely undisturbed by the activities of the ruled? Nicholas, Alexandra, the girls, the boy, they lived a charmed life in their palace, so removed from the Russian people.

There was a tightness in the air, sure. But there were visitors still, social climbers here to call upon the tsarina. The servants, the maids, and the cooks were all bustling about their daily routines. There were even workmen here, Mikhail noted as he descended the stairwell to the basements. Carpenters were covering an opening in the ceiling back in the guards' chamber at the end of the hall. One of the men turned, meeting Mikhail's eye as he observed, and Mikhail's eyes widened in recognition. Not a workman. Mikhail knew that face.

In his mind, it was a year ago, and Mikhail was in a different basement, beneath the Alexander Palace in Tsarskoye Selo. It had been that first meeting, arranged by his dissident cousin, Sergei, that had set everything in motion. There had been three men present that day, representing the Narodnaya Volya. Sergei, but he was rather unimportant to the cause aside from his funds and the use of his grand home. Ivan, the group's leader, who had taken charge of the meeting. And another fellow, whose role seemed to be more that of a bruiser, who stood behind the other men wordlessly, a silent threat.

The Silent Threat smiled softly as he saw the recognition on Mikhail's face, nodded, and returned to inspecting the wall.

Unease filled Mikhail, and he couldn't pinpoint the cause at first. Over the hours that followed in the dark solitude of the dungeon, he realized that the Narodnaya Volya's presence in the palace, disguised as workmen for whatever objective, highlighted Mikhail's ignorance of their movements, methods, and motives. And that meant that Mikhail didn't control the game after all. *No,* he thought darkly, *I may very well be a pawn myself.*

CHAPTER TWENTY

"Everyone is afraid. But one person falls to pieces from fear, and another person keeps it together. You see: fear remains the same for everyone, but the ability to bear it increases with practice; that is where brave men and heroes come from."

—*The Garnet Bracelet* by Aleksandr Kuprin

THOUGH THE SUN HAD risen hours ago, it was still quite early for the well-to-do residents of Tsarskoye Selo, who as a rule preferred the midnight sun to the first rays of the morning. Still, I'd thought it best to station ourselves off the road, finding a grassy spot between trees, hidden from the street behind a small shop.

For what must have been the hundredth time, I emptied the rifle of its four bullets and reloaded, having become moderately adept at this task with the repetition. The rifle still felt so foreign in my hands, but I had to teach myself the basics. I had to know I could shoot the gun. That I could chamber another bullet and shoot it again. I hoped I didn't have to.

Wiping my sweaty palms on my dirty blue dress, I gazed toward Molniya, who had sprawled himself across a sunny patch of grass in such a way as to absorb maximal sunrays, resting blissfully. I envied him. Exhausted as I was, I couldn't relax, couldn't catch a moment of sleep. As the rescue mission loomed before me, my mind cycled through countless possible outcomes, none of them good. The confidence and excitement I'd felt while following the feather trail had dissipated into dread as the reality of the situation set in. Other than my familiarity with the Alexander Palace, I had no qualifications for this task. I was a seventeen-year-old girl with an old hunting rifle attempting to rescue a prince from a palace full of regicidal terrorists. It would have been enough to deter me, had I anything to lose.

From our vantage point, I saw no signs of activity at the Alexander Palace. The tsarevich (as I'd come to refer to him within my mind, the name "Alexei" being reserved for my actual brother) would be inside, somewhere. I mentally traced every hallway, placing each room, chair, and portrait. It wouldn't be the same—not the décor, nor the purpose given to each room. But I hoped the palace would be the same in the ways that mattered. It certainly appeared identical to the Alexander Palace I knew, commissioned by Catherine the Great over a century ago. I had to believe that in this world, Catherine had been as devious in her designs as she'd been in my own.

The hidden passage had seemed ancient, and I'd always liked to think that it was a secret between old Catherine and me. I had discovered it when I was a little girl, playing hide-and-seek with my sisters. I had been "it," searching for my older sisters.

Tatiana, being the most kind-hearted of my sisters, had been prone to letting me win. She would hide in quite obvious spaces and I would pretend not to notice, not wanting the game to end so easily. Maria had usually been a pretty good hider, though she used her favorite spaces too often. The greatest challenge had been finding Olga. The oldest of my sisters, and most like me in her tendency for mischief, she had been unafraid to hide in forbidden spaces.

It was in my quest for Olga that I had come across the hidden passageway. The entirety of the second floor had been free game, and I had tried to imagine where Olga might have thought I'd be too chicken to look. *The maids' bedrooms*, I'd thought. I'd entered one after another, searching under the beds, inside the closets. I had found some risqué love letters and hidden jewelry, but I hadn't been interested in those. Unable to find Olga, I kept looking.

Rummaging through a maid's closet, I came upon a large iron trunk—*large enough to hide inside*, I'd thought. It had seemed old—older than the typical maids' rooms furnishings—and it was secured with an old rusted lock. On impulse, I grabbed the lock and yanked, and the lock broke right through the crumbling latch, flakes of rust littering the floor. Clearly Olga couldn't be inside—how would she have locked the trunk? But I knew where I would hide in the next game.

Though the lid had been heavy, I'd managed to heave it open. I was delighted to find it empty and had immediately climbed inside, testing my new hideaway. As my shoe pressed against the trunk's bottom, the metal gave way, opening downward. I'd nearly fallen straight down into the vertical tunnel, crying out in surprise as I caught myself with my arms. I'd peered downward, marveling at my discovery. It was dark, but I could see that there were footholds dug into the stone. Meant for climbing down. *To the library*, I'd figured. *The library would be directly below these rooms.* I had completely abandoned the hide-and-seek game. I'd been enthralled. Snatching a candle from the maid's desk, I clambered into the trunk.

Down I climbed, down, down, down . . . too far down. *I should be in the library by now*, I'd thought, *unless . . . was I inside the wall beside it?* My fingers found spider webs in the footholds, but I was too excited to care. When my feet met the floor at last, the light of my candle had revealed a narrow hallway—was I *under* the library? I'd tried to orient myself, unsure which direction I was facing or where I might be going, but unable to resist my curiosity. I'd had to crouch as I stepped into the hallway, my candle burning low.

I'd gone on, ducking through the dark and narrow tunnel until the passageway came to a hard stop. It didn't make sense for it to just stop, though. Surely there was a way out other than the way I came. This passage had to lead somewhere. I'd pressed and pulled on the stones of the wall until one pushed loose. The stone was large and heavy, and it had taken all my strength to push it forward out of the wall. Daylight had flooded into the passage then. I pushed the stone a little farther, far enough that I could crawl outside into a tangle of bushes.

I had been awestruck. I'd found a secret entrance into the palace.

Over the years, I used the passageway many times. As long as the maids weren't in their chambers, I never lost at hide-and-seek. It was my secret. Mine, and Catherine the Great's.

Molniya brayed, bringing me back to the present. We were stationed just a block away from the Alexander Palace, the tsarevich, and the Narodnaya Volya. I knew what I needed to do. I had a plan to get inside and an idea of where to search first. I supposed that was about as far ahead as I could plan—if everything went well, I would find the tsarevich within the servants' quarters and deliver him safely out through the passageway without seeing another soul.

Not for the first time since our separation, I wished Lev was here. He had proven himself to be quite capable—he would at least know how to use the gun. He would probably point out some flaw in my plan I hadn't considered and figure a way around it. I thought of the explosion of bark when the bullet had struck the tree, Lev pinning me to the ground beneath him. Warmth spread to my cheeks as I remembered the heaviness of his body over mine as he'd shielded me. Despite the gunshot, despite the explosion, I'd felt safe. But I was far from safety, now.

I was so hungry, so tired, heartbroken, lost . . . My sense of self-preservation was quite low. Slinging the rifle over my shoulder, I set off for the Alexander Palace. This mad quest was all I had left.

THE STONE SAT heavily in its station. I couldn't even get a solid grip on it to pull, as it was completely implanted in the palace wall. On the bright side, I supposed that meant that the passageway had gone undiscovered all these years. If I just had something to pry it loose . . . I considered my assets. Other than the bedraggled gown I still wore, the horse I'd left cobbled behind, and the tsarevich's hunting rifle, I had nothing. Perhaps if I could wedge the barrel of the gun under the stone . . . could I shoot it loose? It would be loud.

But if it worked, I could get the stone out before anyone came to investigate. I glanced around, confirming that the yard remained empty.

Sharp holly leaves pricked my neck as I lay on my belly, struggling to dig the gun beneath the stone. Several long, frustrating minutes passed as I wrestled the rifle into place. I was quite sure I'd managed to chamber a bullet during my practice earlier. Still, I'd never fired a gun. My finger trembled as I awkwardly gripped the trigger. I counted to three and pulled, and . . . nothing. It was loaded, wasn't it? Then I remembered—the safety. It was on the underside of the rifle, wedged against the ground. Cursing beneath my breath, I buried my face in my hands. I had to start over.

Suffice it to say that by the time I had removed the gun, pulled on the boulder some more, and resigned to turning off the safety and wedging the gun back into place, I was quite irritable, impatient, and certain someone would come along and see me. The sun was rising higher in the sky, people would be stirring, and the Narodnaya Volya would be patrolling their grounds. Aside from a few well-placed bushes, the passage entry was rather exposed.

Again, lying on my belly, my finger still shaking a bit on the trigger, I counted to three and pulled. This time—

BANG.

The sound echoed through my skull, my mind bursting with images of the cellar, the guard, the bullets, the blood. My ears erupted with screaming and gunfire. Sweat slickened my trembling hands. My head swam, my vision blurred, and the images cycled: the guard, the bullets, the blood. It was like a nightmare, only I was awake.

Awake. I opened my eyes, only then realizing they'd been closed. The stone still lay ahead of me, the rifle wedged beneath it, prickly holly leaves scratching my skin. I took a shaky breath. I needed to keep it together. This was not the time for . . . for whatever that was.

I yanked the rifle from the stone—it was easier this time, as the stone had crumbled a bit on the bottom. It was enough for me to get a grip. Wasting no time, I whipped myself around to my back and bent my knees, positioning my feet against the adjacent stones. Using the strength of my legs for leverage, I gripped the stone and pulled with all my might. I sighed in relief as the stone pulled away, revealing a dark hole. My secret entrance.

The gunshot, however, had not gone unnoticed. There were voices, too distant to make out, but alert in their tone—probably guards on the southern entrance. Close. Too close. A bush blocked my view in that direction—and would block their view of me, too, I hoped—but they would follow the sound of the gunshot. What had I been thinking? Shooting the gun was a terrible idea. Still, it worked. I grabbed the rifle and scrambled feet-first into the dark hole.

Feet-first was the right way to go—my boots broke through thick spider webs, and despite my desperate need for a speedy disappearance, I couldn't help but pause when my feet hit the floor, as I imagined spiders crawling up my legs, up my dress. The open hole stared back at me, and I knew I wouldn't be able to get the same leverage as I had to open it, not from down here, but I reached through and pulled it back as best I could. Not quite back into place, but hopefully close enough. It was certainly close enough to minimize the sunlight coming through, blinding me in darkness as I waited for my eyes to adjust.

Would the guards inspect the palace walls? They would be looking for a man with a gun. Perhaps they wouldn't notice the stone askew along the wall. It made me uneasy though. To be followed, or to be intercepted on my way out with the tsarevich would be catastrophic. So I waited, the rifle pointed at the entry. At times I heard activity in the yard, undecipherable voices, movement, though nothing around the stone. I found myself once again quite grateful for that holly bush, and wondered if Catherine the Great herself had planted it there.

It felt like an eternity, waiting there. It could have been fifteen minutes or an hour. When I at last felt as satisfied as I could that I wouldn't be followed, I lowered the rifle, turning toward the path before me. Dark and dirty, yet regal somehow in its emptiness—I supposed I was the first explorer to enter the space in a century. My eyes adjusted to the darkness slightly, but the passageway became darker and darker as I moved farther from the entry. I proceeded slowly, hunching low yet still occasionally bumping my head on the cobwebbed ceiling. I placed one foot cautiously in front of the other, finding the path to be just as I remembered until my foot landed on something hard. It was rounded under my boot, like a strong branch or the barrel of a rifle.

I knelt even lower to investigate, running my fingers along the cold smoothness of the unknown object. It wasn't wood, or metal . . . I reached beyond it, finding that it continued, just as my eyes made out the shape—human. A human skeleton, slumped against the wall. Swallowing a scream, I jumped back, horror-stricken, my face moving through another spider web as I scrambled away from the bones. My heart racing, I ran blindly and awkwardly through the passageway until I tripped on a ridge in the floor and smacked right into the stone wall that ended the path.

As I felt around for footholds, rather immune now to the unknown filth and evidence of arachnids my fingers moved through, I wondered—who? A prisoner? An explorer like me? Could it have been some dissident who displeased my great-great-great-great-grandmother? These thoughts occupied my mind as my fingers and feet found the familiar notches. I climbed upward. Did the poor pile of bones not try to move the stones? I began to feel uneasy. Perhaps it was just the thought of being trapped in the passageway. But I felt that it was something more.

My arms were tired from the climb, from the difficulty of the last few days, from the deconditioning of the last year and a half. I sighed in relief as I reached the top, pulling the trap door downward as I climbed up into the trunk and pressed the top of my head to the metal lid as I'd done so many times before.

It didn't budge.

Of course it was locked. I had discovered the passage from the other end, back in my own world. Here, the trunk remained unopened, undiscovered. Locked. I couldn't help but let out a frustrated groan, slamming the palm of my hand into the unyielding lid. The *bang* reverberated, as though the old stone walls, accustomed to silence, didn't know how to absorb the sound.

Then there was another sound. Footsteps. Above me. Not directly above, but getting closer. Approaching the trunk. Someone was in the room, and they'd heard me. Would they open the trunk?

"What the hell?" a muffled voice inquired from the other side of the lid. And then, the rattling of a pick in a lock. The rattling grew louder, faster, as perhaps the would-be lockpick became frustrated. Good. Time. In my haste, I slammed the trapdoor upward, but it didn't catch, falling open again as I scrambled back down the wall. I swore, too loudly. There was no time to climb back up to latch the door—I just had to get out of sight. I jumped the last few feet, and as my feet hit the stone floor, I heard it. The *yank*, the crumble, the lock falling away from the latch. And then light flooded the passage as the lid lifted away. I squinted, covering my affronted eyes, as I threw myself down the tunnel in a squatting sprint. But my foot caught on the same accursed ridge as before, and I splattered face up on the ground quite gracelessly as another face peered down from the room above.

"Anastasia?"

I blinked, feeling partially blinded by the light shining down on me. Could it be the tsarevich? Could I be so lucky? Who else would know my name?

I blinked again. But that voice wasn't the tsarevich.

"Anastasia, is that you? What the hell are you doing here?"

The face above me came into focus, my eyes beginning to accept the light of the sun once more. It was a handsome face, round with a strong jaw. Dark hair. Green eyes.

"Lev?"

CHAPTER TWENTY-ONE

"Let us not forget that the reasons for human actions are usually incalculably more complex and diverse than we tend to explain them later, and are seldom clearly manifest."

— *The Idiot* by Fyodor Dostoyevsky

THE TSARINA WOULD REMOVE the necklace in the evening hours, surely, Alexei thought. She would be relaxing in the game room, or some parlor, somewhere other than her dressing room, certainly. All day, his mind had remained quite singularly focused on reclaiming the gemstone, despite the chilling confrontation between brothers he'd witnessed that morning. In fact, the nearness of the trial and the increased scrutiny that would be placed on him and his lie only intensified his need to recover the necklace. If everything went wrong, if his lies were exposed, if he could not emerge from this tangled web as tsarevich—the garnet was his ticket onward.

Alexei moved stealthily, counting doors and ducking between the shadows as he moved through the winding hallway toward the tsarina's dressing chamber. The only guards he'd encountered had been whispering among themselves, unaware of his presence. *Some guards,* he'd thought dubiously. Alexei found it exhilarating, sneaking about unseen, unwatched. Moments such as these had been rare for a tsarevich of fragile health, and he found that perhaps what he enjoyed most in this new world was the lack of supervision. No one seemed all that concerned as to how he spent his time. In fact, other than his backgammon game with his mother and his door-watching with Petrov, Alexei had spent most of his time at the Winter Palace completely alone.

The twelfth door stood closed. It was the twelfth, was it not? Alexei considered redoubling his steps and recounting before entering what he hoped was the tsarina's empty dressing chamber. He pressed his ear to the door. Voices within. He pulled away—surely it was the wrong door—then he changed his mind, giving in to his curiosity.

"A ransom note?" The tsarina's voice, appalled. "Any amount, we shall pay, shan't we? Oh, but Nicky. I just couldn't . . . I just couldn't lose another."

Silence followed, filled only by a soft footstep. Perhaps the tsar, moving to comfort the tsarina. *Lose another?*

"Alexandra," the tsar's voice spoke quietly, soothingly. "That . . . that was quite different from this. It was God's will. If we hadn't lost the baby, we might never have had Alexei. It wasn't meant to be, my love. You mustn't compare the two."

Alexei fidgeted anxiously behind the door. Under different circumstances, he'd have been intrigued by their conversation, but as it was, he just wanted them to leave. He had to find the garnet.

The tsarina was crying, her voice shaking between sobs. "But how can I not? There is nothing, *nothing,* more devastating than losing a child. No ransom I would not pay." Her sobs became louder, her voice rather hysterical. "How could you let this happen? How could you trust Dina with our girls, when Mikhail stands trial for poisoning our son!"

Despite his focus on his mission, Alexei raised his brows, his interest piqued.

"I don't trust her, Alexandra. I pray that indeed our daughters are safe and shall appear as witnesses for this trial. My men have not found them, not in their searches of Luga, St. Petersburg, nor the forests between. What else can we do but search and hope?"

The tsarina was crying now, her voice shaking. "We pay the ransom, Nicky."

Silence. Then the tsar's voice again, unwavering. "For several reasons, we cannot."

"But our girls—"

"The note does not mention the girls." Alexei pictured his father, standing on the other side of the door, hands clasped behind him, his back to his sobbing wife, his gaze fixed on the wall.

"Out with it then. What?" Exasperation in her voice.

"The hostage. Not our daughters, but our son. It is nonsensical." The tsar's deep voice covered the sound of Alexei's sharp gasp on the other side of the door.

A short laugh from the tsarina, her tone shifting. "By our Father in Heaven, Nicky, why have you distressed me so, over nothing? Garbage, that letter. What foolishness. Alexei is here with us and nowhere else."

Another silence. "It is certainly strange."

"There's something else, isn't there? Who is the note from? How much do they demand?"

A heavy sigh. "The Narodnaya Volya. And they demand everything. Abdication. Exile."

"Oh, Nicky, don't stress so! Their demands are meaningless. They don't have our son!"

"Meaningless, perhaps. Still, this note unsettles me greatly, and my instinct is to not disregard it." A rattling of the doorknob. *Pizdets.* Alexei pressed himself against the wall just in time as the door swung open, concealing him from view, as the tsar stepped into the hallway. "I must think."

The tsarina trailed behind him, attempting in vain to reassure the tsar, who marched swiftly down the hall. As the two disappeared down the winding corridor, Alexei slipped from behind the door and entered the now-empty room. He brought his head to his hands as a storm of thoughts blew through his mind. *I'll be found out, I'll lose my chance—my double, he's . . . where?* But there was no time for this now.

The garnet, first. Then Alexei could sort out his jumbled thoughts.

The chamber was nearly dark, illuminated only by a single candle left burning on the vanity. As good a place as any to begin the search. Alexei glanced between the jars of creams and lotions that lined the countertop, before landing his eyes on the great mirror above it. His own eyes stared back at him, hollow, tired. As had often occurred when Alexei studied his reflection, he felt startled by his own youth. Surely he had endured more than a man twice his age. The pain of his illness, his family's imprisonment, the shock of their brutal execution. The loss of his destiny. His inevitable betrayal of his sister to salvage it. She would never forgive him—had it been for naught? He clung to his place in this world by a thin thread.

With the trial looming, Alexei had known that his deception might soon be revealed. And the tsar was suspicious of him now, was he not? "*This unsettles me greatly,*" he'd said as he'd marched from the room. Alexei wanted so desperately for this world to work. Everything he needed was here. Didn't the universe owe him this chance? After all he'd endured . . .

Perhaps it was the universe responding to his silent plea. Or perhaps it was simply that Alexei had chosen the right place to search. But as he lifted the half-burnt candle from the vanity, the light caught a gleam of red—the garnet, the thin golden chain hanging over an ornate hook on the opposite wall. Back to movement, back to stealth, Alexei seized the necklace and hurried from the room, leaving behind the mirror and his bleak thoughts.

CHAPTER TWENTY-TWO

"But the line dividing good and evil cuts through the heart of every human being. And who is willing to destroy a piece of his own heart?"

—*The Gulag Archipelago* by Aleksandr Solzhenitsyn

I N THE TIME IT took me to roll over and push myself up to sit, Lev had shimmied down the wall, his boots landing soundlessly beside me. Kneeling, he extended his hand and pulled me to my feet. For a moment, neither of us let go, only staring at each other. Then he brought his hand to my cheek, his calloused fingers brushing gently across my face. My skin tingled, a shiver traveling up my spine as I held his gaze. "Spider." The corner of his mouth lifted in a half-grin as he flicked the wretched creature into the air, dropping his hand to his side.

Shaking my head in disbelief, I still stared at him, unfazed. "You're here."

He nodded. "Well, I was taken prisoner in the woods at Luzhsky—Mikhail's prisoner, and now a prisoner of the Narodnaya Volya it would seem. I would recommend the latter over the former—it's been rather luxurious, if boring, thus far." He smirked, but his eyes searched my face for some clue.

I was quite pleased that for once, I didn't have to hide the truth. "I'm here for the tsarevich. We were ambushed in St. Petersburg. We had just left from . . ." Well, some truths would remain hidden. "We were almost to the Winter Palace when they got him. The Narodnaya Volya. And I'm quite sure they brought him here." I glanced at the opening above. "Recommendation aside and luxury notwithstanding, I'd rather not be taken prisoner myself. If someone comes to fetch you . . ."

He followed my gaze to the open trapdoor, then met my eye. "You're right. Come on."

Lev scaled the wall effortlessly, and I followed, equally adept for once, the familiarity of the task trumping my exhaustion. He climbed out of the trunk ahead of me and turned, offering his hand. I didn't need it, but I took it anyway, and as our hands touched, my tense shoulders released. Perhaps it was simply relief that I was no longer acting alone, that I had someone on my side, that it was Lev.

The rifle bounced at my side as my feet hit the floor. There I was, in this alternate version of my childhood home, standing in the old maid's closet once again. Lev stood before me, watching me as I glanced around in wonderment that surpassed the magnificence of the room. His mouth formed a half smile, his eyes warm. Cocking his head to the side, Lev raised a dark brow as I hopped from the trunk. "You've a habit of sneaking in and out of this place, then?"

Then he dropped the smile, his jaw tensing as though he'd just remembered something unsettling, something that darkened his mood. His grip tightened on my hand, and I flinched. When I opened my mouth to answer, he cut me off.

"No, wait. If you're in the mood to answer questions, that one is actually quite low on my list." He released my hand and turned, pacing to the other end of the room. "I don't even know who you are."

I raised my eyebrows, placing my hands on my hips indignantly. "I'm Anastasia."

Lev turned, his green eyes searching mine. Piercing, as though his eyes might see deeply enough into mine to truly see me, to learn me, to know me. "And who is Anastasia?"

For once, I was speechless. How could I answer? I was not Grand Duchess Anastasia, not the daughter of Nicholas and Alexandra, not the youngest sister of OTMA. Nothing I'd done had ever happened. This world contained no series of events that had transpired just so, to result in my existence. And everything seemed to be just fine—better, even—without me.

"She's . . . no one." I dropped his gaze, turning my eyes to the floor.

Lev's face flashed frustration, exasperation, disappointment, and then that moment of one person seeking sincerity in another had passed, and the corner of Lev's mouth lifted in a smirk as he lounged onto his cot, stretching his arms overhead. "Well, No One, let's get to business then. You're here to rescue the tsarevich. What's your plan?"

I stood, still staring at the floor. What was my plan? To find the tsarevich and get the hell out of here, back through the passage. To return him to the palace. To sneak him in, and force my *zasranets* brother to give it up, to leave the palace. *And after that?* A mocking voice in the back of my mind nagged me. *And what then? When your quest is over, when you stop moving, what then? What does No One do, then?*

"I used to be someone." I hadn't consciously formed the thought before the words were out of my mouth, and I found myself walking toward the cot until I stood just an arm's reach from Lev. My eyes found his. "In another world, I was someone. I had a family and a purpose. The execution—" My voice broke, and I paused, considering for a moment stopping, but I was so tired of lying and hiding and being alone. What did I have to lose? "—I told you about the execution. That I escaped. Well, I escaped to an alternate universe. Or from one, I suppose, depending on your perspective." I half-smiled at my own dedication to semantics. "Another world, anyway. Another and another and another, until my brother and I arrived here. In your cabin, to be precise. I don't know how . . . but it was the garnet. I think maybe it was seeking yours."

As I spoke, the look on Lev's face moved through a series of emotions, from empathy to incredulousness to realization. I saw his logical mind taking this bizarre explanation and applying it to his many questions, piecing the story together.

"But here . . . Here I am no one. I'm just a girl trying to fix what she's broken, to return the tsarevich to his home." I steeled myself and smiled then. "And to find her brother and kick his ass for trying to steal the throne in an alternate reality."

It was Lev who sat speechless now, still weighing the insanity of my revelation against the otherwise inexplicable events of the last few days. Just as he opened his mouth to speak, a key rattled in the doorknob. His eyes widened, and he sprung from the cot, pulling back the blanket and motioning me to climb in, quickly. I sprawled as flatly as I could on the cot as Lev pulled the blanket over me, hiding the world from view. Then his weight sank into me as he returned to his casual lounge on the cot, or rather, on *me*. He was careful not to squash me as his body pressed against mine through the thin blanket.

The door swung open. Heavy footsteps grew louder as at least two pairs of boots entered the room. Boots containing the feet of the Narodnaya Volya.

"It's time for your interrogation; don't jump up from your comfort on our account," the speaker's voice dripped with amusement and sarcasm.

"Ah, wasn't planning on it, sir." Lev managed to keep his voice calm, nonchalantly cheeky.

"No need to be a wiseass." A second voice, less amused. "This can be painless, or . . . not."

"An excellent reminder, Dmitri," the first voice chirped. He addressed Lev with equal joviality. "Now first, your name."

"Lev Lukavich," Lev answered without hesitation.

"And Mr. Lukavich, why were you in the woods on the grounds of Mikhail Romanov's estate on the night of July eighteenth?"

"My companion received word that the tsarevich had been kidnapped. We went to find him, and we did." Again, without hesitation. He'd thought about these questions, clearly.

"Were you sent by the tsar?"

"No."

A sigh. "Then who sent you?"

"As I said. The tsarevich wrote to my companion, requesting help."

"And who," the first voice drawled, "was your companion?"

Lev shifted in such a way that his hand landed over my mine, warm through the blanket. "No One," he answered.

A footstep, and then *SLAP*. I felt Lev tighten in response to the smack, his hand leaving mine, perhaps to touch his own face. "Try again," growled the second voice. Dmitri.

"My companion," Lev spoke slowly, "was simply my employer. He told me what I told you, but I suspect he was a ransomer. At any rate, I was hired to assist."

Though Lev was a good liar, the man behind the first voice was not convinced.

"Paid handsomely and in advance, I must imagine, to sacrifice yourself for your employer's escape with the hostage."

"Indeed," Lev answered, his voice tight.

A laugh from the first interrogator. "The things we do for money. We work, we fight, we kill. But we do not sacrifice ourselves, not for money. For honor, perhaps. For loyalty. For love. Oh, I hope it wasn't for love. It would be sadder then, when he breaks, wouldn't it Dmitri? Ah, I see you're ready."

Lev's body stiffened and he shifted, sprawling himself in such a way that squashed me quite thoroughly. I bit my tongue as what must have been his elbow dug into my belly. And then, a gunshot.

In that instant, the darkness under the blanket became the darkness of that cellar. There was my father, dropping to the floor as bullets filled his chest. My sisters, screaming. The barrel of the gun, pointing at my chest. I dove to the floor, shoving . . . shoving someone off me, and there was the sound of a man, howling in pain . . . Where was I?

Not the cellar. No, the bedroom. Lev's room, where he was a prisoner of the Narodnaya Volya. Lev, howling in pain on the floor.

Scrambling to my feet, I pulled the rifle from my side. I didn't have time to think, only to react. As I fumbled for the safety, Dmitri pointed his gun at me, and I was breathing too fast. In and out and in, and the room was a haze—a crowded bedroom, a dark cellar, bedroom, cellar, bedroom, cellar, and bullets, bullets, bullets . . . I staggered back, my knees weak.

From the floor, Lev grabbed for Dmitri's foot, pulling it out from under him just as the brute pulled the trigger, the bullet straying wildly. "Anastasia—" Lev's voice strained as he wrestled for Dmitri's gun—"shoot!" I followed his eyes to the other man—the interrogator—who raised his own handgun as he stepped toward Lev.

"*You are to be executed.*" The guard's voice filled my mind, and I whirled to face him, stunned. The *yobanyy* safety be damned. I raised the rifle, smashing it over the back of his head, dropping him to his knees. He bellowed in pain, but I didn't stop. I raised the rifle again, slamming it down, again and again. The cellar. The bedroom. This world. My own. The scene shuffled before my eyes like a blood splattered kaleidoscope, and I raised the rifle, bringing it down on the Narodnaya Volya, the Bolsheviks, the interrogator, the guard. Again. He stopped moving, but I kept going. Raising the rifle, slamming it down. For my sisters. For my parents. For Alexei. For myself. Again and again and again.

He became silent. The room, silent.

And I stopped. Blinked. The rifle dropped from my shaking hands, thudding to the floor.

I stared numbly at the bloodied mess of a man, lifeless on the floor. The interrogator, not the guard. We were in the bedroom, not the cellar. I took a breath. Lev and Dmitri were still interlocked on the floor behind him. Both men had a hand on the gun, Dmitri rather weakly. I saw then that Lev's elbow was digging into the man's thick neck. Dmitri's eyes were bulging, his face bloodred, and then he went limp.

Lev removed his elbow from the dead man's strangled throat, grunting in exhaustion.

I took in the scene before me, as though seeing it for the first time.

"What . . . what have I done?"

Lev glanced up at me, an odd look on his face. "You saved my life, for one. Rather messily, but I'm in no position to complain." Despite the levity of his words, his tone was gruff, straining as he pulled himself to a seat.

"So I . . . I killed him . . ." my voice broke, barely audible ". . . to save you?" Had I? I pressed my lips together tightly, shaking my head. No. It hadn't felt like heroism. I'd felt only anger. Hatred for another man in another world.

Wild, uncontrollable rage that I'd brought down upon my victim mercilessly. My whole body began to shake, and I sank to my knees.

Lev brought his fingers to my chin, tilting my face to his and locking his eyes on my own. "You killed him to save me." He nodded slowly, and I did, too. I needed the words to be true. I needed to know I was not a monster.

"I killed him to save you," I repeated, holding Lev's gaze.

A moment passed in silence, and I studied the green irises of Lev's eyes, so sure, so certain. He lifted the corner of his mouth in a grim half-smile. "Thank you, by the way." Then he released my chin, bringing his hands to his lower leg. Applying pressure to a wound through his blood-soaked pant leg.

"Lev, you were shot!"

"I'm aware. You need to get out of here, quickly."

"I—I can't . . ." I looked once more to the dead men on the floor, swallowing my nausea. "*We* need to get out of here. Quickly . . ." I glanced toward the door. How long before more men of the Narodnaya Volya would come bursting into the room? My heart raced, adrenaline overtaking my shock. We had to get out. And we couldn't be followed.

"Lev, I need your boot."

He winced, still applying pressure to the wound. "You'll need to get it yourself."

And so I removed the left boot as delicately as I could in my haste, as Lev tried to stop the bleeding. I wrung the blood from his pant leg onto the sole of the boot, and then pressed it to the floor, creating a trail of bloody footprints to the door. I didn't dare open the door. Hopefully, the ruse would be enough to inhibit any investigation into other means of escape from the room.

Satisfied enough, I then turned back to Lev, kneeling beside him.

"Anastasia—"

"I know we need to wrap it, but if we can just tuck your pants leg into your stocking for now so it doesn't drip blood everywhere—"

"Anastasia—"

"Come on, grip my shoulder, stand up on your good leg. Come on."

"Anastasia—"

"Hurry up, Lev, come on!"

"Anastasia."

My eyes met his, and I saw his meaning before he could speak it.

"No way am I leaving you here, Lev Lukavich. For Christ's sake, I *killed* someone to save you . . ." I made myself believe it. "I'll drag you to that chest, if I have to. But it'll be a hell of a lot faster if you get up!"

Perhaps Lev could see that I was barely holding it together. Or perhaps he could see that I would indeed try to drag him—ultimately wasting a lot of time and getting myself caught—if he did not comply. Lev heaved himself to his feet, or rather, to his foot. "Go on then, I'm coming. Get the guns."

I silently peeled Dmitri's gun from his stiffening fingers and slung my own rifle over my shoulder. The interrogator's body lay crumpled in a slowly spreading pool of blood, his gun hidden beneath his corpse. I shuddered. That was certainly where it would stay.

"The climb—" I started, lifting the lid of the trunk, refashioning the busted lock on the latch.

"I can do it." Lev spoke impatiently, motioning me along as he hobbled toward the chest. "But you're going first."

I didn't argue, scrambling through the trapdoor and down the wall. I waited as Lev hauled himself into the trunk, pretended I didn't hear him cursing under his breath with every movement. Then we were both blinded by darkness as he pulled the lid closed behind him. I let out a breath I hadn't realized I was holding. He was in. His boot scraped the stone wall, searching for each foot hold as he made the slow, one-legged descent.

"Where does this lead?" Lev landed beside me in the darkness.

"Are you familiar with the Alexander Palace? We're under the small library now, heading for the southern courtyard."

"That's where we are? Fancy." He spoke between raspy breaths. It was too much exertion—the fight, the climb, all while in immense pain, all while losing blood. "The southern courtyard, you said. We'll be exposed?" I heard the sound of his back sliding against stone as he maneuvered to sit on the hard floor.

Ah. Yes. Alarms would be raised. The Narodnaya Volya would be looking for us—or at least, looking for Lev. The well-placed bush in the courtyard would not be enough. How could we get away from the palace wall without being spotted?

"We may have to wait here. In the passageway. Until dark." I shivered. Dark was a long time away. What if Lev lost too much blood? "I'll wrap your leg." I began to tear at the bottom of my filthy dress, ripping the dirt-caked fabric into strips as I knelt beside Lev.

"Oh, I'll be all right." Despite his nonchalance, Lev took my hands, guiding them toward the wound in the darkness. "I've always healed quickly." He flinched slightly as I rolled up his pants leg, finding the wound. From what I could feel, it seemed that the bullet had struck through his calf muscle. I supposed that was a good thing—he hadn't shattered the bone. As I worked, I found myself thinking about blood, grateful that Lev's was clotting as it ought to. I thought of my brother, his life dictated by his blood in so many ways. And I imagined the pool of blood above us. I imagined it soaking into the floor, dripping into the passage below.

The wrap was dirty but efficient enough. I wiped my hands on my ruined dress and sat back against the wall, sighing involuntarily.

"What are you thinking about, Anastasia?"

Blood, family, alternate universes, failed rescues. Brutal murder in front of my eyes, brutal murder by my own hands. Beds. Food.

"Food, mostly."

"Ah." A brief moment passed, and then Lev produced something from his pocket, handing it to me.

A beat up and mostly squashed half-eaten roll of bread.

I took it and settled into my seat amongst the spider webs, hoping we'd make it until dark, trying not to think about the third body resting in this passage, and praying for a better fate for us all.

CHAPTER TWENTY-THREE

"Power is given only to those who dare to lower themselves and pick it up. Only one thing matters, one thing; to be able to dare!"

—Fyodor Dostoyevsky

O BSERVING FROM THE DARKNESS of the imperial opera box, Alexei could view the stage perfectly as the scene progressed, the man in black pacing the front edge of the stage, the actor portraying the tsar standing solemnly, his back to the audience, his voice carrying effortlessly across the theatre as he spoke.

"The hostage. My son. The tsarevich. You will return him to me."

The man in black spoke softly, but harshly. "Do you forfeit your reign, your throne, your country, your home?"

"I do, for the life of my son, my heir, who will rule in my stead."

"Then have him." And the man in black disappeared, replaced with the image of Alexei, almost, if he were a bit bigger, stronger, more carefree. The Other Alexei clapped the tsar on the back, and the tsar spun, and it wasn't an actor or even the tsar but Alexei himself—how had he gotten on stage? He pulled the garnet from his pocket, looping the golden chain around the other boy's neck, and then he was holding a gun, pointing it at the gemstone—

Alexei awoke in a sweat, his blankets rumpled around him. Thrust back into reality, into the darkness of his bedchamber, it took a moment for him to remember where he was, what had happened. It came back in waves. The execution, the garnet, the worlds, the lies, the ransom note. The last sands of the hourglass trickling downward as his façade neared its end, the inevitable revelation of his fraud.

Unless . . .

The dream was already starting to fade from his waking mind. Could there be a way? Could he use the ransomers to lead him to his double? Could he find the Other Alexei and remove him from this world? He sat up to the edge of the bed, drawing the blanket around his shoulders. He didn't have much of a plan to go on, but there was a glimmer of light now where before he'd seen only darkness. He had the garnet. Now he just needed his doppelgänger, and a gun. First, though, he needed the ransom note. *No time to waste*, Alexei told himself, shrugging the blanket off his narrow shoulders and slipping from the room.

The palace was quite a different place in the darkness of night, the unfamiliar hallways shrouded in shadow . . . it was eerie. Alexei shuddered, wrapping himself in his arms, suddenly chilled. *A ghost walked through you*, Olga would tease. Maria would roll her eyes, assuring her little brother that ghosts did not exist. Alexei tried to remember if this interaction had ever occurred, or if it was the ghosts of his sisters that lived on in his mind. He hoped his memory of his sisters still reflected quite truthfully who they were. But he suspected that death would morph those memories, creating caricatures, amplifying some single piece of a person to become the whole.

He thought of these things often as he considered his own death, having been on the brink of it more than once. As a future tsar, he pondered the legacy he would leave behind. Would it be greatness, like Peter before him? Or gentleness, like his namesake? What single act would history remember him for? Or would it be nothingness, a tsarevich who simply faded away?

No. He refused to be nothing. He would matter. He would be tsar. Uncrossing his arms, Alexei rolled his shoulders back, adopting an air more confident than he truly felt. He had found the garnet. The universe was on his side. He would find the note. It came to him, then, where the tsar would hide a troublesome letter. *The Box*. Alexei's father had been a man for nostalgia. He'd kept all sorts of snippets from his childhood—notes from his mother, praise from his educators, jokes from his brother. From a young age, he'd cherished these bits of his past, these memories of a simpler time, and he'd stored them in The Box. That had been the start of it. But over the years, The Box had become home to all sorts of special scraps: newspaper clippings, photos, documents that Nicholas valued. And, Alexei had discovered in his forbidden rummaging, letters his father had wanted no one to see: letters from his cousin Kaiser Wilhelm in Germany, letters from his former lover, a heartbroken ballerina. The Box would be in the tsar's study, Alexei thought, quickening his pace, counting doors as he arrived in the corridor.

The tsar's study was not exactly as it had been at the Alexander Palace, a world away. Still, the man's tastes and tendencies remained the same. The desk was tidy, the bookshelves neat and organized. Any hiding place would be deliberate and efficiently accessible, if not the most creative. Alexei approached the bookshelf, wasting no time. When Alexei had first discovered The Box, he'd been a child of only eight or nine. He couldn't remember now exactly his purpose in intruding the off-limits room—perhaps for the sake of rebellion itself—but he'd found himself standing before his father's personal bookshelves, the works alphabetized by author from floor to ceiling. Alexei had been most interested in the book covers and any illustration he might find within, and had pulled book after book from the shelf, sometimes stopping to admire a particularly beautiful cover, sometimes flipping through the pages. He had stopped when he had gotten as far as the Ds—it had been the works of Dostoyevsky that had hidden The Box.

The bookshelf in this office, in this Winter Palace, in this world, was taller and wider than the other. Yet the books were organized in the same way, A to Z, floor to ceiling. Alexei traced his finger along the dusty spines until arriving at *The Brothers Karamazov*, the first Dostoyevsky in line. Holding his breath, Alexei pressed his finger to the spine of the book, exhaling disappointedly as the book slid easily to the back of the bookshelf. *Is it ridiculous to imagine that there even is a Box here?* Alexei closed his eyes. *Is this whole plan mad?*

It's the only chance you have, an answering voice within his mind snarled.

Or I could give up. Quietly, from a smaller, calmer place in Alexei's brain. *I could accept that I won't be tsar. Escape before I'm found out. Find my sister.*

And what then? the stronger, louder voice shrieked. *You would be no one, nothing. Weak, doomed to die unremembered, unremarkable.*

As Alexei fought the battle within his mind, his head beginning to ache, his finger moved absently to the spine of the next book, tracing the lettering along *Crime and Punishment* before pressing gently. It did not move. Snapping back to the task at hand, Alexei pressed more firmly; the book did not budge. It was pressing against something behind it. The Box.

Dumping the next few books from the shelf, Alexei pulled the simple wooden box into his lap, gingerly flipping back the top to reveal its contents. A line of photos sat atop the pile of papers within, as though lain carefully to hide the documents beneath. Taking care to remember the placement of each, Alexei scooped the photos—a bride and groom, a mother and daughter, a father and son—and set them aside. And there it was.

To Nicholas and Alexandra—Simply said, we have your son Alexei. We wish him no harm and rather greatly wish to return him to you, but find ourselves loath to do so whilst you remain Tsar and Tsarina of our great country. We thus propose a trade, the boy for the man, the Tsarevich for the Tsar. Unless the need for violence should arise, we ask only for your abdication, followed only reasonably by your exit from this country, which we shall accommodate most proficiently. The trade shall take place an hour after the sun sets, the 21st night of July, upon the steps of the Church of the Savior on Spilled Blood. We ask that you do not attempt any foolishness, as we are quite prepared to resort to violence beyond your imagination.
Sincerely, NV

Alexei read the note again and again, until he could see the tidily scrawled words in his mind, committed to memory. He replayed each line in his mind as he navigated the dark hallways back to his bedchamber. The 21st night of July. He paused for a moment, counting—it had been four days in this world. Only four days . . . meaning that the next night, an hour after sunset, he would have his chance. His opportunity to remove his double from this world, to secure his role as tsarevich.

And less than twenty-four hours to concoct a plan to do so without getting killed.

CHAPTER TWENTY-FOUR

"I can see the sun, but even if I cannot see the sun, I know that it exists. And to know that the sun is there—that is living."

—*The Brothers Karamazov* by Fyodor Dostoyevsky

COLD METAL PRESSED INTO my cheek as I shifted in my sleep, the sensation awakening me abruptly. My eyes flashed open to find myself in the dark dampness of an ancient hidden passage, propped against Lev's chest, awakened by the silver button of his military coat.

"You must have been more exhausted than hungry, Anastasia." He spoke in a whisper and placed something soggy into my hand as I rose to sit. "You were mid-chomp when this fell from your mouth."

I lifted the soggy something to my nose. Ah. "Poor bread roll. It's been through so much, wouldn't you say? I'd better eat it now, put it out of its misery."

"Most compassionate. But then I'd like to hear more about your . . . travels."

I finished the bread roll in two bites, my mouth occupied by chewing long enough to think about my response. My travels. In my mind, I went back over what I'd told him in the maid's room above. "You think I'm insane, don't you?"

A moment passed in silence, as perhaps Lev considered whether or not he thought me insane, and if so, how he might phrase it delicately.

Then, "No. And maybe I'm insane not to. But I felt that . . . you were telling the truth. Finally."

My shoulders relaxed a little, where I hadn't realized I was holding them tight. "Well certainly you understand why I didn't lead with that when I met you. 'Oh hello, I'm Anastasia, your princess of another realm.'" Then, another thought struck me. "Lev, how is your leg? Is it bleeding still?"

He laughed quietly, and I pictured the smile on his face, hidden by the darkness. "Oh, it'll be fine. Probably needs some movement." He shifted, moving his leg about from his seat beside me on the stone floor. "My princess, you say. I'd come to that conclusion—the only explanation for your brother, Alexei. But Alexei already existed in this world, too. Now there are two." He thought for a moment, piecing it all together. "No memory-wiping magician. Two different boys. One at the palace, your brother. And one here, the tsarevich, held hostage." Another moment of silence, and then, "I'm afraid there is only one of you, Anastasia Romanov."

I snorted. "A blessing, surely."

"You mentioned the garnet. Your garnet." He paused, acknowledging that I had a gemstone of my own. That I had not stolen his after all. "You said your garnet . . ." He paused again, shaking his head in incredulous acceptance. "Your garnet was how you traveled, from one world to the next. You said that you thought perhaps it was seeking my own."

The theory had been forming in the back of my mind, not quite translated from thought to words. Where to start? I supposed that to explain my theory, I would need to tell him about my detour with the tsarevich.

"Ah Lev, I'm sorry. But the note—you see, I thought my brother knew something I didn't. And he wrote that I would need to use the garnet, but I didn't have it anymore. From your accusations, I had gathered that you had one too, and I . . . I'm sorry. The tsarevich and I went to your cabin and I looked for it. I think I found it. In an iron box, beneath the floor. I didn't take it, I didn't even open the box, but I was going to, if I hadn't realized

just then that the tsarevich was not my brother. I was going to take it—
Lev, I'm sorry."

Another moment of silence passed. Then, "I suppose thievery was not
your greatest concern in the moment. Forgiven."

I sighed in relief, feeling just an ounce lighter as one of the many weights
on my shoulders lifted. "You see, your garnet, it was beneath the floor. My
brother and I used our garnet many times to travel, over and over, landing in
the most bizarre versions of our world, but each time we landed just there.
On the floor of your cabin, just above the iron box, the other garnet. So I
think that mine was somehow drawn to yours."

"Uh-huh."

"Uh-huh?" Surely he had something more to say, given the magnitude
of my revelations. "That's it?"

"Let me think a moment, won't you?"

We sat silently, my eyes having adjusted to the darkness well enough to
make out the shape of him. He sat with his left leg extended, rocking his an-
kle back and forth. His hands were raised, rubbing his temples. I supposed
it was a lot to take in.

"Somehow the answers to my questions have only led to more questions. If you had opened the box, if you had taken it, you would have used it,
you and the tsarevich, and traveled on to another world?"

"Assuming yours works as mine does, yes."

"And how do you use it?"

"You shoot it."

I expected some level of disbelief at this admission. I, for one, found
shooting a gemstone to be quite a strange method of trans-universal travel.
But Lev let out a low whistle. "You realize you just answered a question
people have marveled over for years. Not only have you possessed an actual
kolodets, but you've discovered how to use them."

That word again. "And what exactly is a *kolodets*?"

Lev paused for a moment, as though reluctant to answer my question.
Then he sighed, speaking slowly. "According to the lore, a *kolodets* is a sort

of storage vessel. Like a well, but holding magic. And until now, I would have laughed at anyone who claimed they exist."

I waited for him to continue.

"Magic used to just hang in the air." He paused again, as though trying to find the words to explain. "Like heat or cold, it just . . . existed. And sometimes it acted of its own accord, like how the wind blows. But there were people, magic-wielders, who could control it. They could take it and mold it, shape it to perform certain tasks. And again, according to the lore, some wielders could infuse that magic into gemstones, creating a *kolodets*. Or many *kolodtsy*, I suppose. And for people who couldn't control magic, this idea of magic-infused gemstones that anyone could use was really enticing."

I followed, sort of. People wanted to believe in *kolodtsy*. And *kolodtsy* clearly did exist. "So why all the skepticism?"

Lev nodded. "Yeah, well, it would take an enormous amount of power to create a *kolodets*. Most wielders' abilities were limited to cheap charms and party tricks, and even they were relatively rare. There were a ton of phonies out there, though, taking advantage of people's desperation for magic. I guess that's how *kolodtsy* became such a joke. All these fake magicians peddled cheap polished rocks, claiming they had some sort of magic power. And people ate it up."

From his tone, I could surmise that Lev thought very little of these rock-peddlers and purchasers.

"Idiots," I offered.

He smiled.

"There were some people, though, who weren't idiots and still believed in *kolodtsy*. People who knew you couldn't just buy one at a store." He swallowed. "Like my brother, Luka. He was certain our garnet was a *kolodets*, but he never figured out how to use it. I don't suppose he ever tried to shoot it."

My turn to swallow. "He was right, then, wasn't he? If our garnets are twins, if mine is drawn to yours, we each have a *kolodets*." Or had, anyway. Where was my garnet, now? A minute or two passed in silence as we each considered all we'd learned. I had so many questions swirling about in my mind that I hardly knew where to begin.

Lev broke the silence, returning to a more practical subject. "Your brother, he wrote that note so you would find the tsarevich, shoot the garnet, and take him to another world?"

"Yes. So that I would find the tsarevich and take him *out* of this one. Leaving only one Alexei in this world. Allowing my brother to assume the role of tsarevich, and eventually, tsar. Nevermind that he'd be losing his sister. Anything for his crown, I suppose."

"Evil little bastard."

"My thoughts, precisely. That's part of the reason I'm here. To help the tsarevich, of course, but also because I need him. I need to return him to the Winter Palace in order to get my brother out. To stop the evil little bastard from stealing the throne."

Lev raised his brows, nodding. "And then what?"

I sighed. "Oh, I'll give him hell. Make him wish I *had* left this world." The corner of my mouth lifted in a sad smile as I realized my answer. "And then I'd forgive him, I suppose. What choice is there? He's my brother."

"I know what you mean."

I thought of the drawings, then. The cabin, the dog. The woman, cradling an infant in each arm. The two identical little boys, one smiling, one solemn. And the drawing rolled up in my pocket, with his long beard, his hypnotic eyes, piercing through the parchment. Each signed "Polina."

"Lev, I didn't take the garnet. But I took something else." I pulled the rolled parchment from my pocket and placed it in Lev's hand, so he could feel it. Would he know what it was? "Who is Polina?"

I held my breath as the room became silent. Lev stopped moving.

"Which one did you take?" Lev asked as though he already knew the answer, his voice flat, cutting the silence.

"Who is Polina?" I asked again. I'd told him so much, wasn't it his turn?

"Which one did you take?" he asked again, speaking slowly but impatiently.

"Not the dog. Who is Polina?"

"Not the dog," he answered, that hint of a smile in his words despite his serious tone. He cleared his throat, and then—"Polina was my mother. Which one did you take?"

"Rasputin. I would know his eyes, in any world. The beard, longer when I knew him, but it was him. In my own world, he was a healer, a mystic. He gave me my garnet."

"Rasputin." Lev was quiet for a moment. "I don't know that name. But the man in the drawing was our father, mine and Luka's. The garnet was the only thing he ever gave us."

Of course. As he said the words, it made sense. Rasputin was at the center of all of this, wasn't he? He was the connection. And he was Lev's father. Was Lev's father the *same* Rasputin I knew? He must have been. Was it he, then, who had possessed such a magnitude of power to create these *kolodtsy?* Had he infused the garnets with the magic of this world and then traveled between worlds as Alexei and I had? My brain began to hurt. There was so much to take in.

"I'd better change your wound dressing." I started to rip another strip from my skirt. "We've an impossible escape ahead of us, and we can't have your leg falling off."

HOURS HAD PASSED and it would still be hours more before the sun set, offering that brief period of darkness that exists in St. Petersburg in July. I had crept to the end of the passageway and nudged the rock, just enough to see that the sun was still quite high in the sky. It had been risky, but we had agreed, Lev and I, that it would be the only way to tell the time in the darkness of the passageway.

In addition to being stuck for hours beneath the Narodnaya Volya stronghold whilst having just murdered two of the group's members, we had another problem, which was becoming quite consuming. Thirst. Lev insisted that despite the discomfort, we could live for days without water. However, I pointed out that he had lost a lot of blood, that we needed strength for our escape. That I could listen for anyone in the room before pushing up through the trunk. That I wouldn't even have to enter the hall-way—the room had its own bathtub, after all. And that maybe while I was at it, I might find the tsarevich. Lev was just beginning to concede until I stretched it too far.

"No, this is crazy. Are you crazy? He'll be so heavily guarded, especially now if not before. The place will be crawling with Narodnaya Volya—prob-ably waiting for me to make an attempt at rescuing the tsarevich. We were lucky to get out alive the first time."

Lucky. Lucky that I smashed a man's head in, while Lev strangled an-other? I shuddered, certainly not wishing to relive that scene. But if I was careful . . .

"It's a deathwish, Anastasia. We wait here until dark and make our es-cape. I want to save him too—I do—but that's not how it would go, if we tried."

"Just the water, then. I'll listen at the top, before I go through the trunk. If I hear anything, anything at all, I'll come right back down."

Lev sighed. "And you promise not to leave the room? Just get to the tub, fill whatever receptacle you can find, and come back down?"

"Promise!" I was already on my feet, moving toward the wall.

"Take the gun," Lev's voice was uneasy, clearly not convinced of my plan's soundness.

With the rifle at my side, I began the climb. Driven by thirst, by the need to *do* something, I reached the top in less than a minute. Through the trap-door, and I was inside the trunk, listening for any movement in the room.

Footsteps. Voices. I held my breath.

"—a bloody mess, is what it is. And without Ivan, tomorrow night could go poorly. No one negotiates like Ivan."

"Negotia*ted*. He won't be negotiating anything now, with his head beat in. Who'll take the lead then, on the hostage exchange?"

"Dunno yet. And the *yobanyy* Church of the Savior on Spilled Blood— a place only Ivan would have chosen. Dunno who else knows it well enough to stay sharp. Especially in the dark."

"Not me. Help me with Dmitri, here, will you? God rest his soul."

The sound of trudging boots, of a body being dragged from the room.

"And close the door behind us. Nobody needs to see this mess."

The door closed with a click. And it was quiet. My mind was racing with all I'd heard—the hostage could only be the tsarevich. Tomorrow night. The Church of the Savior on Spilled Blood. At dark. I swallowed, my dry throat reminding me of my mission. Quite certain that the room was now empty, I pressed the top of my head to the lid of the trunk, raising up into the room.

A bloody mess, indeed. The bedsheets were splattered with Lev's blood, the boot prints trailing to the door. The man's—Ivan's—body had been removed from the room, thankfully, but his blood remained on the floor, on the wall, on the ceiling. Looking away, I repeated the words in my mind once more. I'd killed him to save Lev. I'd done what I had to. Now I needed to keep moving. On the other side of the room was the wash closet, the bathtub.

I crept as quietly as I could from the trunk, across the room. A bath pitcher sat in the tub, just what I needed. Turning the faucet on, I stole a drink in my cupped hands before holding the pitcher to the spigot, impatiently waiting for it to fill. Tapping the faucet urgently with my index finger, I willed the water to pour more quickly. Half full. My heart raced. Would the men come back? Full enough. I grabbed the pitcher and kept my step light as I rushed across the room, back to the trunk.

Just as I knelt to open the lid, the doorknob turned, and the door popped open. Kneeling by the trunk, I set down the pitcher, raising the rifle with shaking hands. I flicked the safety off as I aimed at the door. I would do what I had to do.

"—already got him? Thank the *yobanyy* Lord." Then the door closed again.

I lowered the gun, releasing a heavy exhale and sinking to the floor in relief. But Lev was right. There was too much activity, too many people nosing around the room, around this whole wing. I quickly slid into the trunk, closing the lid behind me. The climb was slow and awkward with the water pitcher, and quite a bit of water sloshed over the sides as I kept switching hands, but I was so relieved to be back in the safety of the hideaway that I didn't care.

When I reached the last few footholds, Lev's hands found my waist, steadying me as I lowered my feet to the ground. He turned me around to face him, as though he were taking inventory, ensuring that I was indeed Anastasia, that I was still in one piece. "You're a bit soggy, Romanov. Any water left in the jug?"

I took another swig from the pitcher, then handed it to him. He reached to take it, his other hand lingering for just a moment, then dropping from my waist.

"You're welcome, Lukavich." Or Rasputin, wouldn't it be? Had he ever had a real surname?

As we passed the pitcher between us, I relayed to him what I'd heard, what I'd made of it. I repeated the conversation as well as I could remember it, the bits about Ivan and all. The important pieces I remembered clearly— the hostage exchange, tomorrow night, the Church of the Savior on Spilled Blood. My opportunity to free the tsarevich, to try again to set things right.

"The lack of leadership should be to our advantage," Lev observed, a rather calculated assessment of the perks of me having bludgeoned a man— Ivan, it would seem—to death with the butt of a rifle.

"*Our* advantage?"

"You prefer to do this alone?"

"I wasn't aware it was a matter of preference."

He set the pitcher down and took my hands in a strong but comforting hold. "I'd prefer that you don't get killed."

"I—I didn't know it mattered. To you. Or anyone." Heat rushed from my hands to my face, and I was grateful for the darkness to hide the redness of my cheeks, the tears in my eyes. That was it, wasn't it? I was No One, because there was no one with any tie to me here. Just my brother, who had already tried to trick me into leaving this world. And now, Lev. Who was apparently willing to hop on one foot to a potential slaughter to protect me. I looked up at him, wishing I could see the green of his eyes, piercing, like his father's, but . . . warmer.

He squeezed my hands. "It does." Perhaps he could sense that I was overwhelmed. Perhaps he was, too, because he cleared his throat, dropping my hands. "And of course, I would see the tsarevich to safety," he added gruffly.

The moment passed and we returned to our seats on the hard stone floor. There were hours yet before we would make our escape. Better to use the time to sleep, because we were going to need it.

Between naps, plotting our escape, and chatting (about food, trans-universal travel, and brown bears' general preference for salmon over roasted pheasant), I took several trips to the end of the passageway, peeking outside the stone, waiting for the sun to set.

Lev insisted that he take a turn, that his leg was fine, that he needed to move prior to our upcoming escape.

"Lev—"

"No, it's fine, really." He pressed a hand to my shoulder as he lifted himself from the floor.

"It's just that, you haven't been through the passageway yet."

"You seem to come and go easily enough." His dark silhouette moved toward the tunnel.

While I'd gotten rather used to the presence of our deceased companion, or as used to sharing space with a decayed body as one can be, it felt like a bad omen given our current predicament, and to speak about it seemed . . . foreboding. I had known that I would need to alert Lev to its presence eventually, but had been procrastinating this revelation quite successfully until then.

"Lev, you should know . . . we aren't exactly alone down here."

He stopped. "What does that mean?"

I drew in a breath, steadying my voice. "There's a . . . body. The remains of one, anyway. Mostly bones, really."

He was quiet for a moment. Then he crouch-limped back to me, reaching his hand to mine. "Let's go together. Maybe we can . . . put him to rest, somehow."

I took his hand, pulling to my feet. "Doesn't this feel like a sign? Like a bad omen? Like we could be trapped here too, until we waste away?" I imagined the Narodnaya Volya, noticing the stone, noticing the trunk, smiling smugly as they barricaded both ends.

Lev tugged me along. "He—or she—was a person, who by some unfortunate circumstances may have died in the tunnel, or maybe not. Their remains might have been brought here later, to be hidden. We'll never know. What I do know is that this body being here doesn't say anything about me and you and our chances of making it out of here."

I nodded. Logical, rational, but I still felt uneasy.

"And anyway, if we don't make it out of here, we could live off of spiders, start a family, start a whole village down here, couldn't we?" Lev spoke with laughter in his voice, and I pictured that half-grin, hidden in the darkness. I was simultaneously repulsed at the notion of living off of spiders and intrigued by the idea of starting a family and all that was implied in that suggestion. My cheeks flushed, and I was grateful once again for the darkness.

"We'll go together, then." I led the way, ready to alert Lev when we arrived at the corpse.

The shape of it was just discernible, sprawled right where I'd left it. Thankfully. I shuddered. It was immature of me, I supposed, or perhaps just disrespectful, to be repulsed. Lev seemed to approach the remains with more reverence, and while I found that admirable, I couldn't get past the creepiness of its presence.

Lev stopped when I did, taking a deep breath as he took in the shape of the bones, legs outstretched, propped against the wall. He took my hand.

"Who might he have been?" While Lev voiced the question rhetorically, I'd wondered the same.

"A prisoner? An explorer? A murder victim, his body hidden here, undiscovered until now?" As I spoke, a chill went through me, and I was grateful for Lev's hand, strong and comforting.

Lev was quiet for a moment, and when he spoke, his voice was distant, thoughtful.

"There would have been someone—family, a friend, a lover— someone to whom he never returned. Someone who never knew what happened, if he lived or died, what became of him. What happened to his body." He knelt to the floor, still holding my hand, but extending his other to touch the bones. He let out an exhale. "Old. Very old."

I fought the urge to vomit and knelt beside him, unsure what to say. It was one of those rare occurrences when I chose to stay quiet, to just listen. I squeezed his hand, and he continued.

"I've been that someone before. When Luka died, we never learned how, or why. We never saw his body."

Forgetting my choice to just listen and not probe, I blurted, "How can you be sure he's really dead, then? Your brother?"

While it was certainly not the right thing to say, Lev seemed unbothered by my impoliteness.

"You aren't the first to ask me that. My mother refused to believe it, when we got the letter. But I knew. I could feel it—his absence. It's hard to explain. It had always been as though there was a part of me that existed within him, a part of him that existed within me. That's why I felt it, before we even got the letter, I knew. The part of me that existed outside of myself, in Luka? It was just gone. Vanished. I felt . . . simpler. Lighter, honestly, though it sounds terrible to say."

"It's not terrible to say," I tried to speak comfortingly, though I did think it was rather terrible.

"Well. I don't suppose I'll ever have the chance to bury his body properly, but I hope that someone has, or will." He dropped my hand and stood, pulling off his coat. "Not that we can properly bury these bones, but we can pay our respects." He knelt again, tucking the bones of the legs so that they didn't protrude into the pathway. Then he laid his coat over the sitting skeleton, and we stood quietly for a moment, heads bowed. We were paying our respects, I supposed, though my thoughts were less on the body before me and more on Lev and his loss, his resilience, his goodness.

"Rest in peace," he said simply and looked up.

Wordlessly, he turned and we continued on to the end of the passage. I peeked out from behind the rock.

"The sun is setting. It's still pink out, but . . . soon." As anxious as I was to get out of the passageway, I was loath to leave the relative safety, this place where Lev and I had been able to rest, to relax, to even laugh a bit. I dreaded what came next.

Lev leaned in beside me, peeking out for himself. "We'll stick close to the walls, then make a break for it toward the street. Take cover in the trees. Get to Molniya."

I hoped Molniya was still there. "How's your leg? Up for sprinting?"

The small amount of light entering the passageway from behind the rock illuminated Lev's face. There was worry hiding behind his nonchalance. "I'll be fine."

That light diminished with the setting sun, shrouding us in utter darkness once again. I checked the laces of my boots, feeling that they were tied tightly. Secured the rifle at my side. Readied myself.

"It's time to go, Anastasia," Lev whispered.

"You're sure you don't want to stay, live off spiders, start a family, start our own village down here?" I turned his words on him in jest, but there was a part of me that was really warming to the idea, distaste for spiders aside.

"You can have all the spiders you want when we get back to my cabin, I promise. First, we've got to bust out of here." Lev pushed the rock from its station, hoisting himself up and through the opening. His face gleamed in the moonlight as he turned, reaching his hands for mine, pulling me up from the dark hole.

The night air was crisp and fresh, awakening my senses after hours in the stale passageway. Though the yard was quiet, I knew not to be fooled. Two men were dead, their prisoner on the loose. The Narodnaya Volya would be vigilant. Lev kept hold of my hand and we stayed low, our backs pressed to the palace wall; we moved with stealth. A cloud covered the moon, a thicker darkness filling the courtyard as we hurried beyond the bushes. If there was anyone in the courtyard, I couldn't see them. I hoped that meant that they couldn't see us, either. Under the cover of darkness, we reached the end of the wall easily, but my heart raced. It was time for the part of our plan I dreaded the most.

The road was about fifty feet away, a short run, but right in front of the palace. I had left Molniya cobbled another block away, off the road in a somewhat hidden spot, to which I hoped no horse thieves had wandered.

A sliver of the moon was just edging out from behind the cloud, illuminating a ruffled outline in a silvery glow. "Now or never, Romanov," Lev whispered. He squeezed my hand, then let it go. And took off. I watched him for just a moment, his sprint uneven but fast, his sturdy frame too visible in the July night.

Then I took off after him.

The silence of the night was broken by a shout of, "Who's there?" We didn't stop. We kept running for the road, just thirty more feet. "Who's there?" the voice shouted again. We didn't answer, running on in silence. Twenty feet to the road.

Gunshots—one, two—we kept running, never turning to see where the shots may have landed. My heart pounded in my chest as I darted across the courtyard . Ten more feet. More gunshots, and in my mind I saw my father, the bullets filling his chest. Fixing my eyes on my boots as they pounded the grass, I kept running, my legs moving impossibly fast.

Then there was the hardness of the road beneath my feet—we'd made it. Not safe, not really, but trees lined the road, casting their shadows,

providing some cover. A small amount of protection from the rebel marks-
men. With each running step we were farther from the palace, closer to safety. Time seemed to slow, and I was aware of every sound. The beat of Lev's
boots hitting the bricks in an uneven gallop, his injured leg disrupting his
gait. The shouting of our pursuers as they rushed toward the road. Gunshots
and the spattering of bullets hitting the bricks behind us. As the trees thickened and we shifted off the road into the trees as we'd planned, hope crept
into my fear-filled mind.

But Lev was slowing down, so I did, too. "Almost there, Lev," I spoke in
a whisper between heaving breaths.

"Full speed, Romanov. Get to Molniya. I'll be right behind you, just
go." He was still running, or galloping, or whatever one might call it, but he
was losing speed, putting even less weight on the left leg then, as though he
could hardly tolerate touching his foot to the ground.

There was no time to argue, and I would need to untie Molniya anyway. I sprinted ahead, glancing back over my shoulder to be sure Lev still
followed.

Another hundred feet or so to where I'd left the horse that morning.
Please be there, please be there, please be there . . . I sighed in relief as I spotted Molniya's regal silhouette, grazing in the darkness. He lifted his head,
acknowledging my sudden reappearance and then returned to his grazing.

Hastily untying the cobble, I gave Molniya a firm pat on the flank.
"It's me, you great beast, and we've got to go, as soon as Lev . . ." I glanced
around. Had he gotten so far behind me? I swung up onto the horse, taking
the reins. Where the hell was Lev?

More gunshots. What if he was shot? In my mind, I could hear what he
would say. "Anastasia. Just go."

I'd sprinted away on Molniya once before, leaving Lev for the rebels.
But I wouldn't do it again. Because I had a teammate in this wild adventure
now. Lev, who had stood in the path of the rebels, so I could ride away. Who
had sprawled himself overtop me, a shield, when Dmitri had pulled the gun.
Who would hop on one foot to a royal hostage exchange teeming with the

men who'd held him prisoner, questioned him, shot him . . . for me. I pulled the rifle from my side. Flicked the safety. Held it ready. I kicked Molniya into a run, back toward the palace, back toward Lev.

A cluster of frenzied men on foot patrolled the road in front of the palace, desperately shooting their guns in all directions, clueless as to where the running figures had gone.

"*Pizdets,* Romanov, what are you thinking?" Lev emerged from the trees, hobbling unsteadily. The men must have spotted Molniya's unmissable silhouette then, because they started moving toward us, shooting at us. I tugged the reins, but Molniya had already decided to stop, rearing onto his back legs. I swore as I threw my arms around the horse's neck, fighting to stay in the saddle as he bucked. Bullets struck bricks—we were just out of range.

Using the strength of his arms, Lev swung himself up onto the wild horse, landing in the saddle behind me. He wrapped his arms around my waist, holding me tightly as Molniya let out a feral bray. "Let's go the other way, shall we?"

And we were off, Molniya living up to his name as we bolted down the road, bullets striking the road in our wake. Our pursuers had no chance, not on foot, as we took odd turns, zigzagging our way through the city until we were quite sure that no one had trailed us.

From behind me, Lev relaxed his hold at my hips and leaned forward, murmuring into my ear, "I think it's safe to slow a bit now. To head toward the cabin. Left, up here."

I tugged the reins, slowing the horse to a walk, turning left.

"You saved me, Anastasia. I know you didn't come there for me, but you saved me. And then, you came back for me." We swayed and bounced slightly with the horse, and as he spoke, his lips brushed my ear, sending a chill through me. "You came back for me. That was stupid, but I don't know how to thank—"

Before he could finish, I turned my head, so that my lips found his. He stopped talking, surprised, but then he pressed his lips to mine, kissing me quite thoroughly, and the chill became a shiver and then this amazing warmth, filling me completely.

He pulled away slowly, his eyes finding mine, sparkling green in the moonlight. I was struck by the rightness of it. I could have kissed him again, kissed him all the way to the cabin. Surely Molniya could steer himself? I could have deflected these feelings that overwhelmed me, making some joke about how we might have passed the time in the passageway more pleasantly, had we thought of it sooner.

Instead, I held his gaze, and said what I was truly thinking. "Yes, I saved you. But I'm sure you'll save me, too."

And we rode along, winding through small streets lined with cabins like Lev's, the brief darkness lifting as the sun began to peek back around the horizon, promising another day.

CHAPTER TWENTY-FIVE

"And even within hearts overwhelmed by evil, one small bridgehead of good is retained. And even in the best of all hearts, there remains . . . an unuprooted small corner of evil."

—*The Gulag Archipelago* by Aleksandr Solzhenitsyn

HOT BREAKFAST ARRIVED, A silent guard pushing the plate beneath the bars of Mikhail's dark cell. Fried eggs, warm black bread with honeyed butter, porridge—signifying that morning had come, beginning the Grand Duke's second day of imprisonment. He supposed that the breakfast, much like the cot and the wash basin, were luxuries beyond those offered to a more typical prisoner.

As a boy growing up in the Winter Palace, Mikhail had snuck about the castle, exploring the darkest hallways and the most hidden nooks. He'd crept down to the dungeon on occasion, but never when they'd had a prisoner. Most prisoners were kept across the water, at the Peter and Paul Fortress. Mikhail shuddered at the thought despite himself, grateful that he hadn't landed *there*.

Some immeasurable amount of time passed—Mikhail had long since finished his breakfast and was just beginning to think about lunch—when the sound of footsteps brought him to attention. *Lunch, already?* Mikhail supposed time must be passing more quickly than he'd thought, a pleasant surprise. However, the approaching footsteps were not those of a palace guard, rather those of a carpenter. *Or at least, a man dressed as a carpenter.* Mikhail had thought extensively about the Narodnaya Volya, the Silent Threat and his companions, disguised as carpenters repairing the palace basement ... but *why*? Mikhail's eyes narrowed as the carpenter approached, not recognizing the man, though suspecting he represented the rebels.

Forgoing any greeting or introduction, the man stopped before the cell and stated bluntly, "Ivan is dead."

Mikhail blinked. Ivan. Ivan had been Mikhail's primary contact with the Narodnaya Volya, the closest thing to a leader that the group had known. Ivan. The man with whom Mikhail had negotiated his relationship with the rebel group, his role in Russia's future. And it was Ivan who had promised the safety of the Grand Duchesses, Mikhail's witnesses, his nieces.

"Dead, you say." Mikhail kept his voice casual, looking to the carpenter expectantly, curiously, anxiously.

"His head was beaten in by the prisoner you sent us."

Mikhail fought to maintain a cool demeanor, not to react to the gruesomeness of the statement, nor the implication. The man's voice was accusatory, as though the prisoner had been acting on Mikhail's orders. Where did Mikhail stand with the rebel group, without Ivan?

"Horrific." He paused, as the weight of the revelation set in. "Ivan's death pains me. As ... as I know it pains the Narodnaya Volya." Would the rebels be leaderless, now? Mikhail thought of the group's history, their recent evolution from scattered anarchic cells, ranging from actionless grumblers to willing regicidal martyrs, to a semi-organized band of revolutionaries. Ivan had managed to rally them around the idea of ending absolute tsarism, creating a new representative government that worked *with* the Romanovs. Specifically, with Mikhail Romanov.

"The Narodnaya Volya is bigger than one man. Bigger than Ivan. Certainly bigger than you." The man gave Mikhail a hard look, assessing him.

"I have come to speak with you about a troublesome matter. You are aware of the tsarevich Alexei's presence in this palace?"

Mikhail thought of the boy, standing smugly by his father, watching as his uncle answered for crimes not committed. Answering for the boy's lies. "Yes."

"Troublesome. The boy simultaneously resides with us in the Alexander Palace, awaiting his use in a hostage exchange tonight."

What? How could that be? How could the boy exist in two places at once? Was it a doppelgänger? A mistake? Mikhail's mind raced. It was like magic—but magic didn't exist anymore.

"A hostage is not of much use if he is not believed to be kidnapped. It has been agreed that in order to achieve our intended goal, we will require the use of the Grand Duchesses Olga, Tatiana, and Maria. They have been removed from Luga and will no longer be available to serve as your witnesses."

As Mikhail opened his mouth to reply, to demand, to plead—to say something, anything, to sway the man—the carpenter turned, leaving the dungeon. In desperation, Mikhail gripped the bars of the cell, shaking them, kicking them. "Wait! Surely we can come to some sort of agreement?"

The carpenter didn't look back, strolling down the long hallway and out of sight, leaving Mikhail alone once again in his cell.

Alone to ponder his upcoming trial and who, besides Dina, might speak on his behalf. To imagine his nieces, hostages of an untamed rebel faction. To consider his nephew, to wonder *how*.

While there was much to occupy his thoughts, Mikhail found himself to be most consumed by regret.

CHAPTER TWENTY-SIX

"Happiness always looks small while you hold it in your hands, but let it go, and you learn at once how big and precious it is."

—Maxim Gorky

MORNING SUNRAYS POURED IN through the little window across the room, the brightness of the day quite welcome after unknown hours of darkness. I didn't mind the lumps of the hay mattress, nor the scratchiness of the wool blanket over me. I was grateful for a bed, this bed, safe and snug with Lev's arms wrapped around me, and so I remained curled on my side, smiling to myself as I replayed the events of the night before within my mind.

Behind me, Lev yawned, rousing himself awake and pressing up to his elbow. Looking down at me, his sleepy green eyes found mine, his dark curls framing his face like a lion's mane. With his other hand, he reached to brush a lock of hair from my face, twirling it around his finger.

"Good morning, Anastasia."

I smiled. After all I'd endured, I hadn't thought it possible to feel truly happy for even a moment. I felt the need to explain it to myself, to tell myself that it was okay to feel joy. That this moment of happiness didn't lessen the trauma of losing my family, nor the devastation of my brother's betrayal. It didn't erase my own descent into a darkness I'd never known existed within me. It was okay. It was valid. I was allowed to smile, basking in the morning sun, cozy in Lev's arms.

So I did.

"Good morning, Lev."

As I spoke, my stomach did too, letting out quite a demanding growl.

"I thought you said you'd never be hungry again, after our feast." Lev snickered, tugging the little lock of hair he'd been twirling. "Believe it or not, we managed to leave a bit uneaten." He rolled to his feet, jerking just slightly as he remembered his injury. His back faced me as he strolled across the room toward the kitchen, and I took the opportunity to assess his condition. Strong and lean, he walked with only a slight limp, the bandage around his calf still clean.

The night before, we'd chatted and laughed and snuck a few more kisses as we'd ransacked Lev's cabinets for food, finding an apple apiece, a portion of salted fish, and enough potatoes and carrots to fill a pot of boiling water. With our bellies full and exhaustion then replacing hunger as our most urgent need to satisfy, it had taken an enormity of willpower to clean and rebandage Lev's wound before collapsing into bed.

My stomach growled again, prompting me to drag myself from the coziness of the blankets to follow Lev into the kitchen. He was scraping the remaining boiled vegetables from the pot, filling two small tin plates. We sat together at the small table, where Alexei and I had sat just days before, scarfing down dry bread and dreaming of chocolate.

"I thought we could head down to the stream, have a nice wash before bloodying ourselves up again tonight. What do you say, Romanov?"

I knew I was filthy. Suddenly self-conscious, I scraped my scraggly fingernail along my dirt-caked forearm. How had Lev possibly wanted to kiss me, coated as I was in mud and blood and sweat? Puffing up my chest, I swallowed my self-doubt. "And here I was, thinking you only liked me for my signature scent. Didn't you know that bloodstains and body odor are all the rage in Paris? Ladies would kill for a gown like this." As I made the joke,

I realized what I was saying, and my voice broke on the word "kill." For a moment, my mind flashed to the room above the passageway, where I'd beaten a man to death with the butt of a rifle. I steeled myself, determined to stay in this moment of happiness, not to be dragged away by guilt, hate, grief. Couldn't we revel in the light of morning for just a bit longer, before dealing with all the darkness?

Lev must have seen the change in my face, heard the strain in my voice. His lazy smirk disappeared, his eyes full of concern and empathy as he leaned toward me, taking my hand. "Anastasia. You saved my life. And you preserved your own. All we can do now is use them well."

I nodded, forcing a smile. His words made sense, and they eased my guilt. Still, beneath the guilt, there was fear—fear for what I might become, stripped of all that had made me who I was. Fear of my own mind, and the thin veil separating *me* and the person I'd been when I'd . . . done what I'd done. Could that darkness be a part of me, without consuming me?

Lev held my gaze, his eyes unconvinced by my strained smile, but he lightened his tone.

"And to answer your question, Romanov, I rather like the smell of you, though surely you're offending your own royal sensibilities in that dress?"

A hint of a genuine grin fought its way onto my face despite myself. "The stream sounds marvelous. Just as soon as I finish stuffing my face." I popped a potato into my mouth, and another into Lev's. He held it in his mouth, crossing his eyes in imitation of a stuffed pig, and we both laughed, clinging to the easiness of it, cherishing the lightness before the inevitable night.

<hr />

"Have we walked into a fairy tale, Lev? This place is absolutely dreamy." I looked up through the canopy of trees above, the sunlight shining through oak leaves and pine branches to glisten on the still surface of the water. The creek was an offshoot of a stream that had broken away from the Neva, pooling in a clear, deep, swimming hole in this empty pocket of the forest.

"It's quite romantic. If I didn't know better, I'd think you were trying to get me to kiss you."

Lev smiled over his shoulder as he navigated the path ahead. Though limping slightly, he held back branches and pinned briars beneath his boot to ease my journey. "I wouldn't need to bring you out here for that, Romanov. All *that* took was getting myself arrested by rebels, taking a bullet to the leg, strangling a man, spending the day underground, and wrapping it up with a quick one-legged escape from the Narodnaya Volya." Shrugging, he smirked, tossing his bag aside and reaching for my hand as we arrived at the water's edge. "You're rather easy to impress."

I stopped, jerking Lev to a stop, too, and pulled him toward me, placing our linked hands against his chest. His face was just inches from mine, his exhale a cool breeze against my brow as he dropped the cocky smile. "And you," I whispered, leaning in close so that my lips brushed his as I spoke, "are rather easy to dunk." I shoved him into the pool, disrupting the pristine surface with a splash, filling the quiet nook of forest with my uncontainable laughter.

His head popped up a moment later. "Well played, Anastasia. But you're missing out— come on!"

Eying the pool skeptically, I pulled off my boots and stockings and dipped a toe in the water. "It's freezing!"

Lev only laughed. "You mean, refreshing."

"No, I mean freezing!"

After a bit more back and forth on the matter, Lev successfully convinced me that the only way to escape my fate as a smelly, dirt-covered coward would be to submerge fully in the pool. "Just jump in all at once. It's best, and what I would have chosen anyway, had I any choice in the matter."

I approached the water's edge. Fear can be quite an irrational thing. After all I'd seen and done in the last week, jumping into uncomfortably cold water was what gave me pause? I was reminded of the moment days ago, when I'd sat atop that old mare. "*Just faint,*" Alexei had whispered. The fear, the anxiety, the panic I'd worked myself into as I tried to will the nerve to fake a faint. And then I'd woken up, Lev's face over mine, and it'd been okay. I'd been okay.

Lev skidded his hand over the water's surface, splashing me. I shrieked, taking a step back as he grinned.

"5, 4, 3 . . ." He counted tauntingly, and I glared at him. ". . . 2 . . ." If I could just do it, then I could splash him right back. ". . . 1."

I jumped, and was underwater, my skirt floating up around me as my body submerged. The water was freezing, but refreshing, too. The caked dirt and dried blood loosened from my skin, my hair releasing a week's worth of grime. My feet found the rocky bottom of the pool, and I stood, drinking in air as my head rose from the water.

Wiping the water from my face, I slicked my dripping hair behind my ears. "I believe it's my turn." I raked the pool's surface, splashing a wall of water right at Lev's face as he ducked under water, finding my feet, pulling them out from under me. I kicked, and a ruthless war of splashing and dunking ensued. I forgot all about the cold.

A few minutes later, when I came up for air, I caught Lev wincing for just a moment as he reached down toward his wounded calf. He transformed the grimace to a smile, but I'd already seen that he was hurting. "Lev. Time to clean it, I think."

He nodded, and moved toward the pool's edge. He heaved himself from the water, pulling off his shirt as he limped toward the bag he'd brought. I caught myself staring rather shamelessly as water rolled off his lean muscled back. He removed a few garments from the bag and sat them by the water's edge. "For you. I'll go a bit away and change, give you some privacy." And he wandered into the trees.

As I peeled off the heavy wet dress, I found myself thinking of the night I'd put it on. It had been in haste, when my family and I had been awakened, instructed to get dressed. "*You will be moved tonight,*" they'd said. "*Out of Yekaterinburg.*" We'd readied ourselves, and I'd found myself oddly grateful to the men for their protection. Grateful to the same men who had patrolled the house, confined us to our rooms, and rationed our food. I'd been grateful to the evil men, as my family and I were unknowingly marched to slaughter.

Shaking myself from the memory, I examined the bunched-up bundle of garments, finding a woman's white blouse and plain brown dress, well-worn but sturdily sewn. Unsure how long I'd sat in reverie, I moved quickly, buttoning into the blouse, lacing the brown bodice. The skirt was a bit long on me, but the dress was otherwise a near-perfect fit. Once dressed, I walked to the water's edge, the surface still once more, and set to brushing out my wet blonde locks with my fingers. I hadn't realized how badly I'd needed this, and was amazed how much better I felt. A bath and some clean clothes had truly worked wonders.

"Looking good, Romanov." I turned to see Lev emerging from the trees, appearing quite reputable in his clean white *kosovorotka* and sand-colored trousers, his wild curls tamed by the water. The stubble darkening his cheeks and chin, the slight hitch in his gait—these were the only evidence of the unusual week he'd had.

Maybe it was that he looked so dapper, or maybe it was that he'd thought of everything, known just what I'd needed to feel human again. But I didn't respond, and instead stood there smiling stupidly, overtaken by the desire to kiss him again, to rub my own cheek against his stubbly one.

"It was my mother's. The dress." He had a strange look on his face as he approached me, as though he couldn't quite stand to look at me, yet couldn't look away. Was it wrong for me to wear his mother's dress? He'd given it to me, after all. Perhaps he hadn't anticipated how it might affect him.

"Should I change?" I eyed the mangled wet dress I'd left piled in the grass.

"No—" He wiped the look from his face, eyes dropping to the ground. "No, of course not. I just . . ." He paused, looking up at me again, finding my eyes. "When I remember my mother, I remember her wearing this dress. It's why I didn't get rid of it, when I sold her things."

I took his hand, not sure what to say, but needing to say something. "How long has it been?"

"Over a year now. It's . . . don't worry about it. I didn't mean to make you feel odd about the dress. It fits you well."

"Lev. You can miss her. It's not . . ." *It's not weak. You can feel, you can grieve.* Those were the words I wanted to say. But they caught in my throat, as I turned them upon myself, and it was too overwhelming. There was just too much to feel. I squeezed his hands. "It's okay. However you need to . . . it's okay."

He sighed. "I do miss her. I loved her. And then . . . then I hated her, toward the end. I was all she had, and . . . it wasn't enough. Not enough to live for. So she just . . . stopped." He cleared his throat, looking away. "So I had to try to be enough, for myself."

"You're enough." Was I enough, for myself?

His eyes met mine again, the corner of his mouth lifting in a half smile. Then he leaned in, his stubbly cheek pressing against mine as he found my lips with his. Tender, at first, then more hungrily as we both sought and found solace in one another.

I had been such a scrambled mess—lost in grief, in fear, in anger. The bullets had ended my family, torn me from my world. But I'd been torn from my world long before then, hadn't I? When my life as a Grand Duchess had been ripped away. When I'd become a perpetual prisoner. I'd lost everything. And then, the bullets. And the worlds, the lies, the search for a purpose. But then there was Lev. And it was all . . . better. Not healed, but better.

THE SUN HUNG high in the sky, reflecting off the ornate onion domes of the Church of the Savior on Spilled Blood. The church stood magnificently, so extravagant in its design, like something out of Moscow. My grandfather had built it, sparing no expense in memoriam of his father—my great-grandfather, for whose spilled blood the church was named. The church appeared exactly as I remembered it, built in just the spot along a busy stretch of road alongside the canal, where townspeople bustled about their daily business. In the very spot where my great-grandfather had been murdered. Curiously, I looked to Lev.

"Tsar Alexander II . . . you said he was killed by the Narodnaya Volya. In my world, a bomb was thrown at his feet on this very street. And here? I mean, in this world?"

Lev tore his eyes away from the magnificent structure, looking at me. He nodded, following my train of thought. "Close, but not quite. It wasn't a bomb. The Narodnaya Volya had magic-wielders in their ranks back then, and they . . ." He shook his head. "They sort of turned him inside out. It was gruesome, from what I've heard."

I tried not to picture it, but my mind's eye moved faster than my self-control. These magic-wielders had just pulled this power from the air, shaped it into such evil, and thrown it at their tsar? The thought was terrifying. My horror must have shown on my face because Lev reached out, taking my hand.

"But magic doesn't exist anymore. Other than our *kolodets,* it's gone." His tone was confident, reassuring. "Whatever power the Narodnaya Volya have gained—it's not the power to do that. Yes, tonight will be dangerous. But it won't be . . . it won't be *that.*"

He was right, of course. Still, the notion was little comfort. Unfathomable violence was certainly possible without magic, too. I supposed I wasn't so frightened by the methods, so much as the merciless hatred behind them. Magic or not, these men hated the tsar, hated the tsarina, and hated the tsarevich, even though he was just a child.

What did these rebels hope to accomplish with this hostage exchange? Were they looking for money? Were they luring the tsar here to kill him? And what about . . .

"My brother!"

Startled by my sudden outburst, Lev looked around, as though searching the crowd for Alexei. Not spotting any sickly versions of his tsarevich amongst the crowd, he looked at me quizzically. "Your brother?"

"Alexei, he's at the palace, isn't he? Or—he was." I'd assumed he remained there, but much had happened since we parted, since he'd sent that deceitful note. "If he is, if he's still at the Winter Palace, and there's this hostage exchange—it will be obvious there's two of him, won't it?" I stumbled over my words as I struggled to keep up with my thoughts, not to mention my feelings. Although Alexei probably deserved the worst of fates, he was my brother. Whatever punishment should befall him, it ought to be coming from *me*.

Lev stood for a moment in silence before responding, characteristically rational. "Anastasia, I think there are two possibilities. The first is that he remains at the castle, in which case the Narodnaya Volya have no bait. No one will come to negotiate for a hostage who is thought to be safe at home. In that case, it will be up to us to rescue the tsarevich, to deliver him home stealthily, to sneak your brother out of the Winter Palace."

I nodded. It made sense. "And the second possibility?"

"The second possibility is that your brother is not still at the palace. In which case the tsar and his men will come here to the church, to bring the tsarevich home. That would make our job much easier. If that's the case, all we'll need to do is find your brother."

I wasn't so certain about the ease of finding my brother, who, if he wasn't at the Winter Palace, could be anywhere in Russia. Anywhere in the world. But Lev's reasoning did comfort me somewhat.

"I suppose you're right."

We wandered the street, circling the church, taking in the setting in the light of day. We gazed out over the canal—the water was high, promising storms upriver—and we formed our plan. It had seemed the most useful way we might spend the daylight hours, given the quest that awaited us after sunset.

Tugging my hand, Lev turned me toward him. "We're so close, Anastasia, to being done with all of this. Then we—me, and you, and your brother—we can just live. We could all stay at the cabin, figure things out. Or we could travel. We could do whatever you want." He smiled, so optimistic, so *hopeful.* It was contagious—I smiled back. Despite all the many reasons I had not to be optimistic, to abandon hope, to see the world through a jaded lens—I smiled back.

As we sauntered back toward Lev's cabin, I found myself fantasizing about what life might look like, living here in this world with Alexei and Lev. I was just imagining all the ways we might alter Alexei's appearance to distinguish him from his doppelgänger, when Lev cleared his throat.

"Anastasia?"

"Yes?"

"Could you . . . tell me about him? About my father?"

I paused, unsure what to say.

"Anastasia, was he a good man?"

I looked at Lev. "I . . . I'm not sure. He was complicated."

Lev said nothing, waiting for me to continue.

I went on, voicing my doubts about this man who'd been like family. "And he was powerful. Even without the magic of this world. His eyes were hypnotic. He could influence people, and the way things happened. Like my father and his rule." I paused as Lev took in my words, thinning his lips and raising his brows as he digested my words. "He may have been our downfall. I thought he loved us. I thought he cared about my family. Looking back . . . I'm not sure anymore."

Lev scanned the sky, where clouds had moved in, threatening a July thunderstorm.

"I don't know, Anastasia. Maybe I have it all wrong. But he cared enough to give you the garnet, didn't he? He's got some . . . vested interest. In you being here, I mean. He wanted you to escape, when the time came. You said he told you to find him. He must be . . . findable. Why would he have said that?"

"He's dead, Lev!" I snapped. "The Bolsheviks shot him in the back. He's not *findable.*" The words spilled out too quickly, before I could give any consideration to how they might land. A gust of wind rustled the trees ominously, and I felt a drop of rain on my forehead.

Beside me, Lev swallowed, looking down. For how many years had he wondered about his father? What had he hoped to hear? Certainly not the answer I'd given.

Though for all Rasputin's faults, he'd had one undeniably redeeming quality.

"But Lev, without him, Alexei would have died. Rasputin saved his life, more than once. He was the only one who could."

Lev looked at me curiously. "What was wrong with your brother?"

"He has—" Just then, thunder boomed, lightning flashed, and the clouds let the rain loose in sudden sheets of water, pouring from the sky. "Argh, let's run!"

Lev was moving well on his wounded leg, and we sprinted through the rain all the way back to the cabin, leaving behind any talk of Rasputin, my brother, and hemophilia.

We had hours before sunset—hours to relax, to eat, to enjoy each other's company. And we did just that, relishing the comfort of the cabin, hoping with unreasonable optimism that we might return to it in the morning, not daring to consider the alternatives.

CHAPTER TWENTY-SEVEN

"When I go to confession, I don't offer God small sins, petty squabbles, jealousies . . . I offer him sins worth forgiving."

—Grigori Rasputin

"ALEXEI, YOU HAVEN'T EATEN a morsel." The tsarina set her glass on the table delicately, the juice within undisturbed.

"Neither has . . . Father," Alexei hesitated over the word. Would it ever feel right, to think of these people before him as anything more than the tsar and tsarina? *It's the closest thing you'll ever get*, he told himself. Pushing a runny yolk across his plate with his fork, he speared an egg white to a bit of black bread. His stomach was in knots, his mind consumed by what he must do.

Never doubting that he would succeed, his mind churned over the *how* of it more than the *if*. He would meet the Other Alexei tonight at the Church of the Savior on Spilled Blood. He would use the garnet, casting his double to another world, securing his own place as the tsarevich in this one. And he would escape the Narodnaya Volya and return safely to the Winter Palace. But how?

"A benefit of being tsar," the tsar rumbled from his seat at the head of the table, "is that I can fill up on sweets before breakfast and no one can scold me." His mouth widened in a grin, but Alexei knew the man was stressed. How couldn't he be? His son poisoned, his brother accused, his daughters missing, his crown threatened. He'd been unsettled by the ransom note. But if he was suspicious of Alexei's identity, he hid it well.

Just then, a messenger stepped into the dining room, accompanied by two guards.

"A letter for you, Your Majesty."

The tsar dropped his grin, set his fork down. "A letter from who?"

The messenger shuffled nervously. "Your pardon, but I could not follow its trail. It was brought to me by another messenger, who received it from yet another. If I may be so bold, Your Majesty, I would suggest that the sender is someone who wishes to remain unknown."

Silence sat heavily in the room, the tsar and tsarina exchanging a glance. Alexei shifted in his seat. It could only be the Narodnaya Volya.

The tsar sighed, beckoning the messenger to come forth and then breaking the uncomfortable silence. "Very well, deliver it here, then."

Alexei's mind raced, imagining the possibilities, what words that letter might contain. Surely the rebels weren't canceling the meet up? What else could the letter be about?

Once the guards and the messenger had left and it was again just the three of them at the long table, the tsar opened the letter, his brow furrowing as he read. He reread the note several times before looking up, his face hard.

His turned to his wife, meeting her eyes. "The girls, too." She gasped, bringing her hand to her heart.

Then he looked at Alexei, his eyes unreadable. "You'll accompany me tonight on an unusual outing. It is quite important—you might say our future depends upon it. Are you prepared to join me on such a mission?"

Across the table, the tsarina stood. "But Nicky—why not the men—"

"It must be done." He cut her off, holding up the note as his basis for the statement as he rose to stand. He turned back to Alexei, his face still a hardened mask. "Son?"

Alexei fidgeted, unsure what was meant by this new development—whether it would assist or complicate his own mission.

While it would certainly simplify the matter of getting out of the palace and getting to the church, it would be more difficult to slip away. And what if the tsar saw his double, became aware that there were two? Alexei could weigh the options all he wanted, but based on the tsar's face, his tone, it was clear that Alexei didn't have much choice in the matter.

"Of course, Father. Whatever is needed. I am your tsarevich."

THE BEDROOM DOOR flew open, the tsar stepping through the threshold, clad head to toe in midnight black. Alexei tossed aside the Dostoyevsky he'd borrowed, his knee giving slightly as he swung hastily to his feet. It was time, then.

"It is wrong, Alexei, what we must do. I need you first to understand that."

If you only knew, Nicholas, Alexei thought grimly, the garnet sitting heavily against his chest beneath his buttoned coat. Inhaling a sharp breath, he nodded. He was ready.

"In this case, however, we must do wrong because of the wrongs done unto us—we must do wrong to protect our family, to protect our empire. Do you understand?"

And to protect myself, my birthright, my legacy. Understanding all too well, Alexei lifted his chin. Met the tsar's eye. "Yes, Father."

"And which is more important, Alexei? Protecting our family or protecting our empire?"

Alexei's brows shot up, and he paused, studying the tsar's face. He knew what his father's answer would have been. His father had answered that question when he'd abdicated the throne for himself and for his son. Weak when he should have been ruthless, he'd ended the Romanov reign in a last desperate attempt to save his family. Family, always, his father had chosen.

And still he'd failed.

But the man who stood before Alexei, now? There was kindness in his eyes. Love, even.

And a fierceness that Alexei had never seen in his actual father. *Strength,* Alexei thought, *that might have saved us.*

"You've already answered this question, Alexei. You answered this question when you left your sisters behind, taking what opportunity you found to escape your uncle. Self-preservation, when you are heir to the throne, is preservation of the empire."

Was it pride that Alexei saw in the tsar's eyes? Unsure how to respond, but wishing the tsar to continue, Alexei nodded again. "Yes, yes I did, Father."

"Fortunately," the tsar continued, "we shall achieve both protection of our family, and protection of our empire tonight. Do you know our quest?"

Of course, I do. I've snooped and snuck and learned all that I could. Alexei supposed that the boy the tsar knew might not be as resourceful as him. He chose his words carefully.

"I've an idea."

"The note I received came from the rebel group who call themselves the Narodnaya Volya. They have gained strength in recent months and have thus become arrogant. They claim to hold your sisters as hostages. Do you know, Alexei, who else they claim to have captured?"

Your son. "An imposter, pretending to be me. Is it not, Father?"

The tsar watched him, assessing his face, noting his reaction to each word spoken. "Indeed. Strangely, they also acknowledge your presence here at the palace and have demanded that you and I arrive at this hostage exchange together. You and I, and a messenger to deliver news of my abdication to the world. We shall arrive, us three, appearing to meet their demands."

"Appearing to, Father?"

"The canal by the church will hide our men, already in place in low boats, veiled by darkness. We will retrieve your sisters. We will annihilate the rebels. And we will never, never abdicate the throne. Are you ready?"

Again, Alexei nodded, his heart pounding as he imagined the scene. His voice tightened, outwardly calm as his insides stirred with anxious longing. *This must work. It must.* "Yes, Father."

"Then let us walk." And the two left the room, tsar and tsarevich, off to preserve their reign.

CHAPTER TWENTY-EIGHT

"Revolutions are meaningless without firing squads."

—Vladimir Lenin

T HUNDER STILL RUMBLED IN the distance, and though the rain had stopped, storm winds churned the air as night fell over the city. The dome-capped towers of the church were black orbs against the dark clouded sky, silhouetted by the moonlight.

"One more time, Anastasia."

I whipped around to face Lev, drawing the gun, finding the trigger, my hands steady.

"Good. And the garnet?"

"In my pocket," I answered, feeling the sharp angles of the iron box through the fabric of Polina's dress. It had been Lev's suggestion that we bring it.

"If you own a magical gemstone, it's only logical to bring it along on a life-risking mission," he'd said. I hadn't argued. I'd watched as Lev pulled the leather tab beneath the creaky board, exposing his hideaway. I'd taken the iron box when he'd handed it to me, pocketed it. But there was no way I was leaving this world without my brother.

The gun, however, could be useful. We were both armed, Lev holding the tsarevich's heavier hunting rifle, and I with the late Dmitri's handgun. Lev had given me a knife to keep in my boot, and I'd used it to chop off the too-long dress at the knees, so I could move about unencumbered. I'd been hesitant to desecrate Lev's mother's dress, but he'd insisted. Using the extra fabric, I'd fashioned a little brown shawl to cover the bright white sleeves of my blouse. To better blend into the night.

Lev wore a plain black coat, dark pants, dark boots—a shadow. He stopped suddenly, turning his ear to the road behind us, placing his hand on my shoulder. "Get down."

In the darkness, a large truck rumbled down the road, passing us by as we crouched at the roadside, nestled together beneath the low wall bordering the canal below. Vehicles were uncommon—this truck could only be the Narodnaya Volya, the tsarevich.

"Quite a cargo space, for one boy," Lev whispered.

He was right. "Come on," I whispered back, and we stayed low, creeping behind the truck, approaching the Church of the Savior on Spilled Blood.

Our plan was vague, as we knew very little as to the specifics of this meeting. We'd agreed that our best chance was to stay as close to the tsarevich as possible. When the opportunity arose, we would grab him and slip into the canal. We'd hitched Molniya just a short swim away, on the other side of the church.

Arriving before the church, the truck lurched to a stop. Lev and I nodded at each other and moved silently, crawling beneath the truck, each of us pressed against a rear wheel. As close to the tsarevich as possible. Our view was limited from this post, but we could hear the truck door open and close quietly, the footsteps of several men. The soft *click* of readied guns.

"There they are," a hushed voice spoke, "standing before the doors."

I swallowed. "They" could only mean the tsar. The tsar and whomever he'd brought along. He'd come. By Lev's earlier reasoning, then, my brother could be anywhere.

As the footsteps moved away from the truck, toward the church, toward the tsar, I looked to Lev, raising my eyebrows. *Now?*

He shook his head, pointing behind me. From my crouch beneath the truck, I turned, peeking around the truck's wheel to see the boots of several guards, the men standing silently as they guarded their precious cargo.

"We've come, as you asked. My son and I." The tsar's voice boomed across the silent churchyard.

My son? Alexei was here? *But why . . .?* "Now, my daughters. Release them to me, and I shall continue to comply."

My eyes widened as I held in a gasp—my sisters, well, the Grand Duchesses—they had been kidnapped, too? Another Olga, Tatiana, and Maria, separated from me only by the rusted metal undercarriage of the truck? There was nothing I could do but look across at Lev, crouched against the opposite tire, his eyes equally alarmed. "Daughters?" he mouthed wordlessly. It was not a possibility we'd considered. "My son and I?" I mouthed back, palms up as I shrugged, shaking my head in disbelief.

"Ah, Nicholas, but you see, we have four bargaining points, while you have just the one. First, send your telegrams. Your abdication to all the papers. Do that, and we give you Olga. Once the news reaches the ears of the people, once it is irrevocable, we give you Tatiana."

Movement from the boots by the truck. They were so close, I could have reached out and touched them. The truck gave slightly as one of the men leaned against it, whispering to his companion. "The way he's speaking, like he thinks he's Ivan. Abdication, pish. This whole plan is ridiculous."

"Less than generous," the tsar quipped. "And what of Maria? What of this supposed second Alexei? No, before I comply with your wishes, I must see the four of them. Confined in your truck, I presume?"

"This plan," the booted companion whispered back, "is much smarter than any alternative."

I held my breath, not daring to move an inch, afraid to imagine what "alternatives" had been considered.

A second voice boomed across the churchyard. "Even at our mercy, tsar, even with your children at stake, you speak like an arrogant—"

That first voice, the voice of the Ivan Impersonator, rose an octave as he interrupted—"Put that gun down, you idiot! Put it—" And then a shout, and gunshots. Lots of them. There were more guns than there had been men, where was it all coming from?

My heart pounded, my head swam—it was happening again. The screams of the rebels, the shooters, my sisters, my parents, myself—it was all melding together, a symphony of horror across time and space. Gripping the gun by its handle, I took a long, deep breath. Forced my eyes to remain open. Commanded my mind to remain *here*. Universes away from that cellar. Here, beneath a truck full of hostages, another world's version of my brother and sisters. My actual brother was here, somewhere. I peeked out from behind the oversized tire.

The boots of nearby rebels took off running toward the church. Lev was already rolling out from beneath the truck—"Now, Anastasia!"

I scrambled to my feet, taking in the scene as I threw myself around the back of the truck. There were men climbing up from the canals, over the walls, men leaning out windows of the church—I couldn't tell who were Narodnaya Volya, who were Imperial Army. A bomb had been thrown, something was on fire—it was complete chaos.

Lev tore open the cargo container, his mind set on freeing the tsarevich and his sisters. It was them: Olga, Tatiana, and Maria, all tied up and gagged, at the mercy of these barbaric traitors. I followed behind Lev as he stepped toward them. Then, out of nowhere, he was knocked to the side as a scrawny boy clambered into the truck.

"Alexei!"

At the sound of my voice, my brother stopped for a moment and turned, his eyes finding mine.

"Ana . . ." His face was surprised, confused, ashamed—but then he kept moving, moving toward the tsarevich as he reached into his shirt, pulling out the garnet, brandishing a gun—

"Alexei, no!" My heart raced—I had to stop him, but how? The tsarevich struggled against his ties, using his bound hands to swat at the gun my brother held. My brother didn't stop moving, looping the necklace's golden chain over the tsarevich's fists as he pointed the gun at the jewel. "I'm sorry, Ana. I have to." He looked at me then with sad eyes as his finger found the trigger.

"Alexei, you *zasranets*, listen to me! I forgive you—I *forgive you!*"

His finger found the trigger, but he hesitated, his whole body trembling.

"Just stop, Alexei, please! I'll get you out of here, I'll—I'll—"

BANG.

The gunshot reverberated through the truck, deafening me to my own scream.

The next moments were a whirlwind, and I stood frozen in shock.

Lev lunged past me toward the Grand Duchesses, pocketing his gun and drawing his knife as he began slashing their binds.

The tsarevich still struggled against his ties, still very much in this world. The garnet necklace slipped from his bound hands as he thrashed.

And Alexei collapsed to the floor, groaning in agony as he reached for his foot. Blood was spurting through his leather boot.

What just happened?

Lev spoke hurriedly as his fingers worked furiously to free Maria. "Anastasia, he'll be fine, it's just his foot—quickly, help me with these ties!"

It took a moment for the words to sink in. *It's just his foot*—"Lev, you shot him?"

"I had to—he'll be fine. He needed to be immobilized while we get these four—"

"You *shot* him?!"

Lev had set Maria free, and she jumped from the truck, looking back over her shoulder to her sisters, her brother, her liberator.

"He'll be fine, Anastasia, we have to hurry—"

"You *shot* him? Lev, he'll die, he's going to *die!*"

Lev bit down on the rope restraining Tatiana as he loosened it, straining to keep the frustration from his voice. "I had to do something! *Pizdets*, it's only his foot! We'll take care of it at the cabin, but we have to *get* back to the cabin. I need your help—come on!" Tatiana leapt from the truck, joining Maria.

My attention had turned to Alexei, kneeling beside him as he lay bleeding on the floor. I propped his foot on my knee, trying to keep it elevated as I stroked his sweaty blonde hair, trying not to think of Spala, when we'd almost lost him.

"It's okay, Alexei, it will be okay, I won't let you die here, I won't." I tried to believe the words as I spoke them, tried to keep the shaking from my voice, to hold back the tears in my eyes. "I'll get you to a doctor—to the best doctors, to the palace—just hold on, Alexei, can you do that?"

His voice, raspy and weak, was barely audible as I leaned in over him.

"Find him, Ana. Find Rasputin."

I nodded, fighting back tears. "I'll find him. I promise, I'll find him." I snatched the garnet from the floor, looped the chain over my neck. It was an empty promise though, wasn't it? Rasputin was dead. And if somehow he wasn't dead, if somehow he existed in this world, I wouldn't know where to begin to look for him. But Alexei looked so pitiful, so desperate.

"He said . . . he said anything is possible." Alexei's voice was barely audible.

"I'll find him," I repeated, keeping the tremble from my voice for Alexei's sake. I acted quickly then, doing what I could to save my brother. Pulling my makeshift shawl from my shoulders, I attempted a quick tourniquet as Lev cut the last rope binding Olga. Hurrying from the truck, she joined her sisters, standing huddled, waiting for their brother. Then Maria's voice cried, "Father!" I squinted, just making out the tsar's shadow sprinting toward his daughters.

In almost the same moment, a bomb skidded across the road, perhaps aimed toward the tsar, but it caught in Maria's feet as she stepped out from behind the truck. In one moment, the girls were tasting freedom, filled with hope . . . I knew that feeling. And I knew how it felt for it to be ripped away. In the next moment, the bomb exploded.

The blast was blinding, the burst rattling through my skull. Three distinct screams pierced through the ringing in my ears, but for just a moment. Then their screams were swallowed by the flames, their lives stolen in an eruption of blood and limbs. Where the girls had stood just moments before, an angry fire raged.

Time seemed to slow, the chaotic scene before me unfolding soundlessly like a silent film. There were rebels and soldiers shouting and firing guns. There was the tsar, still running toward his daughters' burning, broken bodies. And there was my brother, bleeding in my arms as tears poured from my eyes.

It couldn't be real. How could life be so fragile? How could death snatch my sisters away so swiftly yet again? I'd vowed to save them, to protect them from the unjust fate they'd met in my own world. And I'd failed.

The tsar's howl could be heard over the gunshots, his men shielding him as he ran to the scene of the explosion, wailing in anguish as he took in the horror, his three daughters' dismembered corpses burning to ash.

"My girls!" he cried out, dropping to his knees. The sound of more gunshots as soldiers found the bomber, as the rebels fought back.

I still knelt by Alexei, frozen in horror as his blood pooled around us.

"Ana," he rasped, "Ana . . . please."

I looked into Alexei's blue eyes, so much like my own, and knew what I must do. He needed doctors, immediately. The tsar couldn't see the Other Alexei. He had to take my brother back to the palace, or he would die.

He would likely die anyway, but I shoved away the thought.

I scooped Alexei in my arms, looking back at Lev, who was moving with manic speed as he sliced the tsarevich's restraints. My heart split in two. And I did what had to be done, hating myself for what I was doing, hating Lev for what he had done.

As I jumped from the truck, Lev looked back at me, his eyes widening. "Anastasia, no!" But he stayed with the tsarevich, racing time as he sliced away the ropes.

Tears were pouring from my eyes.

"Anastasia, what are you doing?"

I pulled down the hatch, Lev and the tsarevich disappearing from view. "Your Majesty, your son—he's been shot!"

The tsar was on his knees before the mangled bodies of his daughters, sobbing in grief. And he looked up to see me, perhaps appearing as a ghost, so like his own daughters, so *similar* . . . but just a girl, holding his bleeding son in her arms. On top of everything else, my heart ached as I looked into the man's face, my father's eyes, finding no recognition. It was as though there was some part of me that expected him to know me, to say, "Ah, Anastasia, there you are. Not to worry, I'll handle it all from here."

I shook the useless wish away, steeling myself. "Your Majesty, he's bleeding badly, you must understand, the bleeding must stop, or he will die! Do you understand? He needs doctors, immediately, or *he will die!*"

The tsar rose in an instant, taking Alexei into his own arms, barking orders to his men. His eyes met mine for just a moment, curious, grateful. "Who . . ." but he didn't finish his question, looking to the road as a shiny black car plowed through the crowd of battling Narodnaya Volya and soldiers. I recognized the car, remembering my father's lavish collection of vehicles, how on our drives he would command the driver to go faster, faster, faster.

With the arrival of the car, the tsar didn't give me a second glance as he turned abruptly to load his last living child into the automobile, then climbed in himself, slamming the door. And just like that, they were whisked away, leaving behind so much horror, so many bodies, so much blood as they zoomed toward the palace, to doctors, to safety.

I stood at the road's edge, looking down over the canal. The sound of a few stray gunshots pierced the otherwise silent night, the action having died off with the departure of the tsar.

He'd shot him. I still couldn't wrap my head around it. I turned, looking back toward the truck, where Lev and the tsarevich remained trapped. I could have freed them then. The tsar was gone. Alexei was getting help. I could have freed them. But I was numb, unable to think through the weave of rage and shock and grief that overtook me. He'd shot him. The thought kept repeating, an agonizing mantra. He'd shot him.

I stood, unable to clear my mind enough to make a decision, and the decision was made for me. Two men of the Narodnaya Volya rushed to the truck. Throwing open the hatch, one of the men shouted, "Still here!" And then—"Luka? Luka Levich? Didn't know you were here!"

I couldn't hear Lev's reply, but he emerged from the truck, clapping hands with the man who'd greeted him, walking with him around the front of the truck, climbing in to the passenger's seat. The engine roared to life, and the truck moved forward, turning away from the church and lurching down the road. I stood there at the road's edge, staring. Lev was gazing out the window as the truck rolled past, and we locked eyes for just an instant, in a moment of mutual understanding. We'd both made our choices. I held his gaze as I stepped backward, over the edge, plunging into the canal.

I had no fear of the water, not this time. There was only one thing left for me to do, for the only person I had left. *Find him,* Alexei had pleaded. I'd promised. *Take it, and promise you'll find me,* Rasputin had instructed. I'd promised him, too. I had to try.

CHAPTER TWENTY-NINE

"My soul bleeds and the blood steadily, silently, disturbingly slowly, swallows me whole."

—*Complete Letters* by Fyodor Dostoyevsky

H E WAS LOSING BLOOD. Too much blood. Alexei lay across the back seat, his foot propped. Anastasia's hasty tourniquet was doing some good, but not enough. Blood pooled across the leather seat and leaked onto the floor.

"Faster, Orlov, as fast as she'll go!" The tsar turned, looking to the back seat, his face lined with grief, his brow furrowed in concern for his son. "The bleeding will stop soon, son. We'll get you taken care of, my boy."

Alexei closed his eyes. "It won't . . . it won't stop. And when it . . . when it looks like it's stopped . . . it hasn't. Not on the inside."

The tsar was silent for a moment. "Don't be afraid, Alexei. Our doctors are the best." That was all the tsar said for the rest of the car ride. He was in shock, Alexei supposed, having witnessed the brutal, sudden deaths of his daughters. Having been handed his only son, bleeding profusely. How had the night gone so wrong?

The car arrived at the Winter Palace, and things moved quickly. Doors flew open, Alexei was hauled by strangers from the back seat, held over the shoulder of some unknown palace guard, rushed through the halls. And then he found himself supine upon a hospital cot, surrounded by doctors. Had he lost consciousness? It was so loud, all the voices striving to be heard, arguing with one another as to whose methods were best.

As the doctors worked to stop the bleeding, Ana's tourniquet was cast aside, discarded to the floor. Alexei fixed his eyes on the bloody wad of fabric, perhaps his sister's last gift to him, as his vision began to blur. She'd been working to free the tsarevich, to bring him back to the palace, hadn't she? Then she'd abandoned all of that, for Alexei. Did that mean she'd forgiven him? She'd said she did—but did she mean it? She'd done everything she could to save him. She'd promised to find Rasputin.

Rasputin. He could be anywhere, or he could be nowhere. Finding him would be impossible. Still, she'd promised. And she was his sister.

"*I would save our family,*" she had said. "*I would do whatever it took to keep them alive.*"

Alexei allowed his eyes to close, and his thoughts lost coherence, circling around his sister, Rasputin, forgiveness, and remorse.

CHAPTER THIRTY

"Much unhappiness has come into the world because of bewilderment and things left unsaid."

—Fyodor Dostoyevsky

"WELL THAT WAS A bloodbath. We must have lost more than half of our crew." The driver's own face was smeared with blood, one eye swollen, his knuckles bloody as he gripped the steering wheel of the lumbering truck. Glancing toward Lev with his good eye, he let out a sigh. "I didn't know you'd be here, Luka, but I'm glad you are. You just disappeared, man. It's been what, a year? Or longer?"

Lev eyed his new companion warily. Still in shock from what he had witnessed, from what Anastasia had done—it was difficult to muster the presence of mind necessary to navigate the situation he'd found himself in.

This ruse, being Luka, how far could it go? Could he use it to free the tsarevich?

As his mind worked to answer these questions, another unanswerable question continuously interrupted his train of thought. *Why, Anastasia? Why would you do that?*

Keeping his voice low and quiet, in his best impersonation of Luka, Lev returned his companion's gaze. "Over a year, I think." This fellow seemed to have been an acquaintance—maybe even a friend—of Luka's, but was ignorant of his death. Would the others be unaware, as well?

Though Lev tried to focus, his mind kept replaying the image of the cargo door closing, of Anastasia stepping back, disappearing like a ghost, out of his life as peculiarly as she'd entered it.

"Well, it's just us now, and Pyotr, and whoever of Herzen's crew made it. They'll meet us at the base. God. What a nightmare."

A nightmare indeed. Lev shook his head, releasing a heavy exhale. The Grand Duchesses, all dead. So many fallen soldiers, fallen rebels. *So much blood, for nothing . . .* He thought again of Anastasia, cradling her brother in her arms as she jumped from the truck.

"Shame about Ivan, isn't it?" The man's voice was full of disbelief. "I don't suppose you ever got to meet him. But I told him about you. About your theories."

Lev hardly heard him. *She just gave her brother to the tsar, abandoning the true tsarevich. Abandoning me.* He shook his head again. Then, noting the silence in the truck, he saw that the driver was looking over at him expectantly.

"Mm. Yeah. Right," Lev mumbled. *Why, why, why would she have done that?*

"It's certainly fascinating. I thought you'd lost it at first, to be honest, with all your talk about *kolodtsy*." The man gave a short laugh, and then his tone became rather serious. He spoke quietly, as though someone might overhear. "But if they truly do exist, and if they don't have to be gemstones, but anything—you could be right. If magic wasn't really destroyed . . ." He glanced at Lev again as the truck rolled to a stop.

If . . . what? Lev wrenched his mind away from Anastasia, away from the image of her stepping back into the canal below, and looked to the driver curiously. What had Luka discovered?

"That's what Ivan was most interested in," the man continued. "Your theory about the Winter Palace." He raised his brows knowingly, then cut the engine. "Anyway, we're here. Help me unload the kid?"

As Lev's mind raced to make sense of all the driver had said, he squinted out the window, making out the outline of an enormous columned mansion in the moonlight. He noted the familiar courtyard, where just the night before, he'd sprinted for his life, dodging bullets as he made his escape. And from the back of the truck, Lev heard the tsarevich, struggling against his restraints.

There would be time to reflect on Anastasia and to ponder Luka's theories later, but now Lev's duty was clear. He would have to escape the Alexander Palace once again—this time, with the tsarevich in tow. Opening the heavy door, he set his mind on the mission before him and hopped from the truck.

NEVER HAD A group of men looked so out of place as the bedraggled, tattered assortment of surviving rebels who sat gathered in the grandiose entry hall of the Alexander Palace. Their numbers were few—other than Lev, there was the driver of the truck, whom someone had called Kirill, his comrade Pyotr, and four other men who Lev figured to be "Herzen's crew." Lev kept quiet, holding his hands behind his back, observing from the corner of the room as the remaining men of the Narodnaya Volya discussed their next move. The tsarevich remained gagged, tied to a wooden chair positioned in the middle of the room.

There had been a moment of recognition, back in the truck. The tsarevich's eyes had widened when Lev had appeared, and he had known Anastasia's voice. He'd relaxed his brow a bit, relieved, when Lev had started loosening and slashing through the ropes binding his sisters and him.

Lev looked across the room to meet the tsarevich's eyes, now full of confusion and fear, not knowing who to trust. Wishing he could say something to comfort the kid, Lev tried to communicate through his eyes—*I'll get you out of here. I'll get you back to your family. It will be okay.* Perhaps he was imagining it, but Lev thought the boy's shoulders dropped just a bit.

"I say we take him to the door of the Winter Palace, demand to see the tsar, and finish the job."

"Or bring him to the funeral for those girls, that'll be a hot spot of royal *svolochy*."

"No," spoke the more authoritative voice of the bunch, the others quieting to listen. The voice belonged to a hulking man, his frame powerful, his face merciless. A leather patch covered the brute's right eye, adding to his generally menacing effect. "No, St. Petersburg will be hell after tonight. We, and whoever this boy might be, need to get out of the city. Nearly half of our St. Petersburg men were on this mission. Half our men—arrested, scattered, or corpses in the canal." Shaking his head, he spit on the gleaming floor. "Our numbers remain strong in Moscow and in Yekaterinburg. We take the first train out in the morning."

Lev supposed the speaker to be Herzen, as the three men he'd arrived with were nodding in agreement, deferring to his leadership.

Kirill was scowling. "And what, take the little tsarevich look-alike on the train? Wouldn't quite be discreet."

The tsarevich looked up, bewildered.

Herzen shook his head. "We must render him temporarily unrecognizable."

"And how—" but Kirill stopped, as Herzen was stepping toward the tsarevich, tied in his chair. The brute moved rather quickly, delivering a powerful blow to the boy's right eye, immediately followed by a knock to the left. An uppercut to his nose. A final solid knock to his chin. The boy nearly choked on his gag as he reacted, unable to cry out and instead emitting a muffled howl.

Herzen's men cheered, Kirill and Pyotr watching in silence. Lev would have tackled the monster, but Luka? *Would Luka have approved? Would he have stood by as a grown man pummeled an innocent child?* Lev fought to keep his face neutral.

Herzen stepped back to admire his work, then cracked his knuckles as he looked back at Kirill. "This will have swollen nicely by the morning. Unrecognizable." He turned then, looking to each of the men, his eyes pausing briefly on Lev, who remained silent and watchful in the background. "Eight tickets. We leave in the morning." Herzen eyed Kirill, as though awaiting dissent.

Kirill only shrugged. "Fine."

As though securing his role as de facto leader of the mishmashed group, Herzen pointed to Kirill, to Pyotr, to Lev. "You three. Untie the tsarevich, take him to a room. Then tie him, again." He turned to his men. "And you three. Find whatever's in the kitchen. Find some vodka."

No one objected, the men setting about their tasks obediently, perhaps motivated by the prospect of vodka.

And so Lev, Kirill, and Pyotr marched the battered tsarevich from the entry hall. Clapping Lev's shoulder, Kirill snorted. "This place is over the top, isn't it? The worst part is that the imperial *svolochy* don't even live here. Such a waste, while people starve." Grateful that Luka had been a man of few words, Lev merely grunted in reply. Kirill's words were traitorous, but . . . he wasn't wrong. Pushing the conflicting notions from his mind, Lev spoke with his brother's low voice. "Where will we keep the boy?"

It was Pyotr who answered. "Good question. *Pizdets*, Luka, you missed a hell of a day yesterday. Wish we'd had your marksmanship. We had a prisoner here, well, Ivan and Dmitri did. You've heard of Ivan, I take it, and his alliance with Mikhail Romanov?"

Lev nodded tightly. *Someone is going to recognize me. Someone is going to figure it out.*

But Pyotr continued. "Well, the prisoner was some guy Mikhail Romanov sent here—said he had taken the tsarevich from his mansion out there in the Luzhsky. Anyway, the guy killed Ivan, bashed his head in, it was *yobanyy* brutal. Strangled Dmitri. And then he escaped. Got out of the palace without being seen somehow, and then later that night, he goes running across the yard and jumps on a horse. We never found him." Pyotr paused, waiting for some reaction to his unbelievable story.

"*Pizdets*." Luka would have said something like, "Really blew that one."

Kirill laughed sharply. "Indeed. But I think Pyotr's point is, that room is still a bloody *yobanyy* mess. And maybe a bit unlucky. So. We'll keep him close to our own rooms, to be safe, and we have been enjoying the fancy rooms." He gestured down the hall as they arrived at a suite of rooms fit for royalty. In another universe, this palace had been home to the tsar and his family. Would these be the rooms Anastasia and her sisters had grown up in, a world away?

As the men retied the tsarevich in his temporary bedroom, Lev looked to Pyotr. He supposed some amount of curiosity as to the details of Pyotr's story was to be expected. "So this prisoner—what did he look like?"

Pyotr shrugged. "Never saw him. Kirill?"

"I only saw him as he escaped. I shot at him, but I was out of range. Too far, too dark to see his face."

Lev nodded, masking his relief as he knelt by the tsarevich, knotting another rope in place. "And does anyone have any theories as to how he escaped?"

"You want the honest answer?" Kirill raised his eyebrows. "Not a *yo-banyy* clue."

"Hmm." Lev fought the urge to smile, rising to his feet, following Kirill and Pyotr to the door. Lifting the key ring from its hook and locking the door behind him, Lev slipped the key into his pocket. *Too easy. This will be too easy.* He lifted the corner of his mouth in a sarcastic smirk, an expression he'd shared with his twin, though Luka's smile had always seemed a bit more sinister than his own. "Vodka, then?"

CHAPTER THIRTY-ONE

"If thy brother wrongs thee, remember not so much his wrong-doing, but more than ever that he is thy brother."

—Epictetus

I POPPED MY HEAD OUT of the water, sucking in a breath of air and noting the growing distance between myself and the church before ducking beneath the water again. I walked my hands along the canal wall as I kicked my feet. Just a bit farther. I needed to get to Molniya. Then I would give it a try.

I hadn't noticed the sensation at first. When I'd taken the garnet from Alexei and placed it around my neck, I'd been in such a hurry, such a panic. But now, as I crept through the water along the canal wall, I couldn't deny the pull. It was as though the garnet in my pocket was drawing the garnet around my neck toward it, like a magnet. Surely something magical would happen if I brought them together, right? It was a desperate hope, but these twin *kolodtsy*, the magic, Rasputin—they were all connected, weren't they?

I came up again for air, tracking my progress toward Molniya's hitch by looking back toward the church. My eyes widened at what I saw. What were those men doing, climbing down to the canal? Swearing silently, I craned my neck to look out over the water's surface and noticed the empty low boats floating, awaiting their captains. Though I had a decent head start, the men would catch up to me quickly once they started rowing. In the darkness, I couldn't tell if they were soldiers or Narodnaya Volya, and at that moment, I wasn't sure which would be worse.

Lowering myself farther into the water, I sunk my chin and mouth beneath the surface so that I could still breathe through my nose. And I watched. If I kept completely still, if I stayed silent in the shadows, perhaps they would not see me as they rowed past.

The men moved soundlessly, down the wall, into the boats—there were more boats than men. They would come back for the bodies, then. So many bodies.

I realized I was crying, my tears mixing into the murky water of the canal. It had been the second time I'd seen them die—Olga, Tatiana, and Maria. The second time that men—men who didn't know them—somehow confused the murder of innocent girls with political justice. I cried for my sisters, for these versions of them that had existed here in this world. For all the girls, in all the worlds, who suffered at the hands of self-righteous men.

I cried for my brother, who had lost so much blood. Who would still be bleeding. Who had survived so much, against all odds, to likely die from a completely avoidable gunshot. And I cried for Lev. I had found peace, comfort, a connection to this bizarre world in him. But he'd shot him. He'd shot Alexei. He'd *yobanyy* shot him. Perhaps all we'd had was a shared mission. And now we didn't have that. So, we had nothing.

There was sadness in my tears, and frustration, and guilt, but mostly I cried in anger. I was so angry—at my brother, for risking his life for his stupid throne. At Lev, for shooting the gun, for clapping hands with those murderers and riding away in their truck. I was angry at the Bolsheviks, in my own world, for what they'd done to my family. Angry at my parents, for not having seen it coming. Angry at myself, for thinking I could save them, for thinking that this world would be any different.

The most angering part of it all was that I didn't know who to blame. All of the horrible things that happened were everyone's fault. And no one's.

Was it simply that the world—all the worlds—were inherently terrible? Was it that *people*—all of them—are irredeemably flawed?

I wanted to see the goodness in the world. I wanted to see the best in people. But there had been so much violence. So much hatred. So many lives lost.

As the men rowed by, moving slowly, dragging the empty boats along with ropes, the moonlight caught the silver buttons of a black coat. Soldiers, then. They held lanterns, even a few flashlights, and were scanning the water, looking for rebels as their boats crept along. The nearest boat couldn't have been more than ten meters away, close enough that I could hear the soldiers' swearing, cursing the Narodnaya Volya as they rowed.

"What's that, there?" One of the soldiers lifted his lantern in my direction. Had I been seen? I took a deep breath and plunged beneath the water, creating a small splash but hopefully disappearing from view. Perhaps they'd think me a large fish, splashing to the surface for a midnight snack. Underwater, I found the wall with my hands again and kept moving.

How long could I hold my breath? I had to make it to Molniya, to somewhere safe, where I could bring out the garnets. It was just a trace of a plan, but with some time to think, I could figure it out. It would work. It had to.

Twenty seconds underwater.

Alexei told me to find Rasputin. And what had Lev said? Rasputin had to be findable. It would work, it had to, if I could just make it out of the canal.

Forty seconds . . . I needed air.

Slowly, carefully, I raised my mouth to the water's surface, tipping my head back to stay as low as possible and looking through the water to the dark sky above.

The soft light of the moon illuminated the blurry edges of storm clouds, the outlines of tall pines, the onion-domed towers of the church—and the silhouette of a wooden paddle gripped by burly hands, raised high above me, then crashing down, striking me square in the face. And then I saw nothing at all.

IMAGES OF THE St. Petersburg streets, bleary through my heavy lashes, weaved into the blackness. There were voices—loud, angry voices, coming from behind me.

Wrenching my eyes open, I made to sit up, but I found that my wrists and ankles had been tied. My aching body was strewn across the passenger's seat of a large cargo carriage.

"The girl's awake," the driver told his companion.

"Fine. If she tries anything, I'll toss her back with the others."

"Oh, they'd tear her apart. We're almost to the Fortress anyway. See, there's the bridge, just ahead."

My head was pounding, my eyes begging to be closed. But the words shocked me to alertness. The Fortress? The Peter and Paul Fortress? The prison was a legendary horror, a setting for nightmares.

I had absolutely zero interest in visiting the place, much less being locked up within. And more importantly, the garnet beneath my dress and the garnet in my pocket still pulled toward one another, as though begging me to bring them together, promising me that *something* would happen. I had to try it. Before I could consider the uselessness of argument, I opened my mouth.

"Excuse me, but I am not in any way associated with the Narodnaya *yobanyy* Volya. You can't just arrest me for no reason!"

The driver kept his eyes on the road as we bumped across the long bridge to the creepy little island where the prison stood. "Just taking a midnight swim, then, were you?" He didn't wait for an answer, laughing as he glanced at his companion. "Water's high, we ought to get in and out of here before the storm rolls in." A gale of wind swept through the pines, as if on cue.

His companion only grunted in reply, swiftly grabbing me by the head and stuffing a wadded rag in my mouth as I continued to protest. Thrashing my tied wrists and bound ankles, I screamed into the gag—but it was useless. There was no one around, just the driver and his companion and a cargo carriage full of angry rebels, plucked from the streets as they fled from the church. As the winds grew stronger, the carriage bumped along the road, bound for the fortress prison.

CHAPTER THIRTY-TWO

"The law of self-destruction and the law of self-preservation are equally strong in mankind!"

—*The Idiot* by Fyodor Dostoyevsky

I N THE DARKNESS OF the dungeon, Mikhail paced, unable to sleep as he awaited his trial. He presumed it to be nighttime still as no breakfast had yet arrived, but it was impossible to track the hours as they crept by. The hostage exchange would be happening, or would have already happened— would the girls have been brought back to the Winter Palace? Could they serve as his witnesses, yet? Would this mystery of the two Alexeis have been resolved?

The uncertainty made him uneasy. His nieces and nephew in danger, his brother blackmailed—he didn't like it, not any of it, now that it was happening. In theory, forcing his brother to abdicate the throne had sounded noble, the right way to enact change. His brother and their late father were ancient relics, stone statues, unwilling to embrace progress in an ever-changing world, an ever-changing Russia.

Yes, Mikhail told himself, *the time has come for tsarism to end. And I can do it, while preserving the Romanov legacy.* But to do so by risking his nieces? It had been one thing keeping them at Ivan's family home in Luga.

It was quite another now that Ivan was dead. *"His head was beaten in by the prisoner you sent us,"* the man had said. Mikhail shuddered. *What have I gotten myself into?*

Loud footsteps echoed through the empty dungeon, tearing Mikhail from his pondering. Leaning into the bars of the cell door, he craned his neck to see who was approaching. His brows shot upward at the sight of his brother, storming through the long hall. The tsar appeared before the cell, dressed in black, blood on his boots. His face was severe and fuming with rage.

"Tell me what you know." Nicholas spoke with a quiet resolve, a steely surface beneath which fury boiled.

Taken aback, Mikhail raised his brows. "What I know?"

"Tell me what you know about the Narodnaya Volya. I know you are connected with them. I am not blind. But I had not perceived them to be a threat." Nicholas cleared his throat, a look of heartbreaking pain crossing over his face for just a moment before it passed, replaced by cold ruthlessness. "My daughters are dead. Killed by the traitors you patronize. You will tell me what you know."

Mikhail could only stare, stunned. *No. It wasn't possible. Not his nieces, no, Ivan had said . . .* Mikhail looked to the floor. Ivan was dead. His nonviolent revolution was dead. His nieces . . . they were dead. His head was spinning, unable to process the news. Everything he had worked for, planned for, sacrificed for . . . had it all been so fragile? Had the Narodnaya Volya's union shattered when Ivan died? Had the group devolved to its former chaotic self, more interested in murder than meaningful change? An act of such violence certainly suggested such. They'd believed in Ivan, and Ivan had believed in Mikhail, in a new Romanov dynasty with a constitution and a parliament. He'd believed in accomplishing these things without bloodshed. It had been within reach, and then . . . then it had fallen apart. With Ivan's death, the group had unraveled. In less than a day, it had all fallen apart. *And my nieces . . . dear God.*

"I-I am sorry, brother." Mikhail looked up, meeting Nicholas's eyes, finding them devoid of the humor and compassion that had been his brother

—not the tsar, but his brother. "I'm sorry." His voice cracked, the magnitude of Nicholas's words landing upon his shoulders, nearly dropping him to his knees.

"If you are sorry, if you ever loved my daughters, you will tell me. Tell me their numbers. Tell me their leaders. Tell me where I will find them."

Mikhail's head was pounding, a battle of guilt and anger and fear raging within his mind as his world crumbled around him. He'd put his faith in this volatile group. He'd risked everything. And he truly had no idea what they might be plotting.

"Their numbers . . . I do not know. But they are vast, across Russia, in the cities, in the countryside."

The tsar appeared unsatisfied. "My men have recovered thirty bodies, thirty dead traitors from the scene at the church. Are there more in this city?"

Mikhail let out a low sigh. Thirty men. "Yes, there are more. I don't know how many. I think perhaps . . . perhaps one hundred operative men. Minus the thirty."

"Leaders?"

"I didn't know their names. I corresponded only with a man called Ivan. And he is dead. Killed yesterday . . . by your man."

Nicholas raised his brows, as though to ask *what* man, but he would not detour from his interrogation. He stared at Mikhail coldly, clearly frustrated with his brother's lack of information.

Love of family, love of country. Pride in the Romanov name, pride in himself. Mikhail was conflicted, wishing to tell his brother everything, wishing to preserve the revolution, wishing his wishes didn't directly oppose one another.

"There are several crews, each with a leader. Perhaps four or five in St. Petersburg. Ivan, he was the leader of one of these crews, and sort of the leader of the whole group. He was charismatic, he united the group, he wanted to . . ." Mikhail trailed off, Nicholas's stony face displaying how little he cared to hear praises of a dead traitor. Mikhail tried again. "Ivan's crew, they were operating out of the Alexander Palace."

Nicholas's face darkened. "The Alexander Palace. Our cousin Sergei, then, would be involved. Have you any other names for me?"

Mikhail opened his mouth to respond, closed it again. Guilt for his nieces, love for his brother, skepticism of this Ivan-less Narodnaya Volya—these feelings conflicted with his loyalty to his ideals, his certainty that change *must* come. All he could do was choose which side of history he resided on.

The tsar found his answer in Mikhail's tormented silence. "I see." He turned, moving slowly but purposefully as he left his brother's cell. "For your association with the traitors who have murdered my daughters, you will spend the remainder of your days imprisoned. Prepare to be moved to the Peter and Paul Fortress."

Mikhail gaped. "You would . . . you would send me *there*?"

Nicholas paused mid-step, looking back at his brother. "You. Your wife. Every person in this city found to have any connection with the traitorous murderers. I will find you all." And then he was gone, and Mikhail crumpled to the floor in sorrow, for all he'd said, for all he hadn't. He broke down in pity, for himself, for his brother, for Russia. Because whatever would happen next would surely punish them all.

CHAPTER THIRTY-THREE

"I have outlasted all desire, my dreams and I have grown apart; my grief alone is left entire, the gleamings of an empty heart."

—Alexander Pushkin

S HIVERING IN A POOL of his own sweat, Alexei thrashed in his sleep, images of a night lit by explosions and screaming mixing with memories of a quiet cellar with his family, waiting, waiting, and then he was in Spala, certain he was dying.

Spala. Where the hemophilia had almost taken him, where he had spent weeks in agony as he'd bled internally, a case beyond the capabilities of the best doctors in all of Russia. In his mind, he was there again, his blood a rushing river overflowing its basin, flooding his joints, his body erupting with unimaginable pain. As he'd floated in and out of consciousness, he'd seen his mother—or had he been dreaming of her? —standing over his bedside, praying, cursing, stroking his sweaty hair. And then he'd heard the door open, and his mother's voice, *"Oh thank God!"* A strong hand had laid upon his chest, and he'd felt those eyes, penetrating his skin, his veins, and everything had slowed. The rushing river became like mud, too much blood to absorb, still, but it was as though those eyes had found the source, tightened the spigot.

Alexei awakened, the memory fresh in his mind, and he tried to recreate the feeling. To tighten the spigot, to muddy the river, to stop the bleeding. But it was useless without Rasputin. So he thought of his mother, his father, and his sisters. He thought of their trips to Livadiya, cruising the sea on the family yacht. And as he slipped out of consciousness again, he clung to these thoughts, and they became his dreams, and for a while, he slept peacefully.

CHAPTER THIRTY-FOUR

"Man lives consciously for himself, but is an unconscious instrument in the attainment of the historic, universal, aims of humanity."

—Leo Tolstoy

THE VODKA HAD BEEN plentiful, and the men all too eager to numb their senses, to drown the evening's losses in drink. *I wouldn't mind a stiff drink, myself,* Lev thought as he downed the remaining water in his vodka glass and set it on the table, looking around the entrance hall, observing the unconscious men. Kirill and Pyotr were sprawled across an expensive-looking sofa while Herzen slouched in a stuffed chair. His men were passed out on the floor amongst an empty bottle and toppled glasses. Snoring, for now.

Lev stood, stepping over one of Herzen's sleeping men as he quietly moved across the room toward the entry.

He backed up to the threshold. And then he walked, counting the steps as each boot hit the marble floor, remembering when to turn, tracing his steps through the hall, up the stairs to the room that had been his luxurious prison, the room where he'd strangled a man, the room that housed the metal trunk.

The secret passage. *Anastasia's passage.*

As he made the walk, unblindfolded this time, he took in the elegance and extravagance of the halls and rooms as he passed. Kirill hadn't been wrong. The Alexander Palace was over the top, and it wasn't even the tsar's home. *How many palaces, how many opulent homes, and cars, and boats . . . how much of Russia's wealth has been utterly wasted over the centuries?*

Lev pushed the thought from his mind. The tsar was entitled to such luxuries, wasn't he? He and his family. The tsar was chosen by God. The tsar was Russia incarnate. Was he not?

Anastasia's words, spoken in the dungeon beneath the Winter Palace days ago—*God, had it only been days?*—echoed in his mind. *"My family had developed many enemies over the years,"* she'd said. *"People who . . . didn't like the way we lived."*

Yes, Anastasia, he thought. *The way your family lived—it was wrong in your world and it is wrong in this world. But so were the men who imprisoned your family, who killed them, in your world. And the men who kidnapped the tsarevich, killed the Grand Duchesses, in this world. All of it, all of it is wrong.*

Lev was disturbed by these thoughts, having always considered himself a patriot. He'd embraced tsarism despite his brother's passionate opposition—or maybe even because of it. Luka's rambling about a Russia without tsars had been as mad as his obsession with *kolodtsy*, hadn't it?

But he was right about the kolodtsy, Lev thought, picturing the garnet in its iron box. *And Kirill had said . . . what had he said? That Ivan had been interested in Luka's theories that magic could be contained in anything. That magic was never destroyed. And . . . something about the Winter Palace?*

Lev shook his head. However valid Luka's thoughts about magic may or may not have been, he'd been absolutely wrong to support the Narodnaya Volya.

There was no justification for such ruthless violence. But while Lev certainly didn't support the rebels, it was also difficult to justify such wastefulness, such excess as he witnessed then. He thought of his own cabin, where his mother had worked endlessly to scrape by, to keep her boys fed and warm. There had to be a better way. Better than the savage methods of the

Narodnaya Volya. And better than people starving, while golden vases gathered dust in unused palaces.

He glanced down to the vase in his hands, having mindlessly taken it from atop the dresser, the drawers still splattered with blood. On an impulse, he stuck the vase in his jacket. Politics aside, his mission remained the same. An innocent child was held prisoner in this palace and now was the time to free him and escape. And one never knows when one might need a golden trinket to trade, when on the run.

Lev peeked in the closet, ensuring that the trunk remained undiscovered. It seemed that if anyone noticed it, they hadn't thought to look inside. The bloody footprints from the bed to the door, where Anastasia had stomped his empty boot across the room, remained the rebels' only clue as to how their murderous prisoner had escaped.

Taking one last glance around the room, Lev exited, closing the door behind him. The tsarevich would be right where he'd left him, tied to his chair, locked in his room. Lev felt for the room key in his pocket, his fingers closing around the jagged metal and he walked, more briskly this time. This rescue needed to happen quickly.

Arriving at the tsarevich's room, Lev slid the key into the lock, and as he opened the door, he held a finger to his lips, meeting the boy's swollen eyes. "Sshhh, I'm going to get you out of here." The tsarevich tried to smile, rather unsuccessfully given his busted lip and bloodied chin, but Lev smiled back and set to work slashing the ropes, removing the gag.

"I knew you were—"

"Sshhh!" Lev rolled his eyes. *Perhaps I should have left the gag.*

The tsarevich attempted a sort of apologetic face, his face too damaged from Herzen's blows to show much expression, and then whispered, "I knew you were a good guy—not just because you tried to set me free, back in the truck—but you were in my uncle's forest, too. With Anastasia."

At the sound of her name, Lev winced slightly but nodded. "I have a way out. Don't say a word, move as quietly as you can, and stay close to me. Got it?"

The boy stood, stretching his limbs. "Got it."

The two moved stealthily from the room, Lev locking the door behind him, pocketing the key. The second story corridors remained quiet, empty, as the men slept in the entrance hall below. *We made it.* They arrived at their destination, and the tsarevich dropped his jaw as he took in the blood-stained floor, the room in disarray.

"My gosh, what happ—"

"SSSHHH!" Lev was beginning to think it had been quite miraculous that he'd made it through the halls with this clueless kid without getting caught—but through the passageway? Away from the Narodnaya Volya stronghold, to St. Petersburg? Into the Winter Palace? Would he be able to explain to the tsarevich why they must sneak into the boy's own home—that there was another Alexei who must be snuck out?

There was no turning back now. Lev lit a candle and opened the trunk. He stomped the trapdoor open, cringing at its noisiness, and gestured toward the opening. "Go on," he whispered. "Climb down, I'll be right behind you."

The tsarevich widened his blackened eyes, surprised, unsure as to the wisdom of climbing into a dark hole with a near-stranger, but seemed to arrive at the conclusion that there was no better alternative and began the climb. Lev followed, closing the lid behind them. He breathed a sigh of relief as he descended into the darkness, the murder scene disappearing from view.

"Well, it's Lev, if you'd forgotten. And this passage will take us out of here, but we'll need to be quiet and quick and smart. The others had quite a bit of vodka and are sleeping for now. But we can't be too careful. Someone could wake up. More Narodnaya Volya could arrive. Do you understand?" Lev leaned against the wall for a moment, unweighting his wounded leg.

"I do . . . but . . . you must tell me. Um, I couldn't see very well, in the truck. But, my sisters . . . are they . . . ?"

Lev swallowed. He couldn't risk the tsarevich getting emotional, acting in anger, doing something stupid. Something risky. He clapped the boy on the shoulder. "I'll tell you everything you need to know, but we need to get out of here first. Come on."

Down the tunnel. Lev silently saluted the unknown corpse as they passed, but didn't mention his presence to the tsarevich. There was no time for distraction.

Through the entry. Lev boosted the tsarevich through, then climbed out himself. Still no sign of anyone stirring in the palace.

Along the wall, across the yard, to the road, meeting only empty quiet. But as they reached the road, the sound of galloping horses interrupted the stillness of the night. Lev stepped back into the trees, pulling the tsarevich with him, and crouched low as he tried to discern who approached. The uniforms, the horses, the emblem on the carriages—they were the tsar's men. They'd learned of the Alexander Palace then. Of the Narodnaya Volya's ironic stronghold.

The tsarevich recognized the men as soldiers too and opened his mouth to call out to them. But Lev clapped his hand over the boy's mouth, feeling more like a kidnapper than a liberator as he restrained him, pulling him along, farther from his father's regiment.

"I'll explain later, I promise," Lev whispered, "but we have to get away from here." *Right? Or should I just drop him with the tsar's men, call it a night? Let them sort out which Alexei is which?* That didn't feel right, either. Herzen had rendered the boy nearly unrecognizable, especially in comparison to the Alexei in the Winter Palace, who had been playing tsarevich, fooling the tsar and tsarina for days. No, it could be bad for the young tsarevich to stray from the plan. And it could be bad for the other Alexei, evil little *zasranets* he may be, but . . . Lev thought of Anastasia's face as she scooped her brother into her arms. "*You* shot *him*?!" She had sounded so horror-stricken, appearing genuinely frightened for his life, as though Lev's calf wound had shown her nothing about the nonfatality of a bullet to the lower leg.

"Come on." Lev pulled the tsarevich along through the trees.

"But they're looking for me, aren't they? They've come for me." The tsarevich kept his voice down at least.

Lev supposed they would have to talk and walk, as he didn't see how he could delay the explanation any longer. "They . . . they aren't looking for you. There's . . ." *How do I tell the kid that he's been replaced?* "There's another boy. A boy who looks just like you. He's in the palace. Pretending to be you."

Even with his face swollen, bloody, bruised, the tsarevich looked utterly appalled. "You're joking, surely. My parents wouldn't fall for that."

"I'm not joking."

"And even if they did, they'd know when they see *me*, and the imposter would go to prison."

Lev sighed. "That's the other thing. The imposter is . . ." *Do I tell him it's Anastasia's brother? Would he care?* ". . . someone I have to protect. I've rescued you from the rebels. Can you just . . . trust me on this? When we get to the Winter Palace, I need to sneak you in and sneak him out. Then you can tell your parents whatever you want, just let me get the boy away from the Winter Palace first. Will you do that for me?"

The boy paused to think. "I suppose I owe you."

Lev relaxed his shoulders a bit. *Thank God.* Then he swallowed, remembering the other truth he had promised to share. It could wait, though, couldn't it? It could wait until they were farther from the Narodnaya Volya. It could wait until the tsarevich asked again.

The sun neared the horizon, the overcast sky lightening to a pinkish gray as the two moved out from the trees to the empty streets of Tsarskoye Selo. On foot, the journey to St. Petersburg would take around five hours, Lev supposed.

A journey he didn't look forward to, as his wounded calf still throbbed. He thought of Molniya, wondering if Anastasia had ever made it to the horse. Wondering where she'd gone.

Lev pushed Anastasia from his mind. Pushed the pain in his leg from his mind. And he walked, the tsarevich trekking along beside him as a light drizzle thickened into a steady rain, washing away the blood from the boy's face. The blood, but not the sorrow. Though the tsarevich hadn't asked again, he clearly knew his sisters were dead. Lev could tell from the way the boy carried himself, the way he trudged onward, determined but deflated. It was a feeling familiar to Lev, as he wrestled with his own sentiments toward tsarism and the rebels, as he struggled to understand why Anastasia had done what she'd done, and as despite it all, he continued on his mission. Onward, to the Winter Palace.

CHAPTER THIRTY-FIVE

"Prisons are universities of crime, maintained by the state."

—*Russian and French Prison* by Peter Kropotkin

A S THE SOLDIERS MARCHED me through the dark, damp hallways of the Peter and Paul Fortress, the garnets still pulled toward one another. And to my immense surprise, the cold metal of Dmitri's gun still pressed against my leg, tucked into my stocking. In fact, I was more disturbed than delighted by this discovery, as it was no testament to the capability of the tsar's soldiers, nor the prison guards charged with confining the Narodnaya Volya. While I needed to bust out of the wretched place, I quite hoped that the violent rebels shouting in the hallway behind me would rot in their cells.

My head was still pounding, aching from its encounter with the paddle, and churning with conflicting notions as to what I should do. I could try to draw the gun, wrists bound as they were, but the guards had guns too and were certainly more adept at using them. Would I have another chance to escape? My mind wrestled itself as I trudged through the prison.

"Found this one in the canal." The soldier shoved me toward a pair of prison guards, who assumed me as their charge.

"Just a girl, eh?" The younger of the two took hold of my bound wrists with firm, clammy hands.

His partner scowled. "Not *just a girl*, Kozma. A murdering traitor. Haven't you heard what these people did?" The stocky guard's voice was full of disgust, seemingly in agreement with the tsar that anyone associated with the traitorous group deserved the grimmest of fates.

Through my gag, I tried to protest. But my words were indecipherable yowling.

"Of course, the poor Grand Duchesses. Still . . . a girl? *Here?*" The younger guard—Kozma—eyed me with something like pity.

"From what I hear, he's tracking down the whole lot of them, the rebels, anyone associated with them. Told us to expect a full prison by nightfall tomorrow."

Kozma's face whitened. "A full prison?" he repeated. Perhaps he was imagining, as I was, what atrocities might befall a young woman in a crowded prison. Perhaps he was doubting the morality of tossing a girl into a prison full of dangerous criminals. I memorized his face—brown eyes, boyish chubby cheeks, sandy blonde hair cut short, accentuating the largeness of his head. I took a mental photograph and stored it away in a new file in my mind, labeled "possible allies."

As we arrived at an empty cell, the stocky guard pulled a key ring from his coat, opening the door as Kozma nudged me forward into my new lodgings. Frowning, Kozma closed the gate behind me and locked it. "She should remain in a solitary cell, to preserve . . . decency."

"Decency?" The other guard spat on the floor. "None of these people deserve decency. And there won't be room, anyhow." A horn sounded. "There's another load of prisoners now."

As the two left me, Kozma continued, "A women's cell then, at least, if there are more." The other guard grumbled something in reply, but I could no longer hear them, could no longer hear anything but silence and rain, pouring heavily against the cell's small window, washing away my optimism, drowning my hopes for escape. For finding Rasputin and saving my brother.

IT WAS NOW or never. I knelt in the corner of the cell, my back to the barred door. Taking a deep breath, I drew the iron box from my pocket. It was heavy for its size, but at the same time, strangely delicate. I struggled to work the tight latch, breaking the clasp in my haste. This was it. I opened the box.

There it was, a dark red gemstone identical to the one around my own neck, its many sides gleaming in turn, dancing in the lantern light flickering from the hallway. A *kolodets*, a well for magic, infused with power by Rasputin himself.

The inside of the box was iron too and sat much shallower than the box itself, the center having been shaped into a little alcove to display the gemstone. Fascinated, I tugged at the thin gold chain, lifting the garnet from its nook. With my other hand, I lifted my own necklace overhead and held the two to the light, the twin garnets gently swinging. The pull between the gemstones grew stronger, as though the magic recognized itself in the other and craved reunion. A soft otherworldly hum filled the air, surrounding me, moving through me.

I took a gemstone in each hand, grasped between my forefinger and thumb, and I closed my eyes for a moment. It was time. My breath caught in my chest as I brought the two garnets together, touching.

And then I opened my eyes. Nothing had happened. There was the hum—quiet but perceptible. And there were the gemstones, gently reaching toward one another. Nothing had happened. I wasn't sure what I had expected to happen, but I had thought surely . . . surely something. I let out a sigh, closed the two necklaces in my fist, and grabbed the iron box from the floor. Bleakly disappointed.

As I grabbed the box, the inside shifted slightly. Strange. I pried at the edge, and the iron inlay lifted up from the box, exposing a second layer, identical, empty. A nook for my own garnet. I dropped each gemstone into its home, acknowledging the confirmation of what I'd already guessed. Rasputin had indeed used the magic of this world to empower the gemstones.

Then he'd left this world, bound for my own, and given the garnet to me. But why?

I was frustrated and dismayed and at a loss for what to do next. I hadn't even realized what I was doing, but I found myself prying at that second layer, where my garnet sat snug in its nook. The iron sheet popped from the box. And beneath it, lay a third, final layer at the bottom of the box. Another iron inlay, another empty alcove, just the size for a gemstone. A third garnet, missing. Too depressed to theorize, I restacked the inlays, two filled, one empty, and closed the box. Pocketed it. That was it, then. Nothing. Of course nothing had happened. What had I thought? That I'd rub a couple of gemstones together and summon Rasputin? I pressed my palm to my forehead, sinking into despair when the whooping and clapping of my fellow prisoners disrupted my self-pity.

"Down with the tsar!" A booming voice was followed by more cheers and then a loud *crack*. The overwhelming smells of vodka and vomit overtook my senses as the new arrivals were pushed past my cell, the six prisoners outnumbered doubly by guards. A towering man with a commanding presence and an eyepatch looked at me with his single eye as he lumbered past and spat blood, splattering the bars of my cell. "Down with the tsar!" He shouted again, his cry met with another round of cheers from the prisoners and another loud, bloody *crack* as the guards struck him across the jaw. The prisoners passed, leaving a drippy trail of muddied rainwater in their wake.

Moments later, the prisoners erupted in noisiness again, an even mix of applause and jeers. Through a horde of guards, I spotted a single prisoner this time, and though he hung his head, I recognized him instantly. It was my Uncle Mikhail—this world's version of him, anyway. He responded to neither the shouts of support nor the beratements as he shuffled along, looking quite defeated.

Lev's words, spoken in the forest of the Luzhsky Uyezd, echoed in my mind. *"That Mikhail still lives is testament that the tsar has no idea how deeply involved his brother has become. Well, perhaps until now."* Yes, the tsar would know now that his own brother was a traitor. That the rebels had become a true threat. That they would act mercilessly. And he was responding. I wondered again how my own father might have responded differently when the Bolsheviks emerged. If there was something he could have done that would have saved us.

I became used to the commotion that arose from the prisoners with each batch of men paraded through the hall and settled into the solitude of my own cell, as Kozma's instruction had thus far been upheld. Slumping against the cold damp stone wall, I allowed my eyes to close as my mind swam with incoherent images. Bombs and bullets and bodies exploding. Maria's face, smiling and then screaming. My own hands bashing a man's head with a rifle. My little brother dying in a pool of blood. The images swirled as I faded in and out of consciousness, lulled by the sound of continuous rain.

I JUMPED, STARTLED by the jingling of a key in a lock and the creak of rusted hinges as the cell door inched open. It was Kozma. But he hadn't come for me. He was delivering another prisoner to my cell.

The prisoner was heavily cloaked, their hooded face hidden in the shadows. I squinted, trying to discern something about my new cellmate by the dim light of Kozma's candle. Could it be Rasputin? Had I summoned him, after all?

Kozma stepped aside, ushering the mysterious prisoner into the cell wordlessly. I tried to make eye contact, but he kept his eyes on the new arrival until the gate was closed, the lock in place. He looked to me briefly then, through the bars. His face was grim, as though it had been a long night. Young—he couldn't have been a prison guard for long. How had he arrived at such a bleak post? I opened my mouth to speak—as I often did, without quite knowing what words might come out—but he turned and was gone. And so I was alone with the enigma who stood before me.

"Is it—is it you?" The question escaped my mouth before I could think to stop myself. Oh, how I hoped it was him. It was a hope founded in nothing but desperation, in the notion that I was due for something to go right.

Tossing back the hood, the cloaked figure shook out long chestnut locks and puffed out her chest as she appraised the cell. The woman was quite beautiful and seemed to be unshaken by the unfavorable circumstances she'd arrived in. "It is me, indeed, though doubtfully the 'me' you meant." She smiled, as though entertained by her own wit, and looked me up and down in assessment. "I'd hoped to be jailed with my husband, but I suppose I could have landed a much worse cellmate than you."

I sighed. Definitely not Rasputin.

"Oh, cheer up, pretty darling. It's all happening now. I knew I married Mikhail for a reason."

I blinked, taken aback, and stammered, "Don't call me—what all is hap—wait—Mikhail? Mikhail Romanov? He's your husband?" She certainly wasn't the Aunt Natalia I'd known in my own world.

The woman rolled her eyes, misinterpreting my surprise for veneration. "You indeed find yourself in the presence of a Romanov. But no need to bow. Nor spit, for that matter." She cocked her head to the side. "You can call me Dina. And you are?"

No one, I might have said, had she asked me two days ago. But I was through with that nonsense. I puffed myself up, lifting my chin to look down my nose at this self-proclaimed Romanov.

"I'm Anastasia," I answered.

She smiled then, catlike, and purred, "Pleased to meet you, Anastasia. And tell me, Anastasia, which side of this divide do you find yourself on?"

It was my turn to raise my brows. "Divide? You mean, do I stand with the tsar or the rebels?"

Dina scoffed. "If you stood with the tsar, I should hardly imagine you'd be *here.*" She laughed. "Unless the monster is throwing everyone into prison, which is quite possible."

I kept my face neutral, waiting in stony silence for some elaboration.

"This divide, this chasm that threatens the success of our revolution. Do you stand with the violent idiots who murdered my darling nieces? Who simultaneously managed to cast us as villains in the hearts of the people, while failing to eradicate the tsar?" She scowled, shaking her head indignantly. "Or"—she reset her face, smiling once again—"do you stand with Mikhail and his grand vision for a new Russia, in which a representative government works *with* the tsar?"

It was rather clear on which side of this divide Dina found herself. Perhaps it would have been best just to agree with her, but I blurted out questions of my own. "A representative government working with the tsar. And how does that work? The tsar, if you weren't aware, is not looking to forfeit his div—" *his divine right to rule*, I'd almost said. I didn't suppose that would go over well. "His power."

"Right you are. And that is precisely why this tsar's reign must end."

I opened my mouth to protest, but she rolled her eyes, waving her hand dismissively, and continued. "Don't be naïve. Tsars come and go, do they not? They get themselves blown up, they die of illness, some make it to old age, but still they die. And so it is silly to place so much power in the hands of one mortal man."

"It . . . well I wouldn't say it's silly. It's hundreds of years—"

"Hundreds of years of subjugation! Of the few, living in opulence, dining lavishly, and laughing carelessly while the masses starve. You're right. It isn't silly. It is wrong."

For a moment, I could only stare. People truly thought that way? They thought our family didn't care about the people? That we laughed while they starved? My kind father, my loving mother, my sweet sisters—never in any world would they be that cruel. That they were so hated was heartbreaking and unfair and infuriating. Still holding Dina's gaze, I narrowed my eyes and scoffed.

"You may call yourself a Romanov, but you know nothing of the tsar. He's a good man. He would never—"

"A good man? Pah!" Her expression grew cold. "Goodness does not matter. Intentions do not matter. Results are what matter, and the results of this lavish tsardom are poverty and suffering. The right tsar would see that and use his power to disperse it to the people."

I rolled my eyes. "That's insane. You actually believe that goodness doesn't matter?"

Dina paused, appraising me once again. "Think of the worst thing anyone has ever done to you."

I didn't want to appease her. But my mind began listing the betrayals before I could stop it. The guards and the execution. Alexei and his note. Most recently, Lev, firing that gun.

"Now imagine that awful thing was done with *good intentions*," she continued. "Does that make it all better?"

I opened my mouth then closed it, thinking of Lev. He hadn't known about the hemophilia. He saw my brother about to transport his tsarevich to another dimension, and he stopped it. He'd done what he'd done with good intentions. And no, that did not make it all better. But . . . it mattered.

Misinterpreting my silence, Dina smiled. "Exactly." Then she launched into her grandiose manifesto once again. "It is time for Russia to evolve, to grow beyond the nineteenth century. The tsar shall remain as a figurehead. A symbol. A beacon of hope, inspiration, and unity for Russia. But the power, the power mustn't reside with one man, rather with an ever-evolving governing body chosen by the people, serving the people."

She paused, looking me up and down. "Who are you, Anastasia?" By the way she examined me, she didn't have to say "*because you clearly aren't with the Narodnaya Volya.*"

Who am I? A worried sister, who just wanted her brother by her side. An ex-princess of another world, who just wanted her family to live. I sighed. "I'm just someone who is here by mistake. Wrong place at the wrong time."

Her face changed, the look of wary suspicion morphing into callous disregard, as she seemed to sense the truth in my words and apparently found my answer quite boring. "Shame. Well, you've chosen an awful time to get yourself locked up in prison." Her eyes moved around the cell, up and down the damp stone walls to the barred window that separated us from the storm outside, appraising. In a brief moment of transparency, her nostrils flared and her eyes widened, as though an alarming thought had just occurred to her. Just as quickly, her face resumed a mask of arrogant indifference. "But fear not. We don't intend to be here long."

Dina then peeled off her cloak, folded it into a neat pillow, and turned, bringing her hand to a rounded belly, as though to indicate just who she meant by "we."

CHAPTER THIRTY-SIX

"My dreams, my dreams! What has become of their sweetness? What indeed has become of my youth?"

—*Eugene Onegin* by Alexander Pushkin

I N THE EARLY HOURS of the morning, Mikhail found himself curled on the floor of a different cell—smaller, dirtier, and damper than the palace dungeon. Blood oozed from his lip. His ribs ached. His head throbbed.

"Perhaps you'll fare better in a solitary cell . . ." The guard trailed off, as though unsure how to address the traitorous brother of his tsar. He finished the sentence instead with a single curt nod, setting a jug of water on the stone floor and exiting the cell.

The traitorous brother of the tsar. Mikhail had never wanted to hurt anyone. His eyes swept the empty cell. How had he gotten here? He traced a finger through the pool of blood he'd awoken in. And then the memories of what had happened came rushing back, flooding his mind with misery.

There were memories of Nicholas, the look on his face as he'd condemned his brother to the fortress prison. *"You would send me there?"* Mikhail had implored. Nicholas's eyes had shown his heartbreak for just a moment, but then his face had changed, overtaken by a merciless hunger for vengeance. "*You. Your wife. Every person in this city found to have any connection with the traitorous murderers. I will find you all.*"

The guards had come, dragged Mikhail from his cell beneath the Winter Palace, and brought him here. Across the bridge, to this wretched island. The Peter and Paul Fortress. He'd been handled roughly, shoved along past cell after crowded cell. Some of the prisoners had cheered; more had taunted and teased. Mikhail had realized, then, that he had allied himself with a group that hated him for the very blood that flowed within his veins. The guards had stopped as they'd reached the end of the row of cells, unlocking the last cell on the hall and shoving him in. The small windowless cell was already occupied by six other men.

"The Grand *yobanyy* Duke himself, gentlemen." The speaker had been a big man with an eyepatch, smelling strongly of vodka. "Forgive me for neglecting to bow." Three of the men had laughed nervously, the other two sitting silently in the far corner of the prison cell. "As I likely won't be present to see the tsar's head explode with his *yobanyy* palace, I'd settle for beating his brother's."

Before Mikhail had been able to ask for more details on this matter of the tsar's head exploding with his palace, a voice had emerged from the corner of the cell. "*Pizdets*, Herzen." The man had spoken slowly, deliberately, as though he were trying very hard to communicate coherently despite his drunkenness. "Ivan trusted the man. He's with us."

"Ivan is dead. And no *yobanyy* Romanov prince is with us."

Mikhail had looked up then, meeting the brute's single eye. He had mustered his remaining self-respect, speaking with more confidence than he felt.

"Herzen, is it? I understand your wariness. But I'll tell you what I told Ivan. I seek the throne only so that I might share it with the Russian people and change the structure of our government, giving the people real representation. My only demand in this transition has been that no harm befalls my brother, his wife, or his children, as they are my blood. But it would seem it is too late, now, for that."

Herzen had laughed, a look of vicious delight in his single eye as he slowly approached Mikhail. "Too late, indeed. There may have been some men—" he cast his eyes toward the two in the corner, "—who supported Ivan's plan to give you your throne in exchange for some vague promise of change. But the rest of us, we will only stop when the tsar is dead. In the meantime . . ." He glanced toward his companions, and in the next moment a giant fist had collided with Mikhail's jaw. Herzen and his men had pummeled Mikhail while the other two tried to stop them and, in an instant, the cell became a tumble of fists and boots and blood. There was another punch to Mikhail's jaw. A kick to his ribs. Another. Screams, guards, blood, and then darkness.

That's how I got here, Mikhail thought, answering his own question. *I trusted a loosely united group of radical miscreants. I allied myself with regicidal rebels who seek to murder my brother. Who murdered my nieces. Who would murder me.* He'd only wanted what was best for Russia. And yes, that meant removing Nicholas from the throne, making changes. It had seemed possible to accomplish real change without violence—when Ivan had been alive. He remembered how excited, how enthralled he'd been, when Dina had introduced him to Ivan. The de facto leader of the Narodnaya Volya, Ivan had promised a bloodless transition of power from one Romanov to another, so long as that other would listen to the people and hand them the power they deserved. But as Herzen had so eloquently stated, Ivan was dead.

Finding little motivation to move, Mikhail remained curled on the floor in a pool of his own blood, wallowing in his misery, allowing the sharpness of his suffering to be dulled by the sound of the rain.

CHAPTER THIRTY-SEVEN

"I don't want to prove anything, I just want to live; to cause no evil to anyone but myself. I have that right, haven't I?"

—*Anna Karenina* by Leo Tolstoy

T HE RAIN HAD THICKENED into a steady downpour, the summer air heavy and humid. Lev's boots were soaked through, rubbing blisters on his aching feet as he limped along the muddy street, the tsarevich trudging along silently beside him. The boy had been uncharacteristically silent, but Lev supposed that the severity of the situation had begun to sink into the tsarevich's rather thick skull.

"It was a bomb, wasn't it?" The tsarevich broke the silence, revealing the subject of his thoughts to be the sudden explosion that had killed his sisters just hours before.

"It was." Lev looked to the boy, hoping his eyes might convey an offering of comfort beyond his words.

"Why?"

Lev took a breath. Why, indeed. "Well. It appeared that the bomb was meant for your father."

A look of deeper confusion crossed the boy's face. "Why would anyone want him dead? He's the tsar."

Sighing, Lev resigned himself to having this conversation, accepting that someone needed to explain to this kid that the world was in fact quite complex, quite cruel. He supposed the tsarevich had lived a rather sheltered life, and that the last two tsars' untimely deaths via magic-wielding terrorists was not a common topic for discussion over tea at the Winter Palace.

"There are those who want him dead *because* he is tsar."

The boy was quiet for a moment. "They want him dead because he's tsar. And then I would be tsar, and they'd want me dead? And then my uncle, and then whoever is in line after him?"

Lev nodded. "That's how it's been. Your grandfather and your great-grandfather were both killed by the Narodnaya Volya all those years ago. Now it seems different. There's more talk now about a new system of government. I don't know how it'd work. These people—they don't want another tsar. They want change. But the lengths they'd go to for it . . ."

"You mean like what they did to my sisters?" The boy's voice broke a bit on the word "sisters," and he looked away.

Wishing to impart some sort of comfort, Lev wasn't sure what to say. He placed his hand on the boy's shoulder and felt it relax slightly. The rain became heavier, louder, filling the silence as the two walked the long road to St. Petersburg.

DESPITE THE UNCEASING rain, the streets buzzed with nervous energy as Lev and the tsarevich neared the center of the city. Men and their families, some carrying traveling bags, others looking as though they'd just rushed from their homes, hurried through the streets, looking over their shoulders as though expecting to be followed. The busy city street may not have appeared unusual to the tsarevich, who, despite his exhaustion, trudged along as ceaselessly as the rain. Lev, however, was filled with a sense of unease. Reaching for the tsarevich, he pulled the boy aside as he stepped off the road, backing toward the trees.

"What are you—" the boy started to protest.

"*Shhhh*. Wait." Just in time.

It was as though the tension in the air had tightened and tightened until it burst, and then there was the galloping of horses, the splashing of carriage wheels through the puddled street.

Soldiers, like a swirl of blackbirds across a clouded sky, were swarming the streets in their black coats. "Ilyin!" a soldier bellowed, and the frightened crowd pointed out a man who had been hurrying through the streets, and the soldiers descended upon him, making their arrest. "Gusev!" another soldier bellowed, and the scene repeated.

Some men were arrested on sight alone, others identified by the crowd. Men were arrested alone or with their families, their children. Businesses were raided and suspected rebels were dragged from their hideaways in the shops and cafés, the business owners then dragged out as well, and loaded into the carriages.

From their crouch at the roadside, Lev and the tsarevich backed farther into the woods, moving quietly, carefully, until the scene on the street was out of sight, the sounds a blur of horses and carriages and men, muffled beneath the continuous sound of the pouring rain.

The tsarevich looked to Lev, his eyes wide. "What now?"

Lev held his gaze and took a deep breath, as a plan started to form in his mind.

"I will get you to the Winter Palace, I promise, but I think first we must go to my cabin. From the look of things, we'll need to dress as soldiers."

Through patches of pine trees and winding backroads, Lev led the tsarevich along a meandering path from the pandemonium of the city to the quiet row of small cabins, where well-worn laundry waved on the lines, where people—neither rebels nor soldiers—planted their vegetable gardens. The peacefulness along Lev's road was in stark contrast to the scene in the city, just as the extravagance of the Alexander Palace highlighted the destitution of the cabins before him. Lev was struck by the unfairness of it all. While the tsar sat in his palace, while the Narodnaya Volya schemed their attacks, it was these people, people like his neighbors, people like his mother, who suffered.

"Are you a soldier, then?" The tsarevich looked Lev up and down, perhaps remembering the uniform he'd been wearing at their first meeting, in the woods of the Luzhsky Uyezd.

"Well, yes." Lev swallowed. *How long has it been since I've reported for duty? A week?*

So much had happened in the last week—even in just the past day. As Lev's cabin came into view, he thought of the day before, when he'd held Anastasia's hand as they'd sauntered down the road, talking about his father. Talking about her brother. About how the one had healed the other, over and over. *"What was wrong with your brother?"* Lev had asked, and then the thunderclap, and the sky had let loose, the beginning of this unending rain. As he relived that scene, as he pictured the look on Anastasia's face—*"You shot him?!"*—Lev thought there must be something he'd missed. Some explanation.

Lev swung open the door to the cabin, the tsarevich trailing behind him, looking ready to collapse. As was his habit, Lev paused at the entry, sweeping the cabin with his eyes before proceeding. Looking for signs of anything amiss. And, he realized, hoping she would be there. He hadn't noticed he'd been holding his breath, but somewhere deep within his mind, or perhaps his heart, he'd hoped he would arrive home and find her there, waiting for him. Waiting to explain why she'd done what she'd done. Waiting to take him in her arms, to—

"Oy Lev, you're alive after all!"

The voice called jovially from around the side of the house, taking Lev unawares just as he was supposed to be practicing vigilance. And the voice certainly did not belong to Anastasia.

"You know, the men figured you'd left town, or died. I asked them though, if anyone had bothered to come looking for you, and they hadn't, so. It's all hands on deck, over at the Winter Palace—*Pizdets*, you look rough, man."

Viktor had always been a nice enough guy, close to Lev in age and out-going enough to know every soldier of the regiment. While Lev wouldn't quite consider Viktor or any of his fellow soldiers to be his friend, he appreciated that the man had bothered to check on him before presuming him dead. Even if the timing was less than ideal.

"I would imagine I do, Viktor. Not as rough as my companion here though." He gestured toward the tsarevich, who had just stepped through the doorway, dripping wet and clearly exhausted, looking quite pitiful with his blackened eyes and swollen lip.

Lev thought quickly and kept talking, before the tsarevich could say something thoughtless. "This is . . . Alek. A soldier who's . . . just recently come from Moscow. He was attacked by rebels, and I interceded, and here we are."

Viktor seemed to accept Lev's story, suspicion not being of his nature. While he hadn't necessarily been invited inside, he followed them through the door. "And good to meet you, Alek." The tsarevich opened his mouth to reply, but Viktor chattered on. "The two of you look as though some hot tea and dry clothes would do you some good. May as well get your uniform on, anyway, Lev. We're on guard duty at the Winter Palace."

The soldier turned his attention back to the tsarevich. "I suppose you ought to join us, if you haven't any assignment. Better to be on guard duty than arrests, for certain. And, no offense, but you really do look awful, and if you were to go your own way with no one to vouch for you, you'd likely end up getting hauled off to the Peter and Paul. Guard duty is certainly better than that." Viktor continued to prattle on about the arrests and the tragedy at the church and the abundance of rain as he took it upon himself to set the tea kettle to boil, aimlessly opening this cabinet and that in search of food. Lev, who couldn't get another word in, found himself closing cabinets behind Viktor as he located some bread and dried fish.

The tsarevich had gravitated to the kitchen chair, burying his face in his arms as he drooped into the seat. Viktor cocked his head to the side and clicked his tongue, his eyes full of pity.

"Poor fellow's gone right to sleep, hasn't he? Well, a brief rest then, but soon we must really be off, before the raids start out this way if we can. Not that we ought to have any trouble—just to avoid the nastiness."

Lev looked up, wrenching his mind from Anastasia and back to the scene before him. "The nastiness?"

"Oh, yes, it's been getting ugly out there. With the arrests, I mean. They say it's quite like the exile of magicians, all those years ago, though who knows. Of course, what else can the tsar do, after what happened to the poor Grand Duchesses. Everyone's angry, everyone's a suspect, and it's been violent. Ugly. Nasty."

Lev nodded. "I see—"

"So," Viktor interrupted. "Best to be on guard duty. And best to leave soon."

The tsarevich stirred as he emitted a loud snore and then nestled his head into his arms where they rested upon the table. Lev raised his eyebrows. "A brief rest, as you said, and then we'll be off."

Lev had not yet decided whether Viktor's presence was a burden or a blessing. Either way, the wheels seemed to be in motion. The Winter Palace awaited.

CHAPTER THIRTY-EIGHT

"The inner state of his soul might be compared to a demolished building, which has been demolished so that from it a new one could be built . . ."

—*Dead Souls* by Nikolai Gogol

"T HE BLEEDING HAS STOPPED, but the boy does not appear to be improving, Your Majesty."

Alexei emitted a soft groan, his foot feeling as though a pin prick would pop it in an explosion of blood and skin and tissue. Throughout his lower leg, it felt as though his severed veins were punctured fire hoses, flowing with the force of a tidal wave.

"But the bleeding has stopped?"

No, no, it hasn't stopped.

"Yes, but—"

"Then he shall recover! Why have you upset my wife so?"

"I-I only asked if the boy has ever shown signs of the bleeding disease . . . that which affected her brother."

"And you call yourself a doctor. Have you not seen the boy for countless injuries, all more severe than Friedrich's fatal fall? No, if my son had the bleeding disease, he would not have lived to be thirteen."

"It's just that—"

"He shall recover." The tsar placed a strong hand over Alexei's sweaty forehead. "You will be just fine, my son. The bleeding has stopped."

No, no . . . In his semi-consciousness, Alexei couldn't form his rising panic into thoughts, nor thoughts into words, but could only let out a small sound which his father interpreted as confirmation that yes, he would be just fine.

"The men who did this to you are being arrested as we speak. The city will be swept of traitors and sympathizers, proof be damned." The tsar patted Alexei's forehead and swept from the room.

Alexei's mind was a cyclone of images: his parents, his sisters. Anastasia. Rasputin. Bullets, blood, the garnet. Anastasia. *Anastasia, I need you!* He had needed her many times in his life, to lie for him, to defend him—he'd always needed to use her, for one thing or another. And she had always been there for whatever he'd needed. But he needed her now because she was his sister, the one person in this world who knew him. Who loved him. And he needed that, more than he needed Rasputin, more than he needed to fit into this family. More than he needed to be tsar. More than anything, Alexei needed his sister.

CHAPTER THIRTY-NINE

"I am who I am and that's who I am."

—*The Government Inspector* by Nikolai Gogol

B Y SUNRISE, AN INCH of murky water lined the cold stone floor of the prison cell, wetting the soles of my boots as I stood slumped against the wall. The slow trickle of water would have been but a minor threat to our relative comfort had it not been backed by a wall of water splashing against the high barred window of the cell, threatening to break through the glass. In my own world the prison had flooded before, I recalled, and in my mind I became Princess Tarakanova in her famed portrait. An heiress to the throne, wrongfully imprisoned by a mad ruler, awaiting her death in a dreadful island dungeon as the floodwaters raged.

Dina paced, hands resting on her swollen belly as she thought aloud, seemingly speaking to my unborn cousin within her womb.

"You will be tsar, my darling, you will be tsar, and I shall rule by your cradle, we will change the world, we will. We will escape, we must . . ." She trailed off, and then began muttering again. "You will be tsar. You'll be tsar, my love. You will be tsar."

I glanced up, my interest piqued. "What about Mikhail?"

Dina stopped pacing and balked, as though just remembering my existence.

"I assume you're speaking to your spawn." I gestured to her pregnant belly rather pointedly. "I've gathered that you wouldn't mind knocking off your brother-in-law, and your nephew too, I suppose, to get who you want on the throne. But after the tsarevich, it's Mikhail. Your husband is next, not the kid." I raised my eyebrows. Was the woman mad?

She smiled that catlike grin again, instantly transforming her face, shedding the appearance of an anxious madwoman and becoming once again the formidable presence I'd met the night before.

"Inquisitive, are we, Anastasia?" She appraised me, her sharp mind apparently finding no reason not to answer my question. "Men are disposable. If it's Mikhail, fine. If it's my son, even better. Means to an end, don't you see?"

She was insufferable. "You think you're so noble, don't you? Were the lives of Olga, Tatiana, and Maria disposable too? Were their deaths just *means to an end?*"

Dina's eyes flashed with anger, her upper lip curling into a snarl as she opened her mouth to reply, but our exchange was interrupted by shouting from a neighboring cell. A gunshot echoed through the hall, followed by the whooping of rowdy prisoners. Then another gunshot. This time followed by breaking glass. Rushing water. Her eyes widened then as they met mine in a moment of realization before we both turned toward the little barred window overlooking the cell. The pane of glass was a thin barrier between our confined space and the wall of water outside, demanding to be let in.

A panic was rising within me, my heart quickening, its beat throbbing through my veins. I clenched my fists. No longer was I Princess Tarakanova, serenely awaiting my doom, but Anastasia Romanov, unwilling to accept this fate. I hadn't come this far to drown in some dingy dungeon. I had to get back to Alexei. Perhaps if I were by his side, if I could make the doctors understand his condition, I could save him still. Even without Rasputin, I had to try.

Gunshot. Glass. Water. The sounds cycled repeatedly, as though some-one were systematically shooting out the windows and flooding the prison. The noise grew louder, closer, and then a towering prisoner—it was the brute with the eyepatch—lumbered drunkenly to our door.

"No—" I started, but Dina interrupted me.

"Get down, you idiot girl!"

I obeyed, diving to the floor as the brute fired into our cell—not aiming for us, but for our window. He laughed barbarically as the window burst and water rushed into our cell, pouring in as though someone had pulled a plug at the bottom of the sea.

The cell was filling quickly, shin-deep in a matter of moments, and the halls were chaos. There were prisoners attacking guards, taking their guns, taking their keys, opening cell after cell, freeing the Narodnaya Volya. The halls were filling with riotous men and rushing water as I watched helplessly from behind the barred door. I didn't suppose any of the men cared to free the Duchess and an unknown girl.

None of the rebels, anyway. Somehow, amidst the violence in the hall, a familiar face appeared at our door. Kozma jammed his key into the lock, swinging open the cell door. He glanced over his shoulder at the chaos be-hind him, then up to our window, where the water poured in. "God bless the tsar, but traitors or not, I won't leave you ladies trapped here, doomed to drown. Go . . . go quickly. These men, they are animals." And with that, he ducked back into the hall, disappearing into the madness.

I shuddered at what was implied, wishing by no means to find myself backed into the cell at the mercy of these rage-filled imbeciles. Dina certain-ly wasted no time, holding her skirts as she raced through the open door without giving me so much as a last glance. I followed, splashing across the cell and sloshing into the hallway, taking in the cacophony of escaping pris-oners and overwhelmed guards.

There was no time to stop and observe—I had to keep moving or be trampled as the prisoners barreled through the narrow hallway like a stam-pede through a rushing river.

Fighting my way down the hall, I battled the water as I pushed forward, but the water continued to rise. My legs were too short and I couldn't move fast enough, not faster than the men behind me. A large hand shoved me sideways, my head colliding with a muscled shoulder, and then my feet slipped from under me, my knees finding the hard stone of the floor beneath the rushing water. This could not be how I died. Not like this. My breathing grew rapid. Couldn't die. Not like this. Couldn't die. Frantically, I tried to push to my feet, fighting the force of the water. But it was too much. Moving bodies kept cramming down the hall, and I slipped again, this time submerging, taking a mouthful of muddy water as I cried out. Not like this . . .

And then a hand grabbed the back of my dress between my shoulder blades, lifting me up like a mother cat, moving her kitten by the scruff of its neck. I gasped for air as my head lifted out of the water, and I willed my feet to find the floor, to move, one in front of the other as my savior pulled me along through the madness. One foot in front of the other, stumbling forward, the hand at my back not allowing me to sink beneath the water again. The hallway seemed an endless hell, a mob of frantic bodies, moving mercilessly forward through the raging sludge. But between the moving bodies, I caught a glimpse of a stairwell ahead, and an open door, and then we were upon it, moving up, out of the water, and . . . outside. Into the open air, where the water swirled at our feet and the rain pounded down upon us, but there was space, there was room to move, there was time to stop.

We stopped.

The hand released me, and I turned to thank my rescuer. My eyes widened as I looked upon the bloodied, beaten face of my uncle Mikhail. Or rather, the tsarevich's uncle Mikhail, as the man was truly nothing to me but a stranger. A stranger who'd betrayed his brother, his tsar, his country for the Narodnaya Volya. A stranger who'd saved my life. I didn't know what to say to the man, but as usual, that didn't stop me from speaking.

A simple "thank you" would have been the most appropriate response, but the words that tumbled from my mouth were instead, "You look awful."

And to my surprise, Mikhail offered me a broken smile, though it didn't reach his blackened eyes. Perhaps his pain, physical and otherwise, wouldn't allow it. "I would imagine so," he answered, speaking gently, searching my face as though seeing in my features the faces of my sisters. Something like regret shadowed his face for a moment, but he wiped it away and extended his arm toward me, a small iron box clenched in his hand. "This, erm, fell from your pocket."

I patted at my skirt, feeling for the gun, and found it missing. I looked at Mikhail. He worked to maintain a mask of innocence, and I narrowed my eyes as we studied each other. He had returned the box, not knowing its contents, its value, or perhaps not caring. The gun, though . . . the gun he might need.

Perhaps it was the exhaustion, or sympathy, or gratitude—but I didn't pursue it further. I didn't care much about the gun. What I needed was Molniya. I needed to find the horse, and then, Alexei. Holding Mikhail's gaze, I reached for the box. "Thank you."

Mikhail opened his mouth, perhaps reconsidering his thievery, but whatever he might have said was interrupted by the sight of Molniya galloping toward us, hooves splattering mud and water in his wake. Had the wild beast *followed* me here?

I was elated to see him—but then immediately livid, because sitting atop the unruly horse, somehow maintaining control of the reins, was Dina, peering out at us from beneath her dark hood.

"Mikhail, my love, come. We must get out of this city!" Looking past me, she spoke with urgency but sweetly—not the arrogant woman I'd met in the dungeon. I stood there staring, my arm still outstretched, clutching the iron box. I was in disbelief—the *svoloch* had stolen my horse.

"That's my horse—"

"Dina, we must get to the palace—my brother, my nephew, they'll die—"

"Get off my horse—"

"The palace—nonsense, my love. For Nicholas? Nicholas threw you in this prison, and he would do the same again."

"And I would deserve it—but there's some plot—the rebels, they're not honoring the agreement, Dina, they were *there*, disguised as workmen—there's, I don't know, a bomb or something—I haven't pieced it together—"

"Then let them explode, darling."

Mikhail stopped speaking, took a breath. He looked at his wife, really looked at her, and appeared shocked at what he saw. On her face, indifference. She truly did not care if his brother was blown to smithereens. In her eyes, ruthlessness. She had her agenda, and she would not be deterred. The moment of transparency was brief, as Dina quickly rearranged her features into a mask of sweet sincerity once again.

"That sounded harsh, my love, I know," she spoke evenly, quietly, as she brought her hand to her belly. "But we can't risk the child."

I rolled my eyes. "Wherever you're going, get off my *yobanyy* horse!"

Ignoring me and my grievances, Mikhail kept his eyes on his wife. "The child . . . yes, of course. You . . . you get to safety. But I'll go. I have to go."

There was no way I would just stand there and let this awful woman ride away on my horse. I needed to get to the palace, before Alexei lost too much blood. Before . . . before he died. Before everyone in the palace died, if Mikhail was right about the bomb. And so in a less-than-dignified display of exasperation, I raised the iron box and brought it down on Dina's kneecap with a satisfying *bonk.* "Get *off* my horse, you thieving traitor!"

Dina cried out—in rage more so than pain—and grabbed me by the wrist just as Mikhail yanked me backward by the waist. Still clutched in my outstretched hand, the iron box fell open, exposing Lev's garnet, sparkling red amongst the wet gray drear. Mikhail's eyes widened at the sight of the gemstone, and Dina stopped cursing me, her mouth hanging agape. In that moment, with Mikhail gripping my waist and Dina clenching my wrist as I clung to the open iron box, a voice rang out from a group of escaped prisoners, moving toward us from the prison stairs.

"The Grand *yobanyy* Duke!" It was the man with the eyepatch, pointing a fallen guard's gun in our direction. Mikhail was pulling a gun—my gun—from his pocket as the one-eyed-man roared profanities, and both men fired. It all happened so fast—Dina was screaming, Mikhail was shielding his face, and I watched as the bullet struck—missing its mark, but striking Lev's garnet, gleaming in the open box.

I screamed, squeezing my eyes closed as though by not watching, I could resist the pull from this world.

No—I couldn't leave this world—not for fear of entering a new one, but— Alexei! I couldn't leave him, couldn't let him die alone. And Lev! So much was left unsaid, no, no, no . . .

But I didn't feel a pull.

I felt my feet, still grounded in the mud. I blinked my eyes open and gasped. We . . . we were still here. But the scene around us was frozen, as though time itself had stopped. The man with the eye patch was like a statue, stopped in mid-stride. Mikhail's bullet floated in the air, suspended in its path. A bolt of lightning sliced the dark sky like a photograph. Nothing and no one moved, except—Dina recoiled, releasing my wrist and cursing. Mikhail staggered backward, unbalanced. I dropped the iron box to the ground, where it disappeared beneath the muddy water. Molniya brayed, clearly growing impatient.

"What . . . what happened?" Mikhail looked around, mesmerized, and lowered the gun.

Quite stupidly, I answered. "Well, the garnets have powers, you see, and apparently this one stops time—well, for everyone but us, it would seem, since we were touching it—so when you shoot it—"

Dina interrupted me. "You were carrying a *kolodets*? And you've used it?" And then her eyes flashed to the ground, where the box lay hidden beneath the shallow stream of murky water. We moved for it at the same time—I dropped to my hands and knees as she swung down from the horse, and we were both crawling through the mud, feeling beneath the surface for the little iron box.

Mikhail hardly reacted, still looking around in awe. "This . . . this is perfect. This is just what we need. Now we have time to reach the palace, find the bomb, and stop it. This is a gift from God, and I will not waste it."

Dina rolled her eyes. "It's not a gift from God, my sweet idiot love. It's a gift from Russia. And it's not for you." With that, she flung her hand into the air, snapping the box closed and waving it victoriously as she sprung to her feet. Except she wasn't so nimble as she thought, or perhaps her balance was thrown off by the extra weight of her belly, because she stumbled. And in that moment, all that mattered was keeping the garnets from this woman. I lurched for her, grabbing her by the arm as I struggled to wrench the box from her grasp.

I was prying at Dina's fingers as she yanked me by the hair, pushing my face into the muddy water.

"You *yobanyy svol*—" Mud filled my open mouth as she plunged my head to the ground. I kicked at her, and she swung at me, and it was a splashing, muddy mess of flailing limbs.

"Stop—the baby—the box—just stop—" Mikhail flapped about in exasperation, and then, BANG. He shot the gun into the water. "Stop, I say!" BANG.

Bold, but effective. I froze, Dina staring wide eyed at Mikhail, the box still clenched in her hand. He kept the gun pointing toward the muddy ground, and as though to emphasize his point, fired again. BANG. And this time, the gunshot echoed across the sky as thunder boomed, the scene around us springing to life. The raindrops suspended around us fell in sheets. I hadn't realized how quiet it had been until the noise of the rain and the wind and the men resumed.

Our time was up.

Dina seemed to find her agility once more as she swung atop the horse, and Mikhail lunged toward her. "No—we need the time—the *kolodets!*" He gestured toward the iron box in her hand. "You must, we must shoot it again, my love—the bomb—"

She peered down at her husband, who stood pleading in the mud.

"We let them explode. You will be tsar. And if you won't"—she smiled sweetly, bringing her hand to her belly—"*he* will." She tucked the box into her cloak as she dug her heels into Molniya's flanks. The horse reared back, his hoof catching Mikhail across the forehead and knocking him to the ground. Unhampered by Mikhail's misfortune, Molniya released a fearsome bray and broke into a run, carrying Dina and the little iron box off into the storm. In the same moment, there was a scream across the yard as the bullet Mikhail had released minutes before resumed its path, striking the big man with the eye patch, blood spurting from his massive torso. He fell to his knees, wailing in agony as his comrades dropped to the ground around him, one of them offering comfort in his own way. "You got him, Herzen, the Grand Duke—he's dead."

I glanced at the Grand Duke. Mikhail did appear quite dead, I supposed, as he lay unconscious on the ground before me. The men wouldn't have known the bullet had missed its target, striking the garnet instead. They wouldn't have known that time had stopped and started again. No, they saw Herzen shoot his gun, and they saw Mikhail collapsed on the ground.

Another group of prisoners burst from the flooded fortress, seemingly outraged at the sight of the big man with the eyepatch.

"Herzen, you *yobanyy* fool!" The voice belonged to a prisoner, a man vaguely familiar to me. And then I remembered—he'd clapped hands with Lev, calling him Luka. He'd driven the truck as Lev's eyes had found mine through the window, one last look before I'd stepped from the wall, plunging to the canal below.

And then, from another door, a team of guards rushed into the yard, led by none other than sweet, pudgy Kozma.

"That's him, the attacker!" Kozma's voice called to his fellow guards as he pointed to the big man bleeding on the ground. Herzen.

For the moment, attention had been diverted from Mikhail and me, as the three groups of men turned toward each other. And with one last glance at Mikhail, prone on the ground before me, I turned and ran. I ran as fast as I could, away from the prison, away from the prisoners and the guards, and toward the palace, toward my brother.

The plot Mikhail had spoken of—the bomb, the workmen—it sounded familiar. And if it were anything like the bomb I'd learned about back in my own world, it needed to be stopped. My brother was in that palace, fighting for his life. The tsar and tsarina were in that palace—not my parents, not really—but I could save them. I had to save them.

THE CARRIAGE PATH I'd ridden in on the night before was now a shallow stream winding between the pines. Shallow, but deepening with every stride as I ran through ankle-deep, shin-deep, and now knee-deep water.

Thoughts of my brother, bleeding in the hospital ward at a palace full of dynamite, wrestled with thoughts of Dina, riding away on Molniya with the iron box and the power it held within. In Dina's hands, the power of Lev's garnet would be terribly dangerous. What havoc might she wreak, with the ability to freeze time? And then there was my garnet, the *kolodets* that brought me to this world. It remained hidden within the second layer of the box, where she would discover it eventually. Would she use it? As much as I loathed her, I pitied the little one in her womb. It wasn't his fault that his mother was a traitor, after all. *"He'll be tsar,"* she'd said.

The words were concerning, given the number of deaths that would have to precede the boy's coronation. The tsar, in his palace, doomed to explode if I didn't make it in time. The tsarevich, whom I'd last seen trapped in a truck, riding away with the Narodnaya Volya and Lev. The Grand Duke, unconscious on the ground outside the prison, where I'd left him. The words were concerning, yes, but not so farfetched.

I sloshed through the water, dragging my heavy limbs through the mud. My body ached with hunger, thirst, and exhaustion—but I had to get to the palace. I had to. That single thought overpowered everything else, filling my body with a strength I didn't know I was capable of, propelling me forward through the sludge. And when I reached the island's edge, where the bridge lay hidden beneath the rushing river, that strength carried me across. I'd felt for the bridge's railings, clinging tightly as I made my way step-by-step out onto the bridge and at the mercy of the wild Neva.

As the river raged around me, I was reminded of how I'd felt before sneaking into the Alexander Palace, before finding Lev... A sense of desperate resignation, an acceptance of the impossibility that lay before me, and the notion that live or die, I'd had nothing to lose.

The difference now was that I'd had a glimpse of what life might be like if I succeeded. There had been moments in those last two days with Lev, moments in which I'd smiled, and laughed, and felt that maybe I was not No One after all, but that I was Someone who could heal, who could find happiness and meaning once again. I'd imagined my future, maybe with Lev, with my brother, but *my* future. That I could go on living, without my sisters, without my parents, without my crown, without my world. Despite the nightmares that haunted me, there was more for me still. And so as I crept across the underwater bridge, hand over hand, I did have something to lose.

My heart was pounding, my veins coursing with adrenaline. I was quite honestly terrified. Terrified for myself and terrified for Alexei. Terrified that he would die, that I would never see him again. If he died, would I ever forgive myself? There were so many things I could have done differently. If I'd told Lev about the hemophilia, or if I'd gone for my brother rather than the tsarevich that night after Luzhsky . . . if I'd done a better job of protecting him, maybe he wouldn't lie bleeding to death in the Winter Palace.

I'd tried to do the right thing.

Dina's words echoed in my mind. "*Goodness does not matter,*" she'd said. "*Intentions do not matter. Results are what matter.*"

The results of my mistakes, of Lev's mistakes—the results of my parents' mistakes—were horrendous. But Dina had to be wrong. Goodness had to matter. Intentions had to matter. Because despite my failures, I wanted to be better. I wanted to grow from my mistakes. And that mattered—it had to.

I moved one hand over the other, inching my way across the underwater bridge as the river swirled around me, as though angry I'd dared attempt to outrun its rage. Fighting the water required a strength I didn't know I possessed. Perhaps it was my conviction that there had to be some reason

I'd survived thus far. There just had to be. And if there was no reason designated by fate or God or Rasputin, then there was the reason I'd found for myself. It was my desire to be good. To do good. To make the world better by being in it.

I gritted my teeth. That meant stopping this bomb. Finding my brother. Saving my family and everyone else at the Winter Palace.

But being good, doing good—that didn't just mean grand acts of heroism. No, it meant letting go of anger. It meant forgiveness. For myself, for my brother, for Lev. For my parents. For . . . I pictured that guard, once again, the cellar, the gun, the bullets. I shook my head, pushing the image from my mind. I wasn't sure if I could ever forgive those guards. I could try, in time.

My fingers nearly slipped from the rail as a small tree branch swiped my side, tearing my dress and the skin beneath. I cried out in pain, and the gash in my side burned, but I tightened my grip on the rail, refusing to give up. Blood mixed with the water around me for a moment, but then it was gone, the blood and the branch carried onward.

I paused for a moment, watching as the offending branch disappeared down the river. And I allowed my anger—all of my anger—to go with it. I realized I was crying, not from sadness or grief this time, but because the feeling of release was so powerful. Everything I'd endured in the last week—in the last years—had weighed so heavily on me, compounding into this unmanageable load I'd carried. And I couldn't erase it. But I could choose to let it go. To move forward.

Energized, I moved faster through the swirling water.

Alexei, I'm coming for you. I forgive you, and I'm coming for you.

CHAPTER FORTY

"Intentions are deep waters in a human heart."

—*The Garnet Bracelet* by Aleksandr Kuprin

AN EERIE SYMPHONY OF gunfire and violins echoed off the looming domes of the church as Alexei sprinted from the tsar's side, racing across the starlit pavilion toward the cargo truck. The music grew louder, blaring inside his head and urging him faster. Faster, as his boots beat against the stone. Faster, as he whirled past soldiers and rebels and . . . three strangely familiar faces, leering at him from amongst the rebels. He skidded to a halt. *Familiar, but from where?*

As if in answer, the music stopped abruptly, and a wooden podium topped with a visitors registry appeared before him. Alexei skidded to a halt, his heart still pounding, his breathing still ragged, and he gazed down at the registry. Line after line of Petrov's untidy scrawl, and then, there at the bottom, was Alexei's own neatly printed entry. "*Workmen,*" he'd penciled in the log. *Those familiar faces . . . what were the palace workmen doing with the Narodnaya Volya?*

But then the podium was gone, and Alexei wasn't standing, but lying against the cold metal of the cargo truck. There was an explosion of flames, and his sisters' screams, and his own blood, pooling around him. "My girls!" It was his father's voice, and then, as Alexei looked up, the scene changed once more.

There was a dark stairwell, leading to an even darker dungeon. It was the basement beneath the Winter Palace. A basement he'd never explored, because he'd never lived there, not in his own world. It was unsafe. *Unsafe, but why?* He squinted to see in the darkness, and saw that there was dynamite, stacks and stacks, and there were those workmen again, laying the explosives like bricks. A clock ticked, a match was struck, and there was another explosion of flames, blasting down the palace walls. He heard his father's voice again, but this time screaming, this time dying, this time . . . lecturing, as he paced in front of the chalkboard, delivering the day's history lesson. Alexei and his sisters sat attentively at their desks, hanging on their father's words.

"There have been many attempts to end us, my children. Most of them failures, but only one success is required to alter the course of history. Today our lesson shall be about the Winter Palace bomb, an act of a group called the Narodnaya Volya in the year 1880. The rebels, traitorous as they were, were rather clever in this instance. Over a course of time, men of the Narodnaya Volya snuck what amounted to quite a lot of dynamite into the basement of the Winter Palace, building it into the walls and ceilings in the guards' chamber, just beneath the dining room. The clever part, you see, was that the men dressed as carpenters, and as there were repairs to be done in the palace basement, no one suspected a thing. Using a clockwork contraption, the men set the bomb to explode at six o'clock sharp, just when the tsar would be sitting down to dinner. It was mere luck of course, that dinner had been delayed that evening . . ."

A crack of lightning illuminated the sky, immediately followed by a booming rumble of thunder, and Alexei thrashed awake. *The basement.* The details of the dream were fading, as dreams do, but Alexei's mind grasped at the main points, held tightly to the essence of it. *The carpenters.* In the dream he'd seen them, the carpenters—their faces those of the men he'd let through the palace entry days ago. *The bomb. God, the bomb!*

Alexei peeled himself from the sweaty sheets of the hospital bed, lurching to stand. His leg was throbbing, red and swollen, and his head burned, swimming with incoherent thoughts. *The basement, the carpenters, the bomb*—the words repeated like a mantra, the only sensical thought his foggy brain could conjure. He hobbled across the room, out the door, through the halls. *The basement.* He moved in a feverish daze, and he could hardly see except for a narrow tunnel of vision, but his hands and his good foot guided him along as he leaned to the wall, dragging his caustic limb behind him.

The door, the staircase, *the basement.* As he closed the door behind him and stepped down, his leg collapsed beneath him and he tumbled down the staircase, his scrawny frame feeling every bump along the way until the pain was blinding. It was too much to bear. He lay crumpled on the basement floor, slipping from consciousness, his mind still screaming in warning, "*The bomb!*"

CHAPTER FORTY-ONE

"All the variety, all the charm, all the beauty of life is made up of light and shadow."

—*Anna Karenina* by Leo Tolstoy

HOT TEA AND DRY uniforms had provided only brief warmth and comfort, as Lev, Viktor, and the tsarevich soon found themselves drenched once again, riding through the endless downpour toward the Winter Palace.

As they'd prepared to depart, the tsarevich had appeared utterly crestfallen at the notion of walking once more through the relentless rain. Lev was considering how he might procure a horse when it dawned on him that he'd never returned the old mare he'd borrowed from his neighbor nearly a week ago.

And so he didn't borrow the younger mare he now rode upon, but bought her and her older, slower sister, who presumably remained at the palace stables. He'd overpaid, as the value of the horses was certainly less than that of a solid golden vase from the Alexander Palace itself. Still Lev supposed that was fair, seeing as the seller had not been consulted on the matter. His neighbor was a clever and reasonable enough fellow. When he discovered his stable to be empty but for a golden vase and a hastily scribbled note reading simply, "Sorry," he would understand that a transaction had been made.

The tsarevich had not opposed his new identity as Alek of Moscow, perhaps finding any identity more desirable than his own as he struggled to assemble the circumstances of his situation into any sort of acceptable reality. Because how could he accept his sisters' deaths, his uncle's betrayal, his father's rampage, his mother's belief that some other boy was her son? He rode quietly in front of Lev, a thick blanket draped over them to shield the rain.

Viktor rode beside them, chattering about their various shared acquaintances in the regiment. Lev did his best to steer conversation away from the topic of the Tragedy at the Church, as the Grand Duchesses' deaths had come to be known, and found himself less worried that "Alek" might have difficulty remaining discreet as it became ever more apparent that Viktor would be doing most, if not all, of the talking.

Winding their way through the quiet backstreets, the three avoided the nastiness of the main roads for as long as they could until they emerged near the Winter Palace. They found the city streets empty of rebels and townsfolk, but bustling with soldiers such as themselves.

The palace grounds hosted the largest gathering of soldiers that Lev could remember having seen. The atmosphere was rather cheery despite the rain as men moved purposefully about the grounds, some on foot, some on horseback. Viktor seemed to be enjoying the scene quite thoroughly, greeting his fellow soldiers. More than once, he offered a laughing "Told you I'd find him!" to the faces familiar to Lev, while Lev nodded and smiled apologetically.

Occupied as Lev's mind was, he found himself grateful for Viktor's endless ability to fill a silence, to dominate a conversation. Lev and the tsarevich were thus able to remain relatively inconspicuous as Viktor interrupted other soldiers' questions about Lev's absence and Alek's beaten face.

"Rebels, wouldn't you know, as the boy had just arrived in the city, too. Shameful. But such is the nature of these beasts, wouldn't you agree, beasts, more so than men, who would attack a lone soldier. Traitors to the tsar, traitors to Russia. Quite sad, how it has escalated. And those poor girls!"

Amongst the crowd of soldiers, Lev found himself listening to multiple conversations at once, catching snippets of similar sentiments. "Those poor girls," the soldiers would say, their tones more indignant than sorrowful, and Lev sensed that the Grand Duchesses were morphing from victims to martyrs as the tsar's men found in their deaths justification for a ruthless annihilation of political dissenters.

The tsar's men. Lev was one of them, was he not? He was a soldier, a patriot, loyal to the crown. *Aren't I?* Disturbed by his analysis of the soldiers, disillusioned by the excessiveness of the Alexander Palace, but also disgusted by the violence of the Narodnaya Volya, Lev found himself conflicted.

A crack of lightning immediately followed by a booming rumble of thunder interrupted Lev's reverie. There was no time to ponder such questions anyway, not when the window of time for finding his way inside the Winter Palace was closing. Soon, there would be guards on every door, making impossible his already slim chances of getting to Alexei. Glancing around the crowd, Lev noticed several officers, observed the resolve on their faces as they spoke to one another, solidifying their plans before calling the men to order. *Better to slip away now,* Lev thought, *and take advantage of the disorder.*

Leaning forward toward the tsarevich as though to tighten the mare's reins, Lev kept his voice to a murmur. "Stay with Viktor. Give me until the end of the day, if you can, and then reclaim your title. Tell them the truth, tell them whatever you want." Lev paused a moment. Then, "Good luck, Your Highness."

"Wait—" the tsarevich started, as Lev slid from the horse. But Viktor had actually stopped speaking for a moment, pausing his chatter to take a swig from his flask.

"I'll be right back, just off to stretch my legs and say hello to an old friend," Lev spoke loudly, waving to a nonexistent pal in the distance. The plan was flimsy and hastily constructed, but could perhaps be successful if carried off with confidence. Lev held his shoulders back and fixed his eyes on a point just above the heads of a group of soldiers, waving, smiling, and walking with purpose. As he walked, he could sense the tsarevich watching him as Viktor resumed his chatter. He was tempted to look back, having become rather fond of the tsarevich in their time together. While not particularly clever, the boy was kind, an optimist, persevering despite having been kidnapped and beaten by the men who'd killed his sisters. A boy with honor, having chosen to keep his promise to Lev, to fulfill his debt by trudging hours through the rain, keeping his true identity hidden behind a muddy soldier's uniform and a busted face while his parents sat warm and dry within the palace walls.

Lev had reached the outskirts of the crowd and positioned himself out of view of Viktor and the tsarevich when a deep voice bellowed over the noise, bringing about an anticipatory hush. Lev didn't recognize the man, but could identify him as a higher-ranking soldier than himself by his uniform. "Those of you on horseback, form lines! You are the greatest wall protecting our tsar from a rebel attack! Those of you on foot, gather into groups and await assignment!"

Commotion ensued as horsemen and footmen ended their conversations and began dividing into new groups. Lev attached himself to a nearby group containing no one he knew—or more importantly, no one who knew him—as an officer rode toward them. Without stopping his horse, the officer merely barked, "Northeast entrance!" at the men and continued on to the next group.

Lev managed to remain inconspicuous, bending to retie his boot to stall, and then tailing behind the group of eight or so men as they slogged through the mud toward the northeastern entrance. The north side of the palace overlooked the Neva, the river rushing wildly as the rain poured down. He recognized this side of the palace—the door would be along this wall, the door he and Anastasia had exited through after their night of imprisonment. Lev's mind raced with one impossible plan after another, and he concluded that his best course of action would be to slip away unnoticed, to get through the door before its guards arrived. Looking over his shoulder, he could see a small group of soldiers moving this direction—would they be bound for the little door? Or some other post?

The soldiers of Lev's own group walked quickly—perhaps eager for some shelter from the rain amongst the trees of the northeast garden—and left Lev straggling behind. None of them looked back. It was his chance and he took it, veering off the path and moving hurriedly to the palace wall. Muddy water sloshed around his ankles, permeating his boots as he reached the little door. He opened it, slid through, and sighed with relief as it closed behind him. He had done it. He was inside.

From the corner of his eye, Lev caught a glimpse of movement as the neighboring door, the door to the basement staircase, pulled closed. Lev's immediate thought was "Pizdets, *they'll have seen me.*" But then, who was this "they"? And why would they slip silently through the doorway to the staircase if they had seen a soldier sneak into the palace through a side door? The only logical conclusion would be that they also did not wish to be seen.

Perhaps it was an instinct, or perhaps it was Lev's realization that he had no clue as to the whereabouts of the hospital, but Lev found himself moving stealthily in pursuit of this mysterious person, through the doorway, down the staircase.

The heavy door closed behind him, and he slowed his steps, allowing his eyes to adjust to the darkness. As he reached the bottom of the stairwell, he could just discern the shape of a body splayed on the basement floor. A scrawny teenage boy. Alexei lay unconscious, his ragged breathing the only sound in the otherwise quiet dungeon.

Lev was reminded of a small bird he'd found as a boy, a hatchling that had fallen from its nest, lying broken and helpless on the ground below. He'd known better than to touch it, but had been drawn to it. Though the bird had lain silently, motionless, Lev had sensed the life within it still. Unsure how to help, he'd merely sat with the bird, tried to picture its delicate little bones rejuvenating, its sporadic heartbeat stabilizing, its body filling with life.

And so as he gazed down at Alexei, whose face so resembled his tsarevich, whose veins carried the same blood as Anastasia, he thought of the bird. How its bones had rejuvenated, how its heartbeat had stabilized, how its body had filled with life. How it had begun to move, chirping softly until its mother came to reclaim it.

He had never thought himself to have played any part in the bird's recovery, but had rather considered himself a witness to the miracle of nature. Because what was more natural than the perseverance of the spirit, the regeneration of life?

CHAPTER FORTY-TWO

"The mystery of human existence lies not in just staying alive, but in finding something to live for."

—*The Brothers Karamazov* by Fyodor Dostoyevsky

D ARKNESS, AT LAST, HAD replaced the ceaseless frantic dreaming within Alexei's mind. Darkness and deep throbbing pain were all that filled him, as he lay unconscious at the bottom of the staircase. Darkness, as the rivers of blood overflowed their banks within his leg. Within his elbow and hip—every place in his body that had bumped the staircase as he'd fallen. He welcomed the darkness, certain he was dying, and he was ready if it meant an end to the unbearable pain.

Until. Until the smallest fleck of light began to permeate that darkness. Faint, like a distant candle on a foggy night, but still, the darkness was no longer complete.

Leave me alone, his weary mind mumbled, his lips unmoving. But the light grew larger, as though the candle-bearer approached still. A presence, separate from Alexei and yet . . . within him. And it felt familiar. Alexei had been infiltrated like this before—just not quite like *this*. When Rasputin had laid his hand upon Alexei's chest, he had swept through Alexei like a powerful surge, locating the area of bleeding immediately and clogging the flow, thickening the blood, stopping it. But this was not that. It was not the forceful entry nor the surge of power that had been Rasputin. It was rather as though someone had gently slipped through an open door, quietly observing, offering a bit of light.

Take a look around, then, Alexei's mind grumbled soundlessly. *But watch out, or you'll drown in all this blood.* Alexei sensed the presence smile then, inquisitively.

This blood! Can't you see? It's filling my body and will soon kill me. You'll want to be out then.

The raging river seemed to calm just a bit, the candle becoming like the sun, peeking through the clouds to suggest an end to the storm within Alexei's leg. The puddles that had begun to form at his elbow, his hip—those dried up in the ever-growing light.

It was like a summer day on the beaches of Livadiya, lying in the sand as the sun soaked into his skin, warming his body, soothing his mind. Time became meaningless, it could have been seconds or hours. There was nothing but light and warmth and the smooth, gentle lapping of the sea. So content was Alexei to lie peacefully after countless hours of torturous pain that he hardly noticed the continued company of the gentle intruder. The presence seemed to nudge him then—no, someone *was* nudging him, nudging his shoulder.

"Can you wake up, Alexei?"

The voice was familiar to Alexei's ears, and he realized that the presence had withdrawn, that his senses were perceiving the world outside of his own body once again. His awareness returned to his body, to the hard cement beneath him, to the dampness of the basement. He opened his eyes.

"Lev?" He recognized his voice more so than his face in the dim light of the basement.

"Indeed." Lev spoke casually, despite the situation.

"What are you doing here?"

"I came for you."

"What . . . what am I doing here?"

The corner of Lev's mouth lifted in a half smile. "Good question. It would seem accidental, if I were guessing, as most tsarevich imposters do not make a habit of napping sprawled at the bottom of a basement staircase." Despite the sarcasm and the accusation, Lev's voice remained good-natured.

Alexei blinked, trying to remember. He had gotten to the truck, he'd had the garnet, the gun, the tsarevich. And then, Anastasia. Lev. The gunshot. An explosion. Anastasia, holding him. Anastasia, promising to find Rasputin. Anastasia, handing him over to the tsar. There had been a car. There had been flashes of dreams. And there had been pain, so much pain, and then here he was. No more pain, but for the dull ache of an injured foot, a bumped elbow.

Tsarevich imposter, Lev had said. Alexei peered at him warily. "What did she tell you?"

Lev extended his hand, helping to pull Alexei up to stand. "Enough to know that we've got to get you out of here, before the true tsarevich returns."

Alexei shifted weight to his injured leg, wincing slightly. "I was shot, was I not?"

"You were."

"And I've lived."

"It would certainly seem so."

"Without Rasputin."

"Apparently, he was my father. Anastasia recognized him in my mother's drawing."

Alexei balked. "Your *father*—"

But Lev stopped him, bringing his finger to his lips as he raised his eyebrows, listening. "We aren't alone down here." He looked over his shoulder. "Quickly, up the stairs."

Before Alexei could react to Lev's words, unknown hands emerged from the darkness and grabbed him, yanking him down the hallway, away from the stairs. Lev immediately sprung at the man, but was charged by a second foe, then a third.

"It's the little tsarevich—get him into the dungeon cell."

"This one, too?"

"Yes, and quickly. We've got to set the timer and be gone."

Lev and Alexei fought their oppressors, but were nonetheless wrestled into the dungeon cell, the men slamming the barred door behind them.

"They have no key, push!" Lev instructed Alexei, and he threw his body weight into the cell door, the two of them pushing with all of their strength as their imprisoners pushed back.

"Wedge the door!" While two of the men held Lev and Alexei at a gridlock, the cell door not budging, the third man grabbed a guard's stool and jammed the metal seat against the door, the legs pressing into the stone wall across.

Laughing cruelly, the men eased off the door and stood back, admiring their work. Lev stared back at them through the bars, wrinkling his brow as he noted the workmen's uniforms. *Carpenters? Did we just get caged in a dungeon by carpenters?*

Then one of the men, the oldest of the three, raised his brows. "I'll be damned. Luka? Thought you'd died." Unlike Kirill, this man did not appear particularly pleased at the notion of a still-living Luka. Assessing Lev skeptically, he added, "What are you doing with the tsarevich?"

Alexei looked at Lev curiously, while Lev scrambled to make sense of the situation. *Not carpenters. Narodnaya Volya.* Before he could answer, one of the other men chimed in.

"Trying to sneak him out of here, clearly!"

The older man eyed Lev coldly. "This whole plot was your idea—and you're working against it?"

Lev was momentarily stunned by the man's words. Before he could stop himself, he asked, "What whole plot?"

It was Alexei who answered, his eyes widening in recognition, his face horror-stricken. "The carpenters. The basement. The bomb!"

"A bomb?" Lev struggled to remain calm, to think. This was Luka's idea? His mind scrambled to piece together the scraps of information he'd learned in the last days. Luka had a lot of ideas, hadn't he? About *kolodtsy*—they could be anything. About magic—that it wasn't destroyed. He'd had some theory about the Winter Palace. And now, a bomb.

Twisting his mouth in disapproval, the older man nodded. "I knew you were *yobanyy* nuts. You had one good idea though. We've snuck enough dynamite in this place to take out half the building. Whether you were right or wrong about a blast releasing magic from this place, we know one thing for sure. It'll take out the tsar." He glanced at Alexei. "And the tsarevich." Then, eying Lev, "And you, if you're trying to stop it."

The other men were already backing away from the cell, content to leave their former comrade and the tsarevich to die. Lev had to say something, anything, and the only explanation that he could think of was the truth. Or at least, part of it.

"This boy is not the tsarevich—he's a double, it's complicated, but you've got to let us out—"

The older man shook his head, laughing humorlessly. "*Yobanyy* nuts." Then, addressing his companions, he spoke decisively. "Let's set the clock and go."

The three men turned, heading toward the guards' room beyond the staircase at the end of the hall. One of them checked his watch, his voice barely audible as they disappeared down the hall. "It's four now. Give it two hours."

Moments later, the men exited the guards' room, the older man casting one last glance in Lev and Alexei's direction. "Repairs are all done, Your Highness!" he called tauntingly, and they hurried up the staircase, leaving Alexei and Lev alone in their cell. Alexei jiggled the door, the metal stool not budging. Lev gaped at the empty stairwell in disbelief.

Thunder boomed once more, and a drop of water rolled through a small crack at the base of the wall, trickling along the floor within a groove between stones. Lev noticed it too, and the two watched silently as the water inched toward Alexei's bandaged foot.

There was a note of humor in Lev's tone as he sighed. "By fire, or by flood."

Alexei shook the cell door, trying to squeeze his hand between the bars. Useless. "By fire, or by flood," he echoed, and slumped to sit beside Lev against the damp stone wall of the dungeon.

SOME UNKNOWN QUANTITY of time had passed, measurable only by the rising water in the cell, now lapping around Alexei's knees, soaking his bandaged limb and promising infection. Alexei grimaced. But the bleeding had stopped. He looked to Lev.

"Can you explain . . . everything? Why they called you Luka? What they meant about magic?"

So Lev explained. He explained how magic-wielders had once stored power in *kolodtsy*, in gemstones like the garnets. He explained how the Narodnaya Volya had used magic to assassinate the last two tsars, all those years ago. And he explained how Tsar Nicholas had commanded his wielders to destroy all of Russia's magic, before exiling them all from the country. He told Alexei about the snippets he'd gleaned from his twin brother's theories—the theories that Ivan had found so interesting. And as Lev spoke, he began to piece it all together.

Alexei, clever as he was, beat Lev to it. "So those magicians—they didn't destroy the magic. They stored it in a big *kolodets*." He paused, looking around the dungeon contemplatively. "A big *kolodets* that's going to explode in an hour or so. Releasing its magic back into the air. And killing us."

Lev agreed, still dumbfounded by the unbelievable truth. "I suppose that sums it up."

Alexei mulled it over silently, his expression difficult to read.

"This happened in my world, too, you know. I mean, the palace wasn't a giant storage vessel for magic in my world, but the bomb happened the same way. The carpenters, the dynamite, the basement. Long ago." Then he raised his brows, his calculating mind always working. "They said this was Luka's idea. Your brother."

Lev nodded, knowing that for Luka, it had been all about releasing magic into the world once more, no matter the casualties. The tsar, the tsarina, the palace workers—all expendable to him.

Would he have stopped the bomb, knowing it would kill his twin brother? Was he so ruthless?

"It's interesting," Alexei continued, "that it should happen the same way here, all these years later." Rubbing his chin, he appeared puzzled. "Luka's idea," he repeated, and then he became quiet, thinking. A long moment passed in silence, as they each contemplated the strangeness of the situation that would inevitably lead to their deaths.

Minutes later, Alexei broke the silence, speaking matter-of-factly. "I always thought it'd be the hemophilia that killed me. The bleeding. I never imagined it would end like this."

Lev smiled wryly. "I can't say that I've thought much about how my life might end. But I don't suppose I would have imagined myself stuck in a flooding prison cell with the tsarevich of another dimension, counting down the hours 'til the palace explodes."

Alexei didn't laugh, didn't even smile. "What would you do with it, if it doesn't end here? Your life, I mean."

"What's there ever to do with it? Try to live well. To be happy, to make . . . to make someone else happy." Lev swallowed. "And you? What will you do?"

Alexei sat quietly for a moment, considering his answer as he stared into the swirling water around his knees. "I—I don't know. It's always seemed so simple. That I'd either die, or I'd become tsar. Those were the only two possibilities. Death or tsar. It wasn't a choice—it was an inevitability. Until I got here, and I had to start making choices, and . . . I want it, I do. I want to be tsar. I want to be somebody, to matter, to be remembered. But it's not just death or tsar now, it's not such a . . . such a duality, not here. I—I've had to make all these choices, and I've made bad ones. I hurt people. I hurt *her.*" Alexei looked up suddenly, meeting Lev's eyes as though he'd just remembered that he wasn't talking to himself, but rather, to another human being.

"So now, I don't know. I guess I'd . . ." he looked down, mumbling the last bit embarrassedly, ". . . be better. I'd make it up to Ana, somehow."

Lev sighed. "Well, with luck, you'll get the chance." Though he smiled, the grin didn't meet his eyes.

Alexei didn't bother to pretend the situation was anything but hopeless. "It will take something more than luck."

CHAPTER FORTY-THREE

"Don't tell me the moon is shining; show me the glint of light on broken glass."

—Anton Chekhov

RAIN CONTINUED TO POUR in sheets. Thoroughly soaked and covered with mud, I kept my head down as I ran along the silent street toward the Winter Palace. I panted with every splattering step, my body already pushed to its physical limit. Still, I continued my wayward route to the palace. Having anticipated streets teeming with soldiers and prison wagons, I'd looped around away from the river, crisscrossing through less prominent roads. But all the streets were eerily empty—the shops appeared closed, and some of the storefronts were damaged, as though they'd been ransacked.

I rounded the corner and skidded to a stop. There it was. The Winter Palace stood before me, its front lawn packed with soldiers on horseback. Resting my hands on my knees, I breathed heavily as I took in the scene. Of course the streets were empty. The soldiers were all here, guarding the Winter Palace. They didn't know, then, about the bomb. How many people would die in the explosion? Not only the tsar and tsarina—there were the soldiers, the staff, and my little brother in his hospital bed.

I had to stop the bomb. I had to find my brother. Somehow, I had to make it into that palace.

The northern rooms of the Winter Palace sat perched on the Neva, and the banks had overflown, spilling at least a foot of water onto the grounds. The horses were clearly not pleased with the situation and appeared to be growing increasingly difficult to manage. In fact, the soldiers seemed agitated themselves, restless, losing zeal for their station as water bombarded them from both sky and ground.

The Winter Palace was enormous—the grandest of all the Romanov castles. Countless windows opened into countless rooms, one of which would house my little brother, bleeding in his sickbed. And behind some other window, the tsar and the tsarina, the closest likenesses to my own father and mother in existence. And deeper within the palace, the dynamite. A ticking time bomb. It was difficult not to become overwhelmed.

I took a slow breath, exhaling through my mouth. One step at a time. First, I needed to get inside the palace. I needed to find that door. The one that Lev and I had exited through—I could find the staircase to the basement easily from there. The basement, I'd determined, was the most prudent destination. This bomb Mikhail had spoken of—it could explode at any moment. I needed to find it first, dismantle it, drown it, destroy it somehow—and then, locate Alexei.

And so I needed to find that door. I conjured the memory of Lev and I, exiting the palace in haste, Alexei's note in hand. We'd been strangers, united in our mission to save my brother, Lev's tsarevich, ignorant of the lies that drove us as we'd sprinted from the palace, alongside the river, toward the stables. My chest deflated as I swore under my breath. The river.

I gazed out toward the northern wall, where the boundless Neva splashed against the stone. It had swallowed the door and with it, my only semblance of a plan.

Sighing, I turned my gaze to the front lawn, where tired soldiers worked to calm their horses as the water continued to rise. I squinted. It appeared that two horsemen had broken away from the group—were they abandoning duty? —and had thus been stopped by a leader of some sort, I supposed, and there was some yelling, an altercation, and then—chaos. They were joined by more men—I couldn't tell if they were deserting as well, or if they'd gone after the two—but it erupted in a brawl of tired, angry men and frightened horses, splashing and punching and shoving in the relentless rain.

This was it—my chance. It was the best distraction I could hope for, to shield my dash for the palace. A hundred meters to the closest wall, I guessed, with no trees, shrubs, or well-placed bush courtesy of Catherine the Great—not this time. Only water. Better to stay low, hidden beneath the water. Feeling rather ridiculous, I dropped to my hands and knees, sinking my body into the cold muddy water, my face just barely above the surface. And I took off in an awkward scampering crawl, moving as quickly as I could across the exposed yard, praying that the soldiers would be too preoccupied with each other to notice me.

Halfway there. I had to get to the wall. Then, south. Find a door. And pray that I could find the basement from there. The soggy earth squished beneath my knees, mud consuming my hands as I crawled, my eyes skimming just above the surface. Seeing only the wall, only my destination, only . . . another head, floating just above the water's surface as the body crawled beneath, moving toward the palace.

I stopped for a moment, looking back toward the soldiers, fully engaged in a chaotic brawl. Then I looked again to the head, or rather, the person, who had now reached the palace wall and was turning toward me. Cursing to myself, I dropped my chest to the ground and plunged my head beneath the surface, but not before my ears caught the sound of a familiar voice.

"Anastasia?"

Too late. I raised my head from the water, wiping the mud from my face as I opened my eyes.

The face looking back at me was busted, with blackened eyes and a swollen lip. But beneath the bruises, I knew those gray-blue eyes, that narrow nose, the soft chin.

"Alexei?" As the name left my mouth, I realized my mistake. Alexei—yes, but no. It was not my brother, but the tsarevich who crouched beneath the flood waters with the Winter Palace at his back. It had to be, because my brother never would have survived the beating that marred this boy's face. Not without Rasputin. And the gunshot had been so much worse. Glancing to the palace, I wrinkled my brow in anxious helplessness. *Are you still alive, little brother?*

"Didn't you hear me? Anastasia?"

I blinked, drawn back to the present and the Alexei before me.

"I said, did you come to find Lev?" The tsarevich watched me inquisitively as I gaped. Lev? Was he here?

"I . . ." I looked over my shoulder, where soldiers were still fighting one another, or else riding off into the rain. Distracted for the moment, but I knew that my chances of making it into the palace undiscovered lessened the longer I lingered.

"I need to get into the palace, Your Highness." Your Highness. The words did not taste so foreign in my mouth as they once had. I must have been growing used to my new position in the world, without a title of my own. Not a princess, not a rebel, just Anastasia. Just a girl trying her best to save the people she loves.

Refocused on the mission before me, I turned my gaze to the palace's southern doors, the nearest accessible entry. Despite the disturbance that preoccupied the soldiers in the yard, sentries still stood guard at the entrance.

"Well, so do I. I'm afraid I'll need to sneak in, though." The tsarevich glanced at the palace and then to me. There was a sadness in his gray-blue eyes that hadn't been there before. He was a changed boy, it seemed, from the silly child Lev and I had met in the woods of the Luzhsky Uyezd. Witnessing the brutal murder of one's sisters had that effect upon a person. I winced, my own dark thoughts cutting deep.

"Supposedly there's some other boy here, pretending to be me," he continued. "No one seems to recognize me—no one but you, anyhow. I'm afraid I'd be turned away if I tried the main entrance. Anyway, I'll be going in through the basement. Swimming in, you might say. Rather unsuitable for a lady, but . . ." He trailed off, the look on his face implying that the drenched, mud-covered mess before him hardly qualified as a lady.

I cocked my head to the side with a smirk and flicked a glob of mud from my shoulder. "Oh, but Your Highness, I'd just hate to sully my dress!"

He chuckled, though the grin did not quite meet his eyes, and motioned for me to follow him. "Come on, then."

And we ducked our heads beneath the muddy water, submerged as we felt our way along the grimy wet stone of the palace wall. I followed the tsarevich, this boy I'd written off as a sweet but incompetent idiot, who was now my only hope of finding my brother. And maybe . . . finding Lev.

The tsarevich stopped suddenly, having found the drop he was looking for, where the stone wall extended downward to an underwater basement door. I toed the top step of the staircase, then popped my head above the water.

As the tsarevich pulled a soldier's rifle from his side, his eyes lit up with that certain type of joy exclusive to thirteen-year-old boys preparing to blow something up. "Our key," he explained with a grin and disappeared again beneath the water. A muffled bang, and then he resurfaced, appearing satisfied. "Ready, my lady?"

I nodded, and we dove down, blinded beneath the murky water, but my hand found the slick metal of the door. On cue, I rammed my bodyweight into the hard metal, pushing with the tsarevich to lurch the door open.

We fell into the open air of the wet basement, gasping for breath as a wall of water crashed through the open doorway behind us. The water poured in, submerging me to my shoulders. Paddling my arms like a dog in a river, I kept my head above the water as the current swept us down the hallway toward the stairs.

"*Pizdets!*" A familiar voice shouted a series of expletives from down the quickly flooding hallway, growing louder as we neared its source. My brother could swear like a war seasoned Cossack. But how . . . wasn't he supposed to be bleeding to death in the hospital ward? What was he doing in the basement? I felt a brief sense of relief that he was well enough to have made it to the basement, followed by horror as I remembered that aside from the bleeding, there was the flood, there was the bomb, there were the guards.

The force of the water kept washing us down the hall, and my arms were already tiring.

"Alexei?" I yelled frantically as I pushed my feet off the floor, working to keep my head above the water.

"Anastasia?" The tsarevich's voice melded with my brother's in answer.

And then I saw them. My brother and Lev, neck-deep in water and clinging to the bars of a prison cell as the water continued to rise.

"Alexei!" I seized the bars, pulling as though I might rip the door from its hinges, tearing down the barrier that separated me from my little brother. He was alive, kicking frantically as the rising water swept his feet from the floor. If we could just get out of this basement—

"Holy God, Anastasia, you're here." Lev's deep green eyes found my own, searching. "You're here," he repeated. "I'm sorry. If I'd known, I never would have . . ." He glanced at my brother. "I didn't—I just—I'm sorry, Anastasia."

I held Lev's gaze, remembering his face, hurt and confused, disappearing behind that truck door as I slammed it down. "I'm sorry, too," I said quietly, and for a moment, we just stood there, neck-deep in floodwater, staring at one another with tentative hope in our eyes. Hope that if we survived, we might put this behind us. Hope that we might still have a chance.

Beside me, the tsarevich gripped the cell door, staring at the face floating before him, identical to his own. "I—you—how—?"

"Anastasia, the door! It's wedged—" My brother, the smallest of the four of us, failed to keep the panic from his voice as he clung to the cell bars, craning his neck to keep his nose above the water.

Immediately, I plunged beneath the water, gripping the cold metal bars of the cell door with one hand and feeling around blindly with the other. As I swatted through the water, my hand found a saturated wooden stool, lodged between the door and the wall. With both hands, I grabbed it and shook. It took all my strength, pulling and pushing until the stool slipped free and the cell door swung open.

I kicked to the surface, gasping for breath as I wiped the muddy water from my eyes.

Lev was already helping my brother move through the water, following the tsarevich to the stairwell. I made my exhausted body keep moving, swimming after them down the hall. At the dry stone steps, Lev reached for my hands, pulling me from the water and into his arms.

For a moment, I just allowed myself to be held, resting my head against his sturdy chest as I caught my breath.

My brother and the tsarevich were perched on the step above us, in discussion of the next urgent matter—the bomb. The tsarevich wrinkled his brow. "But wouldn't the dynamite be quite wet?"

Alexei rolled his eyes, unimpressed by his counterpart. "Carpenters, you prat. They won't have just left a bomb on the *floor*." He paused, as though searching his memory for some specific piece of information. Then— "They'll have snuck a lot of dynamite in, and they'll have built it into the walls, into the ceiling. In the guards' chamber."

Frowning, Lev looked to the guards' room at the end of the hall, where the rising water was still feet from the ceiling. "Does anyone have the time?"

"Ten 'til six," the tsarevich answered, wiping water from the face of his heirloom pocket watch.

"Ten minutes," Lev muttered. "We have ten minutes." His eyes darted to the guards' room, then darkened, his brow furrowing as he shook his head. "It's not enough time. We've got to get out of here."

Ten minutes. My mind reeled. *It's not enough time.* Not enough time to try to stop the bomb and still get out of here if we failed. I knew that was what he meant. But how many lives would be lost when the bomb exploded? We had to at least warn them, didn't we?

What had I told Alexei, days ago, worlds ago? *"I would save them,"* I'd said. *"I would do whatever it took, to keep them alive."*

Lev motioned us up the stairs, and I pushed ahead, leading the way through the door out of the dark, wet basement. Muddy sludge splattered on the bright marble floors as I burst into the Winter Palace's resplendent hallway. The exit was just to our left, but I turned right, sprinting deeper into the palace.

"Anastasia! There's no time—we've got to get out!" But Lev turned right too, racing behind me.

"There's a bomb!" I yelled for whoever might hear me, my desperate warning echoing down the hall. There was no time for royal etiquette. "Get out, now! Anyone, everyone, get out!"

Looking around frantically as I ran, I saw no one but Lev. Where was my brother? The tsarevich? Then footsteps pounded down an intersecting hall, a voice calling out, "Intruders!"

"There's a bomb!" I yelled again, grateful to encounter someone, anyone who might help us spread the word before we ran out of time. Then more men appeared, running at us as though *we* were the intruders. I looked over my shoulder just in time to see Lev tackled to the ground, and more guards running at me. One of them reached for me, and I ducked, shrieking my warning once more.

"There's a bomb! It's going to explode any minute—everyone must—" I gasped as a guard collided with me, knocking the breath from my lungs and my feet out from beneath me. My back hit the floor, my head whipping backward against the marble with a dizzying smack.

As drums pounded within my skull, I could still hear Lev trying to reason, trying to explain. But the guards were not interested in our words.

"Take them to the throne room," one of the men instructed. "His Majesty wishes to address intruders directly."

Yes. Take me to him! I need to tell him—was I speaking out loud? My head throbbed and my vision blurred. I made my mouth move, made it make sounds, my voice a faint murmur as I repeated once again, "There's a bomb."

CHAPTER FORTY-FOUR

"Mere existence had always been too little for him; he had always wanted more."

—*Crime and Punishment* by Fyodor Dostoyevsky

A LEXEI STOOD FROZEN ON the stairs alongside his double, considering the impossibility of what must be done.

Anastasia had already disappeared through the door, with Lev right behind her. "Ten minutes. We have ten minutes." Lev's voice sounded far away as he bounded up the stairs. "We've got to get out of here!"

The urgency of the situation was not lost on Alexei. But neither boy moved.

"Built into the walls and ceiling, you say." The tsarevich no longer stared at him in astonishment. Now, he had a far-off look on his face—perhaps remembering the explosion that had ended his sisters' lives. "I have to . . . my parents—" His voice broke and he looked away, blinking back his tears.

Alexei glanced upward as Lev followed Anastasia through the door at the top of the stairs. *He'll take care of her,* Alexei thought. And he looked back to the tsarevich. "And if you fail?"

The tsarevich met Alexei's gaze, his face perplexed.

"I . . . I would die. My parents, everyone in the palace, we would all die."

Alexei nodded. "And who would rule?"

"I dunno, my uncle, gosh—you, I suppose. It doesn't matter—I have to—"

Both boys stood frozen on the stairway, each looking into the face that so mirrored his own. The same eyes, the same nose and mouth, but a different life, a different soul. Each born to rule, and never meant to coexist, never meant to meet.

Or were they? Was everything that had happened, the execution, the garnets, all the lies that had led them here—was there some purpose to it all?

"In some world, I could be tsar," he'd said. Universes ago.

"I would save my family," she'd said. *"I would do whatever it took, to keep them alive."* And she would. She was. But there wasn't enough time.

One boy looked to the other, an understanding passing between them. "Go," the boy whispered, his gray-blue eyes resolute. "You go. I . . . I have to save them." The other boy hesitated, but nodded, and followed the others up the stairs.

CHAPTER FORTY-FIVE

"It is impossible to expel evil from the world in its entirety, but it is possible to constrict it within each person."

—*The Gulag Archipelago* by Aleksandr Solzhenitsyn

I CAN DO THIS, Alexei told himself, treading water as he kicked his feet, searching for the step up toward the guards' chamber. *I can save them.* His bandaged foot met stone and he winced in pain. But only winced. Though the wound was still there, the bleeding had stopped. Dried up, like a rain puddle in the sun.

The imagery contrasted sharply with the scene before him. The guards' room, though elevated several steps higher than the rest of the basement, was still full of water. Submerged to his waist, Alexei trudged into the room, his eyes searching for some sign of the dynamite.

Alexei closed his eyes. What had his father told him?

"The rebels, traitorous as they were, were rather clever in this instance. Over a course of time, men of the Narodnaya Volya snuck what amounted to quite a lot of dynamite into the basement of the Winter Palace, building it into the walls and ceilings in the guards' chamber, just beneath the dining room."

Built it into the walls and ceilings. The interior walls would be all wooden—he could tear them down, if he had a tool. Even if there was an ax in the room, could he find it beneath the water, break through the walls, and sink enough of the dynamite before the clock struck six?

The clock. I just need to find the clock.

Alexei searched, dragging his injured leg with its waterlogged bandage through the waist-deep sludge, scanning with his eyes, feeling with his hands, thinking, *thinking*, while somewhere within that room, the clock ticked.

Five minutes. Four minutes. Ticking, ticking.

Scanning, searching, feeling, thinking.

Ticking.

Three minutes. Two.

I have to find it. I have to, or they'll die. The tsar, the tsarina. The tsarevich . . .

He'd had his opportunity, hadn't he? To let them all die. To release the magic into this world once again. To run free. The lone survivor, they'd have said. A gift from God, they'd have said, that the heir to the throne had survived. The youngest tsar to be crowned in Russian history, they'd have said. He would be cherished. He would be revered. And when he died, thousands would mourn.

But he'd made his choice, and he would not be those things. He would be a better brother. He would be a better person. *I have to save them.*

One minute.

And he saw it. A loose panel in the wall, up high and slightly crooked, as though someone had shoved it hastily into place. Pressing himself into the wall, Alexei stretched his arm, reaching—no, he would have to climb.

Splashing frantically through the water now, Alexei found a chair, one he'd stumbled into minutes ago, and dragged it across the room. He couldn't help but cry out in pain as he pressed through his injured leg, climbing up, reaching—he had it, the board slid away easily enough, and there it was, the clock, the secondhand ticking toward the hour mark as he reached—

Thunder rumbled across the sky in a long, drawn-out bellow.

And the clock struck six.

CHAPTER FORTY-SIX

"... the earth quietly swam away from under my feet."

—Ivan Turgenev

EVERYTHING PULSED WITH SPECKS of light, like the sun reflecting along the surface of the sea. Bright and shiny, the marble floor gleamed between muddied boots as I kicked and thrashed, my head bursting as the guards dragged me along.

I was vaguely aware of Lev, still fighting the guards and shouting about the bomb. And the tsarevich, racing down the hallway behind us, pleading to be heard. But there were louder, adult voices speaking over him, drowning out his frenzied warnings. He was still feverish, they said. He ought to be in bed.

Alexei. Where was Alexei? Had he turned left? He must have. He . . . he must have.

My ears were ringing, the sounds all converging into a white noise, a fuzzy hum that filled my head. My head, argh, it was so *full*, as though it might burst, exploding from atop my neck in a flurry of glimmering light and mud and blood. With all my remaining strength, I still struggled against my captors as they shoved me through an enormous gilded doorway.

Stumbling forward, I heaved my chin from my chest, rolling my head back to see, and then I knew.

I must have died. My head had split open, and I'd died.

But it was okay. This was surely heaven, this place.

I was standing in an opulent hall, in a glimmering haze. Honeyed light gleamed off the glass of magnificent arched windows, framed with decorated columns. An enormous chandelier hung from the ceiling high above, lit with hundreds of tiny, flickering flames. And across the room, on their gilded thrones, sat my parents. My mother, her long amber hair hanging loose over her shoulders as she gazed toward me. My father, his mustache curled atop an amused smile as though he were waiting for something.

Waiting for me, here in death.

So I knew I must have died.

There were more voices, but I didn't hear them.

I only heard the thunder, rumbling across the sky in a long, drawn-out bellow.

Then Lev's face, next to mine, and he said something. Asked me something, I thought. When I didn't answer, he took me by the shoulders and pressed his lips to mine.

Maybe not dead. Maybe dreaming.

Because then there was another boom, and the earth shook, and I was sitting on a grassy hilltop beside Lev and my brother. A spellbinding chime seemed to grow from the ground, vibrating through the air and into my very bones. A force, both foreign and intimately familiar, swept through me, filling me with tingly, beautiful, raw *power*. But just for a moment, and then it was gone, leaving me utterly dazed as golden beams of light shot across the sky, swirling through St. Petersburg in a glittering flurry. And as bricks and marble erupted in a burst of bright flames, I watched the Winter Palace explode.

CHAPTER FORTY-SEVEN

"Everyone thinks of changing the world, but no one thinks of changing himself."

—Leo Tolstoy

I T WAS LIKE A dream, but one of those unpleasant sorts, where one realizes that one could awaken, if only his eyes could peel open. But they wouldn't. Were they sewn shut? No . . . no, he could lift his lids a bit. They were not sewn shut. They were caked in mud.

In fact, Mikhail was not dreaming. He was quite awake. And he knew it to be so, because someone was pinching him, right on the cheek, and he could feel it.

"St-stop." He uttered the word hoarsely, as though the mud caking his eyes and ears and nostrils had seeped into his throat, coating his voice in sludge.

Mikhail wiped the mud from his eyes, blinking them open to find himself prone on the deserted prison grounds, alone in the desolate swamp. No one had been pinching him, then, but something pointy had punctured his cheek—he could feel the warm wetness of his own fresh blood streaking down his face, in sharp contrast with the cold slurry that covered the rest of him.

He reached beneath the mud, his fingers searching the ground for the culprit, until they closed around something hard, angular—a prism. *Could it be? Had it fallen from the iron box? Could fortune have smiled upon me finally?*

Mikhail was afraid to open his hand. Afraid he might open it and find just a rock. Just some jagged pebble and not the gemstone that could save his family and his soul. Lightning flashed, thunder rumbling across the sky in a long, drawn-out bellow. He unclenched his fist and swallowed a sob when he saw it, the deep red gemstone gleaming against his mud-caked palm.

The *kolodets*. He wasted no time, taking the gun from his side and pulling the trigger.

～～～～～～

WITH EVERY STEP, it was as though Mikhail was splashing into a pond, the suspended raindrops waiting for him, then sticking to his skin, rolling down his face. He had hurried at first, running toward the Winter Palace, and then slowed, realizing that there was truly no hurry. Not with time frozen.

Should time start again, he had his gun and the garnet. But he was thinking that it wouldn't start again, not on its own. Not until he shot the gemstone once more. Because that was what had happened. He had pointed his gun at the ground, and the bullet had found the *kolodets* where it waited, hidden in some muddy puddle. No, he was the master of time, as long as he held that gemstone.

He toyed with the garnet in his pocket, his fingers tracing the edges of the prism. *Unbelievable.* For over eighteen years, he'd believed that all magic had been destroyed. But it hadn't—not all of it. He marveled at the evidence in his hand. Magic still existed, if only in this one tiny remnant from the past. A *kolodets*. They existed, after all. Could there be more? And if there were more, what could that mean for this revolution?

Mikhail scowled at the thought, so contrary to his current mission. The revolution. His family. Maybe someday, he could have both. But not today.

When he arrived at the submerged bridge, Mikhail imagined Dina, gazing out at the raging river from atop that wild horse. Had she reopened the box, intent on stopping time once more for her passage, only to find the inlay empty? Had she dared cross as the water pushed forward as relentlessly as time itself? Or was she still here somewhere, a beautiful statue of a woman he'd thought he'd known? A woman he thought he'd loved. Had loved. Still loved. A woman who shared his dreams of a democratic Russia. A woman who valued that dream over everything. Over her family's lives. Over her own husband's life. He shook his head and waded across the bridge, continuing toward the Winter Palace.

Pine branches curved from tree trunks at odd angles, stopped mid-wave as the wind halted with time. Fat rain drops shaken from the trees hung suspended in the air. The scene was like a painting, like a snapshot. A blip in the perpetuity of time, preserved. The main street was nearly empty, but for a sullen shopkeeper, frozen at his shattered storefront window. His was not the only damaged storefront—broken glass lined the street. There'd been violence, clearly. Mikhail wondered briefly if the soldiers' raids or the rebels' riots were to blame for the vandalism.

He didn't know how long he'd been walking. It had been hours, and it had been no time at all. He supposed he existed outside of time. Around it. If time was a wool blanket, Mikhail existed between its woven fibers. *No, Mikhail thought. Not a blanket. An orb weaver's web. And entrapped in the web lies the spider's prey.* He conjured the image of those rebels who'd assaulted him. Of the guards, who'd dragged him from his cell. Of his brother, who'd condemned him to prison, who'd spent fortunes on foreign automobiles while his own people starved. *My brother,* Mikhail corrected himself, *whom I betrayed. Whom I owe. Whom I love.*

Mikhail reached out, plucking a pine needle from a low hanging branch as he neared the palace, the branch reverberating from the release, oscillating gently until rejoining the stillness of the scene.

Such power, Mikhail thought, *holds the orb weaver.*

But such shame. Such shame.

Mikhail began to run. Not to outrun the bomb, not to outrun time. But to outrun his own conflicting thoughts, his own mind as it threatened to betray him.

There was a certain weakness within him. An indecisiveness that spurred him to make half-choices. To believe ridiculously that he could have it all. That he could be both a Romanov and a revolutionary. That he could take the throne peacefully, that he could sit upon it as leader of the Narodnaya Volya. But he hadn't formed those ideas all on his own, had he?

Dina had seen him for what he was. A gullible optimist, a vulnerable idealist. A puppet.

These thoughts swirled in Mikhail's mind as he ran through the static streets toward the towering Winter Palace, offensively ornate in its enormity, but *home.*

As he reached the intricate iron gates, Mikhail didn't stop, ramming through the gilded doors. He stepped into the grand hall and coughed as the smell of smoke hung heavily in the air, overwhelming his senses. Thicker, stronger as he reached the basement door and followed the smoke down the stairs, into the murky water that filled the space.

Then he saw the flame. It was just the beginnings of the explosion to come, the dynamite having just burst through the walls of the guards' chamber in a still-frame explosion of wood and stone and . . . something else. Mikhail sniffed the air, but he couldn't quite place it. He was reminded of those moments of stillness before an electrical storm, when the air buzzes with restrained energy. Through stagnant clouds of thick smoke, through the spark and ember nebula hanging in the air, that energy began to seep through its restraints. Time remained frozen, but it was as though this mysterious force—this pulsating power—was not subject to the laws that govern the natural world.

Mikhail knew this feeling, this presence. The humming *kolodets* in his pocket knew it, too. Knew it, came from it, and called to it. Its source. *Could it be? Has it been here, all this time?* He sank against the stone wall of the dungeon hall, his mind reeling. Like the bullet to the gemstone, this explosion was releasing magic into the world once more. Releasing power from the palace. *What could this mean for the revolution? For Russia?*

Exhaling slowly, Mikhail allowed himself a moment to ponder. Magic would change everything. If the revolution could find wielders and use them wisely, perhaps his dream for Russia was possible, after all. But that meant restarting time, allowing the explosion to continue, allowing the Winter Palace's fiery destruction. He gazed toward the guards' chamber. And there, at the center of the budding explosion—there was the little tsarevich, helpless, frozen mid-scream. The boy was the heir to the throne, the barrier between Mikhail and the power to enact change. The boy . . . the boy was his nephew, trapped in the web.

I am not the spider, Mikhail told himself. An idea struck him, then, and he moved through the smoke, into the burning heat of the guards' chamber. Coughing, he collected the boy and climbed the stairs, trudging down the glistening marble hall and out of the gaudy palace. He hiked up to a dry hilltop, propping the boy's limp form against a tree. The first of countless trips. In and out, one body at a time. The tsar and tsarina on their golden thrones. And with them, a boy, his face badly bruised, but beneath the swelling was the face of his nephew. Another boy, identical to the boy he'd dragged from the basement, another Alexei. It was true, then, the whispers. But Mikhail didn't stop to marvel—no, he'd witnessed far stranger phenomena that day. This boy, whoever he was, was just another body to carry from the palace. Another life to be saved.

And so he continued, from the palace to the hilltop and back again, and again, and again. His family first, and then the guards, the staff. A soldier, his face familiar . . .

And the girl. Mikhail brought his hand to his pocket, his fingers grazing the smooth surfaces of the magical garnet within. How had this girl come to possess such a gem? Mikhail brushed her hair from her face as he loaded her onto his shoulder. Her face . . . her face was familiar, too. Not just from the prison. But . . . Mikhail found himself thinking of his nieces. Those sweet, innocent girls, whose pretty faces had been engulfed in violent flames.

I am not the spider, Mikhail told himself again.

And once the Winter Palace sat empty, its ornate halls housing not one soul, Mikhail stopped moving at last. He sank against a solid oak tree, gazing out at the red-walled palace in the distance—the legacy of the Romanov empire.

For centuries, those walls had housed love and family, seen young boys grow to be men, grow to be tsars. But those walls had been a barrier, too, drawing a thick boundary between the rulers and the ruled. A barrier, containing power that ought to be shared—power that ought to be *released*. With somber resolution, Mikhail found his gun. Found the gemstone. A single tear rolled down his cheek as he whispered good-bye to his childhood home.

And then he pulled the trigger, smiling as the *yobanyy* monstrosity burst into flames.

CHAPTER FORTY-EIGHT

"Love destroys death and turns it into an empty phantom; it turns life from nonsense into something meaningful and makes happiness out of misery."

—*The Circle of Reading* by Leo Tolstoy

N O EXPENSE HAD BEEN spared. The caskets were maple, embellished with rubies and emeralds and diamonds that glittered under the bright morning sun.

The sun had reappeared several days ago, and had since set to work drying up the submerged St. Petersburg streets. And as the sun dried the earth, a softly smiling sparkle illuminated the city. Every surface seemed to shine. Magic rode the air like a pleasant hum, waiting to be activated.

You would never know, now, that the city had been underwater days ago. Unless you were one of the thousands who lost a loved one, or one of the hundreds who lost their homes. They had come, all of them, to mourn their loved ones, their homes, all that had been lost.

And of course, to mourn the Grand Duchesses.

Behind the three caskets stood the tsar and tsarina, draped in black silk and dark lace. And beside them sat the tsarevich, the bruising on his face having healed to reveal a deep sadness in his eyes, a grim determination in the set of his jaw. There were dark circles beneath his eyes, as if he hadn't slept in days. He gazed out at the masses assembled, his eyes searching, but never landing upon us.

Alexei, Lev, and I sat perched on a dilapidated rooftop, overlooking the assorted congregation of the poor and the wealthy and everyone in between. Though the crowd was dotted with armed soldiers, there was no sign of the rebels. They had faded back into the periphery—for now, anyway.

In the aftermath of the bomb, and as the floodwaters drained away, the tsar had acted quickly. His soldiers resumed their raids, arresting and rearresting as many suspected Narodnaya Volya men as they could find. Some had slipped away, though, according to Lev. His unit had been assigned to arrests, and it seemed that Mikhail and Dina, at least, had not been found. They were out there somewhere with the garnets and with the knowledge of how to use them. I stiffened at the thought, and behind me, Lev's chest expanded against my back as he inhaled and placed his hand over mine.

Then Tsar Nicholas stood. A hush fell over the crowd as thousands of heads lifted, turning to look upon their tsar, eagerly awaiting what he might have to say. When he spoke, his voice boomed through the amplifiers, filling the city square.

"Perhaps the worst moment a father may experience is the death of his child." His face remained unreadable as he turned toward his wife, who stared blankly at the caskets, as though still not believing they housed her daughters' dismembered remains. "And certainly, the worst moment a tsar may experience is the reckless disobedience of his nation." He looked out to the crowd, his expression one of carefully controlled rage.

"The bomb that ended my daughters' lives was a coward's cry for attention. And so I speak now to the Narodnaya Volya when I say that you have my attention." The tsar swept his hand upward with the word "attention," and in response, the soldiers in the crowd raised their guns, as though ready to shoot on command. "You will be found and exterminated," he said simply, growing silent for a moment as he scanned the crowd. Then he waved his hand again, and the soldiers lowered their guns. His message was clear.

But if the threat of the imperial army wasn't enough to solidify the tsar's unbroken authority, his next words were.

"The bomb that razed my palace, however, was my own doing."

I startled, intrigued by the tsar's false claim.

A murmur passed through the crowd and then quieted as the tsar continued.

"The Winter Palace, as you have all undoubtedly ascertained, was a *kolodets,* storing all of Russia's magic for the last eighteen years, eight months, and fourteen days. The power it held was released with the bomb. And the power it held is now mine."

With that, he raised both hands, gesturing dramatically. In a golden swirl, the glimmer in the air coalesced around the jewel-covered caskets, and they rose from their stand, levitating in the air. My jaw dropped, my eyes fixed on the spectacle before me.

Alexei nudged me, nodding toward the tsarevich. Still sitting beside his mother in the background of the scene, the boy was sweating profusely with his eyes squeezed tightly closed. When he opened them and saw the caskets floating in the air, his face alighted with immense relief, and the caskets lowered once again.

Without missing a beat, the tsar lowered his hands, his eyes flashing briefly with what looked like annoyance, or perhaps disappointment, that his performance had ended so soon. But he quickly reset his features to exude an authoritative confidence. He looked out at the crowd once more. "Mine," he repeated, gesturing toward the now-scattering light, "and mine alone."

The crowd beheld their tsar silently for a moment, and then erupted with an applause too raucous for the somber occasion. But perhaps against the backdrop of such tragedy, the people took comfort in their tsar's display of strength. I glanced again at the tsarevich, who appeared rather pale.

His demonstration of power now complete, Tsar Nicholas turned toward an old priest in traditional robes. "And now, a blessing from our Priest Patriarch." He then returned to sit with his wife, clapping his son's shoulder as he passed. The applause ended abruptly, and a reverent quiet fell over the square as the funeral proceeded.

For another moment, the three of us stood in shock, until I broke the silence, keeping my voice low.

"What a liar."

Alexei snorted. "What else could he do? It looks pretty weak, being the victim of two bombs in two days. A liar, sure, but it's a smart move. Lucky for him, his son is a magic-wielder."

I blinked. Though I'd come to the same conclusion, to hear it voiced aloud was rather startling.

Behind me, Lev clicked his tongue. "I'm curious if others noticed, or if the crowd was too distracted by the tsar's theatrics."

"Either way," I said, "it was effective."

We stood quietly then, listening as the priest delivered his blessings and scriptures. Despite the disturbing display I'd witnessed just moments before, I found myself rather entranced by the service. Thousands of voices joined in a sweet, sad hymn, and the sound of song held a sort of magic of its own, rising from the crowd below. My heart panged, as I knew that in my own world, my sisters had not been honored with such a memorial. I didn't let myself imagine what might have become of their remains. Shaking my head, I remembered the guilt I'd felt before.

Guilt that I'd survived. But as I'd crossed that raging river, as I'd watched that tree branch disappear down the Neva, I'd let go of the guilt. I'd let go of the anger and the self-doubt, and I'd chosen to move forward, just as my family would want me to. There had to be some reason for it, whether designated by fate or Rasputin or myself. I had a purpose. I just hadn't quite discovered it yet.

The song came to an end, and the priest sprinkled holy water upon the coffins. Then the crowd began to wind into circles around them, and from our aerial viewpoint, it was like watching a slow swirling dance.

Keeping his gaze fixed on the maple caskets at the center of the assembly below, Alexei spoke thoughtfully. "It's . . . nice, in a way, to see them buried. I mean, it's not *them,* but it's something like closure." He was silent for a moment. "Do you know what I mean?"

I met my brother's eyes. For once in my life, I thought for a moment before I spoke.

"I know what you mean. It helps. It's taking time to stop, to stop moving and look back and try to accept what has happened." It would take a long time to grieve. In the days that had passed since the bomb, nightmares still haunted my sleep. They still crept about during daylight, too, but hadn't overpowered me as they had before. Shaking my head, I looked to the sky. "I still have so many questions."

Alexei nodded. "Like how we got out of the Winter Palace, for one."

All three of us turned our heads, looking to where the Winter Palace still stood under a haze of smoke.

Half of it, anyway—the northern wall of the colossal palace had crumbled in the explosion, the embers still smoldering. It had been spectacular to see, and delirious as I'd been on that hilltop, I could still recall the image of orange flames and golden light illuminating a purple sky, showering the soggy earth with scorched stone.

Lev shook his head, removing his hand from mine as he began to pace. "Perhaps it was the magic. When the force of the bomb released it from the palace, maybe the magic was . . . I don't know, feeling *nice.* Maybe it chose to save us."

I shrugged. "Or the tsarevich—if he's a magic-wielder, maybe it was him." Could it have been, though? Magic-wielder he may be, but a novice. Even now, he was hardly a master of his newfound ability. He seemed to be straining quite a bit to levitate the coffins, and to teleport a large quantity of people from the palace seemed like a much more difficult feat.

Alexei wrinkled his nose, unimpressed with our theories. "I think it had to be the Time Stopper." He spoke, of course, of the second garnet, using the nickname he'd coined for it during one of our numerous discussions of the events that had transpired. "How else? Time must have been stopped, and we must have been moved."

It was my turn to shake my head. "Dina wouldn't have moved anyone. I told you, she's homicidal. Regicidal, I should say. She wants her kid to be tsar. There's no way she would have cleared anyone out of the way of that bomb." I paused, thinking.

"Mikhail, then." Alexei still gazed at the Winter Palace, where it smoldered. "Mikhail would have done it."

"Would he though?" Lev raised an eyebrow. "Last I checked, he was a prop of the Narodnaya Volya. And next in line to be tsar, had the bombing gone as planned."

"He was a prick." Alexei swallowed, an odd look on his face as he looked to me. "He was selfish. And stupid. He betrayed his closest family. And he . . . he did all he could to make it right again."

I smiled softly. "Then he succeeded."

Unaware of the tender moment passing between brother and sister, Lev continued. "Maybe. But even so, it's unsettling to think of such power in the hands of Mikhail and Dina Romanov—"

Alexei returned my smile, then smirked, holding my gaze as he quipped, "Maybe we get lucky, and they use World Hopper instead."

"—and then there's the possibility of a third garnet. Who knows how many more *kolodtsy* are out there, and how many more wielders . . ." Lev trailed off, shoving his hands in his pockets as he stopped pacing. "It's unsettling," he repeated.

Alexei dropped the smirk, becoming quite serious as he turned to Lev. "And what about you? You can manipulate magic, can you not? You healed me."

We'd had this conversation before, and Lev had brushed it off, as though he was still skeptical of magic despite all we'd witnessed. As though he wasn't ready to face his own abilities and what they might mean. He reacted similarly now. "I don't know what I did or how I did it, but I'm glad you're better."

"But you—"

"I don't feel any different," Lev raised his voice slightly, cutting Alexei off. "And I . . . I've tried. To pull magic from the air. Maybe I'm just doing it wrong, but you'd think if the tsarevich can figure it out, I could, too. Anyway, I can't, so there must be some other explanation."

Alexei pursed his lips, as though considering what other possibilities might exist.

My mind was not on the hows and whys of Alexei's mysterious recovery, nor Lev's apparent lack of magical prodigy.

"All good questions, but not the questions I meant." I spoke slowly, finally voicing the question that had nagged me for days. "I need to know . . . why me? Why not Maria? She was the smartest. Or Tatiana, or Olga? Why not our parents? Why did Rasputin give *me* the garnet that night?"

I paused, pensive as I remembered that night, when I'd awakened to find Rasputin standing over me, pressing the garnet into my hand. "Why sneak into my room in the night, to give me that gemstone? 'Take it,' he said. 'When the time comes, *malenkaya*, you'll escape. Take it, and promise you'll find me.' That was all, and then he was gone. No further instructions." I glanced up, meeting Alexei's eyes. "There must be some reason."

We were all quiet for a moment, Alexei shrugging, then casting me a sideways glance as he smirked. "Not destiny, then, I suppose."

He joked, but I knew the weight of his words. The garnet had not delivered him his birthright. Had not healed him of his hemophilia. Had not restored what had been taken from him. I returned his gaze, speaking delicately. "Are you . . . are you okay with that?"

Without hesitation, he nodded. "I've thought about it quite a bit, Ana. And I am. I didn't succeed—I won't be tsar. But you did. You succeeded. You did what you said you'd do."

Bizarre words from my little brother. I'd said I would save my family. Was that what he was referencing? In the wake of so much death, it certainly didn't feel like I'd succeeded. But I sensed his sincerity. I rolled my eyes. "Stop speaking in riddles and tell me what you're talking about."

He bit his lip, perhaps questioning whether to proceed with the words he'd rehearsed in his mind. "Well, you couldn't save them," he gestured to the caskets below. "Nor Mother and Father, nor our own sisters—"

"Yes, thanks Alexei, I'm aware—"

"—but you saved me."

I stared at him for a moment. Hadn't we just discussed this? "Alexei, I didn't—"

"You saved me," he repeated. "There's your reason. You saved me from what I was becoming." He looked down, mumbling the next sentence. "I suppose you saved my soul."

I raised my brows, quite taken aback and unsure how to respond. So I didn't, but rather threw my arms around my shrinking little brother in a loving, if reluctantly accepted, embrace. "I love you, too, you sappy little *zasranets.*" He squirmed, and I planted a kiss right on his thrashing forehead.

"Okay, okay, get off, I take it all back, *I take it back*!" But Alexei was laughing as he pushed me off him—a sound I hadn't heard in quite some time.

Behind me, Lev cleared his throat. "I don't know why Rasputin gave you the gemstone, Anastasia." I turned to face him, finding him watching Alexei and I, the corner of his mouth lifted in an amused half-smile. "I don't know why you're here, in this world. But I'm glad you are."

I stepped toward him, finding Lev to be a much more willing recipient of my affections as I grazed the tip of his nose with my own. His green eyes were full of warmth, full of hope, and it was that hope that had kept me going. That realization that one could lose everything, and still . . . be. That beyond my title and my family, I was still me.

Beyond my own world and the centuries of linked moments that had colluded to produce me, I continued to exist. And I wanted to be me, and I wanted to exist, because there was still so much life to live. There was a whole magical world to discover—so many ponds to swim in, so many forests to explore, so much joy and pain and love and grief and life to experience.

"I'm glad, too."

I took Lev's hand, rewrapping an unsuspecting Alexei to my side with my other arm. Perhaps there was no prescribed purpose. Perhaps it was up to me. To create a purpose. To live fully. Alexei stopped resisting, settling into my embrace. To learn, and grow, and become better.

Life would certainly not be easy. I looked to Alexei, to Lev. Nor would life be empty, nor lonely, nor dull. I couldn't know what hardships or joys might lie ahead. But I was ready to find out. I was ready to face forward.

I was ready to live.

THE END

ACKNOWLEDGMENTS

WRITING AND PUBLISHING THIS book has been a dream of mine for years, and I cannot shout a loud enough thank you to all the people who made this dream possible!

I'm incredibly lucky to have such an amazing support system, and am so grateful to all those who have helped shape *Ricochet* along the way—whether by offering feedback, encouragement, or just by being with me on this journey!

No one has been more invested in this project than my parents, Mike and Jyma Atwell, and my sister, Heather Carpenter. I cannot thank you enough for all you've done to support me in the process of writing my first novel. This book would not have happened without you.

Mom, I believe it was over a lunch break phone call, brainstorming ideas for a short story contest, that you suggested I write something about the Romanovs—and the premise for *Ricochet* was born. And in the last couple years, as I've started, finished, queried, submitted, revised, and now published this book, you've been there every step of the way as my go-to First Reader and that has been absolutely invaluable. It also helps that you read faster than anyone else in (this) universe!

To my dad, and my sister Heather—thank you for all the time you took to read and reread and provide feedback on all the versions of *Ricochet* that I spammed your inboxes with. Thank you for catching typos, asking good questions, and maybe most importantly, believing in this story and my writing!

To all my early readers—Kevin Rowsey, Casey Davis, Mary Martin, Travis Edwards, Tori Frazier—your enthusiasm for this book—even in its early drafts—was a huge motivation, so thank you! And Tanya Condon, I am so *yobanyy* grateful for your help in verifying my use of the Russian language—particularly the swear words—so thank you, thank you, thank you!

To Michelle Rascon, #RevPit editor extraordinaire, thank you for your invaluable early feedback on my first pages and submission materials. Your suggestions and guidance strengthened my storytelling, and helped lead me to CamCat Books! To the publishing team at CamCat Books, I am so grateful to you all for believing in *Ricochet* and for all the work you've all done to get this book out into the world! I especially want to thank Sue Arroyo, Helga Schier, Bill Lehto, Laura Wooffitt, MC Smitherman, Abigail Miles, Elana Gibson, Nicole DeLise, Maryann Appel, Christine van Zandt, Meredith Lyons, and of course, my amazing editor Kayla Webb. Kayla, you are a genius! Your insight into the characters and worlds of *Ricochet* was perfect, and I can't thank you enough for your help in refining this book into its best version!

And to my supportive, encouraging husband, Jimmy: How would I have ever written this book without you? And I don't just mean the countless times you've helped me find the right word or proofread a questionable paragraph. Raising little humans (even the sweetest, most awesome little humans there have ever been) can be utter madness, and yet you still helped me find the time to write and encouraged me to always do what makes me happy. Throughout this whole process, you've never doubted that this whole book-writing endeavor would work out. So for all of that, and for being the wonderful husband that you are—thank you! You, and our little family, are my reason. I love you!

ABOUT THE AUTHOR

K ELLYN CARNI LIVES IN a small town in the mountains near Asheville, North Carolina, with her husband, children, dog, cat, and chickens. When she isn't cuddling one of the aforementioned (usually not the chickens) under a blanket with a good book, she enjoys yoga, camping, and live music. She works as a physical therapist assistant, and graduated from Appalachian State University with a degree in International Politics. While Kellyn has been writing since childhood, *Ricochet* is her debut novel.

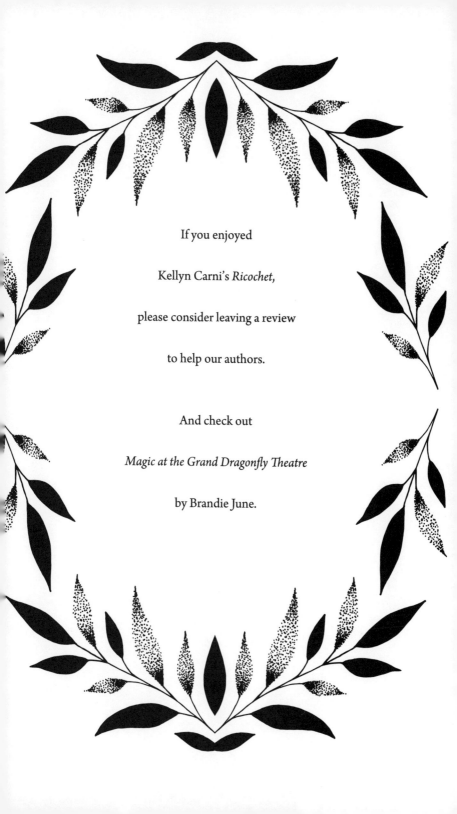

If you enjoyed

Kellyn Carni's *Ricochet*,

please consider leaving a review

to help our authors.

And check out

Magic at the Grand Dragonfly Theatre

by Brandie June.

PROLOGUE

IRIS

IRIS HAD BEEN PRACTICING her trick for weeks, wanting to show her uncle that she could also be a performer. She dreamed of standing onstage instead of watching in the dark. During the ferry crossing to the Isle of Ily, she pulled out her coin and her mother's blue silk handkerchief, the one with her mother's initials embroidered in gold, but the swaying of the boat made her drop the coin instead of hiding it.

"I want to see the magic show!" Violet said when they reached the docks, wriggling in their mother's arms.

"It's not a *magic* show. It's a show of *illusion*," Iris corrected with a six-year-old's sense of superiority.

"That's right, Iris," her mother said, as she set Violet down and went to hail one of Uncle Leo's shiny black carriages, the ones with large gold dragonflies painted on the doors.

"It's important you two know this is a place for illusions only," their mother said sternly when she returned.

"Illusions *and* wonder," Iris added. Her mother had helped her read some of the advertisement posters in the city. One poster depicted Uncle Leo pulling a rabbit out of a hat. In another, he was sawing a beautiful woman in half, but since the woman was smiling, Iris decided that it was nothing to worry about.

Today, she would tell Uncle Leo that she wanted to be an illusionist like him.

Iris draped the blue silk handkerchief over the coin in her left hand.

"Now Violet, blow on the handkerchief."

"Why?" her little sister asked. Violet was a smaller version of Iris with similar chestnut hair, hazel eyes, and a white lace dress that matched the one Iris was wearing.

"Because it is part of the trick."

Violet stared at the silk square, not sure what to make of it.

"Come on, Vi," Iris insisted.

Violet leaned over and blew so hard on the handkerchief that she flecked it with spittle.

"With that breath, I make the coin disappear!" Iris tried to move the coin into her sleeve, but it slipped, falling to the ground. Iris waved the handkerchief around, hoping the effect was mesmerizing as she quickly stepped on the coin.

"And voilà!" Iris said with a flourish, handing the coin-less handkerchief to her sister.

Violet took the piece of silk but wrinkled her nose at her sister. "You stepped on the coin."

Defeated, Iris lifted her foot and picked up the coin.

"You do the trick like *this*," Violet said. A coin appeared in her empty palm. Iris could smell roses and smoke.

"How did you do that?" Iris asked, her incredulity warring with jealousy. Violet hadn't been practicing for weeks to impress their uncle like she had.

"I don't know," Violet said, shrugging.

"Give that to me," Iris demanded.

"Stop it!" their mother said, so sharply that Iris froze. Their mother snatched the coin from Violet. "We don't conjure things, do you understand?" She bent down and held Violet's shoulders. "Understand?"

"Mommy, you're hurting me," Violet whined.

Their mother seemed to melt, almost crying as she quickly wrapped Violet in a hug. "I'm so sorry, sweetheart. Your father had to leave us because bad men saw him conjuring. I only want to keep you safe."

The sun was low in the sky as the carriage jostled them down a winding road to the theatre. Violet whined as their seats shook after hitting a jut in the road, but Iris grinned, knowing this was only the beginning of their journey.

The theatre came into view as they crested the final hill. The building was large and stately, reminding Iris of a palace. Today, the theatre was the perfect shade of butterscotch yellow, making it look warm and inviting against the sunset. Large pillars carved to look like giant stone dragonflies supported the massive domed roof and the great stained-glass windows of amber and green, illuminated by warm light from within. Enormous brass letters above engraved double doors declared that this was the Grand Dragonfly Theatre. Silver and gold stars and moons bedecked the theatre's walls and glittered in the fading sunlight.

"We've arrived," Iris called out in a majestic tone, trying to imitate the booming voice her uncle used when welcoming people to his theatre.

"We are late, so we must get to our seats," their mother said, quickly ushering the girls through a grand mirrored foyer and into their usual box.

Iris hovered on the edge of her seat, leaning as far as she could toward the railing of the balcony, even though all she could see was the thick burgundy curtains that hid the stage.

"Careful, darling. Lean over any farther and you'll fall over the edge," her mother warned.

"No, I won't," Iris argued, but she scooted back a tiny bit to avoid a second scolding.

"When will the show start?" Violet asked.

As if on cue, the lights inside the auditorium went dark.

I could be anywhere, Iris thought and smiled. Her belly filled with happy butterflies as she anticipated the start of the show. With a flash of light and what sounded like a clap of thunder, the footlights along the stage flared to life, casting the stage in bright illumination as the curtain was pulled away. Iris inhaled the familiar scent of gas from the lights.

The stage looked like an extraordinary palace. Gold filigree had been worked into the walls and incorporated in a magnificent throne embedded with rubies and sapphires that sat center stage.

A young boy wearing the regalia of a medieval squire entered stage right and walked to the throne with dignified purpose. Iris wondered if the boy had been made up with white lead paint, since his skin and hair were snow white beneath the bright stage lights.

"Your Highness, one of your subjects requests an audience," the boy said, his high voice surprisingly strong in the vast theater.

A sparkling puff of green smoke exploded in front of the throne, causing gasps of surprise throughout the audience. When the smoke cleared, a king sat upon the great golden chair.

"And which of my subjects comes to see the king?"

Iris recognized her uncle's voice right away. Uncle Leo wore a jeweled crown instead of his usual top hat and a richly embroidered doublet with a bottle-green cape.

The squire introduced a knight, who entered the stage and bowed low to Uncle Leo. As her uncle gave the knight a quest, Iris let herself slip into the story as easily as she slipped into dreams, living in the world playing out in front of her. Iris felt the ocean spray on her skin and tasted saltwater on her tongue as the knight saved himself from drowning after a tidal wave hit his ship in a storm.

She held her breath when the knight fought a three-headed wolf that guarded a witch's hut, the wild animal onstage looking so real that Iris wondered if there really were wolves with three heads. The audience booed when they saw the witch, a hunched woman clad in rags, a giant snake slithering over her shoulders. And Iris shrieked in delight when the brown phoenix that the knight fought so hard for burst into flames, only to reappear golden and mirror-bright. Iris cheered loudly when Uncle Leo rewarded the knight and welcomed him home.

As the actors took their bows, the audience applauded loudly. Iris stood, clapping as hard as she could. Tiny golden feathers no larger than Iris's pinkie finger floated down from the ceiling and the sisters reached out for them, managing to pocket a few of the small treasures so that they would remember this perfect night forever.

"That was incredible." Iris sighed, as the audience began to file out of the theatre.

"Indeed, it was," her mother agreed. "Now let's go see Uncle Leo." Iris's mother led the girls out of the auditorium.

The woman who had played the witch stood in one corner of the lobby surrounded by audience members waiting their turn to pet the large snake coiled around her neck.

"Mrs. Ashmore."

Iris turned to see a strange man approaching them. His dirty trench coat and muddy boots clashed with the finely dressed patrons, and his beady eyes were fixed on Iris's mother.

Iris's mother stepped in front of Iris and Violet, shielding them from the stranger.

"I'm afraid you have me at a disadvantage," Iris's mother said. Her sweet voice had gone cold. Iris didn't know what was going on, but she wanted the strange man to go away. "I don't believe I've made your acquaintance," her mother added, but did not offer him her hand.

The stranger chuckled, a gravelly sound that scared Iris. "How thoughtless of me. Mr. Roman Whitlock."

Iris's mother stiffened and Iris thought she heard her mother say *bounty hunter* under her breath. Iris noticed that the other people in the lobby had stilled their chatter, everyone trying to look like they weren't staring at Iris's family and Mr. Whitlock. Iris peeked around her mother's skirts. Several men in yellow and brown uniforms stood behind Mr. Whitlock.

"Now Mrs. Ashmore, it seems that your husband was not the only conjuror in your family. I have reason to believe you are as well," Mr. Whitlock said. There were several audible gasps in the lobby. Mr. Whitlock licked his thick lips. "Which means you are charged with failing to report yourself for conscription." Mr. Whitlock was grinning, but Iris knew he wasn't friendly.

"What is going on here?" Uncle Leo had finally arrived, out of costume, but still wearing the thick greasepaint makeup. Iris sighed in relief. She was certain he could make the bad man go away.

"Business for the Crown," Mr. Whitlock said, puffing himself up. "You ought to stay out of it, Mr. Von Frey."

"This is my theatre and you are speaking to my sister," Uncle Leo said, stepping right up to Mr. Whitlock, even though he was almost a head shorter.

"And Mrs. Ashmore is a conjuror. I will be taking her in to collect the bounty."

"You have no proof," Iris's mother said, but Iris could hear her mother's voice shaking.

The bounty hunter moved far faster than Iris thought a man of his size could move. Before she realized what was going on, Mr. Whitlock snatched Iris away from her mother, yanking her arm so hard it hurt. Iris screamed as his meaty fingers dug into her arm, but the sound was cut off as his other hand wrapped around her throat, squeezing the air out of her.

A blade appeared in her mother's hand. She slashed at the bounty hunter, a deep cut along his temple and down his cheek. He swore and dropped Iris. She fell to the floor, gasping for air.

Everything hurt. She didn't want to move, but Uncle Leo was already picking her up.

"You don't touch my daughters," her mother said. Iris had never heard her mother so angry. Iris silently cried as she looked over at the terrible, mean man. The cut on his face was bleeding, but he only smiled.

"I love the smell of smoke and roses," Mr. Whitlock said, inhaling deeply. "Using the True Gift always leaves that smell. And that knife trick was all the final proof I needed. Now, will you come with me willingly, or should the Noble Guardsmen use force?" He gestured to the men in the yellow and brown uniforms that now surrounded them.

Iris's mother looked to Uncle Leo with so much fear that Iris cried harder. "I'm so sorry," her mother said. Uncle Leo stepped close to Iris's mother, sandwiching Iris between them.

"I will figure out something, Lynnette," Uncle Leo said.

Iris's mother shook her head. For a moment, she leaned on Uncle Leo's shoulder, and Iris could hear her sobbing. When Iris's mother straightened, tears were running down her mother's cheeks.

Iris pulled out the crumpled blue handkerchief and handed it to her mother. Iris's mother gave Iris a watery smile as she accepted the piece of silk, silently wiping her face as she took long, deep breaths.

Iris's mother turned back to Mr. Whitlock. "I will go with you peacefully but let me say good-bye to my children."

Mr. Whitlock scoffed. "Your husband was carted off years ago. It would be best if they come with us." His grin made Iris shudder. "They will be well cared for at the palace. And maybe one or both will turn out to have the True Gift."

"No!" Iris's mother snapped. "I will come, but you will leave my children alone. The conscription only applies to adult conjurors."

Mr. Whitlock shrugged. "It's only a matter of time."

Iris's mother ground her teeth, but didn't reply, instead turning back to Uncle Leo. "I need you to take my girls."

Uncle Leo nodded vigorously. "Of course, Lynnette. Who do you want me to take them to?"

Iris's mother shook her head. "No Leo. I need you to keep the girls." Quietly, so that the bad man couldn't hear, her mother added, "You know what my daughter is. I need you to protect her."

Uncle Leo's mouth opened but no sound came out. Violet started crying.

"Please Leo, keep my daughters safe. Someday, I will be released from service and I'll come back for them." Iris's mother's eyes were glossy with tears, but she did not look away from Uncle Leo.

"I would do anything for you and the girls," Uncle Leo said resolutely. Iris's unease swelled inside her, giving her a stomachache.

Gently, Uncle Leo set Iris down. Her mother wrapped up her and Violet in a tight embrace. "I love you girls so much. I need you to know that."

When Mr. Whitlock cleared his throat, Iris's mother reluctantly released Iris and Violet, kissing each of them on the top of their heads. "I must go now. Be good for your uncle."

Iris wanted to speak but had no words. Only hours ago, she would have given anything to live in her uncle's theatre, but now she regretted it. She didn't want her mother to leave. Violet kept crying. When their mother rose to leave, Violet lunged to stop her.

"Mama!" she cried. Uncle Leo held Violet back as she kicked and screamed.

Iris reached for her mother's skirts. "Please don't go without me," Iris said. "I don't want you to go."

Her mother bent down, so she was eye-to-eye with her daughter, "I love you and your sister more than I could ever say and I need to keep you safe. Right now, the safest place for you and your sister is with your uncle."

"I don't want to be *safe*. Not if you're leaving."

"But who will protect Violet if you come with me?"

Iris blinked and looked up at her mother.

"I will be back as soon as I can. Until then, I am counting on you, Iris."

"I don't have all night, Mrs. Ashmore," the bounty hunter said.

All eyes were fixed on Iris's mother. Her fists were clenched so tightly they turned white, but still she rose and followed Mr. Whitlock, a line of Noble Guardsmen trailing behind her. Then, she was gone, leaving Iris with her screaming sister and Uncle Leo who was barely able to keep hold of Violet.

Iris ran. The courtyard was dark. Most of the carriages had already left, making it easy for Iris to find the one her mother was in with the bounty hunter. The carriage was already moving as Iris raced outside. She ran after it, yelling for her mother, but her tiny legs were no match for the horses. Iris was crying, her vision blurry with tears. She tripped, skinning her knee bloody as the coach moved farther and farther away. Everything hurt and Iris screamed and screamed.

Mother never came back.

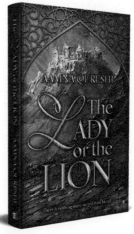
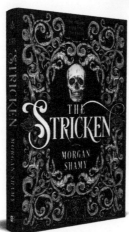

CamCat Books

VISIT US ONLINE FOR MORE BOOKS TO LIVE IN:
CAMCATBOOKS.COM

SIGN UP FOR CAMCAT'S FICTION NEWSLETTER FOR
COVER REVEALS, EBOOK DEALS, AND MORE EXCLUSIVE CONTENT.

CamCatBooks   @CamCatBooks   @CamCat_Books   @CamCatBooks